KT-470-385

Throne of the Caesars: Blood & Steel

ALSO BY HARRY SIDEBOTTOM
FROM CLIPPER LARGE PRINT

Warrior of Rome:
Fire in the East
King of Kings
Lion of the Sun
The Caspian Gates
The Wolves of the North
The Amber Road

Throne of the Caesars:
Iron and Rust

Throne of the Caesars: Blood & Steel

Harry Sidebottom

BRAINSE CARNAN CLOCH
DOLPHINS BARN LIBRARY
TEL. 454 0681

Withdrawn From Stock
Dublin Public Libraries

W F HOWES LTD

This large print edition published in 2016 by
W F Howes Ltd
Unit 5, St George's House, Rearsby Business Park,
Gaddesby Lane, Rearsby, Leicester LE7 4YH

1 3 5 7 9 10 8 6 4 2

First published in the United Kingdom in 2015
by HarperCollins*Publishers*

Copyright © Harry Sidebottom, 2015

The right of Harry Sidebottom to be identified as
the author of this work has been asserted by him
in accordance with the Copyright, Designs and
Patents Act, 1988.

All rights reserved

A CIP catalogue record for this book is available
from the British Library

ISBN 978 1 51001 786 3

Typeset by Palimpsest Book Production Limited,
Falkirk, Stirlingshire

Printed and bound in Great Britain
by TJ International Ltd, Padstow, Cornwall

MIX
Paper from
responsible sources
FSC
www.fsc.org   FSC® C013056

To Katie and Jeremy Habberley

Do not fear god,
Do not worry about death;
What is good is easy to get, and
What is terrible is easy to endure

PHILODEMUS (HERCULANEUM
PAPYRI 1005, 4.9–14)

One could press on or draw back in a private
enterprise, and commit oneself more deeply or
less at will, in accordance with the prospects of
the moment. But in the pursuit of an empire
there was no mean between the summit and
the abyss

TACITUS, *HISTORIES* 2.74

BRAINSE CARNAN CLOCH
DOLPHINS BARN LIBRARY
TEL. 454 0681

CONTENTS

CHAPTER 1

ROME
THE PALATINE HILL

The Day before the Nones of March, AD238

It was still dark. The Praetorian Prefect liked
to walk in the imperial gardens before dawn.
No attendants were with him, and he carried
no torch. It was a moment of calm and solitude,
a time for reflection, before the duties of the day,
the duties that always seemed to stretch away like
a vexatious journey with no evident ending.

Vitalianus often thought about retirement, about
living quietly in the country with his wife and
daughters. He pictured the house in Etruria. The
Via Aurelia and the busy market town of Telamon
were only a couple of miles away over the hill, but
they might have belonged in a different country
or another age. The villa lay between the shore
and the terraced slopes, looking out over the sea.
It had been built by his grandfather. Vitalianus
had added two new wings and a bath house. The
estate now extended inland along both banks of
the Umbro. It was ideal for retirement, for reading
and writing, appreciating the views, for passing time

Leabharlanna Poibli Chathair Bhaile Átha Cliath
Dublin City Public Libraries

with his wife, and enjoying the company of his daughters in the last few years before they married. No place was better suited for a man to lay down the cares of office.

Certainly Vitalianus had earned a time of leisure. His career had been long – commander of an auxiliary cohort in Britain, legionary tribune with the 3rd Augustan in Africa, Prefect of a cavalry unit in Germania, Procurator of imperial finances in Cyrenaica, four years with the Moorish cavalry, leading them through the eastern campaign and then to the Rhine – decades of service, across the breadth of the empire. He was no longer young: past fifty, and needed to rest. But duty still called, and the additions and improvements to his patrimony had not come cheap. The stipend and other profits of another three, perhaps four years as Praetorian Prefect, and he could call it a day.

The white marble borders of the paths shone in the darkness. The cunningly sculpted box hedges and the fruit trees were indistinct black shapes, the plane trees and the ivy that linked them a solid black wall. It was quiet in the Hippodrome, just the rill of water in the fountains; almost hard to believe he stood in the centre of a city with a million inhabitants. Vitalianus was glad he had removed the previous Emperor's aviaries. The murmuring and shifting of the doves – had there really been twenty thousand of them? – had disturbed his morning walks. It was typical of Alexander that he had occupied his time issuing imperial pronouncements about the birds, sanctimoniously boasting how the sale of eggs financed his collection, even produced a modest income, while his mother had stolen fortunes from the treasury, and great swathes of the east were overrun by the Persians, and German tribes put the northern provinces to the torch. Vitalianus had not been party to the plot, but Alexander was better off dead.

Stopping by a marble nymph, Vitalianus absentmindedly ran a hand over her smooth thigh. He could find his way around these twisting walks blindfold. His thoughts took their own course. Risen from the ranks, Maximinus might be uncultured, even crude and violent, but he was a better Emperor than his predecessor. At least the Thracian could fight; for the last three years he had done nothing but campaign beyond the Rhine and Danube. Vitalianus had done well out of the regime; promoted first to governor of Mauretania Caesariensis, then to deputy Praetorian Prefect. It was a remarkable achievement for an equestrian from a backwater of Italy, a man with few significant backers. A member of the second order should legitimately aspire to nothing higher. And Vitalianus continued to serve the regime diligently. The endless court cases that awaited him today and almost every day were only the start.

With the majority of the praetorians accompanying the field army, it had proved difficult for Vitalianus to maintain order in Rome. The remaining one thousand men were not enough to disperse the crowds occasioned by certain arrests, or to clear the mobs occupying those temples whose treasures were to be requisitioned to help pay for the war. Efficiency would be served if he could issue orders to the six thousand men of the Urban Cohorts as well. But that would never happen. The very first Emperor, Augustus, had separated the command of the troops stationed in Rome. An equestrian Prefect led the Praetorians, while a Senatorial Prefect of the City controlled the Urban Cohorts. One officer watched the other, and the Emperor could be reassured that no individual could seize the Eternal City, at least not without an armed struggle. To be sure, things had been better once Sabinus had replaced Pupienus as Prefect of the City. The Urban Cohorts and the Praetorians might have no love for each other, but under firm leadership together they could contain the turbulent *plebs urbana*. The hand of Maximinus lay heavy on the city, but the northern war demanded sacrifices, and so far the Emperor had not struck down those who served him loyally. Safety lay in prompt obedience, no matter what the order. Three or four more years and Vitalianus could withdraw from the fray.

A scream of gulls brought Vitalianus back to his surroundings. The sky was lightening. It was time to take up the reins. He adjusted his sword-belt, the very visible badge of his office, hitched up his tunic, and walked up the stairs to where his secretary

4

and two praetorians waited. Together they set off through the heart of the palace.

Apart from a handful of servants and guards, there was no one in the main imperial audience chamber. The echoing near-emptiness revealed its more than human scale. Three storeys of columns soared up a hundred feet to where the great beams of cedar supporting the wide span of the ceiling were lost in shadow. At the far end of the hall the gathering light outlined the monumental door through which an Emperor would appear to the press of his subjects assembled below on the palace forecourt. Opposite the opening, a seated statue of Maximinus occupied the apse where the living ruler would sit enthroned to receive the Senate and favoured petitioners, should he ever return to Rome. Along the walls, the gods in marble gazed down from their niches at their adamantine colleague.

Vitalianus performed adoration, bowing his head and blowing a kiss from his fingertips. Suddenly he wondered what it would be like to hold court in this hall, not to bow but to receive obeisance, to be lord of all you surveyed. Two Emperors had risen from the equestrian order. As a child Maximinus had herded goats. Vitalianus' mind shied away. Even to entertain such thoughts was treason. A careless word or gesture, something muttered in your sleep, any of them could lead to an accusation. From there events would run their course; a closed carriage to the north, the pincers and claws wielded by skilled hands, until you begged for the executioner's sword. Your head set on a pike. The crows feasting on your eyes. He straightened up, and marched purposefully towards the door to the neighbouring basilica.

When he entered, the hum of conversation died. The first petitioners had been admitted. This hall was smaller. Twin Corinthian colonnades running down the long walls further encroached on the floor space. Among those waiting, he saw Timesitheus.

As he marched down the nearer colonnade, Vitalianus brought the case to mind. The little Greek was embroiled in a private dispute over an inheritance. Timesitheus was in charge of the grain supply. His opponent was a leading Senator. All things being equal, neither was a man one would choose to alienate. But things were not equal. Timesitheus had a sworn enemy in Domitius, the Prefect of the Imperial Camp, and the latter was one of the few patrons Vitalianus had close to the Emperor. And there was a personal animosity. Three years before in the *consilium,* in front of all the councillors of the Emperor, Timesitheus had argued against the appointment of Vitalianus as governor of Mauretania Caesariensis. The *Graeculus* had to be desperate to seek his aid now. The desperation would do him no good.

A centurion of the Praetorians stepped forward as Vitalianus approached the apse where the tribunal stood.

'Soldiers have arrived from the north, Prefect.

The despatches bear the imperial seal. Their officer says he has a private message of the utmost importance from Maximinus Augustus himself. It concerns the security of the *Res Publica*. They are waiting in the portico outside.'

Vitalianus nodded. 'Tell them I will hear them in a moment.' He ascended the raised dais, and faced the hall. 'Forgive me, the court will delay its sitting. Orders have come from the most noble Augustus.' Despite his politeness, a sea of anxious faces gazed up at him. They knew as well as he what it meant: more arrests, more leading men rushed under close guard to the north, never to be seen again. It could be any one of them. The *Graeculus* Timesitheus, his senatorial opponent and every man present would be consulting his conscience, calling to mind every recent conversation, no matter how trivial. They did not fear just for themselves. All knew the dreadful repercussions for the family of the victims: the headman's block, or, at best, exile, confiscation and abject poverty.

Outside the sun had risen. The light flashed back from the highly polished cladding of the walls. Treachery and fear were nothing new in Rome. Long ago the Emperor Domitian had had the white reflective stone brought from distant Cappadocia. Like all Emperors, he had wanted to see what happened behind his back.

Two soldiers were talking to the centurion and the four Praetorian guards by the rear doors of the basilica. They fell silent, and snapped to attention, when they saw Vitalianus. The centurion gestured out beyond the portico into the open space.

An officer was standing by the central fountain. He had his back to Vitalianus, and seemed to be studying how the waters ran down the island that depicted Sicilia and gave the courtyard its name. At the sound of footfalls, he turned. He was young, perhaps in his mid-twenties, dark haired and good-looking. He was vaguely familiar, but Vitalianus could not place him.

'Prefect.' The young officer saluted. Close up, he was pale and looked tired. His tunic was travel stained. Among the ornaments on his military belt was a memento mori, a skeleton in silver. He handed over the despatch.

Vitalianus turned the diptych in his hands: ivory and gold, clumsily sealed in imperial purple with the eagle of the Caesars. He broke the seal, unfolded the hinged block, and read.

Imperator Gaius Iulius Verus Maximinus to Publius Aelius Vitalianus, our most loving and loyal Prefect of the Praetorians. While marching against the Sarmatians, it was with great sadness we received information of yet another conspiracy. The eminence of the traitors precludes writing their names. The bearer of this letter will tell you their identity. Now I entreat you that in the same spirit in which you were chosen

8

as Prefect and have conducted your duties you will spare no efforts in apprehending these evil-minded malefactors and convey them to us, so that with careful inquiry we can ascertain how far they have spread their sacrilegious poison.

Our son Verus Maximus Caesar sends his greetings, and his wife Iunia Fadilla, too, greets both you and your wife. To your daughters we will send a present, worthy both of their virtue and your own. We command you to hold the troops in the city in their allegiance to the Res Publica and to ourselves, my most loyal, most dear, and loving friend.

Below the courtly hand of the imperial secretary was the rough scrawl MAXIMINUS AUGUSTUS.

'Who?' Vitalianus said.

Unexpectedly the officer smiled. 'The Prefect of the City, Sabinus, and he is only the first.'

Vitalianus looked up sharply. A movement caught his eye reflected in the wall opposite. He turned. The two soldiers had drawn their swords.

A whisper of steel. Dropping the diptych, Vitalianus tugged his own blade from its scabbard. 'Guards!' Yelling, he spun back, and blocked the cut aimed at his head.

'Guards!' He parried a thrust. Hearing running feet, he risked a glance over his shoulder. The two soldiers would be on him in a moment. The centurion and the Praetorians had not moved.

A searing pain in his right arm told Vitalianus

that he had paid for his inattention. Somehow he fended off another blow.

'Why?'

The young officer said nothing.

'I have done everything. Never betrayed him.'

Vitalianus felt the steel slice into his left thigh from behind. He staggered. The blood hot on his leg.

'Why?'

Another slash into his left leg, and he collapsed. His weapon gone from his hand, he curled on the ground, one hand half covering his head, the other outstretched in supplication. What of his daughters? They were children, virgins. It was unlawful to execute virgins. Gods, not the fate of the children of Sejanus. No, dear gods, no!

One of the soldiers moved to finish him.

'Wait.'

Vitalianus peered from behind his fingers up at the speaker.

'It is my responsibility.' The young officer rolled him onto his back, put his boot on his chest, the tip of his sword at his throat.

Vitalianus looked into his eyes. 'Spare my children. Please spare my daughters.'

'Yes,' the officer said, and thrust down.

CHAPTER 2

ROME
THE PALATINE HILL

The Day before the Nones of March, AD238

'Follow me.'
The two soldiers moved to clean their blades.

'Do not sheath them,' Menophilus said. 'The blood needs to be seen.'

They walked back, their gory reflections fractured and disjointed in the mirrored walls of the courtyard.

Behind the Praetorians, close-packed faces peered out of the two doorways of the basilica. Silent, round-eyed and open-mouthed, they gazed beyond the military men at the corpse lying at the base of the fountain.

'The Prefect has been executed. Command of the Emperor.' Menophilus spoke to the centurion of the Praetorians. He kept his words low, clipped and military, as if about some oft-repeated routine. 'There is a new watchword: *Liberty*. Remain at your posts. Await further orders.'

'*Libertas!*' The Praetorians chorused without emotion.

11

The first of the civilians wedged in the doorways were ducking back out of sight into the basilica. So far, so good, Vitalianus was dead. He could go over the implications of that again later, but now Menophilus and his men had to get away. Soon the palace would be in uproar. Unexpected bloodshed often unleashed random violence, and there was never any reckoning on the volatility of a frightened mob.

Menophilus raised his voice to address the onlookers. 'The court is adjourned until further notice. The traitor has been executed. There will be no further arrests. There is nothing to fear. None of you will be detained further.'

The main gate of the palace was off to his right. To reach it, you had to go through the great vestibule, and that would be crammed with petitioners, clients and guards; hundreds of men waiting attendance on the Praetorian Prefect. When word arrived of his death, fear alone would create chaos.

Menophilus nodded to his men, and turned left. It was no distance to the smaller western gate, but he found it hard not to run. Walking slowly, the two soldiers marching behind, the bloodied sword ridiculously held up in front, he felt like an unconvincing actor in a tragedy. Perhaps a mask would have helped.

The small, octagonal vestibule was empty. The doormen were nowhere to be seen, and the Praetorians here had deserted their posts. Already discipline had slipped into the vacuum created by the killing of the Emperor's main officer in the city. There was a chance for looting. Avarice was ever a strong passion.

Outside, Menophilus turned right, glanced over his shoulder at his followers, and broke into a run. Cloak in his left hand, sword in his right, he rounded the corner of the palace. A tall wall, marble faced and blank, stretched away. From further up the façade, from among the balustrades, statues and columns, came bursts of noise and half-glimpsed movements. He angled away to the left, across the forecourt, towards the arch that straddled the path down to the Sacred Way and the Forum.

Menophilus started to shamble, his breathing became laboured. The soldiers closed up on either side. Left to their own devices, they would have overtaken him. One had a curious action. Neck craned forward, knees high-stepping, it reminded Menophilus of the big, flightless African birds exhibited in the amphitheatre. The other covered the ground more normally.

Under the arch, Menophilus had to stop. Hands on thighs, he doubled up. The flagstones blurred in his vision. Each breath dragged pain up through his chest. It was not the exertion. They had only run a short distance. It was the enormity of what he had done; the killing of an unsuspecting man. Menophilus hawked and spat. He felt disorientated and sick. There was blood smeared up his arms.

The soldier who ran like an ostrich cleared his throat and shifted his feet. Menophilus knew they should not delay, but could not force himself to continue. The ostriches went into the arena without awareness of their fate. The hunters used a special half-moon arrowhead to sever their necks. Gods, this would not do. Menophilus had to rein in his thoughts, regain his self-control. To Hades with flightless birds and unawareness. Behave like a man. Flanks still heaving like a dog, he hauled himself more upright.

Downslope, what he could see of the valley of the Forum still lay in early-morning shadow. There must have been any number of examples in its history of men who had done terrible things for the right reasons, had committed awful crimes for the good of the *Res Publica*. Sick to his stomach, not one came to Menophilus. There must be innumerable instances of men constrained by their conscience to make choices that had put them outside the law. The Forum had been the heart of the free Republic. For centuries men could speak and act as their principles dictated, until Augustus had seduced power up to the Palatine. That was long ago. It could no more be reversed than the killing of Vitalianus. Neither could be changed by Menophilus. In that light, both were irrelevant. He stood straight, gripped the hem of his cloak, and set off again. Several times at the games he had seen ostriches continue to run after they had been decapitated.

As they reached the Sacred Way, with the suddenness of some fearful epiphany, six armed men emerged from the Arch of Titus. At the sight of the naked steel in their hands, Menophilus skidded to a halt, jerked his own blade up into a blocking position. At his shoulders, the soldiers did the same.

'Is Vitalianus dead?'

'Yes,' Menophilus said.

'We should have executed Sabinus too,' Valerian said.

'Gordian's orders were explicit.' Menophilus lowered his sword.

'A mistake. The Prefect of the City commands six thousand men in the Urban Cohorts.'

Menophilus suppressed his irritation. 'You were there, you know as well as me, neither Gordian nor his father would hear of it.'

Valerian shrugged. 'Potens should have been killed as well. He has another seven thousand in the Watch.'

Silently, not even moving his lips, Menophilus recited the Greek alphabet. After Gordian had been proclaimed Emperor with his father in Africa, the most important of his initial orders had been this mission to take control of Rome. No one but the Praetorian Prefect was to be killed. The new regime was to be one of principle, bound by restraint, different from the bloodstained tyranny that had gone before. Menophilus struggled for the words to make Valerian understand. 'If we had

15

killed them, we would be no better than Vitalianus, and Gordian would be no better than Maximinus.'

'A mistake,' Valerian's complaints continued their ponderous course. 'When the Liberators cut down Caesar, they spared Mark Antony, and everyone knows how that turned out. Why kill Vitalianus, when there are less than a thousand Praetorians in Rome, and leave alive two men just as close to the regime of Maximinus, who between them . . .'

'Enough!' They had been through all this. There was no time now for Menophilus to go from alpha to omega again. 'We have our orders, and we will obey them.'

Valerian scowled. Evidently he did not relish being interrupted by the younger man.

'We all know our roles.' Menophilus nevertheless felt it was his duty to repeat them. Gordian had entrusted this to him. There could be no mistakes. 'Valerian, there is little time, but it is not far to the Caelian. Fulvius Pius will not have left his house yet. With the other Consul away, tell him the *Res Publica* depends on him. When you are certain Fulvius Pius will summon the Senate, collect his neighbour Pupienus as well, and escort them both to the Curia. Everything now depends on how quickly we act.'

Valerian nodded.

Menophilus turned to the one other present who was not a soldier. 'Maecius, when you reach the Carinae, go straight to the home of Balbinus.

16

The patrician is notoriously indolent. He may be reluctant. Flatter him, bribe him, do whatever. Use threats if necessary. Balbinus has many connections among the Senators. We have to have him at the meeting. Only when you are sure he will attend, go to the house of the Gordiani, and warn Maecia Faustina. Lock and bar the windows and doors of the *Domus Rostrata*. Arm the slaves. Stay with your kinswoman. Remember the safety of Gordian's sister rests on you.'

The gold ring on Maecius' hand flashed as he waved to acknowledge his orders. Then both the young equestrian and Valerian turned to go.

Trying to hide any misgivings, Menophilus watched the two men depart. Each was trailed by his utterly inadequate escort of just two soldiers. The next few hours might see them all dead. Duty demanded that he send Maecius to the house of Balbinus before securing the *Domus Rostrata*. Yet it was not an easy decision. Gordian was not close to his sister, but he might find it hard to forgive Menophilus if something happened to her or his ancestral home.

Regarding Valerian's broad back as it receded under the Arch and off up the Sacred Way brought a certain comfort. The older man provided a word-less lesson in duty. Valerian's young son was a hostage in the imperial school on the Palatine. The day held the sure promise of violence; at the least riot, and perhaps savage repression and revenge. And Valerian was going to summon the Consul of

Rome from the Caelian, instead of rushing to protect his son.

It was time to go. Menophilus regarded his two fellow assassins. Filthy, reeking with blood, eyes popping and wild; his own aspect would be no better. He motioned them to follow, and marched out into the Forum.

'*Libertas!*' he roared, and raised his fatal blade to the skies.

'*Libertas!*' the soldiers echoed.

A row of astrologers, dream diviners and others of similar callings sat or stood in front of the House of the Vestals.

'*Libertas!*' Menophilus cried to them. 'Citizens, your freedom is restored. Here in Rome we have cut down your oppressor. The Prefect Vitalianus is dead.'

They regarded him with misgiving, these down-at-heel peddlers of divine foresight. Nothing in their self-proclaimed expertise had given them any warning. They exchanged anxious looks. A couple began to gather up the tools of their trades.

'The tyrant is dead!' Menophilus brandished his sword. 'The news has come from the North. Maximinus has been slain. Beyond the Danube, his corpse lies mutilated and unburied.'

As one, galvanized by his pronouncement, the charlatans scooped and scrabbled up their meagre accoutrements. Wordless, they fled in all directions.

'Maximinus the Thracian is dead!' Menophilus shouted at their scurrying figures.

CHAPTER 3

AFRICA
CARTHAGE

The Day before the Nones of March, AD238

*L*ive out of the public eye, the sage had said.
It was nine days since Gordian had
plunged a dagger into the neck of the Procurator who had been called Paul the Chain, nine
days since he had proclaimed his father and in
return been made Emperor himself. In the nondescript bedroom, in the second-rate provincial
town of Thysdrus in Africa, the crowd had
acclaimed him Augustus, all bloodied as he was,
his toga like a butcher's apron.

A wise man will not engage in politics, Epicurus
had cautioned. Gordian had made his decision.
There could be no return to the shadows. Paul the
Chain had threatened his friend Mauricius with
ruin, and worse. It would have not stopped there.
Gordian had been compelled to act.

The crowds had been waiting several miles outside the walls of Carthage. They were all civilians
and were ranked along the roadside; first the

19

magistrates, priests, and the rest of the councillors, then the young men of good families, and finally all the other inhabitants in their various lower degrees. They had been there for hours, in good order, not a soldier in sight. At long last, in an outpouring of joy and perhaps some relief, the population had had their opportunity to pour libations, blow kisses, and call out words of good omen. To the music of flutes, they had accompanied the cavalcade to the city, spreading the petals of different flowers under the hooves of the horses. Melodious and good-natured in the spring sunshine, the procession had snaked under the aqueduct, between the tombs, through the Hadrumetum Gate and finally to the Circus.

With his father, Gordian stepped onto the purple carpet. They walked with slow and measured tread, befitting their combined dignity and the parent's age. Following the fasces and the sacred fire, they proceeded up the many steps, through the dark interior of the building, up to the imperial box.

The light was blinding as they came out into the Circus. It surrounded them, its marble dazzling under the African sun. The noise and heat rolled up from the tiers, and buffeted the two men. Forty thousand or more voices were raised in welcome. *Hail, the Augusti, our saviours. Hail Gordian the Elder. Hail Gordian the Younger. May the gods preserve father and son.* Nicknames were chanted, respectful for the senior – *Hail, the new Scipio. Hail, Cato reborn* – less so for his progeny – *Hail, Priapus;*

the princeps *of pleasure.* With no soldiers on hand to keep them within bounds, it was their nature to call out what they pleased. The Carthaginians were second only to the Alexandrians in their irreverence.

Gordian solicitously took his father's elbow, and supported him to their thrones. As they settled themselves on the unforgiving ivory, their entourage filed in behind them.

The crowd quietened. Down on the sand, a city elder stood forth. The white of his toga shimmered in the sun, the narrow purple stripe on his tunic an incision as black as blood.

'With fortunate omens you have come, our Emperors, each as brilliant as a ray of the sun that appears to us on high.'

The space was vast, but the orator had a strong voice, and the acoustics were good. The words carried up to the Emperors and to those in the seats of honour. The rest would have to be content with reports and saying they had been there.

'When night and darkness covered the world, the gods raised you up to their fellowship, and together your light has dissolved our fears. All men can breathe again, as you dispel all dangers.'

The enumeration of past miseries would take some time; the iniquities of the deceased Procurator here in Africa, the savageries and stupidities of the tyrant Maximinus Thrax across the breadth of the empire. Amplification was ever the watchword for a rhetor on safe ground.

21

Gordian inclined his head slightly, and regarded his father's profile, the strong chin and aquiline nose. Gordian was glad that at the outset he had thought to have an artist draw them both, and had sent the portraits ahead both to Carthage and to Rome. The coins from the imperial mint would convey a suitable majesty. Here, seated on the throne, Gordian Senior was the very image of an Emperor; serene yet alert. His father had stood up well to the rigours of the hasty journey, but close up Gordian could see the dark smudges under the eyes, the sunken cheeks, and the slight tremor in one hand.

His father was old, possibly too old to bear the weight of the purple. Gordian had neither expected nor wanted his father to elevate him to the throne as well. Yet his father was eighty, and it would have been wrong not to shoulder some of the burden. Now, together, they would see the race out, fight the contest to the finish.

On the evening of the acclamation, when they were as near alone as Emperors could be, in just the company of four or five of their immediate *familia*, they had talked. The conversation remained with Gordian.

'I am sorry, Father. If I had let the Chain kill Mauricius, we would have been next.'

His father had been calm. 'I would have done the same, if I was still young.'

Gordian had been compelled to explain, to try

22

to win his father's approval. 'A life of fear, without ease of mind, is not worth living. To live as a coward can not be endured. Once the Chain was dead, there was no choice but open revolt, the proclamation of a new Emperor. When a tyrant threatens your friends and family, your own equanimity, the very *Res Publica* itself, a man can not continue to live quietly out of the public eye. A wise man will not engage in politics, unless something intervenes.'

'Although I do not share your Epicureanism, you are right.' A long life had armoured the self-control of his father. 'We are wealthy. The *Domus Rostrata* in Rome, the great villa on the *Via Praenestina*, confiscated by the imperial treasury, they alone would fund a legion for the northern wars. Since your sister's husband was condemned for treason last year, we are marked down for destruction. You did the right thing. Your mother would have been proud of you, as I am.'

'But I have endangered us all.'

'There is no time now for regrets. You must act swiftly. Seize Rome. Rally the eastern armies to our cause. I am old and tired. All depends on you.'

'It may end in disaster.'

His father had smiled. 'At my age death holds no terrors. Perhaps it would be no mean thing to end my days on the throne of the Caesars. *Let me at least not die without a struggle, inglorious, but do some big thing first, that men to come shall know of it.*'

*   *   *

23

A flamboyant gesture by the orator brought Gordian out of his memories. Slowly, for imperial majesty precluded sudden movements, and out of the corners of his eyes, he studied those who stood behind the thrones. Brennus, his father's silent bodyguard, as ever was at hand. The persistent rumour that Brennus was an illegitimate child of Gordian the Elder was fuelled by the striking resemblance between his legitimate son and the bodyguard, although the old man laughed the story off.

Gordian took in the rest of the party. Arrian and Sabinianus, the two legates, stood together, as close as the Cercopes, the mischievous twins of myth. Despite the solemnity of the occasion, some hint of patrician amusement could be detected in their faces. Serenus Sammonicus, his old tutor, was the same age as his father, but appeared older and very far from well. Aemilius Severinus, the commander of the *speculatores*, was not young. He must be in his sixties. But he looked tough and fit. Phillyrio, as his scouts called Severinus for some long-forgotten reason, had been scoured and tanned like leather by a lifetime patrolling the desert frontier. At the end was Mauricius, the local landowner whose persecution had been the catalyst. Few enough to support a revolution, none of them, apart from the legates, of any great rank, but loyalty ever counted for more than mere numbers.

'On his father's side he traces his descent from the

house of the Gracchi, on his mother's from the Emperor Trajan.' The oration had moved to the origins of Gordian Senior, another safe topic for fulsome exploration. 'His own father, his grandfather, and his great-grandfather, his wife's father and grandfather, and likewise another of his wife's grandfathers and two of her great-great-grandfathers, were Consuls.'

The offices, deeds and virtues of every one of these individuals would be recalled, exaggerated, or invented. Gordian seemed to have been listening forever, to have been Emperor for eternity.

Gordian had been busy beyond measure. That first day, before the citizens of Thysdrus could swear their oaths of allegiance, majestic regalia had had to be created. It had been easy enough to find both a small, portable altar for the sacred fire and rods to bind around axes to make the fasces. As governor his father had curule chairs which could serve as imperial thrones. A purple cloak already had been taken from the sanctuary of Caelestis, from the shoulders of the goddess, and draped around his father. Another, most likely of similar provenance, was produced for himself. An imperial seal had been more problematic. But the town gaol had contained a forger – as long as there were coins, there would be counterfeiters – and, once pardoned and reunited with the tools of his illicit trade, it had taken him no time to create a simulacrum; in metal not precious stone, but the impression it made had seemed adequate.

From the ceremonial Gordian had turned to the practical. After his father had retired to his chamber, he had worked through the night. Many, many letters had been dictated and signed; to all the leading communities in the Province of Africa, to the commanders of the eight small military units stationed there. More thought had been devoted to those destined for the more than forty governors of other provinces across the *imperium*. Yet the most care of all had gone into the sentiments and wording of those that were to go to the capital, both those that bore Gordian's signature and those that carried a false subscript. Menophilus and Valerian, accompanied by his equestrian kinsman Maecius, had left for Rome at dawn.

The imperial party had remained at Thysdrus for just two more days. Long enough to find recruits to bring the horse guards up to two hundred swords. Renamed the Equites Singulares Augusti, Mauricius had been given their command. A makeshift Praetorian Guard, five hundred strong, had been formed out of the local youth association. The Iuvenes might not be seasoned soldiers, but they had a modicum of military training, and neither their appearance nor enthusiasm could be faulted.

The new Emperors, with escort and entourage, had gone to Hadrumetum, then up the coast road to Horrea Caelia and Pupput, before turning north-west to Ad Aquas, to skirt the gulf of Utica, and so to Carthage. Six days hard travelling, Gordian in the saddle, his father going in a fast carriage before mounting a horse for the entry into the city. The speed of their journey meant that only those communities through which they had passed had yet acknowledged them. But professions of fealty had come from Fuscinus, Prefect of the 15th Cohort of Emesenes based at Ammaedara, and similar messages had been waiting for them at Ad Aquas from the commanders of the Urban Cohort and the detachment of the 3rd Legion Augusta stationed in Carthage. So far things could not have gone better. Gordian was proud of what he had accomplished. Like Mark Antony, he could rouse himself from his pleasures when necessity demanded.

'As Horatius held the bridge, Gordian stood alone amidst the slaughter and held the gate at Ad Palmam. Never tiring, his man-killing hands struck down the foe, threw back the barbarian horde.'

Gordian had been half aware of the flow of the oration: the excellent omens – in fact they had been appalling, for those who believed in such things – the long distant martial exploits of his father. But now it had reached his own triumphs, he was all ears.

'As Alexander scaled the Sogdian Rock, so our young Emperor climbed the sheer cliff at Esuba. Many was the companion he caught as they slipped, saved from a certain death. When he attained the summit, the brigands discovered neither their remoteness nor their inaccessibility provided any defence against the old-fashioned Roman courage of our Augustus.'

All too soon a new theme was introduced. 'Justice is a portion of his humanity: for when victorious, the Emperor did not repay the aggressors in kind, but divided his actions in just proportion between punishment and humanity.'

Gordian stopped listening. Not a dog had been left alive in the lair of the bandit Canartha. His thoughts scouted ahead. They would not stay long in Carthage. Leaving Sabinianus as the new governor of Africa, as soon as word came from Menophilus, they would sail for Rome. There they would muster the military forces in the city: the Urban Cohorts, the men of the Watch, those Praetorians and the soldiers of the 2nd Legion who were not away in the North, the detachments of sailors, and however many *frumentarii* were in their camp on the Caelian. They should raise new troops, perhaps recruit some from the gladiatorial schools. Once they had secured the allegiance of the two great fleets at Misenum and Ravenna, they could hold Italy, and wait for the governors across the empire to declare themselves.

'Just as the sons of Asclepius rescue the sick, just as fugitives obtain security in the inviolate precincts of divine power . . .'

Agitated, despite himself, Gordian could find no meaning in the words. Had the gods existed, Gordian would have prayed for news. Events were beyond his control. Everything now depended on what was happening elsewhere; in Rome, in governors' palaces across the empire, and with the army in the distant North. At least three governors were closely bound to the house of the Gordians. Claudius Julianus of Dalmatia, Fidus of Thrace, and Egnatius Lollianus of Bithynia-Pontus had no legions, but their example might sway the undecided. And in Rome the *plebs urbana* would be well disposed. Some time ago, his father had distributed a hundred Sicilian and a hundred Cappadocian racehorses among the Circus factions. And he had endeared himself across Italy by giving four days of stage-plays and *Juvenalia* in the cities of Campania, Etruria, Umbria, Flaminia, and Picenum, all at his own expense.

'Because of our Emperors, marriages are chaste, fathers have legitimate offspring, spectacles, festivals, and competitions are conducted with proper splendour and due moderation. People choose a style of life like that which they observe in the Emperors. Piety to the gods is increased, the earth is tilled in peace, the sea sailed without danger.'

There was no mistaking the tardy arrival of the epilogue. Gordian shifted his numb buttocks. Not long now. Just the already intimated new honorifics, and the interminable speech would be finished. Gordian was dust-stained, tired and hot; the baths would be welcome.

'We fear neither barbarians nor enemies. The Emperors' arms are a safer fortress than our city walls. What greater blessing must one ask from the gods than the safety of the Emperors? Only that they incline our rulers to accept . . .'

Gordian hoped Parthenope and Chione were not too fatigued from the journey. He had earned the special relaxation from the cares of office that his mistresses could provide.

'Although too modest to share with his father the titles of Pontifex Maximus or Father of the Country, however, let the son also take the name Africanus to commemorate the country of his accession, and that of Romanus to celebrate the city of his birth and make evident the contrast from the barbarous tyrant of hated memory. All hail Imperator Caesar Marcus Antonius Gordianus Sempronianus Romanus Africanus Pius Felix Augustus, father and son.'

As his father stood to accept on both their behalf the not-unexpected titles, Gordian sensed a disturbance behind him in the imperial box. Suillius, the tribune in charge of the detachment from the 3rd Augusta, leant over his shoulder, and spoke in his ear.

'Augustus, the legionaries will not leave their barracks. They are tearing down your new portraits from the standards. Only your presence can stop the mutiny.'

CHAPTER 4

THE FAR NORTH
THE SARMATIAN STEPPE,
TERRITORY OF THE IAZYGES

The Day before the Nones of March, AD*238*

The plain was white and flat and without end. To the east a thin stand of trees, in every other direction the plain stretched untrammelled as far as could be seen. The trees, willow and lime, marked a shallow, marshy stream, now iced over and treacherous. Beyond their bare, frozen and delicate-looking branches the Steppe continued its remorseless slide to infinity.

Enemy in sight!

A rider – his horse labouring through the snow – was coming up from the south. He held the corner of his cloak in one hand above his head in the customary signal: *Enemy in sight!*

Like everyone else in the army with a point of vantage, Maximinus gazed past the lone horseman. The snow was flecked with black where the taller grasses and the occasional shrub showed through. In the extreme distance, it merged with the dirty pale grey of the sky. There was nothing else in sight. The scout had outrun the enemy.

Maximinus dropped his reins and blew on his hands. His breath plumed. It was very cold. A movement to his left drew his eyes to the stream. Where reed beds or the trunks of trees provided shelter from the north wind there was no snow. The ice was black, shining. A flight of ducks clattered up, wheeled, and flew away.

'There,' Javolenus said.

Maximinus looked south once more, to where his bodyguard pointed. A thin smudge of black on the horizon. The Iayzges were a long way off. It would take them an hour or more to reach the stationary Roman forces. They had no reason to hurry.

His fingers were numb. Maximinus flexed them, rubbed his hands together, before taking up his reins. It was time to inspect the troops again. Indicating that his staff should follow, he turned his hack, dug his heels in its flanks, and set off at a slow canter to the right of the infantry front line. Even though the snow had been trampled, the going was both heavy and uncertain.

When he was first promoted to high command, a fellow officer had asked why he still worked so hard, now he had attained a rank where a certain leisure was permissible. The greater I become, the harder I shall labour, he had replied. Back then – the reign of the glorious Caracalla – he had joined his men at their wrestling. He had thrown them to the ground, one after another, six or seven at a sweat. Once a tribune of another legion, an insolent young man from a Senatorial house, but big and strong, had mocked him, claiming his soldiers had to let him win. Challenged to a match, Maximinus had knocked him senseless with one blow to the chest, a blow delivered with an open palm. Back then, even Senators had called him Hercules. Now they whispered he was a new Spartacus, or another Antaeus or Sciron. The only imperial secretary he trusted – despite Apsines of Gadara being a Syrian – had told him the stories about the last two.

As he pulled up by the standards of the 2nd Legion, the Parthian, its commander stepped forward from the other officers and saluted. Clean, well-cared-for armour showed under the Prefect's fur-lined cloak.

'Are your men ready?' Maximinus asked.

'We will do what is ordered, and at every command we will be ready.'

From an equestrian family with a long record of military service, Julius Capitolinus was a fine officer. In Germania, at the battle in the marsh and the one at the pass, he had led his men well, fought like a lion. Maximinus knew he should smile, say something affable. Nothing came to mind. His spies told him Capitolinus passed his time off duty writing biographies. That hardly seemed suitable. Maximinus nodded, knowing he was scowling. His *adorable* half-barbarian scowl,

Paulina had called it. Most likely Capitolinus judged it differently.

With his thighs Maximinus guided his mount a few paces away from the officers. He regarded the legionaries. Where their helmets, scarves and beards revealed anything of their faces, they were pinched with the cold. The front ranks stood to attention, those further back quietly stamped their feet and beat their arms against their sides.

'A long way from the Alban Hills.' Maximinus pitched his voice to carry.

Those who could hear grinned. A murmur ran through the formation, like a wave retreating over a shingle beach, as the Emperor's words were repeated from man to man all the way to both flanks and the rear.

'These barbarians' – he waved towards the south – 'stand between us and warmth, between us and hot food, mulled wine, the baths, women and all the other pleasures of the camp. Defeat them today, and we will have broken the Iazyges, as we broke their cousins the Roxolani in the autumn. Defeat them, and the Danube frontier is safe from the Alps to the Black Sea. Defeat them, and we can cross the river, back into the empire, never to return to this empty wilderness.'

There was a muted noise of approval. Those in the rear had stopped moving, were straining to hear.

'Duty is hard. Those of us raised in the army know that truth. I am no Sophist, no clever speaker from the Forum. I will not lie to you, pretend things are other than they are. This summer we must make one final campaign into Germania. When they too have submitted, when the Rhine also is safe, then, at last, after these long and weary four years, I can lead you home to Italy, to your camp on the Alban Hills, where your wives and children wait for you. Duty is hard, but the end of our labours is in sight.'

Again, the shouts betrayed less than complete enthusiasm.

'Today, remember my orders, keep quiet in the ranks, listen to your officers. Remember you are Romans, they are barbarians. You have discipline, they do not. Give me victory, and I will reward you well. A year's pay to every man who fights. A year's pay to the dependents of any who fall.'

This time even the reminder of their own mortality did not dampen their spirits. As one, the men cheered.

Enrich the soldiers, ignore everyone else, Septimius Severus had said. There was much sense in the words of Maximinus' old commander.

'The 2nd Legion, the Parthian, Eternally Loyal, Faithful and Fortunate. You hold the right of the line, the position of honour. These barbarians' – this time his gesture was one of contempt – 'in their ignorance and blind stupidity, believe they have us at a disadvantage. But we know that the gods are delivering them to us. Kill them! Kill them all! Do not spare yourselves!'

35

Full-throated, the roar went up. Wheeling his horse, Maximinus rode towards the next body of men. The dark stain on the horizon had widened, filled out. He could not delay, but there was time for a few words to each formation in the infantry front line.

From the Ides of January, for a month he had quartered the Steppe, from the Danube to the foothills of the Carpathians. There had been several sharp engagements as he pursued and caught three tribal herds. Then, one night, when the army was far out, the main barbarian force had struck. The Iazyges had taken back their herds, had driven off much of the Roman baggage train. For another month the army had marched south, harassed, short of food. At first a thaw had set in, and they had waded through mud. Then a cold north wind had begun to blow again, bringing blizzards. The temperature dropped, as if the gods had reversed the seasons and midwinter had returned. In the mornings some sentries were found dead from the cold, others disembowelled. Finally, just two days' march north of the Danube, the entire horde of the Iazyges were waiting, drawn up across their path, many thousand horsemen arrayed for battle.

Maximinus had ordered a camp entrenched. The following morning the Iazyges again spread out across the Steppe ready to fight. Although the soldiers had thronged around him demanding he lead them against the barbarians, and the army had trembled on the edge of mutiny, Maximinus had not been swayed. For six days, as the fresh snow fell, the Iazyges paraded across the plain, and the legionaries and auxiliaries near rioted, he ignored all entreaties and threats, and held the army back behind its ditch and rampart. Food, forage and fuel were almost exhausted. Maximinus had the imperial supplies given to the troops, and had commanded all officers to likewise surrender their personal provisions. Apsines had made some flattering comparison to Alexander the Great, but most officers, unaccustomed to privation of any sort, let alone hunger, had not taken it well.

On the evening of the sixth day, when the Iazyges had departed to their distant encampment, Maximinus had distributed his orders, quietly without trumpets or commotion. That night, leaving torches burning along the fortifications, he had led the army out. In the strange glare of the snow, with no lights showing, they went east until they came across this unnamed watercourse, then followed it south. In the gloaming of the false dawn, he had selected his position, and drawn up his men.

The 2nd Legion formed the extreme right of twenty-four thousand heavy infantry stretching back to the frozen stream on the east. Eight thousand were Praetorians and one thousand, at the opposite end, among the trees, German tribesmen. The rest were legionaries, drawn from

across the northern frontiers. Flavius Vopiscus
had them all waiting in separate blocks, sixteen
ranks deep, with carefully measured intervals
between, like pieces on the board of a game of
latrunculi. Close behind them clustered some
two-and-a-half thousand archers, easterners from
Emesa, Osrhoene and Armenia, under Iotapianus.
Scattered among these shivering Orientals were
fifty small carts, their loads still covered with
tarpaulins.

A little way further back, lined up with the gaps
in the fighting line, were two thousand light
horsemen; Moors, Parthians and Persians. Their
mounts steaming in the frigid air, these men from
Africa and beyond the Euphrates would be a little
less cold than the archers on foot. Maximinus had
entrusted them to Volo, the *Princeps Peregrinorum*.
Although the task was unusual for the head of
the imperial spies, Volo had come up through the
ranks of the regular army, and Maximinus trusted
his judgement. The rest of the cavalry, three
thousand regular auxiliaries, a thousand of them
cataphracts, were some way out on the snowy
plain to the right of the infantry. Sabinus Modestus,
their commander, might not be over burdened
with intelligence, but he knew how to fight, and
that was all that was required of him on this
morning.

The reserve, such as it was, would consist of the
thousand horse guards under Maximinus himself
and three thousand auxiliary infantry led by

Florianus and Domitius. The latter also had charge of the mules and donkeys of the pack train. Neither animal being native to the Steppe, it was said local horses were wary of them. If it came down to that, things would be desperate indeed.

Riding down the front line of heavy infantry, Maximinus spoke briefly to each unit: discipline and order, trust and good faith, remember you are Roman, keep in mind the proud heritage of your unit, we have never been defeated, a year's bonus to each man. Under the bare branches of the trees, he told the Germans to think of their forebears, these nomads were their ancestral enemies, a gilded arm ring for every warrior who distinguished himself. Their leaders would have to translate his words. To speak in their tongue would have been a betrayal of his long-dead family, of all those who had died in his native village when he was little more than a child. They may have been from a different tribe, but all northern barbarians were the same; savages incapable of reason, pity or humanity.

As he cantered back to the horse guards, the thoughts of Maximinus were dark and resentful. The Senators called him Antaeus or Sciron. The first was a giant who compelled all comers to wrestle, and, when they were thrown and defence-less, slaughtered them. The second, a brigand, had enslaved innocent wayfarers, forced them to wait on him and wash his feet, and, when he tired of them, had hurled them down from the highest

39

cliffs onto the rocks in the sea. Why could the Senators not see, he did nothing that was not necessary. If the northern tribes were not conquered, Rome would fall. Everything must be subservient to the war.

Once, the Senators would have understood. Horatius had held the bridge, Mucius thrust his hand in the fire, the Decii, father and son, dedicated themselves to the gods of the underworld for Roman victory. But that was long ago. Centuries of peace and luxury, of disgusting eastern habits and quibbling Greek philosophy, had undermined the ancient virtue of the Roman nobility. The rich equestrians were no better. Instead of offering Rome their wealth, let alone their lives, the elite did nothing but conspire. Magnus and Catilius Severus as soon as he ascended the throne, then Valerius Messala in Asia, Balbus in Syria, Serenianus in Cappadocia; the list blurred in his memory, one betrayal ran into another. He would not think of Quartinus and Macedo, would not think of the cruellest treachery, and the death of his beloved wife Paulina.

Nothing would shake his resolve. Every conspiracy had been suppressed with rigour, their estates taken to fuel the war. The traitors served Rome in death, if not in life.

In punishment, as in all else, Maximinus had followed the example of his great patron, the divine Septimius Severus. Perhaps some of the family and friends of those condemned had not been

40

party to treason, but they had been guilty of something. Apsines had assured him that necessary severity was a virtue. Many had been executed, women and children as well as men, but it had brought the empire a measure of security. Maximinus had money to pay the army, and the contumacious should ponder the wisdom of further revolts.

Reining in by the Horse Guards, someone spoke to Maximinus. He waved him away. The mind of the Emperor surveyed his dominions. Rome was in safe hands. On the seven hills Vitalianus and Sabinus watched over disloyal Senators and turbulent plebeians alike. Of course, now he had solved the problems of the grain supply to the city, Timesitheus must die. A pity, for Maximinus had always liked the little Greek. But under torture Balbus had implicated the *Graeculus*, and the arrest warrant had been dispatched. It would be interesting to see how Timesitheus would endure when the closed carriage brought him to the army and he was put to the question. There were no other causes of concern in the West or North. As governor of Germania Superior, Catius Priscillianus oversaw the Rhine, Honoratus held the lower Danube, and no one was more trustworthy than Decius in Spain.

Balbus had been the brother-in-law of the governor of Africa, but there was little to fear from the octogenarian Gordian, his drunk and debauched son, or the other effete upper-class legates in the province. In any event, Capelianus in neighbouring Numidia would keep an eye on the Gordiani, his vigilance focused by an old animosity.

The East gave more pause for thought. Among the many names Balbus had gasped out as he was stretched on the rack, the claws and pincers tearing at his flesh, had been that of the governor of Mesopotamia. In the face of Sassanid Persian attacks, with war raging between the two rivers, it was not a good time to remove Priscus. Regular reports came to the imperial headquarters from the one very close to Priscus that Volo had suborned. So far nothing had supported the allegations. There was always the danger that a coward like Balbus might name anyone in the vain hope of easing his agony. It was unfortunate that Serenianus, himself ultimately a victim of Balbus' confessions, had maintained his silence under the most diligent and inventive ministrations of the torturers. Had he not been a traitor, his resilience would have been admirable. The East was a worry, but Maximinus was somewhat reassured since he had sent Catius Clemens to replace Serenianus in Cappadocia. From there, with two legions at his back, the new governor could supervise the eastern territories. Having been one of Maximinus' earliest supporters and closest advisors, Catius Clemens was intimately associated with the regime. He appeared loyal, as much as any Senator could be counted, and in his brothers, one the governor of Germania Superior, the other in Rome, he had left hostages in the West.

'Father.'

Maximinus regarded his son with disfavour.

'Father, the enemy are near. We should send out our horsemen.' There was no mistaking the note of apprehension in the voice of his son.

Over the heads of the infantry, Maximinus now could see the Iazyges cavalry. Individuals could be just distinguished riding in the gaps between their columns, but he could not yet make out the round dots of their heads. It meant the Sarmatian tribesmen were between thirteen hundred and a thousand paces distant. They were coming on slowly, still moving at a walk. There was plenty of time, but no point in leaving things until the last moment. He gave the order for the cavalry to advance.

A trumpet rang out. Its call was repeated throughout the army. Volo's men swung up into the saddle, and cantered away through the intervals in the line of heavy-armed foot. There was a short pause, and then the light horse out on the Steppe to the right also moved off. The cataphracts remained with Sabinus Modestus, level with the infantry front line.

Maximinus often wondered how he and Paulina had produced such a son as Verus Maximus. Perhaps at the moment of conception she had looked at something weak and perverse, some picture or statue. Certainly – and it was the one criticism he would make of her – she had spoilt the boy. Things might have been different if they

43

had had other children. But the gods had not been kind. While she lived, their son had attempted to disguise his vices. Now she was dead, and he was Caesar, the only thing Verus Maximus tried to mask was his cruelty to his wife. Maximinus felt sorry for Iunia Fadilla. An attractive girl, she seemed amiable and easy going. Most young men would be delighted to have such a wife. Verus Maximus must be a fool to think his father did not know. Of course there were imperial spies in their household. His son was a fool, as well as a coward.

Ahead volleys of arrows arced up into the sky from both sides and fell like squalls of black rain. Squadrons of Persian and Parthian horse wheeled back towards the army, then turned and raced towards the enemy, before wheeling back again; all the time shooting, as fast as they could. Here and there the tiny shape of a man pitched from his mount, or rider and mount together crashed to the ground, as a nomad shaft found its target. Volo's Moors would be closer to the Iazyges, using their javelins. Like all light-cavalry fights, to the inexperienced eye it would look like chaos.

Maximinus called for his warhorse. While Borysthenes was led up, his gaze fell on Marius Perpetuus. The Consular looked as frightened as the young Caesar next to him. Maximinus had given him the signal honour of being one of the two Consuls who had taken up office on the first day of the previous year because once, in his youth, he had served under Perpetuus' father. The son was not the man his father had been. Few Senators matched their ancestors. Virtue was in decline. Was Perpetuus one of those who muttered against their Emperor? Closeted with his ilk, all servants banished, drink imparting a spurious boldness, did Perpetuus call him Spartacus; the Thracian slave, the Thracian gladiator?

Without dismounting, Maximinus stepped from the hack to the charger. He leant forward, smelling the clean, warm horse in the frigid air. He rubbed Borysthenes' ears, patted his neck. The sky was overcast; the wind getting up at Maximinus' back carried a few flakes of snow.

Paulina had been right. The elite hated him, not just for what he did, but for what he was. Maximinus had never tried to hide his origins. He had been a shepherd boy in the wild hills of Thrace. What else could he have been in the small village of Ovile? He had risen through the ranks of the army, via the patronage of Septimius Severus and his son Caracalla, but also through his courage and his devotion to duty. He had achieved high command, but he had never desired the throne. The recruits he had been training had forced the purple on him. He would have been dead within the day, his head on a pike, if the Senatorial triumvirate of Flavius Vopiscus, Honoratus, and Catius Clemens had not ridden into his camp and offered him their oath and that of the legionaries they led.

Maximinus had not wanted to be Emperor. It had brought nothing but tragedy. Micca, his life-long friend and bodyguard, speared in the back as they stormed a ridge in the forests of Germania. Tynchanius, his companion since childhood, cut down by mutineers in the town of Viminacium. Even now, twenty-one months after, Maximinus' mind often shied away from that day. Other times, like now, he faced the horror. Tynchanius had died trying to save Paulina. The old man had failed. Reports indicated she was alive when she fell from the high window. Maximinus would never know if she had jumped or was pushed. But his imaginings of her last moments – the cobbles of the street rushing up – would never leave him.

Shouts and the rumble of hooves brought Maximinus back to the wintry plain. Volo's light horse were steaming back through the infantry. All order gone, each man seemed to ride for his own life, the picture of rout. Off on the right, it was the same with the auxiliary troopers. Like a stream in spate, they lapped around the cataphracts of Sabinus Modestus, circling and pooling behind the motionless iron-clad men and horses.

Now, Maximinus thought, gazing forward. By Jupiter Optimus Maximus, by all the gods, *now*. As if impelled by his will, the rear eight ranks of the legionaries and Praetorians jogged around their fellow soldiers, and filled the gaps between their formations. Where there had been isolated pieces, waiting to be swept from the board, now stood a

46

solid mass of armoured men. Eight deep, shoulder to shoulder, the silent line of soldiers reached out two thousand paces from the wooded stream.

Maximinus spat on his chest for luck. Flavius Vopiscus had done his part. Now it depended on the Iazyges. Everything hung in the balance. The spittle trickled down over the sculpted muscles of his cuirass. Would the nomads take the bait?

Iotapianus was hurrying his archers close up behind the heavy infantry. The covers were being pulled off the carts, men leaping up to man the catapults on them.

Drums and horns sounded out to the south. The Iazyges were ordering their lines, the horse archers retiring, the armoured lancers moving to the fore. Did they believe the Romans were afraid, starving, had attempted to escape them by a night march? Had they taken the flight of the Roman light horse at face value?

In the centre of the Roman line, where Flavius Vopiscus stood with his veteran legionaries from Pannonia, the tall pikes of the front ranks shifted and clacked together like dry reeds when the wind blows. Maximinus smiled. Daemon-haunted, Vopiscus might be, but an intelligent competence lived alongside his many superstitions. One evening in camp, they had discussed the signs an experienced commander can read on a battlefield: how the sounds the troops make and the way they brandish their weapons can reveal their state of mind; how nothing more clearly indicates fear than the wavering of spears. This was an unexpected touch of near genius from Vopiscus – as long as the pretence did not translate into the reality.

The barbarian drums beat a different rhythm, their horns blared, savage incitements to battle. At a slow walk, long, thin lances pricking the sky, the Iazyges began their advance. Numbers were impossible to judge. The armoured warriors in the front rank rode knee to knee. They stretched unbroken from the line of trees to beyond the Roman infantry, and beyond the cataphracts. Sabinus Modestus had the latter arrayed two deep. Say two paces for each cataphract, another two thousand paces. Exceeding four thousand paces, the enemy frontage had to contain over three thousand riders, possibly many more, and their formation was very deep, no telling how many ranks.

'Gods below,' someone muttered. 'Look at them.'

'Silence in the ranks,' Maximinus snapped.

The Sarmatian tribesmen were closing into effective bowshot, some three hundred paces beyond Maximinus' position behind the front line. Bright dragon standards writhed above tall pointed helmets and a shimmering wall of scale armour. They had moved up to a canter. Necks arched, their horses were plunging, lifting their front legs high to break through the standing snow, hooves struggling to find purchase.

It had worked. They were committed. Maximinus

took stock. Volo's light horse were moving close up behind the infantry, and the auxiliary cavalry out to the east had rallied around Sabinus Modestus' cataphracts. Maximinus gave the order for the cohorts under Florianus and Domitius to pivot to the right to protect the rear of the legionaries should, as was only too likely, the riders under Modestus be overwhelmed.

Maximinus and the horse guards stood alone in the lightly falling snow.

A fresh peal of trumpets from the Roman front line. The long pikes that the front four ranks had been issued for this campaign swung down. The rear four ranks hefted their shields above their heads. A moment later the thrum of thousands of bowstrings. The *click-slide-thump* of the ballistae. The air was full of projectiles; arrows arcing, artillery bolts darting. The arrows seemed to vanish into the mass of barbarian horsemen, their effect negligible. Where the ballista bolts struck Iazyges went down, men and horses crashing to the frozen plain. The following riders jostled and bored around them. Some were brought down. The line became ragged, but the momentum was unbroken.

A hundred paces out, every detail was visible. Scale-armoured warriors and mounts – steel, leather, horn – fused together like some nightmarish amphibian beast. The wicked spearpoints bobbing through the cloud of kicked-up snow. Wild-eyed horses, ropes of saliva streaming from their gaping mouths. Fierce bestial faces of the riders, screaming, the sounds lost in the thunder of their coming.

Seventy paces. The archers – horse and foot – shooting as fast as they could over the heads of the legionaries. The artillerymen winding their machines like daemons. All their efforts futile. Nothing human could break that charge.

Fifty paces. A tremor ran through the Roman line. Stand, boys! Stand, *pueri*, stand! Maximinus was yelling. Forty paces. Thirty. The line held, a hedge of pikes, backed by a wall of bodies.

Hauling on their reins, encumbered by their swaying lances, the Iazyges tried to pull up. Horses swerved, skidding on the slippery surface. They collided, fell, took the legs out from under others. In a heartbeat the irresistible charge was reduced to a tangle of flailing, fragile limbs, and the crushing, rolling weight of horseflesh. *Pila* flashed up from the rear ranks of the infantry. The square steel points of the heavy javelins punched down into the mass of rearing, balking horses, and the riders clinging desperately to their necks, punched through armour, down into flesh.

A terrible sound, like a great oak falling in a forest, smashing its way through other trees. Towards the right of the line a lone Sarmatian horse – maddened with fear and pain, perhaps already dead – had run on, impaled itself on the pikes of the 2nd Legion. Falling, its bulk crushed legionaries, hurled others backwards. Its rider was thrown over its head, knocking more soldiers off their feet. Like flood water surging at a crack in a dam, Iazyges poured into the opening.

'Follow me!' Unhooking his shield from the horn of his saddle, Maximinus brought his heels into Borysthenes' ribs. The huge warhorse gathered itself, iron-studded hipposandals biting into the snow and ice, it bounded forward. Maximinus dragged his sword from its scabbard.

The first Sarmatians were through. A dozen or so, no more yet. Lances jabbed down at fleeing bowmen. Long, straight blades swung in deadly, shining arcs.

The leading warrior sawed his reins to meet Maximinus. He thrust his lance. Maximinus turned it with the flat of his sword, urged Borysthenes into the other horse. The Sarmatian's mount was set back nearly on its quarters. Its rider, lance jolted out of his grip, was half-out of the saddle. Another barbarian cut at Maximinus from his left. Taking the blow on the rim of his shield, Maximinus thrust back. The tip of his steel slid off scale armour. The Iazyges on his right had regained his seat, was clawing for the hilt of his sword. Backhanded, Maximinus brought the edge of his blade down into his opponent's shoulder, buckling armour, biting into bone.

The world contracted to the reach of a sword. Maximinus fought with controlled ferocity. Cut, parry, thrust: nothing else existed. Long training and the memory in his muscles guided his hand. Steel ringing on steel. Men and horses screaming

51

in fury and pain and fear. The iron taste of blood in the mouth. The breath torn from his chest, burning. From nowhere a face, insane with terror, in his own. Gone in a moment, down under the stamping, trampling hooves.

Ahead a dragon, red tongue lolling from gaping silver jaws, its scaled, green body twisting in the wind. Below it a chieftain, tattooed forearms protruding from gilded and chased armour. A well-equipped warrior holding the standard, others banded in front.

Roaring an invocation to the fierce deity of his native hills, Maximinus drove forward. The Rider God was with him. A flurry of blows, too fast to be accounted, and he was in their midst. Now other horses impeding his progress. Borysthenes was brought to a standstill. Maximinus' shield was wrenched from his grasp. A clanging impact hit the back of his helmet. Vision blurred, he twisted this way and that, fending off the sharp, questing steel that would take his life. As if through a glass, he saw Javolenus and Julius Capitolinus trying to cut their way through to him. Too late, he was surrounded.

Death held no fear for him. Reunited with Paulina, he would ride the highland for eternity. But not yet. First the chieftain must die. Blocking a blow from his left, one from his right, Maximinus kicked Borysthenes on. The great-hearted beast shouldered through the tumult.

The chieftain swung at his head. Catching the

sword on his own, the impact shuddered up Maximinus' arm. With his left hand, he seized the Sarmatian's wrist, dragged him off balance, then smashed the pommel of his own sword into the snarling face. Something struck from behind, hard enough to drive jagged, broken fragments of armour into his shoulder blade. Ignoring the pain, he brought the pommel down on the chieftain's temple. The barbarian went down, his armour clattering.

Turning, seeking the next threat, Maximinus saw Javolenus hack down the standard bearer. The snarling dragon dipped, and toppled into the fouled, blood-stained slush.

'They are running!'

Julius Capitolenus' words held no meaning.

'Augustus, they are beaten.'

Painfully fighting air into his chest, Maximinus took in the stricken field. The Iazyges were streaming away to the south. Those unhorsed and not too wounded to get to their feet were struggling to catch the bridle of a mount and follow. The rest – the living and the dead – were being butchered, mutilated and chopped into sides of meat.

'Sabinus Modestus and the right?' Maximinus was hoarse, his words a grating whisper.

'Dead or chased off the field. But the auxiliary cohorts on the flank did not break. Maybe Sarmatian horses are scared of donkeys after all. The barbarians are fleeing there too.'

Maximinus felt no elation, instead nothing but

pain and a weary relief. His plans had worked. His delaying had made the barbarians over confident. Exulting, they had thought to ride down a demoralized rabble. Their long approach, and the fresh snow had tired their horses. The battle was won, but now the advantage had to be pressed.

'Open the ranks.' Maximinus found it an effort to talk. His left shoulder was burning. 'Have Volo's light horse pursue them. They must be harried, not allowed to reform.'

As shouts and trumpet calls relayed his orders, Maximinus' son rode up.

'I give you joy of our victory.' Verus Maximus was immaculate, his beautiful face radiant. It could not have been more evident that the Caesar had not fought.

Exhausted, blood-stained and wounded, Maximinus regarded him with disdain.

My sons will inherit, or no one, Vespasian had said. It was the attitude of all Emperors. Even Septimius Severus had let the treacherous Geta accede with his brother Caracalla. The Romans of old had been made of sterner stuff. When Brutus discovered his sons were trying to reintroduce monarchy, he had them dragged to the Forum, flogged, tied to a stake, and beheaded.

Maximinus looked away. High over the Steppe a pair of buzzards were circling, soaring on motionless wings. A man could disinherit his son. Those Emperors who had no son had adopted their heirs. Everyone told him, the will of the Emperor is law.

CHAPTER 5

ROME
THE SENATE HOUSE

The Day before the Nones of March, AD*238*

Pupienus looked up and out of the window high on the opposite wall of the Curia. All the windows were open. The noise of the mob bore in like a spring tide. It buffeted among the gilded beams of the ceiling and broke on the heads of the hundred or so Senators brave or ambitious enough to attend. *Kill them! Kill the enemies of the Roman people! Let them be dragged with the hook! To the Tiber with them!* Pupienus knew too much about the plebs not to despise them. He was glad the doors were bolted.

It was the first thing the Consul had done. After the clerks, scribes and other public servants had left, he had ordered the doors closed and barred. The Lictors stood guard outside. The ceremonial attendants of the few magistrates present would have little chance if the mob determined to force an entrance, none at all if the soldiers intervened. But it was better than nothing.

The religious observances hurriedly completed,

the Consul had declared the Senate in closed session, and required the Quaestor Menophilus read the letter from Africa.

In the shadows, Pupienus sat with his friends and relatives listening. He had forgotten how dark it was inside the Senate House with the doors shut. The gloom smelt of incense and spilt wine, of unwashed men and fear. Pupienus drew strength from those around him: from his two sons and his brother-in-law, and from his two particular *amici*, Rutilius Crispinus and Cuspidius Severus. One could never overestimate the importance of family and friends in Roman politics. All those close to him were ex-Consuls, the last two, like himself, new men, the first of their families to enter the Senate. A solid cohort of men, devoted to duty and the *Res Publica*, they radiated *dignitas*, that untranslatable mixture of propriety, achieved rank and nobility of soul. The Greeks had no such word. That was why they were subjects, and the Romans ruled the world.

Menophilus had been reading the letter from the elder Gordian aloud, and now was coming to the end of it.

'Conscript Fathers: the young men, to whom was entrusted Africa to guard, have called on me against my will to rule. But having regard to you, I am glad to endure this necessity. It is yours to decide what you wish. For myself, I shall waver to and fro in uncertainty until the Senate has decided.'

The elder Gordian had expressed the right sentiments in it. The throne had been thrust upon him. He had accepted not from ambition, but love of Rome. He had raised his son to share the purple from the same motive. He acknowledged the right of the Senate to give an Emperor his powers, to confer legitimacy. But, Pupienus reflected, was it all too weak? Should an Emperor waver to and fro, admit to indecision? Was not a certain measure of ambition laudable? And was there any chance the Gordiani, father and son, could prevail? Menophilus' clever lie that Maximinus was already dead had bought them some time. It had summoned the plebs onto the streets, and sown indecision among the supporters of the Thracian. But now it was clear that Maximinus was alive, and what could stand against him and the might of the northern armies?

Before the Consul could proceed, the other envoy from Africa joined Menophilus on the floor of the house, and asked permission to speak. Up on the Consular tribunal, Fulvius Pius looked relieved the initiative had been taken from him, and he granted the request.

Valerian was a big man, in middle age. Clean shaven, short hair receding above a broad forehead, both his looks and his reputation proclaimed an open, trusting nature, not overburdened with insight. From a traditional Italian family of senatorial status, he had held the Consulship years before, and it had been considered to add prestige to Gordian the Elder's term of office when Valerian had agreed to be one of the governor's legates in Africa. Even so, Pupienus might have been reluctant to accompany him to this meeting – to put himself and those he loved at such risk – if Valerian had not arrived at his house with the Consul Fulvius Pius. In politics, as in everything else, one thing leads to another, like links in a chain.

'Conscript Fathers, the two Gordiani, both ex-Consuls, the one your Pro-Consul, the other your legate, have been declared Emperors by a great assembly in Africa. Let us give thanks, then, to the young men of Thysdrus, and thanks also to the ever loyal people of Carthage. They have freed us from subservience to Maximinus, from that savage monster, from that wild beast, from that barbarian. The family of the Gordiani descend from the noblest Romans, from the house of the Gracchi and that of the divine Trajan.'

So that was how it was to be, Pupienus thought. Valerian would launch ponderous invective against Maximinus and laud the Gordiani with obvious praise. But would it be enough to sway the frightened yet calculating Senators huddled in the close, dark chamber?

Drag them, drag them with the hook! The shouts of the mob rolled around the Senate House, filled the pauses in the speech. Most Senators hated Maximinus and his son, for the confiscations, for the executions of their families and friends, for his casual lack of respect, ultimately for not being one of them. They hated him as keenly as the plebs outside, but, unlike the latter, they lacked the comparative safety of anonymity.

Pupienus ran his gaze over where those openly committed to the Gordiani sat together. Valerian was supported by his brother-in-law Egnatius Marinianus, and a more distant relative by marriage, Egnatius Proculus, the Curator of the Roads and Prefect of the Poor Relief. With Menophilus were young Virius Lupus, a fellow Quaestor, and the latter's elderly father Lucius Virius. One coeval each of the Elder and Younger Gordiani was seated with them, respectively Appius Claudius Julianus and Celsus Aelianus. That was the heart of the problem. Gordian the father was so old that all his closest allies were in retirement or dead. Gordian the son had spent so many years in the provinces – most recently in Syria, Achaea and now Africa – the only associates who remained in Rome were relics of his disreputable youth. Like him, the handful of his friends who had grown into some responsibility were serving the *Res Publica* abroad; Claudius Julianus governing Dalmatia, and Fidus had charge of Thrace. Pupienus had a good memory, and prided himself on knowing such things.

As a faction those backing the Gordiani in the Curia were lacking in numbers and authority – a few greybeards, a couple of Quaestors and, the gods help them, *the Curator of the Roads and Prefect of the Poor Relief*. Yet they must be brave men, or perhaps merely foolhardy. Even the slowest or most senile of them must know that should the decision go against them today, the only way they would leave the Senate House alive would be while they were dragged the few paces to the *Tullianum*. Many enemies of Rome and innumerable victims of an Emperor's animosity had been strangled by the executioners in that dank, repugnant subterranean gaol. Those prisoners who emerged blinking into the painful light only did so to be hurled to their deaths from the Tarpeian Rock.

'Your choice is simple, Conscript Fathers, barbarian tyranny or Roman freedom. Continue to live in a besieged city, always in fear, or recall liberty to Rome.'

Only the other seven diehard Gordiani shook back the folds of their togas and applauded Valerian's conclusion. Everyone else sat very still.

His face as impassive as that of the gilded statue of Victory that loomed over the tribunal, Pupienus surreptitiously surveyed the House. There were next to no Senators here closely tied to the regime of Maximinus. His eye fell on Catius Celer. His elder brothers had helped put the Thracian on the throne, but Celer's expression was as unreadable as Pupienus' own.

Much depended on the absent Prefect of the City. Sabinus had not been summoned. Yet soon, if not already, someone would inform him that the Senate was meeting, and by now he might know that Maximinus still lived. What would he do?

With the Praetorian Prefect Vitalianus dead, Sabinus stood alone as Maximinus' chief adherent in Rome. Potens, the commander of the Watch was of far less import.

No one knew better than Pupienus the latent power of a Prefect of the City. The previous year he had been unceremoniously removed from that office – *insufficient zeal in his duties*, the imperial letter of dismissal had read – and Sabinus appointed in his place. At the time Pupienus had been grateful to be allowed to retire into private life, glad to be left alive, his estates unconfiscated, his family unharmed. Subsequently it had come to rankle. Insufficient zeal had amounted to not turning the swords of the soldiers under his command loose on his fellow citizens, of avoiding a massacre. It remained to be seen if Sabinus would exercise the same restraint now he led the six thousand men of the Urban Cohorts.

In the lengthening hush – even the mob in the Forum had quietened – all eyes turned to Fulvius Pius. The Consul licked his lips, cleared his throat. 'Following senatorial procedure, I would call on the Consuls designate. But in their absence . . .' He looked around the assembly, as if searching for some improbable salvation. Most of the Conscript Fathers looked away, studying the patterned marble of walls or floor. 'I call on the Father of the House to give us his advice.'

An audible sigh of relief came from the benches – let old Cuspidius Celerinus speak, not them.

The octogenarian levered himself to his feet with a walking stick.

'A momentous day, and a heavy responsibility.' His thin, reedy voice struggled to reach the back benches. Those behind him craned forward, turning their heads, cupping hands to ears. The next part of the exordium was drowned as the plebs outside burst into impromptu song: *Fuck the Thracian up the arse, up the arse, up the arse!*

Four Senators, led by the hirsute figure of the Cynic Gallicanus, took it on themselves to unbar the main door, and slip out. If any Senator could quiet the masses, Pupienus thought, it was the demagogic follower of Diogenes, and his like-minded coterie. Sure enough, a short time later the obscene chorus died, and they returned. Pupienus noted with a measure of alarm that they failed to secure the door.

Now quiet had returned, the Father of the House, who had continued inaudibly throughout, also fell silent. His head twisted on his scrawny neck, a display hideously reminiscent of a tortoise. Before continuing, he smiled, as if the new state of affairs were a product of his own oratory.

'Only twice has this august house deposed a reigning Emperor. The first occasion was that disgusting actor Nero. Even I was not alive then.' Cuspidius Celerinus laughed, a gasping, senile sound. 'But the other time I was here. Didius Julianus had bought the throne at auction. Gesturing with his fingers up at the Praetorians on the walls of their

62

camp. A more disgraceful spectacle has never been seen in Rome. We stripped from him the purple he was unworthy to wear. Didius Julianus was a drunk and a fool, but he was not a barbarian.'

The stillness inside the Curia was so profound the silence itself seemed to be listening.

'Maximinus was born a barbarian, and he should die like a barbarian. Bloodthirsty, irrational, beyond all redemption, he will kill us all, if we do not kill him first.'

His powers were failing, Pupienus thought. Three years before the Father of the House had made a far better oration, distinct and sensible, with apposite echoes of Virgil and Livy, when he had recommended the Senate grant Maximinus all the honours and powers of an Emperor. And now . . . Still, when you were as near the underworld as Cuspidius Celerinus, there was little to hold you back from advocating fatal courses.

When it became evident that the Father of the House had no more to say, again all attention focused on the tribunal. Aware he was presiding over a meeting that was slipping towards open treason, Fulvius Pius scanned the room with an air close to panic. 'Senatorial procedure . . .' His gaze fell upon the group of patricians on the front bench opposite Pupienus. 'The Senator next in order of seniority should speak. I call on Decimus Caelius Calvinus Balbinus.'

The man in question appeared to be asleep, or as comatose as made no difference. Most likely he had come to the session from drinking all night. Gods below, Pupienus loathed those indolent, arrogant patricians, detested their endless complacent talk of their ancestors, and hated their sneering contempt for those – like himself – they regarded as their inferiors. Rome is but your stepmother, they said to him. Tell us of your father's achievements. He never replied. Everyone knew about his youth in Tibur, brought up by a lowly kinsman, the Emperor's head gardener. But what happened before, his childhood in Voleterrae, not even his sons knew. As long as ingenuity, subterfuge and money served, he would keep it that way. Dear gods, it must remain that way, or he was ruined.

Balbinus' neighbour, the grossly obese Valerius Priscillianus, touched his arm. Balbinus opened his porcine eyes, and blearily looked around. Valerius Priscillianus whispered to him. Balbinus did not respond. With a strange delicacy, Priscillianus pinched his recalcitrant friend's ear. Balbinus slapped his hand away.

Now that was interesting, Pupienus thought. The superstitious thought the ear lobe the seat of memory. What did one corpulent patrician want the other to remember? Was it that Maximinus had killed both Valerius Priscillianus' father and brother? Could familial feeling stir even the fathomless lethargy of these patricians?

'Let him be slain, that he who best deserves alone may reign.'

Having recited the line of Virgil, Balbinus folded

64

his hands over his protruding stomach, and, with something like a smirk, closed his eyes.

You fool, Pupienus thought, equivocation will not save you. Whichever side carried this debate, and whichever rulers finally emerged in undisputed possession of the throne, would consider all those who had not supported them as their enemies. If the Gordiani were triumphant, the repercussions might be less swift and savage, but all Emperors bear a grudge, and, if their memory fails them, there are always others to remind them of any perceived injury or slight.

Gallicanus was given the floor. His constant companion Maecenas stepped forward from the small philosophical brotherhood, and took a place close behind him. The wool of Gallicanus' toga was coarse and homespun, an ostentatious symbol of his often trumpeted devotion to old-fashioned frugality and morality. From under his rough cut mane of hair, he glared about, fierce censure personified. Given a wallet and a staff, and he could have been Diogenes himself, crawled from his barrel and ready to admonish Alexander the Great. Surely even he was not about to propose the ludicrous scheme he had once suggested to Pupienus of restoring the free Republic?

'Maximinus has murdered our loved ones. No one has escaped. Gordian the Elder mourns his son-in-law, Gordian the Younger his brother-in-law, Valerius Priscillianus his father and brother, Pupienus his lifelong friend Serenianus.'

Pupienus' face remained as blank as the outer wall of a town house.

'A tide of innocent blood, flowing across the empire: Memmia Sulpicia in Africa, Antigonus in Moesia, Ostorius in Cilicia.' As the names rolled out, fired by his own rhetoric, Gallicanus swung his hairy arms, gesturing with angry, simian motions.

'If any spark of ancestral virtue remains in our breasts,' Gallicanus dropped to a murmur, 'any spark at all, we must free ourselves.' Now he shouted. 'Declare Maximinus and his son enemies of the Senate and People of Rome!'

Enemies, enemies. The first shouts came from the faction of the Gordiani. They were joined by mutterings from the darkness of the back benches.

'Proclaim the Gordiani Emperors!'

Emperors, Emperors. The sound swelled, echoed off the panelled walls. Gallicanus had won the house over. As the Cynic dog stood, exulting, Maecenas slipped an arm around his waist.

Not waiting for the Consul to put the question, the Senators began to chant.

Enemies, enemies! He who slays the Maximini shall be rewarded. Let them hang on a cross. Let them be burnt alive. Enemies, enemies!

Pupienus got to his feet. Thessalian persuasion, he thought; necessity disguised as choice. Dear gods, how would this end? With his friends and relatives, he walked to the middle of the floor, the better to be seen. He filled his lungs, and shouted with the rest.

To the gods below with Maximinus and his son. We name the Gordiani Emperors. May we see our noble Emperors victorious, may Rome see our Emperors!

CHAPTER 6

AFRICA
CARTHAGE

The Day before the Nones of March, AD238

'Death is nothing to us,' Gordian said the words to himself, barely moving his lips. The sound of their horses' hooves and the rattle of their armament echoed back from the walls of the unnaturally deserted street. Gordian could smell the sea. They were nearly down at the port.

'Where we are death is not, and where death is we are not.'

A gap in the buildings revealed the turquoise waters of the Gulf of Utica off to the right. A merchantman was beating into the westerly breeze. Its sails shone white in the sun. A string of villas showed minute along the far shore, and behind the mountains rose green and rugged and misted with distance.

Death was nothing but a return to sleep. But Gordian did not want to sleep. The true goal of life was pleasure. The world was full of pleasure, and he had not had his fill. He knew he was scared, and he did not want to die. He was far from virtue, nowhere near the wisdom of Epicurus.

When word of the mutiny spread the crowd had flowed out of the Circus like wine from a broken amphora. Those at the front, still unaware, had been hailing the new Augusti – *May you rule safely, the gods watch over you* – as those at the back were running.

There and then they had questioned the tribune of the 3rd Legion, a makeshift *consilium* in the imperial box. Suillius had provided straightforward answers. No, he could not identify any ringleaders. Yes, the Centurions had remained loyal. The men had not listened to their officers, but so far had offered them no violence. The legionaries had withdrawn to the island in the old military harbour. The Cohort was up to strength, but, with men on detached duties, there were less than four hundred mutineers. They had torn the images of the Gordiani from the standards, but, as Suillius had had them destroyed, no portraits of Maximinus or his son had been available to replace them.

Once he had ascertained that the only other unit stationed in Carthage, the 13th Urban Cohort, had exhibited no signs of disaffection, Sabinianus had argued for tough measures. 'We should deal with them as Septimius Severus dealt with the Praetorians, or Caracalla the Alexandrians. I will get them off the island by subterfuge. Soldiers have little intelligence. Pretending that I have deserted you and reverted to Maximinus, tears of sincerity running down my face, I will lure them here, draw them up down on the racetrack. While I am addressing them from the comparative safety of this imperial box – promising them the heads of you all, or anything else that comes into my mind – fill the stands with the Urban Cohort, our new Praetorians, Horse Guards and the Scouts. Once they are surrounded, outnumbered by more than three to one, you can make your choice; disarm them or kill them. I favour the latter, a salutary dose of severity.'

Arrian had dismissed the need for the dangerous duplicity. Blockade the island; the mutineers could surrender or starve.

'Gods below,' Sabinianus had laughed at his fellow Cercopes, 'I hate it when your simple-mindedness tramples my Odysseus-like cunning.'

Gordian the Elder had been dead set against. Their reign should not begin with treachery and massacre. Gordian had seconded his father. Feeling like a Roman of old, a hero of the free Republic, he had announced he would go and recall the legionaries to their duty. Equally, like characters from a story in Livy, almost everyone else had said they would go with him. Gordian had demurred. He would take just the bodyguard Brennus, to ensure that he did not become a hostage, was not taken alive. He had never felt more noble. If he was killed, he had said, the others should implement the plan of Arrian, and take revenge. Much discussion ensued. In the end, Gordian had agreed to have Arrian accompany him and Brennus, with Aemilius Severinus and his detachment of twenty Scouts as a token escort. Sabinianus had said he would ring the island with the loyal troops, promising to keep them out of sight.

Gordian had called for his armour, and wriggled out of the constricting folds of his toga; better to go to them as a soldier than clad in purple. Arrian and Aemilius Severinus had done the same. Their struggles with straps, buckles and knots were interrupted by an awful dull thump. Serenus Sammonicus had collapsed onto the hard marble. The heat and the tension had been too much for the old tutor. *A doctor, a doctor!* Everyone shouted. *Give him room,* as they crowded around, ineffectually fanning him. Gordian the Elder had knelt by his unconscious friend. Cradling Serenus' head, he muttered, incoherent in his horror. For a moment, Gordian had feared his father would speak of the prodigy or the words of the astrologer. His worries had proved unfounded, a lifetime of reining his emotions like a horse on a curb bit did not fail his father.

The cavalcade emerged onto the quayside. The hexagonal commercial harbour lay to the right, the circular military one ahead. Gordian saw the crowds out on the island. The mutineers stood silent, watching. Gordian led his small party to the left, around towards the one bridge. The dockside was deserted. Not a stevedore in sight, just piles of crates, bales, amphorae, thick coils of

71

rope. No sailor visible on the moored merchantmen. Not a sound except their horses' clopping tread and rigging slapping against masts in the gusting breeze.

Death is nothing to us. The thought did not ease the constriction in his chest.

A dense mass of legionaries blocked the arch at the end of the bridge. They were armed, carried shields, but so far the shields still had their covers on and their swords remained sheathed. They stood in no order, silent and hostile.

'Imperator Marcus Antonius Gordianus.' He announced himself laconically, just the military title, and the first three of his names.

'You can pass, but not the others.' The speaker was an old legionary. Doubtless his back bore the scars of decades of insubordination.

'All or none,' Gordian said.

'Let them in,' another old soldier said. 'Twenty-four men are easily overcome.'

Grinning unpleasantly, the legionaries shuffled aside.

Gordian nudged his mount out onto the bridge, the others following.

The mob closed behind them.

The water on either side was very blue. The air full of the accustomed smells of seafaring; hemp, mutton fat, tar, and salt encrusted timber under a hot sun.

Death is nothing. What would Alexander have

done? He had quelled one mutiny by saying it was more dangerous to turn back than go on. In another he had brooded in his tent. Neither was appropriate. The latter had not worked even for the Macedonian conqueror of the world.

The crowd was dense on the island. There was no tribunal. Gordian walked his horse towards the temple in the middle. The press parted slowly, with ill grace.

Julius Caesar had dismissed an entire legion with one word: *citizens*. They had clamoured to be recalled to the standards. That was unlikely to be the case here.

'Maximinus Imperator!' a voice called from the rear ranks. 'Gordiani traitors!' shouted another.

Brennus closed up on Gordian's left flank. Not a reassuring presence, given his role today.

Something flew past Gordian's head. He jerked back, and his horse shied. Laughter all around. Another missile overshot, rebounded off a mutineer's shield, and rolled across the pavement. A turnip – humiliating, but not lethal.

Gordian held up his hand, palm out, as if in benediction. He forced himself to smile. 'We are in your power. Hear us out.'

'Hear him, hear him,' some of the more respectable-looking muttered.

'Then we nail him to a cross,' yelled a soldier at the back.

At the foot of the steps, Gordian dismounted carefully. He was not so young anymore. The great climactic forty-ninth year was still some way off, but sometimes his limbs felt his age. He hung his helmet on a saddle horn – they would need to see his face – and handed his reins to one of the Scouts. As he ascended, all the Scouts except the horse holders went to follow, but a surge of legionaries blocked them.

Atop the podium of the temple, Gordian stopped and turned. Brennus was on his left shoulder, Arrian his right. Aemilius Severinus and just two of the Scouts were with them. Could they fall back, hold the door of the sanctuary? Gordian dismissed the idea. The *speculatores* were doughty fighters, but no one would wager on these odds. Their only salvation lay with words, not swords.

The front rank of the mutineers was a few steps below; a wall of hostile faces. Discipline cast off for but an hour or so, and already they looked slovenly and dirty. They were packed together without order, standards sloping randomly above. On one of the standards were hung boards with crude drawings: a brute of a man whose jutting chin almost touched his hooked nose, and a delicate youth with bee-stung lips. Lack of draughtsmanship, not lack of affection, had created these caricatures of Maximinus and his son. Words not swords, Gordian thought. Words soldiers wanted to hear. He wished he had had a drink before he left the Circus.

'The gods know, life under the Eagles is not easy. Marching and drill, injuries and wounds are always with us. So are hard winters and hardworking summers, grim war and unprofitable peace.'

Heads nodded. One or two legionaries smiled.

'I first served more than twenty-five years ago, before some of you were born, before your fathers spread your mothers' legs.'

The rising laughter was stifled before it was established. A commotion from the rear, eddying through the ranks.

'It is a trap!' someone shouted. The mutineers were turning away, jostling to see out across the harbour to the mainland. On the wharf troops were moving, forming up facing the island, blocking the bridge. What did Sabinianus think he was doing?

'Traitor!' The mutineers were tugging the covers off their shields, unsheathing their swords. 'Kill them!'

As the boldest took the first steps, Brennus went to draw his blade. Gordian caught his wrist.

'Wait!' Gordian shouted as much at the body-guard as those climbing the steps, but everyone paused.

Words not swords. He had only a moment to master his fear, find the right words. Epicurus was wrong; fear was not just a product of faulty reasoning. It had an existence of its own. Gordian fought it down.

'The troops surrounding you are loyal to me, to my father. If you kill me, you will not leave this island alive. Yes, it is a trap. Would you have a fool for a general? A fool for an Emperor? I have you in my power, and you have me. I came here alone. Would you have a coward for an Emperor?'

The legionaries were still motionless. Gordian had to keep going. Lies, half-truths, it did not matter. He had to win them over.

'You think Maximinus is your friend, because he doubled your pay. He is not your friend. He was trying to buy your honour. You think Maximinus is one of you. He is not. Maximinus is a barbarian from Thrace. You are Romans from Africa.'

Gordian could not read the effect of his words.

'You know me. Three years I have served here in Africa. Ask the Scouts how I fought at Ad Palmam. Ask how I held the gate, captured the chief's son with my own hands. The *speculatores* will tell you how at Esuba I was first over the enemy wall. The Frontier Wolves here will tell you how your fellow-soldiers of the 3rd Augusta scaled the defences when I was cut off by the barbarians.'

A few had put down their weapons. A final effort, and he might have them.

'You all know the rumour. The auxiliaries will be left to hold the African frontier alone, and Maximinus will transfer the 3rd Augusta to the north. It is true. Before I killed Paul the Chain, I forced him to admit the truth. Maximinus has issued the orders which will tear you from your homes and families. You will march and die in the frozen forests and Steppe beyond the Danube,

76

while here in Africa your women and children are raped, enslaved, and massacred by the barbarians.'

A blatant untruth, but now the invention swept through the troops.

'Return to your oath to me, to my father.' Gordian had to shout above their outraged mutterings. 'I swear you will never be posted away from home. There will be no punishments, I give you my word. Return to your *sacramentum*, and each man will receive a bonus of five years' pay.'

A big legionary with a scar across his face spoke up. 'What about the rest of the legion?'

Gordian looked him in the eye. 'My friend Arrian is the best horseman in Africa. If he rides hard, takes just the tribunes Pedius and Geminius as companions, he can be in Lambaesis in three days. In my name, and that of my father, he will make the same assurances to those at the headquarters of the 3rd Augusta. The legionaries here can send men to those Cohorts on guard along the southern frontier.'

'Fair enough, *Imperator*,' the legionary said. Behind him, eager hands reached up to the standard to pull down the portraits of the brutal man and his effeminate son.

CHAPTER 7

ROME
THE FORUM ROMANUM

The Nones of March, AD238

Caenis left the Subura and went down to the Forum. It was early in the morning, and she was not working, not until the ninth hour. There had been stories of riots the day before, but she wanted to see them burning the paintings of the tyrant.

As she got near the Lake of Curtius, the crowd thickened. She had dressed respectably: no make-up, a long, plain gown, a figure-concealing cloak, sensible sandals, bands in her hair, and her only jewellery a bracelet any woman might have worn. The demure costume did little to shield her from obscene comments or wandering hands. It was best to ignore it when men pinched her bottom, more difficult with those who slyly felt her breasts. Men thought any girl alone in a crowd was fair game. Some were with their women, even had their children on their shoulders. Men were unembarrassed, they had no shame.

The paintings were already damaged. The day

before the mob had hurled stones and rotten vegetables, daubed graffiti, and hacked out the face of each depiction of Maximinus. Her gaze ran along the enormous panels. A faceless Maximinus led his army over a bridge, another presided as his soldiers sacked a village, a final one, larger than the others, chased his enemies into a marsh. Her eyes were drawn back to the dishevelled women and children manhandled from their homes. Maximinus was a tyrant. He had treated his own subjects no better than those barbarians. He had cut the grain dole and limited the spectacles. His soldiers had stolen the treasures of the gods from their temples. Those who had protested had been beaten, clubbed to death. All the wealth he had taken had vanished into his northern campaigns, or been lavished on the ridiculous ceremonies proclaiming his ugly, dead wife a new goddess.

Up on the Rostra, the young Senator Menophilus was making a speech. The Gordiani were coming from Africa. Old-fashioned morality would return to Rome. Maximinus would be defeated. The Senate would guard Italy until the new Emperors arrived. The plebs and soldiers would heed their commands. Justice and liberty, free speech and dignity, the ways of their ancestors, all would return to the Seven Hills.

Menophilus was good looking, fresh faced, with short, curling dark hair, but her attention wandered from the meaningless concepts he expounded.

Near her in the press was a young woman of about her age, blonde like her, of similar height and build. A man stood with his arm solicitously about her waist. No one would grab her arse, fondle her tits, without answering to him. She looked a bit like Rhodope. What would have become of Rhodope, Caenis wondered, if that terrible thing had not happened in Ephesus? Would she be standing somewhere with a husband to protect her? Would she have a home in which she could sleep undisturbed at night? Would she have children? Ephesus seemed a lifetime ago, but it was only five years.

The crowd cheered. Thick ropes of black smoke were curling up. Flames licked up to devour Maximinus, his soldiers, and the women and children in an indiscriminate holocaust.

Caenis stumbled as the throng shifted back. The Lictors were pushing people out of the way. Once their attendants had opened a path, the magistrates and other Senators processed to the Curia. Much-obscured by the heads of those in front, Caenis could only see a few of them. She glimpsed the attractive Menophilus. After him went the long-bearded figure of old Pupienus; a harsh man; as Prefect of the City, he had used the Urban Cohorts to drive the people from the Temple of Venus and Rome. Men had died, and the plebs had not forgotten. He ignored the insults that dogged his progress.

Among the very last, she saw Gallicanus in his

homespun toga. He turned left and right, exchanging rough, manly banter with the crowd. Surely it could not be true about Gallicanus? The slave had been drunk, but he was in the household of the Senator, and he had sworn he told no lie. Public morality, and private vice; it was the oldest story. Caenis smiled. It felt good that she knew a secret that could bring down a high and mighty Senator like Gallicanus.

Once all the Senators were safely gathered in, the great bronze doors of the Curia clanged shut. Again the Senate would meet in secret session. The plebs made their disapproval known. The mob surged towards the Senate House. *Libertas! Libertas!* The atmosphere had changed in an instant. The shouts of *Liberty* echoed back off the surrounding buildings with an air of menace, as if the stones of the Forum itself called for blood.

The way back to the Subura was blocked; an angry mob wedged between the Curia and the Basilica Aemilia. Pushing and squirming through, careless of groping hands, Caenis fought her way past the Shrine of Venus Cloacina, and into the comparative quiet of the Portico of Gaius and Lucius Caesar. She would have to take a longer route home.

From the passage by the Temple of Antoninus and Faustina, she emerged into the immense courtyard of the Temple of Peace. The wind had shifted and was stronger, bringing down from the north isolated dark clouds, the forerunners of a storm. But for now the sun shone on neat flower-beds, fountains, statues, and ornamental trees. The stalls of the merchants were closed, and it was pleasantly empty after the Forum, just the occasional stroller. She had most of the day. It made no odds if the rain caught her. She would have to change before going to work.

Calm now, she turned to the right, ambling along under the colonnade. The columns were a pretty pink, with white bases and tops. Most of sculptures and paintings she could not identify. Unable to read their inscriptions, to her they were just a young athlete, a beautiful girl, or a grizzled wrestler. But some she knew. Here was Venus climbing from her bath, and over there was the shrine of Ganymede, with the convenient privacy of its hedges. It was deserted now, but memories of other days at that naughty little shrine made her smile.

She turned the corner, and made her way towards the offices of the Prefect of the City. Sometimes she liked to go into the public room, and look at the great marble plan of the city on the wall. It made her feel like a bird or a goddess gazing down at Rome, as if able to peer into the lives of all those people in the endless buildings, and then soar away. Once an earnest young man standing beside her had said it was odd that South was at the top of the plan. He was trying to pick her up, but she had asked him why. He had looked at her strangely, and said because North was at the top of most maps. When she had again asked why, he had looked put out, obviously not knowing the answer.

The offices were shuttered and chained today. Everyone said that the Prefect of the City had not been seen since Vitalianus had been murdered yesterday morning, and certainly the Urban Cohorts had remained in their barracks. Apparently the Prefect was a friend of Maximinus. Some said he had fled north to the protection of the tyrant.

'I smell a she-wolf.' Three men were sitting by the doors. They were unshaven, dirty, and were passing a jug from hand to hand. Normally the guards would have shooed their sort away.

'Come and have a drink, little she-wolf.'

Caenis ignored them, and went to walk past.

One of them reached out, and caught the hem of her gown. 'Just a little fun, no need to be stuck-up.'

Caenis pulled her gown free, saying she had to get to work.

'Start early,' the man said. 'We have money.'

She walked on.

One of the others laughed. 'Turned down by a *Quadrantaria*.'

Caenis bristled; how dare he call her a quarter-ass whore.

'Come back here.' She sensed the man who had grabbed her getting up.

She walked faster, knowing the others were on their feet too, that they would all follow her. There was no one in sight.

'Come back here, and get what is coming to you.'

They were gaining, she hitched up her gown, and started to run.

'Fucking bitch,' one shouted.

She darted to the left, down between a row of stalls, then right along a flowerbed, cutting towards the nearest gate. Their footfall slapped on the earth behind her.

There were two men, a little way off.

'Help!'

They turned, took in the situation, shrugged, and turned away.

She burst through the gate. No one. The Street of the Sandal-makers was near deserted; just an old beggar off to the left, slumped against the base of the statue of Apollo. Of course, fear of unrest must have driven away the fashionable young men, and shut all the bookshops.

Her pursuers crowding through the gate, she sprinted towards the statue. There was a bar there, The Lyre, if it was open, and she got inside, she might be safe.

Her head jerked back, searing pain as one of them grabbed her hair. Her legs went out from under her. She landed hard, agony driving up her spine.

'Over there, do her up against the wall.'

She was half-pulled, half-dragged across the street. They pushed her into a corner formed by a buttress, crowding in at her.

'You should have taken the money, bitch.'

Hands were hauling her gown up her legs, pawing her breasts, pushing between her thighs.

'Show us what you have got.'

The neck of her gown was torn open, her breast-band yanked up.

'Look at those tits.'

She was forced to her knees. No point in fighting now, they would beat her, perhaps mark her for life.

The man who had first accosted her, undoubtedly the leader, unbuckled his belt, pulled up his tunic, and fumbled in his breeches.

'Get the old beggar. Let him have a go after us.'

The laughter died. The man facing her spun around, his penis still in his fist.

Caenis tugged her gown together, gathered her legs under her, waiting for a chance to run.

'Put it away, and go.' The speaker was her neighbour, young Castricius. The old die-cutter stood with him.

The man laughed, with no mirth and little conviction. 'A boy and an old man.'

One of the others had a knife in his hand.

Castricius shook his head. 'Leave.'

'Run along, boy.'

'Last chance.' Castricius spoke softly, as if saddened by the stupidity of the world.

'Fuck off, and take your grandfather with you.'

One hand stuffing his penis back into his breeches, wrestling with the buckle of his belt,

85

with the other the leader tugged a knife from the sheath on his belt.

In a moment, all the men, even the die-cutter, were crouched forward, balanced on the balls of their feet, steel flicking this way and that.

'The die is cast.' A strange, unreadable emotion slid across Castricius' thin, angular face.

A sudden movement, making Caenis start. A scuffle of feet and a grunt of pain. The die-cutter was down, clutching his thigh. His assailant bent over him.

Neatly, Castricius stepped inside the knife of the third man, and stabbed him deep in the stomach.

Before anyone else could react, with the grace of a dancer, Castricius whirled, and again faced the leader.

The man who Castricius had stabbed dropped his weapon, and curled over, blood flooding out between his splayed fingers. 'He has done for me.'

'Yes,' Castricius replied, never taking his eyes off the other two. 'And now I will deal with your friends.'

The leader backed away. The remaining man joined him. Their eyes flitted between each other, their friend gasping his life out in the dirt, and the long blade in Castricius' hand.

'We will get you one day,' the leader shouted. Then they turned, and ran.

Caenis sprang up to do the same.

'Give me a hand with him.' Castricius was

kneeling by the old man, cutting the material away from the wound, peering closely at it.

She wanted nothing but to run.

'We have to get him away, before the Watch arrive.'

Caenis had to live in the same block with them. Tugging her clothes into some decency, she went to help the die-cutter.

CHAPTER 8

ROME
THE SENATE HOUSE

The Nones of March, AD238

T oday I shall meet with interference, ingratitude, insolence, disloyalty, ill-will, and
selfishness. Menophilus turned over the
words of the *Meditations*. Was Marcus Aurelius
correct that man naturally inclines to virtue, and
so all vice was due to the offenders' ignorance
of what is good or evil, all some sort of near-
blameless mistake? Regarding his fellow Senators,
he judged that the divine Emperor's view could
be true only in the very strictest sense of Stoic
philosophy.

Menophilus had answered Gallicanus' question
with honesty. He could give no realistic estimate
how long it would be before the Gordiani arrived
from Africa. The tone of the query had been offensive, somehow implying both that any tardiness
was his fault, and that previously he had failed to
give proper consideration to the issue. The hirsute
Cynic appeared quick to impute blame, like most
of his kind.

Since he had despatched the summons, Menophilus repeatedly had deliberated on the capabilities of ship and crew, the vagaries of the weather and potential routes, and the parameters of previous voyages. The *Liburnian* was said to be a fast galley, well manned, and its captain recommended as a seafarer of experience. Yesterday, after it had pulled out of Ostia, obligingly the wind had picked up and shifted to the north. It was just possible that it would make Carthage today. But if it had been overtaken by the full force of the storm, it might have been forced to run for shelter in Sicily or Malta, or might have been blown wildly off course, perhaps even to the dreadful shoals of the Syrtes. At worst, it could have foundered. When the storm abated, he would send another ship. Perhaps Gallicanus was right; he should have sent two vessels initially. There was all too much to think about in the midst of a revolt, even if he did not have the killing of Vitalianus on his conscience.

Like countless generations of Senators before, Menophilus gazed out of the window set high in the wall opposite the bench where he sat. Low, black clouds, dragging curtains of rain, scudded across. *Open the doors!* The angry chants were muffled, but audible. *Only conspirators debate behind closed doors!* Someone behind the scenes was whipping up the plebs, Menophilus had no doubt. Normally the first drops of rain dispersed any mob, no matter how riotous. Continued urban unrest best served whose interest?

Gallicanus had the floor. There had still been no sighting of the Prefects of either the City or the Watch, and, in the continuing absence of Sabinus and Potens, with no soldiers on the streets still loyal to Maximinus, many more Senators had found the courage to venture out of their close guarded homes, despite the mob. The Curia was packed. Gallicanus was speaking. Menophilus dragged his mind back.

'Outside the storm rages. The people of Rome grow impatient. They need leadership. There is no telling when the Gordiani will come. Conscript Fathers, it is our duty to bring order to the streets of the city.'

Yes, Menophilus thought, your bluff democratic posturing appeals to the plebs.

'The Gordiani are far away over the seas. Maximinus and his army are close at hand. At any moment the tyrant will cross the Alps.'

An exaggeration, but a real fear. What Maximinus would do to the man who had killed his Praetorian Prefect did not bear thinking. Still, the human condition was that of a soldier assaulting a town; at every moment you should expect the barbed arrow.

'The barbarian and his vicious son will bring fire and sword, murder and rape. In their savage and perverse fury none will be spared. I see the Tiber foaming with much blood. I see shrines and temples consumed with fire; northern tribes-men ruling amid the ruins and on the ashes of a burnt-out empire. Conscript Fathers, it is our duty to protect Italy.'

Followers of Diogenes were encouraged to eschew bookish learning, instead to rely on a god-given education, a bolt of instruction from the blue, something open to all, something far less time consuming and requiring no foreign languages. Replete with reminiscences of Cicero and Virgil, Gallicanus' speech might not fit the ideal of Cynicism, but it was having an effect on its cultured audience. The Senators were receptive. Now all that remained, Menophilus thought, was to discover where it was all leading, and what Gallicanus actually wanted.

'We must elect from among ourselves a new college of magistrates. We must elect twenty men from the Senate to oppose Maximinus, to defend Rome and Italy, to defend the *Res Publica*.'

Amid a general roar of approval, the presiding Consul, possibly not without intention, failed to notice the Father of the House waving his walking stick in an attempt to get his attention. As old Cuspidius Celerinus relapsed into muttered imprecations against modern ways – *it never would have happened in the time of Marcus Aurelius, not even under Severus* – Balbinus was granted the right to speak.

Previous generations respected age, valued experience. The querulous complaints of Cuspidius went unheeded.

Fat, jowly, with a face like a pig, and the manner

91

of an Oriental potentate, Balbinus got up. Paying no more attention to the Father of the House than anyone else, he strode to the centre of the Curia, his habitual lethargy cast aside.

'Roman virtue, true old-fashioned *virtus*, is near extinct. True Roman blood runs thin in this august house. For centuries the Emperors have admitted men whose fathers could teach them nothing of the weighty responsibilities of a Senator. They have scoured the provinces to let in trousered Gauls, yapping little Greeks, and Africans with loose clothing and looser morals.'

Himself a new man, Menophilus thought Balbinus a fool. Great houses died out, new ones took their place. The majority of those present had no Senatorial ancestors; over half came from the provinces. It had always been the way. Unlike Athens, let alone exclusive Sparta, Rome had grown great by admitting outsiders. Romulus had given refuge to runaway slaves who wished to join his new community.

'Once in a while, however, one of these *novi homines* reminds us of our duty. Despite coming from some unheard of village near Carthage, Gallicanus has shone a light on the path of duty. Yet he has not surveyed the path to its end. To command respect, the twenty men elected must have seniority and distinction. I support his motion, but propose an amendment. The election should be limited to those who have held the Consulship.'

Balbinus sat down. He was patted on the back

by Rufinianus, Acilius Aviola, Valerius Priscillianus, and other patricians. None of them attempted to conceal their mood of triumphal cunning. Perhaps dissimulation was beneath them.

Menophilus tasted disgust, like vomit in the back of his throat. Men were despicable; politicians worst of all, no better than animals. Some were wolves, faithless and treacherous and noxious, others lions, savage and wild and untamed, but most foxes, ill-natured and wretched and mean. Menophilus wished he did not have to be among them. The tenets of their philosophy demanded participation, yet several Stoic wise men had never entered politics. Appealing as it was, Menophilus could not follow their example. In retirement they had framed laws for the greater state of all mankind. Menophilus knew he lacked their intelligence. He was bound to serve the temporal *Res Publica*, or abandon any claims to live according to his nature, and thus all hopes of happiness.

The sometime Prefect of the City Pupienus was on his feet. Not exactly pompous, although his luxuriant beard would support such an interpretation, there was something stiff and slightly off-putting about his evident self-control.

'Conscript Fathers, we have heard good advice, both from the scion of a patrician house, and from a man whose *virtus* is its own nobility. Balbinus should be thanked and honoured, perhaps with a statue listing his qualities. Certainly his name must be the first put forward for election to the Twenty.

93

Now, it would be a travesty if the man who conceived this excellent board of magistrates to save the *Res Publica* were debarred from serving in its ranks. Therefore, I recommend that, for the good of Rome, we elect Gallicanus as a Suffect Consul.'

Menophilus calculated rapidly how these measures would affect the following of the new Emperors. Egnatius Proculus was an ex-Praetor, as was Celsus Aelianus, and he was an ineffectual reprobate to boot. Menophilus himself and his friend Virius Lupus mere Quaestors. The latter's father was a good man, and had held the Consulship. So had Valerian and Egnatius Marinianus, although each had his limitations. Appius Julianus was another ex-Consul, but he was old and infirm. As things stood, the Gordiani only had four men here in the Senate House who had held the highest office, and only one of them could be relied on to advance their interests on this new committee.

The presiding Consul was preparing to call a vote.

If only Arrian and Sabinianus were not in Africa, if Caudius Julianus not governing Dalmatia, and Egnatius Lollianus likewise in Bithynia-Pontus; all of them were of Consular status, devoted to the Gordiani, and men who could get things done. No point in crying over spilt wine. Menophilus had to think of something quickly.

'Let good auspices and joyful fortune attend the people of Rome.' On the tribunal, Fulvius Pius

94

had begun the injunction which proceeded a proposal.

Menophilus stepped forward. Romulus and his slaves would provide the answer. With only a hint of irritation at this late intervention, he was granted permission to address the House.

'Conscript Fathers, everything that has been proposed will gladden the hearts of our noble Augusti. Another fast ship will take the news to Carthage.' No point in not reminding them where real power would soon reside, and his proximity to it. 'Although I am but a Quaestor, my respect for the traditions and procedure of this House could not be more profound. As such, I hope my elders will forgive my temerity in reminding them of the date. There is only one mark against the *Nones* of March, and that is the letter *N*. On this day Romulus consecrated the Temple of Veiovis. Whoever you are, he said, take refuge here, and you will be safe. From that small beginning Rome took its rise. Our ancestors believed that no meeting of the Senate or people should be held on a day that is marked *Nefastus*. While fully supporting the proposal of Domitius Gallicanus, the amendment of Caelius Balbinus, and the call from Clodius Pupienus for the election of new Suffect Consuls, I move for a postponement to a more auspicious day.'

As he resumed his seat, every Senator present fell over himself to support his motion. Again, Menophilus tasted the bile of contempt. Nothing could be more urgent than restoring order to the city, and guarding Italy against Maximinus. Yet all the Conscript Fathers rushed to embrace the opportunity of a few days' clandestine manoeuvring. Not one put the safety of the *Res Publica* before factional interest. Of course, much of Menophilus' contempt was reserved for himself.

'Conscript Fathers, we detain you no longer.' The Consul spoke, the doors were opened, and the Senators began to depart.

Outside the rain fell, and the mob jeered.

Menophilus sat very still. The safety of the *Res Publica* must come above everything. He did not like to think about the previous morning, about Vitalianus. All that mattered was the safety of the *Res Publica*. Stern measures were necessary to secure the city. Sabinus had left Rome to the mob. Sabinus commanded six thousand soldiers, and was a friend of Maximinus. Something must be done about the Prefect of the City.

CHAPTER 9

THE NORTHERN FRONTIER
THE TOWN OF SIRMIUM

Eight Days before the Ides of March, AD238

Iunia Fadilla kissed her nurse for the last time. She closed the eyes of the dear old woman, and said her name. 'Eunomia.'

Rain spattered on the window. Through the glass the world was dark and distorted. The rain had come down across the Danube the day before, melting the ice on the eaves and turning the snow in the streets to slush. It had come too late for Eunomia. The cold of the North had killed her. It gave Iunia Fadilla another reason to hate her husband.

Eunomia's decline had been sudden, but there had been time to summon those who prepared the dead from their quarters outside the town. Now, the *Pollinctores* stepped forward in their colourful and sinister caps. They lifted Eunomia from the bed and placed her on the bare floor. They said the ritual words.

The end is to the beginning as the beginning is to the end.

Eunomia had been with Iunia Fadilla since

97

the beginning. A happy childhood, peripatetic yet peaceful; the big house on the Caelian in Rome, the villa in Sicily overlooking the Bay of Naxos, the retreat in the hills of Apulia. Iunia Fadilla's mother had been the granddaughter of Marcus Aurelius. Her father also was rich, and had had the good sense to keep out of politics. Eunomia had gone with her when she married old Nummius. If her nurse had been shocked by the couple's life in their luxurious home on the Esquiline, she had voiced no disapproval. Eumonia had liked Iunia Fadilla's lover Gordian. Sometimes, when she had taken a drink, she had said what woman would not be happy taking an agreeable husband and a vigorous younger man to her bed, separately or together.

If Gordian had proposed when Nummius died, things might have been different. Iunia Fadilla had thought he would, but he had claimed it was against his Epicurean principles, and by then he was more often abroad, in Syria then Achaea. As far as she knew he had not returned to Rome once in the three years since he went to Africa.

Widowed at eighteen, she had enjoyed her independence. Nummius had left her well provided for. She had the house on the Esquiline, and her tutor, her cousin Fadillus, was not the type of man to go against her wishes. In the round of parties and recitals, of visits to the baths and harmless flirtations, of quiet nights reading, she had grown close to Eunomia again.

Everything, except Eunomia, had changed when Vitalianus had come to the house. The deputy Praetorian Prefect had announced that she was to marry Maximus the son of Maximinus. Refusal was not an option when the man seeking your hand was the son of the Emperor. On the long journey north, Eunomia had consoled her with reports of her betrothed. The Caesar was tall, good looking. He was cultured, wrote poetry that rivalled Catullus. Rumour had it he was an attentive lover of women and girls; no danger he would be one of those husbands who preferred page boys, or was held back by stern Stoic principles. When he saw her beauty, he would not desert her bed for concubines or the wives of other men.

There was no denying the beauty of Maximus. At their wedding, he smelt of cinnamon and roses as he leant close to whisper. *They say you have sucked off half the men in Rome; at least you should be good at it.* He had first beaten her that night. She had fought, but he was stronger. *If I have to marry a whore, I will treat her like one.* Since then, he slapped and punched her thighs, her buttocks and her breasts. This new year she had had to wear a veil at the ceremony renewing the oath of loyalty. The night before he had claimed he could smell wine on her breath. *When a woman drinks without her husband, she closes the door on all virtues, and opens her legs for all-comers.*

Iunia Fadilla would have given anything for her husband to desert her bed. And now Maximus was coming back. Laurelled letters had arrived. The Emperor had won another great victory. The Sarmatian Iazyges were routed. The army had recrossed the Danube, and would be in Sirmium tomorrow. Doubtless, Maximus would demand his conjugal rights. No tender kiss of greeting, but a flurry of blows as he took her. No words of end-earment, but insults. *Bitch! What man could kiss a mouth which had sucked so many pricks. Bitch!*

The *Pollinctores* were busy with cloths and bowls of warm water, washing the body. Was Gordian right? Did everything return to peace and sleep, just atoms swirling back into the cosmos, without consciousness? Or were the poets right; the ferry across the river to Hades, murky and sunless? Eunomia had been devout. On the journey north, she had poured a libation at every wayside shrine, added a stone to each of Mercury's cairns. If the dead were judged, there was no question of torments. Yet it was hard to imagine her old nurse disporting herself with the heroes and the virtuous in the Elysian Fields or the Isles of the Blessed. Perhaps she would wander like a shadow among the dark meadows overgrown with asphodel, until she drank the waters of oblivion. At least she was free of pain, her back unbent, her joints no longer stiff, her hand no longer trembling.

Iunia Fadilla was passed the sheers. She hacked off a clump of her hair. She took a pinch of dust from a bowl. *I am what five fingers might gather and carry.* She sprinkled the dirt over her head.

When the corpse was anointed and dressed, it would be carried to the atrium. There, feet towards the door, it would be displayed. A fitting welcome for Maximus: the mournful music of flutes, and the women, filthy in dishevelled black, wailing, beating their breasts, tearing their cheeks.

Eunomia had known her herbs and remedies. She had taught Iunia Fadilla. Seventeen months of marriage, seventeen months of unwelcome and painful visits to her bed, and still no children. And there would be none. Iunia Fadilla would mix the old olive oil with the honey, cedar resin and white lead, and push the mixture inside herself.

Eunomia had served her well, but she had died leaving one service undone. The imperial household was closely watched, spies everywhere. It had been impossible to obtain the necessary poisons. There was no hope in the world. No Sarmatian arrow had found Maximus. No revolt threatened the rule of his father. Every plot had been uncovered and crushed. There was nothing else for it – Iunia Fadilla would have to kill her husband herself.

Everything was ready. Iunia Fadilla put a coin in Eunomia's mouth. The handlers of the dead bound her nurse's jaws shut.

CHAPTER 10

ROME
THE CARINAE

Eight Days before the Ides of March, AD238

The door was shut. No doubt it was locked and barred. The same would be true of the only other entrance at the rear of the house. It was not yet mid-morning, the second hour of the day, still the time of *negotium*, when public business was done. Normally the front door would be open, and the Senator Tiberius Pollienus Armenius Peregrinus would be receiving his friends and clients. The times were far from normal. The plebs were out on the streets. The rain had not checked them. There was nothing else to stop them running riot. Neither Sabinus, the Prefect of the City, nor Potens, the Prefect of the *vigiles*, had been seen in the two days since Vitalianus had been murdered. The men of the Urban Cohorts and the Watch had remained in their barracks. Robbery and murder stalked the Seven Hills. All the luxurious houses in the Carinae district of the Esquiline were tightly shuttered. If Armenius thought it would keep him safe, he was much mistaken.

Timesitheus watched from a recessed doorway, across and down the street. Two bulky men, also hooded and cloaked, stood at his back. It reminded Timesitheus of another time and place. Mogontiacum on the northern frontier, three years before, standing with Maximinus, waiting to burst into the house of Petronius Magnus, and arrest him and his fellow Senators. It had been raining then too.

Some men would say the cases were entirely different. Magnus and the others had been traitors. This thing with Armenius was a personal vendetta. Those men would be wrong. Like everything, both were about self-interest.

Timesitheus despised the hypocrisy of men who clothed their actions in fine-sounding words, even to themselves. Justice was all very well, if it fitted with advantage. Step by step, with infinite care, Timesitheus had led Magnus and his friends into conspiracy. But if they had not been treacherous, they would have denounced him. As Tranquillina had said, best he, rather than another, reap the rewards of exposing their true nature. No one had clearer sight than his wife.

It was the same with Armenius. From obscure equestrian origins on a backwater Greek island, Timesitheus had risen high, the governor of provinces, the councillor of Emperors. He had drawn handsome profits from a succession of military and civil offices, but he had taken no more than was his due. When one of the great patrons of his youth had died, he had left Timesitheus a substantial inheritance. But, on his deathbed, Pollienus Auspex had adopted Armenius. Now the senatorial legacy hunter was contesting the bequest to Timesitheus. Given his connections, Armenius was likely to win the court case.

Timesitheus would not be robbed of what was his by right. Just as Magnus and the others had died because their souls were tainted by treachery, so Armenius would suffer for his avarice.

A squall gusted up the empty street, fat raindrops spattering the pavement. It was near time. Timesitheus hoped that the young cutpurse would be as good as his word. The oaths taken meant nothing, but Castricius had been well paid, and the promise of plunder should outweigh the inclement weather.

Timesitheus thought about that morning in Mogontiacum; the rain falling in sheets, the door splintering, the torchlight glinting on steel. Maximinus could fight, but he had done nothing right since he had become Emperor. The elite hated and feared him for his executions and confiscations. He had never travelled to Rome to attempt to conciliate the Senate. The plebs loathed him for curtailing the games and stealing the treasures from the temples. He had doubled the pay of the troops, but the expense was unsupportable, and soldiers alone could never keep an Emperor on the throne. Maximinus would not survive long. But would this be the revolt that toppled him?

Gordian the Elder was an old man, and Africa held no legions. The Senators were better at talking than fighting. They had neither won over Sabinus and Potens, and thus the troops in their charge, nor liquidated them. The Senators commanded no troops in Rome.

Tranquillina was right. In a revolution, you had to choose your side early. Quietism and procrastination won no thanks with the victors. Either Timesitheus must ingratiate himself with those leading the revolt, find something to offer their cause, or he must declare for Maximinus, ride to join him in the north, or perform some open deed on his behalf here in Rome. Timesitheus had never cared for Maximinus; a big, ugly, stupid and violent barbarian. His blood had boiled every time Maximinus called him *Little Greek*. How dare a hulking Thracian call a true Hellene a *Graeculus*? Yet the very stupidity of Maximinus was an asset. Timesitheus had convinced him of the guilt of Magnus, and been awarded the province of Bithynia-Pontus. He had done the same with Valerius Apollinaris, and received his province of Asia. Here in Rome, the incompetence and venality of the previous incumbent had made it easy as Prefect of the Grain Supply to increase the dole while cutting the cost to the treasury. Another reward could be expected.

It was a difficult choice. Either he had to reaffirm his allegiance to a doomed regime, or throw in his lot with a revolution that showed scant

105

chance of success. And Tranquillina was right, he had to make that decision soon. Still, clarity of thought demanded one thing at a time. Timesitheus packed the problem away down in the hold of his mind. Today he would settle his account with Armenius, and perhaps there might be opportunity enough to deal with the surviving son of Valerius Apollinaris as well. If you plan one murder, you might as well commit two.

The mob could be heard coming up from the Subura before it could be seen. A menacing roar, the individual shouts and chants indeterminate, torn away by the wind and rain. The bolder spirits, or the more rapacious, ran ahead up the steps. Then the street was filled with a bedraggled phalanx of the impecunious.

Castricius had done well. There were at least a hundred, perhaps many more, scoured from the drinking dens and brothels of the slums. Some carried firebrands, sawing in the wind. Most had knives. A knot of men near the front hefted a large beam of hardwood.

Enemies, enemies! Nail the friends of Maximinus on a cross!

Under his hood, Timesitheus smiled. Armenius had been a Praetor under Maximinus, but was no more his friend than most of the dozens who had held office during his reign.

Hostes, hostes! Nail them, drag them, burn them alive!

Young Castricius had shown admirable resource. Even the sordid plebs fought better if they believed they had a motive beyond mere gain. As if summoned by the thought, like an evil daemon conjured by an incautious word, Castricius was in front of Timesitheus.

'The back gate?'

'There are men there,' Castricius said.

'Then get to work.'

Castricius smiled – a look of pure delight on his little pointed, angular face – and skipped away.

Timesitheus wondered if he had met his equal in decisive amorality. He was seized by a transient curiosity. Where had the knife-boy come from? What had brought him to the Subura? He was intelligent, spoke good Greek, had educated manners and no lack of courage. Of course, none of it would do him any good. He was destined for the mines, the arena, or the cross.

Ineptly swung, the makeshift battering-ram struck the door. It did no more than rattle the boards.

In an instant, Castricius was there; darting about, pulling men into place, gesturing, shouting – *one, two, three*. The door jumped on its hinges, groaned. *One, two, three*. On the third blow, the leaves cracked open.

The mob surged through, momentarily choking the throat of the house with their numbers.

Timesitheus turned to the men behind him. It was important to have friends. Alcimus Felicianus was the Procurator in charge of the Flavian Amphitheatre and the Ludus Magnus, the largest gladiatorial school in Rome. Given the unrest, he had been unsurprised when Timesitheus had requested the loan of a couple of gladiators, not demurring when it was stressed that they should be men of discretion, not the sort who would baulk at any order. All Romans had debts to settle.

The gladiator called Narcissus handed Timesitheus the pantomime mask. The silvered leather depicted a young girl, impossibly beautiful, cold, with narrow slits for eyes and mouth. When Timesitheus put it on, his world narrowed, like a horse in blinkers.

The last of the mob were disappearing into the house. Timesitheus went after them, Narcissus and the other gladiator Iaculator following. Toughs from the Subura were fine for looting, spontaneous murder – but calculated killing called for professionals.

The battering-ram lay among the wreckage of the door. Timesitheus stepped over it. The passage into the house was dark, the atrium beyond light. As he emerged into the open space, the noise hit him. Behind the mask, he could not tell its direction. Through the eye holes he saw Castricius' men hard at work in the surrounding rooms. Portable ornaments were thrust into bags, larger ones wantonly smashed. Furniture was broken, mosaics defaced. A man defecated in a corner. In one chamber a girl had been stripped naked, and was held down ready to be gang raped. Everything was going well.

Timesitheus hurried through the open-sided

room that connected the atrium to the peristyle garden. Not many of the mob had penetrated so far yet. A few domestic servants flitted through the columns on the far side, seeking some illusory safety. A handful prostrated themselves before the *lararium*, beseeching the domestic deities. Fools, there were no gods to hear their prayers.

The set of rooms favoured by Armenius were to the left. A suborned slave had drawn a plan. Timesitheus had memorized the entire thing. The outer door was locked. The gladiators put their heavy shoulders to the painted panels. It was their diet, all those beans they ate, that made them so bulky. When the door gave, Timesitheus sprang through, sword in hand. The reception room was empty. A Corinthian bronze of an athlete, sheened with age, stood in the centre.

A connecting door led to a bedroom. Not waiting for the gladiators, Timesitheus kicked it open. The cover on the couch was rumpled. A papyrus roll and a glass stood on the bedside table. Timesitheus put his hand on the couch. It was still warm.

Armenius had fled moments before. Signing the gladiators to silence, Timesitheus wondered what he would have done. There were two choices: run or hide. If the latter, Timesitheus would have hidden in the servile quarters, hoping the mob would overlook them as containing little worth looting. Flight was a better option. There was only the one rear door, and that also was through where the slaves lived.

'Follow me.'

Outside, under the colonnade, Timesitheus ran to the opening on the left. The passage was narrow, the unmortared bricks nearly brushing his shoulders. It was unlit, the air close. His own breathing and the boots of the gladiators were loud in his ears. Tiny cells opened on either side. Check the rear door first. The third opening on the left led there.

As soon as he turned, Timesitheus suspected that he was mistaken. Another corridor led to a storeroom, and no further. Forcing past the gladiators, retracing his steps, he took the next left. A longer passage. It doglegged left then right. The place was a rabbit warren, or a paltry vision of Hades.

More cells on either side. Cheap lamps burnt in some, illuminating tawdry trifles, pathetic attempts to humanize the occupants' servitude. Timesitheus glimpsed a daubed scene on a wall. A large, pale woman sprawled, naked on a painted bed. Between her meaty thighs a diminutive darker man licked her cunt. He was all eyes and tongue, degraded forever by his unnatural desire.

Shouting ahead. A change in the air. Nearly at the door. Timesitheus rounded a corner, and almost impaled himself on the tip of on outthrust sword. Flinging himself sideways – pain flaring where his left shoulder crushed into the wall – the blade missed his ribs by a hand's breadth.

His assailant recovered his balance with surprising grace for a large man. Another gladiator. He dropped into a fighting crouch. Timesitheus did the same. The eye slits of the mask restricted his vision; pantomime artists did not often have to fight for their lives. Sword up, he flipped his cloak around his left arm as an improvised shield. The space was too confined for his own gladiators to help. At least they were not crowding his back.

The bodyguard waited. He was there to delay. Timesitheus would have to take the attack to him. Too narrow to cut, it would have to be at the point of the sword, the steel close and deadly.

Timesitheus felt the rodent breath of fear. He would not let Armenius escape. He steadied himself, forced his terror away, heard the scrabble of retreating claws.

He feinted at the face, thrust to the stomach. The gladiator caught the blade on his own. Steel rasped on steel, high up near the pommel, near their fingers. They were almost chest to chest, an unwanted intimacy. Their breath hot in each other's faces. Garlic and stale beans repulsive in Timesitheus' nostrils.

Both stepped back, careful to give no opening.

Armenius could not escape. Not after all these efforts.

'Ten thousand sesterces, let me pass.'

The gladiator did not answer.

'Twenty.'

The gladiator spat.

Timesitheus did not see if the saliva hit him. Peering out from the mask, his eyes never left his opponent's sword.

'Suck my prick,' the gladiator said.

He talked too much. He was a fool. Everyone had a price. Timesitheus had given him a chance. Now he would have to die.

Timesitheus moved his sword to the right. The man's eyes followed the blade.

Without warning, Timesitheus flicked the trailing edge of his cloak up at the gladiator's head. Instinctively, his opponent brought his weapon across to protect his face. Ducking low, Timesitheus drove the point of his sword into the man's guts, twisted the hilt, and withdrew.

Steel clattered onto the brick floor. Both hands clutching the wound, the gladiator dropped to his knees.

Timesitheus seized his victim's hair with his left hand, yanked his head back. With precision, he thrust down into the man's throat. A painful death, the steel scraping down inside the ribcage, but quick. One convulsion, and it was over.

Recovering his sword, Timesitheus pushed the dead man to the floor.

'Follow me.'

Timesitheus stepped over the corpse. He was covered in blood, his hands and forearms slick.

The rear door gaped wide. No one was on guard. The rain-swept street was bright after the gloom of the corridor. Everywhere men shuffled and stooped, picking things up from the wet paving, like demented farmworkers harvesting some inedible crop. They straightened, bright things in their hands.

The oldest of ruses. Throw a purse in the air, and watch the plebs scramble for coins. They could not be blamed. Like dogs, they had been well trained in such tricks at the spectacles. It was their nature.

Armenius had got away. The rain beating on his back, Timesitheus wondered how to win something from this defeat. The antique bronze statue would go well in his house. No, with Armenius alive, it would be too easy to trace. This had been about principle, not short term gain. Another day.

Timesitheus would take a clean cloak from one of the gladiators, remove his mask in the shade of its hood, and slip away. Only three men knew he had been here, and Castricius and the gladiators had been well paid for their silence. Armenius could wait until another day.

CHAPTER 11

AFRICA
CARTHAGE

Seven Days before the Ides of March, AD238

Gordian the Younger stood outside the governor's residence. The quickening north wind fretted at his dark clothes, tugged at the black fringes of his cloak. They carried the corpse feet first, out through the door decked with its doleful branches of cedar. With much solemnity, they lifted Serenus Sammonicus onto the bier.

It would have been a comfort to believe they would meet again in some afterlife. But that could not happen. This world was just one among an infinite number created and destroyed without design or purpose, just unceasing atoms moving in the void. A soul was so fragile, composed of such minute particles, it dissolved with the last breath.

If death was just sleep, then it could not in itself be a bad thing. A true Epicurean believed that no death could come too soon or too late. Yet, if pleasure was the true aim of life, what of those who died before they had enjoyed all the pleasures they desired? At least Serenus had been old. Devoted to his books, to scholarship, in his quiet way Serenus had lived exactly as he wished: eight decades of reading and writing, eight decades of pleasure. Perhaps, when you lived to be very old, death lost its dread. Gordian found that hard to believe. Unless you were in agony, you would always plead for another year. *All ways of dying are hateful to us poor mortals.* Serenus had no children, but in a sense, a very attenuated sense, he would live on in his books, both those he had written and those he had gathered from all over the empire. It had been an unexpected, yet characteristic gesture of his old tutor to leave Gordian his library. An estimated sixty-two thousand volumes, too many to read in the longest lifetime.

Under the stern, marble eyes of the Capitoline triad high on their temple, the cortège set out across and out of the Forum. In the streets, warned by the sounding trumpets and wailing women, the citizens cleared the way. When the procession passed, they stopped what they were doing, put down their tools, and watched.

First came the torchbearers, their role symbolic in mid-morning, and then the musicians, flautists mingled with the trumpeters. In front of the bier, tearing their hair, scratching their cheeks, ripping their clothes, and beating and gashing their exposed breasts until the blood ran, the hired women acted

115

as macabre midwives to the chthonic life to come. Serenus lay on a double mattress placed on a litter carried by eight strong men. The mourners followed. The locals aside, they were pitifully few in number: just Gordian himself, his father, and Sabinianus. Gordian remembered when the fellowship had been together, when the Gordiani had been gods. A summer evening, not two years before, in the villa of Sextus, outside the city walls, close to where they were going. He had worn the helm of Ares. His father had wielded the thunderbolt of Zeus, Valerian the trident of Poseidon. The winged hat of Hermes askew on Arrian's head. Serenus as Pluto – now the religious might take that as some omen – Sabinianus as Hephaistos, Menophilus as Dionysus. Their women half-naked as goddesses, a wonderful dinner. They had been so drunk, so happy, so very united. And now they were scattered. And they were in danger. And it was all Gordian's fault.

Slowly, they left the city, and in due course, reached the burial ground by the aqueduct, not far from the fish ponds on the Mappalian Way. A member of the city council, a gloomy looking rhetor called Thascius Cyprianus, oversaw the sacrifice, as if he had doubts about the whole procedure. The sow dead, and the grave consecrated, Gordian's father stepped forward to speak the eulogy.

Gordian the Elder was unshaven, his hair unkempt and matted with dirt. It was excessive. Friends were like figs, so Menophilus often said, they did not last. Death was just sleep. Gordian's father did not share his son's Epicurean philosophy, but he put much store in the *mos maiorum*. Gordian thought the way of the ancestors should have curbed this immoderate display of grief, should have held his parent to the restraint of antique Roman *virtus*.

Yet his father was old. Serenus had been his lifelong friend. Gordian knew his father needed his support as never before. Already he had done what he could to use this ceremony to gather popular support. A distribution of meat after the funeral had been announced, and a gladiatorial show would follow in a few days. The populace would appreciate both, the more so if the rituals went well. Gordian just hoped his father would not mention either the portent or the words of the astrologer.

'Where shall I begin my lamentations? How shall I share my grief at what has happened?' The wind plucked away the words, but the voice of Gordian's father contained no more tremor than age should allow. 'Serenus was, as it were, a shining torch lit for our example, and Fate has put it out.'

It was four days since Serenus' death. Gordian the Elder had spoken of attending the ninth-day funeral feast. That would be unwise. Menophilus' messenger had made port first thing this morning, his ship running before the wind. Vitalianus was dead. The Senate had declared for Gordian father and son, voted them all the customary powers of Emperors. Rome was theirs. And yet, Gordian knew, it had to be secured. Valerian was a loyal friend, but not a natural leader, and Menophilus was young. The *plebs urbana* were fickle, and Senators trimmed their sails to the prevailing breeze. Rome needed to see its new Emperors, and Italy had to be defended from Maximinus. And then there were the provinces. Arrian would secure Numidia, Sabinianus keep Africa safe. It was unthinkable that friends such as Claudius Julianus in Dalmatia, Fidus in Thrace, and Egnatius Lollianus in Bithynia-Pontus would fail to come out in their favour, but what of the others? Above all what of the East, with its great armies? Perhaps Gordian could travel ahead to Rome, leaving his father in Carthage? Or go and rouse the East, while his father went to Rome?

'I feel convinced that he who has gone dwells in the Elysian Fields. Let us therefore praise him as a hero, or rather bless him as a god. Farewell, Senerus.'

Gordian's father had done well. The eulogy had been of moderate length, measured in tone, yet full of real sentiment. Now it remained for Gordian to play his part, try not to dwell on it too much, keep his thoughts on superficial actions.

The pyre was well made; the logs neatly layered, each at right angles to the one below. Only the faintest waft of corruption under the scents of cinnamon and cassia. Serenus lay with a scroll in his hands. Gordian took a coin from an attendant, and placed it in the cold mouth. The ferryman would be paid. One hand gripping the waxy, repellent skin of the face, with the other Gordian forced the dead eyelids up. At the last a man should have his eyes open to the heavens. Mastering his reluctance, Gordian leant down and kissed the cold, dead lips.

The papyrus caught easily. The fire spread to the kindling, and with a whoosh to the incense-soaked timber. Tongues of flame licked up at the corpse.

Gordian looked up at the sky, distancing his thoughts. The smoke was pulled away into the interior. Dark clouds scudded high up. A storm was coming down from the North, racing in across the sea. If the gods existed, it was as if they were mocking his plans to leave Africa.

CHAPTER 12

ROME
THE MINT, NEAR THE FLAVIAN
AMPHITHEATRE

Seven Days before the Ides of March, AD238

The die-cutter turned off the Via Labicana and limped into the alley. A man came the other way, and both turned sideways, their backs brushing against the bricks. The door to the Mint was about halfway along, on the left. He went down the steps and out into the open courtyard. Blue sky showed between the grey clouds. It did not lift his mood. The die-cutter had much on his mind. Work would help, it always helped.

Unshuttering his cubicle, he dragged his bench and stool to the front. His leg hurt. The wound had been long, but not too deep. Castricius and Caenis had washed the cut, stitched it, and bandaged it with clean linen. God willing, it would heal well. Man was born to suffer; life a vale of tears.

Sighing, he sat, and picked up the two obverses he had made the day before. He held them close to his face. His myopia was an advantage for his work. Unlike many of his colleagues, he had no need of polished lenses or other optical devices. Near-to, things had a jewel-like precision. He did not think his long range vision had got worse recently, but it was best whenever possible to work in natural light.

The Gordiani, father and son, gazed off to his right. They had a strong family resemblance; the long nose, the unbroken curve of the jaw from earlobe to chin. The cheeks of the older man were slightly sunken, the hair of the younger more receding. They were good pieces; no sign of hurried or careless workmanship.

The young magistrates in charge of the Mint had been amazed when Menophilus had appeared the day before. All three of the *Tresviri Capitales* had fawned on the Quaestor, even though he was little older than them. Toxotius was not too bad, but Acilius Glabrio and Valerius Poplicola as ever were contemptible. Menophilus had addressed them with a weary politeness, but mainly talked to the die-cutter. The Quaestor had said what was wanted and produced portraits that he had brought from Africa.

It was very different from the accession of the last Emperor. Initially no one had had the faintest idea what Maximinus looked like. The die-cutter turned that reign over in his mind. He did not hate the Thracian as did most of the plebs. He had had no objection when Maximinus had curtailed the games and spectacles or taken treasures from the temples, no objection at all. Making reasonable money, he had not suffered when the grain dole was cut back. Most likely the condemnations of leading men had been justified. The Emperor fought the northern tribes for the safety of Rome. The obscenely rich Senators and equestrians should have volunteered their wealth. Certainly the die-cutter had felt keen pleasure at the news of the execution of Serenianus, the governor who had persecuted his brothers in Cappadocia. But that had been before Pontianus and Hippolytus had been taken and sent to the mines of Sardinia. Their arrest had left the Gathering leaderless. He had been afraid before, but in the last year the terrible cellars of the imperial palace had haunted his thoughts and dreams; the ghastly pincers and claws wielded with refined cruelty by men without compassion. Once they knew who you were, they treated you worse than a murderer.

He replaced the obverses and studied the reverse dies he had cut. For practical reasons, as well as the greater variety of messages they carried, there always had to be more of them. Taking a greater strain in the minting process, they wore out quicker. Menophilus had issued general, but clear guidelines: traditional values, the *mos maiorum*, the centrality of Rome, nothing foreign or outlandish, the political experience and the unity of the Emperors. So far the die-cutter had produced *Romae Aeternae*, *Providentia*, and *Concordia*. He wondered how things would be under the Gordiani.

122

They had been appointed by Alexander, and that Emperor and his mother had been gracious to some of the brethren. Better still, three of the freedmen in the *Domus Rostrata*, the great house of the Gordiani on the Esquiline, belonged to the Gathering. If Gaudianus, Reverendus and Montanus had influence, all should be well.

But the war was still to be won. The die-cutter shuffled through the papyri on his desk until he found his sketches: personifications of *Victoria*, *Securitas*, and *Virtus Exercituum*, the latter an innovation of his own, suitable for the circumstances. He took from his bag and unwrapped the three different drills, the burin and graver, the tongs and pincers, the cutters and files, the compass and pouch of powdered corundum. Taking a disc of bronze, he fixed it in a vice. He would start with the *Virtue of the Armies*.

Virtue meant different things to different men. Whatever the definition, the die-cutter knew he was far from it. For four years he had been an apprentice, not a full member of the Gathering. The usual time was two years, three at most. Four years of being watched, his behaviour scrutinized. And for all of them – the watched and the watchers – there was the constant fear of betrayal. As he had heard Pontianus put it, they must consider their closest friends, their own relatives as worse than their enemies, in fear that they would denounce them. The informer could be anyone. It could be Castricius or Caenis.

The die-cutter tried to put away his doubts. This life was good, but the life he longed for better. His own sins had prolonged his apprenticeship. Twice he had been demoted to the status of a Hearer, reduced to standing by the doors of the Gathering. The offence both times had been fornication. Soon he would have to go to his instructor Africanus and admit to the fight in the street. If he expressed true contrition, his punishment might be light.

And he knew in his heart, he deserved much worse. He had been there in the street when the soldiers came for Pontianus. As the mob surged around him, three times he had denied knowing Pontianus. When they howled for blood, rather than attract their anger, he had joined in their chants. *Throw him to the beasts! To the lions!* Should he confess, no amount of remorse would serve. In sackcloth and ashes, he would be led into the midst of the brethren and prostrated, an object of disgrace and horror. Before the elders and the widows, before them all, he would have to grovel, begging for their forgiveness, clasping their knees, licking their very footprints.

CHAPTER 13

ROME
THE FORUM OF AUGUSTUS

Six Days before the Ides of March, AD238

Be a man. Without moving his lips, Menophilus repeated the words – *Be a man*. He was sure that Sabinus, the Prefect of the City, should have arrived by now. The outcome of this clandestine meeting depended on timing. He could go outside, and check the sun, but that might be seen as irresolute. He continued his solitary wait for Maximinus' supporter, pacing, back and forth, back and forth.

The room oppressed him. It was the height, not the floor space. Panels and bands of marble – Numidian yellow, Phrygian purple, white from Greece, the smoky red and black they called Lucullan – revetted all the way up to the coffered slabs of the ceiling, fifty foot or more. A gigantic statue of Augustus, five or six times larger than life, crowded the space. The whole effect was like being at the bottom of a quarry or mine shaft under the gaze of a singularly impassive deity.

Menophilus stopped in front of one of the two

paintings by Apelles. From a triumphal chariot, Augustus looked down on a bound prisoner, a personification. The Emperor had vanquished war itself. The transience of human endeavour weighed heavily on Menophilus. Augustus should have known better. War could not be conquered. The folly and ignorance of mankind ensured war was eternal.

If there was war now in the city of Rome, the Gordiani would lose. Sabinus had quartered three thousand of the Urban Cohorts in the Porticus Vipsania on the Campus Martius, commanding the west of the city. The other three thousand remained in their usual barracks in the Praetorian camp at the north of Rome. The thousand Praetorians left in their camp also followed his orders. The majority of the seven thousand men of the Watch were still at their stations throughout the city, although their Prefect Potens, said to be nervous by nature, had gathered some two thousand across the Tiber, dominating the bridge. The proximity of their camp on the other side of the river, had ensured the detachment of a thousand men from the Ravenna fleet had remained loyal to Maximinus.

To put against those forces, Menophilus had won the oaths of the men stationed in the east of the city; a thousand from the fleet at Misenum in their camp near the Baths of Trajan, the two hundred cavalrymen and the less-than-a-hundred *frumentarii* left in their bases on the Caelian, and the couple of hundred Praetorians who had been on duty on the Palatine when he killed Vitalianus. He had sent Serapamum, an equestrian client of the house of the Gordiani, to try to secure the adherence of the Second Parthian Legion at their base in the Alban Hills. Yet, even if the mission was successful, only a thousand swords had remained when the legion had marched off to the wars in the North, and the camp was twelve miles distant from the city. If it came to a fight now – odds of ten to one against – the Gordiani would be massacred. Other approaches were necessary. Distasteful as it was, this meeting with Sabinus was inevitable.

Still, one thing had played into Menophilus' hands. The messenger from Maximinus had sought the office of the Praetorian Prefect on the Palatine. He had found not Vitalianus, but an officer called Felicio. The day before, Menophilus had appointed this Felicio, another equestrian indebted to the patronage of the Gordiani, to command their vestigial Guard. Among the imperial despatches from beyond the northern frontier – detailed stages of march, dispositions of troops, intelligence regarding the Sarmatians – had been the order for the arrest of Timesitheus.

Menophilus had admired the self-control of Timesitheus, as he read his own purple-sealed death warrant. Unsurprisingly, the *Graeculus* had been quick to pledge his allegiance to the new imperial dynasty. There was much to recommend the little Greek. He was intelligent and personable, good-looking in a restrained way. He had governed provinces in the North and East with distinction. His handling of the logistics of the northern campaign had been exemplary. As *Praefectus Annonae* he controlled the grain supply of Rome. One of his closest friends had charge of the Ludus Magnus and the largest troop of gladiators in the capitol. His links with those in the Subura who could get the plebs out on the streets might prove invaluable.

Yet, on the reverse of the coin, Timesitheus was not to be trusted. He had informed against Magnus, and his fellow would-be tyrannicides in Germania, and against harmless, old Valerius Apollinaris in Asia. He had enemies here in Rome – men the Gordiani would need. None were more fervent than Apollinaris' son Valerius Priscillianus, but the Greek also was embroiled in a protracted and vitriolic dispute over an inheritance with Armenius Peregrinus.

And then there were the schemes Timesitheus had proposed to further the cause he had so recently joined. Unethical was far too mild a word. A courtier around the throne of an Oriental despot would have found them disgraceful. The hypocrisy of his own thinking turned Menophilus on his heel, drove him out of the room into the Forum. He ignored the two soldiers he had posted outside the curtains; the others were out of sight. He sat on the plinth of a statue, trying to rein in his thoughts, master himself.

A fountain played at the foot of the steps of the temple. He heard the sound of another fountain, the sound of approaching footsteps. Sicilia on the Palatine. His boot on Vitalianus' chest, his sword at his throat. The doomed man looking up at him. The last request. *Spare my daughters.* At least Menophilus had sent his ashes back to his widow in Etruria. He doubted his letter assuring the family they were free from any further reprisals had afforded much comfort.

In politics the things you most desire were the things you should most fear. In the last few days frequently Menophilus had wished he had never left his native Apulia. Now there was no going back to the quiet life of an equestrian in the country. The Stoicism he aspired to held that retirement was justifiable if the state was irremediably corrupt. The empire was a monarchy. If the ruler was a tyrant, mad or bad beyond cure or redemption, he could be killed and replaced. Maximinus was both, that much seemed clear. Yet what of the others who stood in the way of pulling the tyrant from his throne? Gordian had sanctioned the killing of Vitalianus, but had the Prefect deserved to die? What of his other supporters?

Menophilus looked past the steps to the exedra on the other side of the temple. Romulus stood there, armoured, carrying spoils stripped from an enemy chieftain. For the good of Rome, he had cut down his brother, and he had become a god. Rome was founded in blood. They were the children of the wolf. Ausonian beasts, as the Greeks called them.

A movement at the southern end of the portico in which he sat. Sabinus had come. The Prefect of the City was not wearing a helmet, but otherwise was equipped for the battlefield; breastplate, military cloak, sword-belt, and boots. He was backed by ten men of the Urban Cohorts. Their swords were sheathed, but the covers were off their shields, showing their emblem, Roma enthroned.

'The agreement was two soldiers each,' Menophilus said.

Sabinus dismissed this with an odd motion of his hand, as if dusting an invisible object. 'The streets are unsafe. The homes of two Senators were looted yesterday, their occupants attacked, several servants were killed. I have more soldiers at the front of the Forum and at both the rear doors.'

'Yet life goes on,' Menophilus said. 'The streets are quiet in most parts of the city.'

With a patrician wave, Sabinus indicated the room should be searched. Two soldiers went behind the curtain. The others remained tight around him until they re-emerged.

'Shall we?'

Menophilus followed him. The curtain fell to after them. They were alone.

Sabinus paused to let his eyes adjust to the gloom. He looked around, as if his men might have overlooked a lurking assassin; nothing but marble panels and the huge statue, nowhere to hide. He went over and studied the painting of captive war.

'The fool Claudius ruined Apelles' masterpiece. He had the features of Augustus painted over those of Alexander the Great.' Sabinus spoke as if instructing a child. 'All too few really appreciate art. When Mummius was bringing his loot back from Corinth, he had a clause inserted into the contract with the shippers, if they lost or damaged any of the old masters they were to provide him with new ones.'

'I am sorry your pictures outside the Senate house were destroyed,' Menophilus said.

Sabinus replied without taking his eyes off the painting. 'They were of little merit, although the artists were proficient, and I had given the composition some thought. They resonated well with their surroundings, the Rostra and the Lake of Curtius.'

Turning, Sabinus ran his gaze over the great gilded statue, and shuddered slightly. 'I had hoped Valerian would be with you. I have always liked him.'

'And I would have welcomed Potens,' Menophilus said.

Sabinus smiled. 'A jumped-up man of little *virtus*, but loyal.' He continued without pause. 'You wish to negotiate your safety. Maximinus is not renowned for the quality of mercy. Old-fashioned severity is more his style. Renouncing Gordian and his father will not be enough. However, if you name everyone connected to the revolt, and you aid me in restoring order to the city, then perhaps I will be able to persuade our Emperor to allow you to return to your pastures and cattle droves in the South, live out your life in obscurity.'

Menophilus counted from alpha to omega before replying. 'Maximinus is a tyrant. He will turn on you.'

Again Sabinus made the strange dusting motion, fluttering his fingers. 'Maximinus is on the other side of the Alps with an army. The Gordiani are on the far side of the sea with no legions. If they sailed into the storm, they may well already be dead.'

'If you join us,' Menophilus said, 'Potens will follow you.'

'If I countenanced such treason' – Sabinus looked at the gilt statue as if struck by the idea that it might be hollow, and contain some witness – 'and, before the gods, I would never entertain such thoughts, the troops who garrison Rome would still never defeat the field army on the battlefield.'

'No set battle,' Menophilus said. 'We block the Alpine passes. If the tyrant gets through, we hold Aquileia. As a final barrier, we fortify the routes across the Apennines. We delay Maximinus until the British and eastern armies rise against him.'

The flutter of Sabinus' fingers. 'I am far from convinced that will happen. Maximinus appointed many of the governors. Certainly Decius and his legion in Spain will remain true to Maximinus.'

A soldier stuck his head through the curtain.

No longer the languid connoisseur, Sabinus was very alert.

'Apologies, Prefect, a mob is gathering in front of the Forum. Several hundred of them, they are throwing stones. The men will not be able to keep them out for long.'

Sabinus pointed a finger at Menophilus.

'No, not my doing,' said Menophilus. 'The plebs hate all Senators. I will leave by the back doors with you.'

'Indeed you will.' Sabinus laughed. 'Guards!'

The curtain was pulled back. Soldiers muscled in, ringed Menophilus.

'What of your oath? You gave me safe conduct.'

'Oaths are very overrated,' Sabinus said. 'Our ancestors knew the safety of the *Res Publica* must come before such technicalities.'

Menophilus was clad in just a tunic and cloak. When they searched him they found no hidden weapons, just the knife on his belt.

'A pity Valerian is not with you. I would have sent you both to Maximinus. Bind him.'

'There is no need.'

'Actually,' Sabinus gestured at the painting, 'I think there is.'

They tied Menophilus' hands behind him, the rope rough, cutting into his wrists.

'Shall we?' Sabinus said.

Outside, they descended the three steps to the floor of the Forum. Menophilus took care, should he stumble, he could not put out his hands. He could see his two soldiers, disarmed and trussed up some paces away. The confused roar of the mob echoed down the porticos, through the statues, as if the great men of the past cried out against such treachery.

A guard on either side, Menophilus followed Sabinus under the Arch of Drusus, up the steep flights of stairs, through the rear gate, and out into the street.

On the *Vicus Sandaliarius* some forty troops were drawn up in a crescent facing the door, on their shields Roma on her throne, or Neptune rising from the ocean.

'Fall in,' Sabinus ordered.

The waiting troops did not move, neither those bearing the symbol of the Urban Cohorts or the Misenene fleet. The soldiers of the former around Sabinus and Menophilus shifted uneasily, looked back over their shoulders. The door through which they had come was now blocked by the marines Menophilus had hidden inside the temple in the Forum.

A tall officer, old and forbidding in appearance, heavy-bearded, stepped forward from the surrounding troops. 'Sabinus, you are relieved of your office,' Pupienus said. 'You men with him, join your fellow-soldiers in swearing allegiance to our noble Emperors Gordian the Elder and Younger. By the authority of our sacred Augusti, I am once again Prefect of the City.'

Sabinus rounded on Menophilus, drawing his sword. Menophilus hurled himself sideways, knocking the soldier on his right off balance with his shoulder. As the man staggered, Menophilus was off. The ranks of the encircling troops opened. He was spun around. Someone sawed through the ropes that bound him. The blade nicked his forearm. The sounds of a scuffle behind him.

Turning back, he saw those who had guarded Sabinus putting down their weapons. Sabinus himself was running to the open door of a store-room a few paces down the street. Marines from the Misenene fleet bundled in after him.

'Do not kill him!' Menophilus shouted, and raced after them.

The dark room was full of lumber, discarded offerings and damaged furniture from the Forum. Sabinus was cornered, his sword gone.

'Leave him, he is my responsibility.' Walking towards the trapped man, Menophilus picked up the leg of a broken chair.

The marines fell back.

Menophilus faced Sabinus.

'I take it there is no point in pleading for my life.'

'No,' Menophilus said.

'For a Stoic, you have a talent for deception and murder.'

'You should have joined us.'

'And been killed by Maximinus a little later. You will lose.'

'All men have to die.'

Sabinus covered his head with his cloak. 'What an artist dies here.'

As Menophilus hefted the improvised cudgel, Sabinus lunged forward, the concealed blade now in his hand. Menophilus brought the chair leg down on the other man's fist. The knife clattered to the floor. Sabinus doubled up in pain.

'Maximinus will kill you,' Sabinus gasped.

'If it is fated.'

Carefully judging the distance, like an attendant at a sacrifice, Menophilus brought the chair leg down onto the back of Sabinus' head. A sickening sound, like smashing an amphora full of something wet and solid. Sabinus went to his hands and knees, blood oozing from his scalp. Menophilus hit him again, three or four more times when he was prone.

Pupienus caught his arms. 'Enough.'

Menophilus stood, panting, beyond words, beyond thought.

Pupienus released him. 'We need his head to be recognisable.'

CHAPTER 14

ROME
THE SUBURA

Six Days before the Ides of March, AD238

Caenis woke softly. Rain pattered on the roof of the attic in the tenement. She yawned and stretched. It was a luxury to be able to sleep in the early afternoon, in her own room, her own bed, alone. She had been dreaming of the voyage from Ephesus. A long time ago now, but it was still fresh in her memory; the strange smells and motion of the ship, the flying spray as it shouldered the waves, the towns and islands shining in the sun, Samos, the Cyclades, Zakynthos, Corcyra, names like poetry. It had been a good time. She had raised enough money to pay for her passage and food. The sailors and the other passengers had left her alone. Superstitious to a man, they held it was unlucky enough to have a woman on board, let alone bother her for sex.

Five years since she had left Ephesus; what would have happened to Rhodope? She would be married, Caenis was certain. Her husband would be the son of a member of the *Boule*. They would live in a grand house with servants. No, that was wrong. Rhodope had never wanted wealth. She would have married a potter, a neighbour from the quarter by the Magnesian Gate. The house would smell of wet clay. It would be under his nails, engrained in the pores of his skin. Perhaps she would have caught the eye of a farmer come to market. In his unsophisticated way, he might have thrown an apple at her. When it came time to talk to her father, he would have brought a cheese, a kid. The wedding would have been on his small-holding on the slopes of Mount Prion, with rustic dancing, roast suckling pig. Or he might have been a blacksmith, like her father. Their home would be warm, ringing with the clangour of his trade. She would worry about the little ones getting too near to the forge. In the evenings she would rub salve into the burns on her man's strong arms.

A raised voice in the street brought her back to the Subura. She would not let it depress her. Things could be much worse. She could have a *Leno*, who would take her earnings, beat her, use her, pass her around among his friends. Girls confined in a *Lupanar* had a harder time; even those who were not slaves were hardly ever allowed out. The other day she had seen a poor slave girl in the street, a collar forged around her neck: *This is a cheating whore! Seize her, she has escaped!*

The bar was not a bad place to work in the evenings. The patrons might be rough, but Ascyltos allowed little rowdiness, and he took no more than half of what she made. During the day she only needed to entertain a few clients in her own room, mostly regulars from the neighbourhood. There was the old die-cutter across the hall. He had grown odder after his wife died. He had turned to the worship of Dionysus, joining a cell of *Iobacchi*. That had not lasted. Since then he had taken to slipping out of his room, down the creaking stairs, long before it was light. He came back late at night, sober. He would not say where he went, who he saw. Whatever he did, it was not within the law. Doubtless the authorities would reward an informer who discovered his furtive activities.

Caenis did not mind the die-cutter. He made no unusual demands. But she preferred the visits of Castricius. The young cut-purse was generous. Often he brought wine and a handful of delicacies. Thin and wiry, when he had finished, he told jokes. Her laughter was not feigned. He spoke educated Greek, and always left a tip.

There were heavy footsteps on the stairs, the rap of hobnails, the jingling of the ornaments on a military belt.

'Open.'

'A moment.' Caenis slipped naked from the bed. She pulled on a tunic, before unlatching the door.

'A modest whore.' The Centurion filled the doorway. There was an air of harmfulness about him. In the room even the inanimate objects – the bed, the one chair, the chest, the chipped bowl and jug – seemed to shrink from him.

'I was not expecting you. With the rioting, I thought the Praetorians would be on duty.'

'Emperors come and go, whores still have to pay the tax.'

Caenis did not like having to prize up the floorboard with him watching. She counted out thirty-one *denarii*, one for each day of the month.

The Centurion put them into a wallet on his belt. 'Two short.'

There was nothing to be gained by arguing. Caenis handed over another two coins. He slid them into a different wallet. The chair creaked as he sat to write the official receipt.

'A *denarius* a fuck.' He shook his head in mock wonder. 'Hardly seems worth it.'

Caenis remained very still. Perhaps he would just leave.

'On your knees.'

He got up, and stood in front of her. 'Get my prick out.'

She pushed up his tunic, unbuckled the belt that held up his breeches.

His penis hung flaccid. She took it in her mouth. It was unwashed, tasted of urine.

'Look me in the eye.'

She did as she was told.

'If only your father could see you now.'

His penis stiffened.

'Over the bed.'

She leant on the covers, as he hauled her tunic up around her waist. He spat on his fingers, pushed

140

them between her legs. She felt him bend his knees to guide himself inside her. Her mind went blank, her thoughts unfocused.

Down in the street someone was singing. Somewhere in the tenement the sounds of furniture being moved. He gripped her hips, grunting as he thrust.

When he was done, he left without speaking.

Caenis tugged the tunic over her head. She squatted over the bowl, washed herself, tried to sneeze. There were some hours before she had to go to the bar.

CHAPTER 15

AFRICA
THE TOWN OF LAMBAESIS,
NUMIDIA

Six Days before the Ides of March, AD238

They rode over the last rise, and Lambaesis was below them; the jumbled town on the lower slopes, the plain beyond, bright with spring grass, and in the middle of it the great, regular fortress of yellow stone, and beyond that the green hills, saw-toothed against the sky. Nothing in the scene lifted the dissatisfaction that was habitual with Capelianus.

He did not hate Africa, but he did not love it, and he had had no desire to return. For four years he had been governor of the province of Numidia. He had been meant for greater things. His grandfather had been Consul, governed Pannonia Inferior, and been friend of the Emperor Antoninus Pius. Admittedly his father had failed to attain the Consulship, and had squandered their money. Capelianus himself had mortgaged the ancestral estates at Cirta to pay the huge bribe to Alexander Severus' mother for a belated Consulship. His

142

patrimony had been almost exhausted by the next payment. He had hoped for one of the rich, major provinces, Asia or Africa Proconsularis, somewhere fitting to his *dignitas*, where he could recoup his losses. Instead that avaricious Syrian bitch Mamaea had sent him here. Numidia was a post for ex-Praetors, not those who had been Consul. It was held by much younger Senators, men not destined for the highest offices. Well into his sixties, and for four years he had been stuck in this backwater.

As he rode down through the streets of the town, the clop of hooves and the tread of the soldiers were drowned by the rumble and squeal of the big game cart.

Capelianus knew exactly when his career had stalled. It was when his whore of a first wife had cuckolded him with that old goat Gordian. No longer a man of promise, he had become a figure of ridicule. It was said the Emperor Caracalla had joked about it with his intimates. The court case had made it common knowledge. As Gordian had been found innocent, against all justice, Capelianus had not even kept her dowry when he threw her out. The threat of prosecution for the beating he had administered had come to nothing. He had not been fortunate with his wives. He had married twice more. Both had proved to be barren. Divorced, they had taken their wealth with them. In front of the required seven witnesses, he had said the words: *Take your things and go.*

They entered the base of the 3rd Augustan Legion by the rear gate and went up the Via Decumana towards the headquarters. The breeze was cut off by the barrack blocks, and the reek of big cat was strong in his nostrils.

At least the hunting had been good. They had been out twelve days in the mountains to the south. They had graded up through juniper and holm oak, up to where there were just cedars. Snow still lay in the hollows of the upper slopes. The steep-cut runoffs had been full of jade and white water tumbling and sliding over smooth stones. It had been cold at night, but the camp had been a pleasure. Big fires flaring bright in the wind. From outside his leather tent had come the ordered murmur of the men; not just soldiers and huntsmen, but bearers, skinners, cooks, grooms, and personal servants.

They had been too high for boar, yet the hunting had been good. Hyenas, two packs of wild dogs, three panthers, one with cubs, but the lion had been the prize. A big man-eater, heavy shouldered, with a fine, black mane. Capelianus savoured the memory of his first sight, as it padded through the trees. The beast had raided a mountain village. It had got into the sheepfolds. Escaping, it had killed a peasant, but taken a slight wound. Capelianus had planned with care. The camp and baggage animals had been protected by zeribas of thorn bushes. The bait, a gazelle and a mare, had been tethered behind the trapping box. Strong nets, secured to well hammered-in posts, had curved away on either side. Everything had been concealed by the fronds of cut branches.

The den was in a thick tangle of undergrowth and fallen boughs. Capelianus had sent in fifteen soldiers with big shields and burning torches. The lion had roared, an ascending thunder, ending in a guttural cough. It had reverberated in Capelianus' chest, made his limbs clumsy with fear. The call revealed an older beast; old, wounded, and accustomed to killing men, dangerous beyond measure.

The lion broke cover. The soldiers came out after. The rough going had broken their ranks. The lion charged an isolated soldier, knocked him down with its great weight. Capelianus smiled, remembering the pinned man screaming. With teeth and claws, the beast tried to tear through the covering shield. Not until the brands singed its hide, did it turn and run into the waiting trap.

They had helped the soldier to his feet. He was not much injured, a few cuts to his arms and shoulders, but his breeches were soaked with urine. Everyone had laughed.

When they reached the rear of the *Principia*, Capelianus issued precise instructions about the care of the big cats. He would send the lion to Maximinus. The Emperor was an uncultured brute. He handled the *Res Publica* like a goatherd who had climbed into a racing chariot. The Thracian had shown no favours to Capelianus. Yet perhaps the peasant-Emperor would be pleased by the beast. Perhaps Capelianus might escape from Numidia.

The carts rumbled away, and Capelianus rode into the forecourt. A groom held the bridle, and he dismounted. A Centurion announced the men were drawn up waiting. Capelianus was back among the tedium of a governor's duties: pointless inspections of troops, endless court cases, disputes over inheritances, complaints of soldiers' greed and brutality, endless pleas for remission of taxes. Still, it was only five days until the *Mamuralia*. The local version of the festival had delighted Capelianus. In other places, they beat the empty hide of an animal. Here the skins were worn by an old man. Capelianus would tour the gaols, choose the prisoner carefully. He should not be too aged or infirm, not go down too easily under the blows. The scapegoat needed to be beaten all through the streets to the city gates. Capelianus wondered what happened to him out in the country. Most likely he died in a ditch.

Capelianus walked through the Basilica, and out into the peristyle courtyard. He went to ascend the tribunal, but a row of soldiers locked his way. An officer he did not recognize stepped forward.

'Caius Iulius Geminius Capelianus, you are dismissed from your command.'

The officer who spoke had a short, stubby beard. His lined face and upturned nose seemed familiar. Capelianus did not recognize the two young tribunes who stood with him.

'You are to be confined under house arrest,' the older of the three officers continued.

Arrian, one of old Gordian's legates. Capelianus knew him now. A friend of Gordian's dissolute son. One of the pair they called the *Cercopes*, the lying, cheating twins of myth.

'Fellow soldiers of the 3rd Augustan,' Capelianus shouted.

'Preserve your *dignitas*,' Arrian said. 'They have sworn their oath to our new Emperors, Marcus Antonius Gordianus Sempronianus Romanus Africanus Pius Felix Augustus, Father and Son.'

CHAPTER 16

ROME
THE CAELIAN HILL

Five Days before the Ides of March, AD238

When the drinks came in they all stopped talking. There was time to study the small room. Like everything in the house of the Consul Fulvius Pius, it was decorated with restrained good taste; the walls painted in blocks of red and black panels, busts of Brutus, Cassius and Cato the Younger on plinths.

Pupienus thought about the portraits. Two Stoics and an Epicurean. Two men who had assassinated Caesar in the name of Republican *libertas*, and one who had killed himself rather than live under his dictatorship; two tyrannicides and a martyr for freedom. Had Fulvius Pius dressed the room to appeal to Gallicanus? On the other hand, if they were a permanent feature of the decor, did it indicate some hankering on the part of the Consul for the long lost free Republic? Not necessarily. Pupienus had read of an equestrian official who had exhibited busts of the same men, while faithfully serving in the imperial administration for nearly half a century, serving under the tyrants Tiberius and Caligula, possibly Claudius as well. It annoyed him that he could not recall the man's name. He prided himself on his memory.

Perhaps Pius's sculptures were merely an assertion of culture. It was possible to read too much into a man's choice in art. Yet, in politics, small details might reveal character; interests, affiliations, strengths and weaknesses. If he was to be harnessed to them, at least outwardly, in the new Board of Twenty, Pupienus needed to know everything he could about the other four men in the room; penetrate beneath the exterior of the young Stoic Menophilus, the gross patrician Balbinus, the hairy Cynic Gallicanus, as well as their anxious looking Consular host.

The servants left, and Fulvius Pius was the first to speak.

'Before we look to the future, the city must be safe. Murder, arson, rape; some people have been afraid to leave their homes. They are not safe even there.'

It was for Pupienus to answer. He took a sip of watered wine, let them wait a moment. The Consul was cautious, irresolute; not to be relied upon, but posing little threat. *Some people*, indeed. He needed reassurance; the calm enumeration of matter-of-fact details of security.

'When he heard that Sabinus was dead, Potens fled; maybe to Maximinus in the north, more likely to his brother-in-law Decius and the comparative safety of Spain.' Pupienus nodded to Menophilus. 'The Watch has a new commander; Maecius Gordianus, an equestrian kinsman of our noble Emperors. The Prefect Felicio has administered the oath of allegiance to those Praetorians still quartered in their camp. Serapamum has the Second Legion ready to march from their base in the Alban Hills. The necessity should not arise. As Prefect of the City, I have put the Urban Cohorts back onto the streets. The ringleaders of the recent troubles are being arrested. Timesitheus, the Prefect of the Grain Supply, has ordered a special distribution. With the stick and the carrot, the plebs should be quiet.'

The others took it all in, sitting still, or toying with their drinks.

Timesitheus had done more than produce a surplus of grain. The *Praefectus Annonae* had shown an extraordinarily detailed knowledge of the identities and domiciles of the plebeian rabble rousers who had led the mobs out of the Subura. Pupienus did not care for surprises, and every conversation with Timesitheus was a revelation. The little Greek was easy and subtle, full of charm, but, for those with eyes to see, remorseless ambition glimmered just beneath the amiable surface. He needed watching, and now, not without reason, he expected a reward. It was a pity that Menophilus had already assigned the commands of the Praetorians and the Watch. Timesitheus had implied that he would like to add one of those Prefectures to that of the Grain Supply. Something else needed to be found to satisfy the *Graeculus*. It would be unwise to alienate such a man.

'Our problem remains.'

Menophilus might be the youngest and the most junior present, but no one objected to his taking the lead. He was close to the new Emperors, and no one was likely to forget that in the last few days he had killed two senior politicians with his own hands. one with a sword, the other clubbed to death with the leg of a chair. The principles of Stoicism had always been malleable, Pupienus reflected.

'The Senate has decreed a Board of Twenty to defend Italy from Maximinus, and we still have twenty-three names.'

'A free vote in the Curia,' Gallicanus said.

'It is inappropriate,' Menophilus said.

'Inappropriate!' Gallicanus bounded up from his couch, like one of the big apes in the imperial menagerie, when they are prodded with a stick. 'Free speech in the Senate House is never *inappropriate*. It is the very cause for which we have put our lives at risk.'

Balbinus raised himself on an arm. His large belly shifted as if some rotund animal, something more slothful than simian, had taken refuge in his clothes. 'If every Senator exercises his choice, do you think most would vote for an ex-Praetor, a

151

man from nowhere, one who ceaselessly parades his austerity?'

Gallicanus wrung his hands with great violence, probably wishing Balbinus' neck was in their strong grip, but subsided.

Pupienus thought Balbinus a fool. A true states-man never gave offence, unless it was necessary, unless it brought him advantage. Bitter words should be dipped in honey.

'When Cato condoned bribery in elections,' Pupienus gestured at one of the busts, 'he accepted that occasionally Roman voters require guidance; that sometimes strict morality and temporal laws must stand down for the greater good, for the well-being of the *Res Publica*.'

Gallicanus did not look particularly mollified or grateful. Oaf, Pupienus thought, yapping Cynic dog.

'A Board of Twenty,' Menophilus resumed. 'Three men, no matter how deserving, must be dropped from our list. Experience of military command should be a prerequisite. As such, for the safety of the *Res Publica*, I am prepared to strike out the name of Celsus Aelianus, friend though he is of our Augustus Gordian the Younger.' He turned to Balbinus. 'Your *amicus* Praetextatus also has never commanded troops in the field.'

'Never.' Balbinus' jowls wobbled with incoherent vehemence.

Gallicanus laughed, an unpleasant sound, fortun-ately seldom heard. 'At least we would be spared looking at him. The only person in Rome uglier is that daughter of his. No matter how large the dowry, he cannot find her a husband, doubt he ever will.'

Balbinus ignored the comments. 'That sniggering little Greek scribbler Licinius has never seen an army. Draw a line through his name.'

'Letters must be written, governors and communities persuaded,' Fulvius Pius said. 'He has been imperial secretary. We need his eloquence. He has been *a Rationibus*. We need his financial acumen. Anyway he governed Noricum, an armed province. What qualifications does your friend Valerius Priscillianus hold? Is he not Curator of the Banks of the Tiber and the Sewers of the City?'

Well, Pupienus thought, our Consul has a backbone after all. Perhaps he wants to build a little *factio* of his own.

'Never,' Balbinus shouted, 'not while I live and breath. What about Egnatius Marinianus. He has nothing to recommend him except Valerian married his sister.'

Pupienus withdrew part of his mind. Long ago Mark Antony, Octavian and Lepidus had met on a small island in a river near Bononia. While everyone else waited on the banks, they drew up a proscription list, trading friends and relatives, marking them down for death. The stakes here were not that high, not yet. But something had to be done to break this deadlock, some concession.

'Appius Claudius is so old, he will be dead by the time Maximinus gets here,' Gallicanus said.

Pupienus regretted that Fortunatianus was outside with the other secretaries. A written list would give certainty to his calculations. He concentrated hard, holding all the names in his mind, arranging them, making patterns of friendship and obligation. Yes, it could be done. If he had counted the numbers correctly, assessed all their attachments, he could make a gesture. He waited for a pause.

'Conscript Fathers, if our history teaches us anything, it is that duty to the *Res Publica* must outweigh love of family and friends.'

They were all looking at him.

'Along with Celsus Aelianus, let the names of my sons, Maximus and Africanus, be struck from the list.'

He would have smiled at their surprise, had his emotions not been schooled by a lifetime of restraint.

A moment of silence, then all spoke at once of his devotion to the cause, his nobility of soul; graceful words masking relieved self-interest.

'It is settled,' Menophilus said. 'Twenty candidates for twenty places. Now for the practicalities. All members of the Twenty have to be ex-Consuls. When the Senate meets tomorrow, Fulvius Pius and Pontius Pontianus will lay down the Consulship.'

'But,' Fulvius Pius spoke up, 'Pontianus is not here.'

154

'He wrote pleading ill health.' Menophilus was brisk. 'We will take that as his resignation.'

No one objected. Feigning illness on a country estate might let Pontianus survive the coming civil war. For many Senators, perhaps the majority, that was all that mattered, but it would not endear them to either camp. The men in this room were putting themselves at risk for power and influence, the highest stakes of all.

'Gallicanus and myself will replace them. At the sixth hour, we too will relinquish office, and Maecenas and Claudius Julianus be elected, the latter, as governor of Dalmatia, *in absentia*. Then, in the afternoon, the Senate can proceed with the election of the Board of Twenty.'

'Consul for six hours,' Gallicanus said. 'It makes a mockery of the constitution.'

'Rome does not have a written constitution,' Menophilus said.

Balbinus heaved himself up to speak, doubtless something offensive.

Pupienus forestalled him. 'The greater good.' He pointed at the stern, marble features of Cato. 'We must all remember the greater good.'

A libation, a toast to each other, and the meeting was over.

Back in his house, a few steps from that of the Consul, Pupienus retired to a private room with Fortunatianus. His secretary handed him writing materials. Opening the hinged wooden block,

Pupienus focused his memory. Smoothing the wax, he took up the stylus, and wrote his list, annotating it only in his mind.

XXviri ex Senatus Consulta Rei Publicae Curandae

Menophilus – *the voice of the Gordiani*
Valerian – *their dutiful, if dull follower*
Egnatius Marinianus – *Valerian's brother-in-law*
Lucius Virius – *father of Menophilus' closest friend*
Appius Claudius – *aged ally of Gordian the Elder*
Five men, only Menophilus and Lucius Virus of any consequence

Balbinus – *repulsive compound of privilege and low cunning*
Valerius Priscillianus – *idem, embittered by the killings of his father and brother*
Rufinianus – *another Patrician, but somewhat thinner, somewhat more capable*
Praetextatus – *rich, ill-favoured, pliable*
Claudius Aurelius – *elderly descendant of Marcus Aurelius, recalled by sense of duty from self-imposed semi-exile on his estates*
Claudius Severus – *indistinguishable from the above*

*Six, united by their estimates of their own
abilities*

*<u>Pupienus</u> – a novus homo, risen to the heights,
his origins carefully hidden; know yourself,
said the Oracle of Delphi
Sextus Cethegillus – his brother-in-law
Tineius Sacerdos – father of the wife of his
elder son
Crispinus – another successful new man,
nothing shaming in his past
Four, all men of substance, especially the novi
homines; Delphic self-knowledge was not to
be confused with humility*

*<u>Gallicanus</u> – a posturing, violent ape or dog
Maecenas – his companion in everything
Two, their dangerous self-righteousness buttressed
by philosophical aspirations*

*Fulvius Pius – the presiding Consul
Licinius – the orator and treasurer
Latronianus – a great noble
Three individuals, or an incipient faction?*

As it read, Balbinus had the largest faction.
Certainly, he had left with an air of ill-concealed
triumph. And yet . . . and yet.

Pupienus tapped the stylus against the ring on
the middle finger of his right hand.

The two Claudii had put their heads on the

block by their own volition. *Virtus,* not loyalty to Balbinus had impelled their return. Descendants of Emperors made bad followers. They would pursue their own line. With persuasion, the *factio* of Balbinus might be reduced to four. And then, with a bold stroke, perhaps, to three.

It was a pity Maximus was already wed. He was the more biddable of Pupienus' sons. Africanus had developed a fine estimate of himself since he had held the Consulship. But there again, he had always been the more ambitious. With the right handling, he might accept the influx of wealth and influence that would come with a less-than-attractive wife. Beauty should reside in her obedience and chastity, not her form. Pupienus would call on Praetextatus without delay.

Twenty Men Elected from the Senate to Care for the Res Publica

And to further their own interests. What a cohort. Still, often in politics it was easier if you did not care for your travelling companions.

Pupienus smoothed the wax clean. He always wrote lightly, taking care to leave no marks on the underlying wood. All gone.

158

CHAPTER 17

THE NORTHERN FRONTIER
SIRMIUM

Two Days before the Ides of March, AD*238*

Mark the day with a lucky white stone. Pour out an offering of pure wine to your *Genius*. Simple birthday rituals, time hallowed. They had always sufficed for Maximinus. But not for his son, not now he was Caesar.

Verus Maximus sat on his throne as if the theatre, the speaker and everyone else in it, as if the whole town of Sirmium and the *imperium* itself, all were arranged for his pleasure.

'Since from you and your love of mankind we receive honour, dignity, glory and protection – in short, all the rewards of life – we would consider it a sin if we celebrated your birthday, the day that brought you into the light for the benefit and happiness of the entire world, more casually than our own.'

The orator spoke from the stage in front of the curtain. His tone was unctuous, the flattery immoderate.

'All your young life, we have wondered what you would look like in the purple. Now, by the foresight of your noble father, we know. The people of Rome, the venerable Senators, the soldiers under their standards, all may be able to take an oath that there has never been a more handsome Caesar.'

A smile of complete and open self-satisfaction was spread across Maximus' features. How had he become this creature?

Maximinus looked beyond his son to Iunia Fadilla. As usual, she sat very still, her face giving no indication of her thoughts. She was not veiled, and no bruises were visible. Yet the spies in their household reported that his son's brutality towards his wife if anything had increased since the return from campaign. Maximinus would have liked to intervene, but there were limits to the powers of even the Emperor. He had never raised his hand to Paulina, but in the usual run of things a wife could expect physical chastisement. When the pervert Emperor Elagabalus had taken the part of a woman in a wedding ceremony, the next day he had appeared in public with black eyes to show it really was a marriage. It was all a question of degree.

At last the rhetor had stopped talking and vacated the stage. The curtain was lowered. The set of the mime was revealed as Mount Ida, a wild and deserted district. It was the story of Tillorobus the huge brigand who had terrorized Asia.

If you were going to celebrate your birthday with a theatrical show, why not something with gravity, something where the actors wore masks, one of the great tragedies? An Emperor was expected to attend such things. Now and then, in winter quarters, Maximinus had sat through some performances. Many of their subtleties might have escaped him, sometimes central parts of the plot as well, but he had understood enough to know that the hero or heroine of a tragedy exhibited fortitude in the face of disaster, even in the face of the gods. If the play had to be a mime, did it have to be a low farce about a cunning criminal? Why not something improving like the adaptation of the *Eclogues* of Virgil that Maximinus had felt obliged to attend the previous winter? It was not how he remembered life as a shepherd, but it had given an improving lesson in rustic resilience and simple virtue. At least this *Tillorobus* was not as filthy as something like *The Adulterer Caught*.

As the players, without masks or dignity, capered on the stage, Maximinus' thoughts drifted. His old commander Septimius Severus had had the good sense not to let his sons arrange their own birthday celebrations. He had understood how such things should be organized. Nothing simpering and unmanly, instead military games: races on foot or horseback, archery, javelin throwing, sword fights with tipped blades, and wrestling. Severus had been touring the Danubian frontier, back from his second eastern campaign, when Maximinus had come into his presence. The games had been for Severus' younger son, Geta, the one who became the traitor, who tried to kill first his father then his brother. Not that anyone had suspected such horrors then. At that point the imperial *familia* embodied concord, at least to those outside the Palace.

If Maximinus narrowed his eyes, the barren Asian hillsides of the stage props blurred and took on the more verdant hues of that day in the valley of the lower Danube. It was long ago, more than three decades. Yet to Maximinus, the memory of meeting Severus for the first time was as fresh as yesterday.

The stories people told about that encounter were wrong in large part. Volo's spies brought reports, Apsines the secretary recounted conversations he had overheard. As Emperor, Maximinus barely recognized the tales told about him. It was like the blurred reflection of himself as a boy in the one tarnished mirror possessed by his home village. He had not been a goatherd straight from the hills. Severus had not set him to wrestle sixteen sutlers from the camp. Maximinus was unsure if the gossip was intended to boast his audacity and strength or reflect unfavourably on his lowly origins. Some said an Emperor was what an Emperor did. Maximinus thought it was more the case that an Emperor was whatever his subjects believed.

He had been a trooper in the auxiliary cavalry.

The Emperor had noticed his great size. Severus had wondered if his stamina matched his physique. Maximinus had run at the Emperor's stirrup until Severus himself had tired of riding. Matched against seven soldiers, Maximinus had laid them in the dirt, one after another. As well as the normal prizes of silver arm rings and belt ornaments, Severus had appointed him to his bodyguard, and handed him the golden collar Maximinus wore around his throat to this day.

An actor had minced to the front of the stage, and gazed up at Maximus as he recited.

Like to the star of the morning when he, new-
  bathed in Ocean,
Raises his holy face and scatters the darkness
  from heaven,
So did the young man seem.

Maximinus watched his son almost squirm with pleasure. When an embassy from Sirmium had greeted them on their return from campaign, Maximinus had stood, showing due respect for their age and dignity. Maximus had remained seated. The *frumentarii* reported that at audiences when his father was not present, Maximus stretched out his hand, and suffered his knees to be kissed, sometimes even his feet.

How had he become such a weak and vain and vicious young man? Maximus had been wilful and petulant as a child, but open and affectionate.

163

Too easy and luxurious an upbringing, that was the cause. The expensive tutors that Paulina had insisted they hire had pampered and spoilt the boy. A relative of his mother had given him the works of Homer, all written in letters of gold on purple vellum. All too often Paulina had intervened when Maximinus had tried to instill some discipline. Maximinus should have beaten him more, beaten the insolence and self-regard out of him before it became ingrained, before he became a man.

The play was coming to an end. For all his tricks and disguises and evasions, Tillorobus had been captured. The big actor playing him stood weighted down with chains.

'Emperor, may I have a word?'

Maximinus inclined his head. Flavius Vopiscus seemed to be getting no more enjoyment from the mime than his Emperor.

'May I urge again that you grant Catius Clemens military command over all the eastern provinces?'

Maximinus pondered his answer. It was never his habit to answer questions of state lightly. 'I do not consider it necessary. As governor of Cappadocia, he has two legions as well as auxiliary infantry and cavalry. Catius Clemens is well placed to watch over the loyalty of the other governors. We receive regular reports from Mesopotamia. Volo assured me the man he has suborned in the household of Priscus is reliable, and will inform us of any attempts at sedition.'

Vopiscus fingered the amulet he wore concealed in his breast. 'Revolt is not our only concern in the East.'

Maximinus scowled. Even a man as experienced as Vopiscus failed to see things in their true light. He placed a massive hand on the thigh of the Senator, a gesture intended to reassure. 'You forget, I served in the East. The Persians are no more of a threat than the Parthians were before them. Had Alexander not been such a weakling, the Persians would have been conquered. The true danger to Rome lies not with painted, effeminate orientals, but here in the North. If we do not crush the hordes of the northern barbarians, they will destroy everything we love.'

Vopiscus was not ready to let the subject drop. 'The Persians claim all our territories as far as Greece and the Aegean. Our eastern armies have been drained by detachments for the northern wars.'

Maximinus mastered his irritation. Apsines often advised him that a good ruler did not speak or act in exasperation. 'The true danger to Rome lies here in the North.'

There was a stir in the theatre. Many of the audience were regarding Maximinus, sly, knowing looks on their faces. An actor was holding forth.

And he who can not be slain by one, is slain
  by many.
The elephant is huge, and he is slain;

The lion is brave, and he is slain;
The tiger is brave, and he is slain;
Beware of many together, if you fear not
 one alone.

Maximinus tightened his grip on Vopiscus' leg. 'What is the meaning of this?'

'Nothing, nothing at all.' The surprise and alarm in the Senator's voice belied his words. 'Some old verses written against violent men.'

Maximinus looked across at his son. The youth had shaken back his toga, the better to applaud. There was an arch expression on his girlish face. Unlike Vopiscus, the lines had not taken him unaware. Did he have it in mind to play Geta? Surely Maximus did not have it in him to bid for the throne over the body of his father?

CHAPTER 18

AFRICA
CARTHAGE

The Day before the Ides of March, AD*238*

'A scholar gets up one night and jumps into bed with his own grandmother. His father finds him at it, and starts giving him a beating. "Hey," shouts the scholar. "All this time you have been screwing my mother without a word from me, and now you get angry when you catch me just *once* on top of yours?"'

The buffoon bowed as the dinner guests laughed. Gordian joined in, gingerly. He had had worse hangovers, but seldom. Yesterday afternoon at the gladiatorial games, he and Sabinianus and Vocula, the new Praetorian Prefect, were already drinking when the messenger arrived in the imperial box. When the news was announced, the crowd had cheered wildly, and Gordian had spared all those out on the sand. After that he had called for unwatered wine. The rest of the day was a blur. Isolated incidents came back to him with absolute clarity – a *retarius* tangled in his own net, an ostrich running a complete circuit after an arrow had

167

taken off its head, being supported back to the Palace, more drinking with just Sabinianus, the girls sliding out of their clothes, Chione and Parthenope busy together on a couch, then servicing both men at once, improbable arrangements of limbs and bodies. There was no narrative to it, only disconnected moments, like scattered scraps of papyri saved from a fire. Still, any man could be forgiven a bacchanalian celebration when he had been told that Sabinus was dead, and all the troops in Rome had declared him Emperor. He hoped he had rewarded the messenger. The man had braved the terrible storm to reach Carthage.

'A scholar's father orders him to put out the child he is having by a slave girl to die of exposure. The scholar says, "Bury your own child, before you tell me to get rid of mine."'

Gordian was sweating. This morning the household had been purified with fire and water, ready for this ninth-day feast. On the way out to the villa of Sextus, they had poured libations at the grave of Serenus. Neither the rituals nor the walk had done much good. He felt hollow, light-headed, his thoughts incoherent.

'The son of a rich scholar dies. Seeing so many people turn up at the funeral, the father laments that he has only one *small* boy to bury in front of such a *large* crowd.'

Gordian did not have a son. He had never married. Epicurus had said a man should take a wife, and sire children, only if the circumstances

168

were right. They never had been. Epicurus had accepted some men would always be diverted. Gordian had provided for all the offspring he had got on servant girls and concubines. Girls as well as boys, none had been exposed. The villa of the Gordiani on the Via Praenestina outside Rome was thronged with slaves with his features.

He had always been compassionate to a fault. As a child, when other boys were beaten by their pedagogue, he had been unable to restrain his tears. Only today he had rejected a petition from the Carthaginians to restore the rites of the *Mamuralia* to their original form. If the gods existed, and noticed mankind at all, he could not imagine what pleasure they would derive from the spectacle of an elderly derelict or criminal dressed in skins being beaten savagely through the whole city. Let the superstitious citizenry thrash the empty hide of an animal.

'A scholar heard that only the judgements in Hades are just. Since his hearing was in court, he hanged himself.'

The buffoon was more suited to a barbershop. He was losing his audience. Gordian looked around at his fellow diners: his father and Sabinianus, the locals appointed to high command, Mauricius, Phillyrio and Vocula, the commanders of the two regular units, Suillius and Alfenus, and Thascius Cyprianus. The latter had been invited out of politeness, as he had conducted the sacrifice at Serenus' funeral. None appeared over impressed by the entertainment.

Sabinianus lobbed a snail at the buffoon as he left. The jokes had been old, but at least they had diverted Thascius and his father from an earnest Stoic discussion of the moral dangers of the theatre. The former had been expounding how people learn to commit adultery, incest and murder by watching it, and other nonsense.

The food had been good so far. Snails cooked in a wine and parsley sauce, eggs stuffed with minced crayfish, a salad of rocket, chervil and lettuce. Often in this state he was ravenously hungry. After his exertions last night, Gordian had concentrated on the snails and picked the lettuce out of the salad. That and quite a few of the hairs of the dog that had bitten him. He required all the help he could get, if he was to perform again later. Parthenope and Chione would expect no less. The next course was to be a wrasse. No fish was keener on copulation. More arse-chasing than a wrasse, as the saying went.

The hangings were pulled back. Instead of a pomp of servants bearing salvers of rainbow fish, an officer entered. It was Pedius, looking tired and travel-stained from hard riding. He was one of the two tribunes who had gone to Lambaesis with Arrian. All the gods, let Arrian be safe, let his friend be alive.

Pedius leant over, and spoke quietly in the ear of the elder Emperor. Everyone waited.

His face impassive, Gordian's father stood, poured a libation. The red wine splashed on the marble floor.

170

'Capelianus is under house arrest. The 3rd Augustan Legion is ours, and with it the Province of Numidia.'

They were all on their feet, clasping hands, slapping each other on the back, tipping wine for the gods. Sabinianus dropped his goblet, staining his toga.

'Father,' Gordian shouted above the noise, 'so much for the soothsayers and their so-called prodigy. Now nothing can stop us reaching Rome.'

The commotion died away. In the embarrassed silence, some of the guests averted the ill-omened words, thumb between fingers.

'Even a follower of Epicurus should not mock the gods.' His father's face was grave. 'And there are the words of the astrologer. The stars predict we will not see Rome again, but meet our deaths by drowning.'

CHAPTER 19

THE WEST
THE PROVINCE OF HISPANIA
TARRACONENSIS, THE SOUTHERN
SLOPES OF THE PYRENEES

The Day before the Ides of March, AD238

In the morning there was fog. A perfect stillness to the shrouded trees. Close up, a drop of water hung on every leaf and branch. Somewhere, out of sight, a songbird sang.

Decius lay on his stomach behind a pine tree, raised on his elbows. The brigands would come soon. He had seen their campfires down the trail last night before the fog descended. They would take their plunder through this pass up to the mountains.

He had nothing but contempt for the mountain tribes. Two centuries since submitting to Rome, they could still barely talk Latin. No better than barbarians, they were the antithesis of *Romanitas*. Armed, violent and unbiddable, they thought their inaccessibility and their wanderings put them beyond the law. They only came down from the heights to drive their sheep to winter pasture or to raid. Shepherds or brigands, they were one and the same.

Even now the kinsmen of these robbers were grazing their flocks in the meadows of the Iberus and the Sicoris, down around Ilerda and Caesaraugusta. Without these spies, traitors to the *imperium* posing as innocent drovers, the raiders would not know where to strike. But there was no honour among thieves. A shepherd had been arrested for murder. Brought before Decius in the governor's court, the man had not denied the killing, but had sought to save his life by betraying his own. Decius looked at him now, trussed up close at hand. His fate was still uncertain. Promises made to his sort were not binding. Decius might execute him yet.

There had been no time to spare. Decius had only had the 1st Cohort Gallica Equitata with him in Caesaraugusta. Of its mounted contingent, sixty were with the standards. It had been two days' hard ride to this desolate place, by Urbs Victrix and Labitulosa, then turning off the road and scrambling along goat tracks, through the timber from one upland valley to another. They had left the horses in a wooded hollow off to the west, made a corral by tying ropes around the trees. No sooner were they in position the previous evening than the scouts had returned warning of the approach of the bandits.

The fog was lifting from the upper slopes. As it receded, depth returned to the view, and with it the first hints of colour. Decius shifted uncomfortably. He was cold, stiff, and his stomach hurt. Now he could make out the other thirty spread across the incline. Like him, they lay in cover, swaddled in dull blankets, their helmets wrapped in rags. The rest of the soldiers on the far side of the path were still invisible, but he knew they were there.

They had taken their rations before dawn; no fires; hard tack and cold bacon, the wine from their canteens sour on their guts. He had ordered them relieve themselves at a distance. The scent of unwashed men might give them away, without the reek of shit. He had stumbled through the darkness, checking every man was in the place assigned the night before.

Some men, the brave as well as cowards, always found the waiting hard. Decius, tight with expectation, was not one of them. This was what it meant to be a Roman governor. Not lolling on silken cushions, composing artful poetry, or listening to elaborate oratory in marble halls, but lying rough, weapons in hand, ready to fight. This was his inheritance. He was from the northern lands up towards the Danube, where antique Roman *virtus* still lived. Generations had passed since his ancestors had migrated from Italy. Every one of them had faced the barbarians. The North bred hard men. None more so than the Emperor Maximinus. There was a man who knew how to fight, knew what it was to be a true Roman.

The sun was a pale white disk. He could make out the opposite slope, tendrils of mist drifting through the trees, but below the pass was still partly obscured. The first noises came to him, disembodied through the fog. A clink of metal, the clop of a hoof, guttural voices; the brigands were coming.

Decius touched a fallen pinecone, the rough bark of the tree. Not long now.

They came up through the haze. Dozens of them, huddled in hooded cloaks against the clammy chill of the morning. They drove mules and packhorses, bulky with sacks. Confident in their territory, they kept no order, had no scouts out.

Decius waited. Let the vanguard pass. Strike the centre of the column, like cutting a snake in half. Come down on them out of the mist, like Hannibal at Lake Trasimene.

Through the dark trunks of the trees, he watched the first of them trudge below him, move off to his right up the track.

Not yet.

More came out of the gloom. Still more. They were strung out. No end to them in sight. At least fifty so far. Some clustered around a big man wearing a helmet with a gaudy scarlet crest. The prisoner had spoken of a bandit leader; Corocotta, the beast of the mountains. The chief and his intimates passed a wineskin from hand to hand.

Health and great joy, to you, Decius thought.

There were four captives with Corocotta, young

women, stumbling in tattered clothes. They would have had a bad time of it over the last nights.

Decius clambered to his feet, shrugged off his blanket. Around him, without orders, the soldiers did the same, like antediluvian beasts emerging from the hillside. Decius nodded to the trumpeter. The soldier took a couple of deep breaths, put the instrument to his lips, and blew one loud, clear note.

A babble of voices from down on the track.

The trumpet call was repeated from the far slope.

The tribesmen had stopped. They pushed back their cloaks, fumbled for weapons, heads turning desperately this way and that. The pack animals skittered and milled, boring into each other, barging the men.

'Throw!'

The soldiers took two or three steps, delicate, almost mincing down the slope. Their right arms snapped forward, and thirty javelins whistled away. A couple of heartbeats later, their steel tips rained down onto the pass. Some thumped into leaf mould, clattered off stones, but several punched deep into flesh. Men and animals screamed.

Decius picked up his shield, hefted it, and drew his sword.

Another flight shot down from the far slope. The brigands wheeled, trying to shield themselves from every direction. A mule bolted back down the path, bowling men out of its way.

'Charge!'

The trumpeter blew again, the sound booming through the trees.

The troopers were off, bounding down the hill like hunting dogs. Decius took it slower. Most were younger than him, and he wanted to get to the bottom on his feet. Looking across, he saw the rest of his men surging down.

The moment's inattention almost cost him. His boot stubbed on a root. No chance of stopping, regaining his balance. Momentum gathering, he ran faster and faster to keep from falling.

On the path, a brigand stood in his way. Shield first, Decius ran into him at full speed. The tribesman crashed backwards to the ground. Another slashed at Decius from the right. A wild, untutored blow, Decius stepped back from its arc. Meeting no resistance, the bandit staggered forward to impale himself on Decius' sword.

The downed man was getting up, another coming up behind him.

Decius retrieved his blade, using his left knee to push the dying brigand away.

His two opponents fanned out, looking to come at him from either side.

Shaping as if to go for the man on his left, Decius sidestepped, and lunged at the other. The bandit blocked. Decius pressed his attack. Two, three round cuts towards the head. The clangour of steel. The rasp of his own breath. Driving him back, allowing him no chance to counter. All the time, listening for the other, trying to glimpse him out of the corner of his eye. Half waiting for the searing pain that would tell him his vigilance had failed.

A quick footfall, and a flash of movement. Decius whirled, dropped to his right knee, and swung, all in one fluid motion. The edge of the heavy sword sheered the left leg of the brigand down near the ankle. Amazingly he did not fall, but hopped, then stood, teetering, looking stupidly at the severed extremity and the exsanguinating stump.

Still on his knee, Decius twisted, hauled his sword around and up behind him. The tribesman chopped down with both hands, like a woodsman splitting logs. The impact forced Decius' blade almost back into his face, thrusting pain through his contorted shoulders.

Taking a few short steps backwards, the brigand raised his sword to strike again.

Decius scrabbled to his feet, got his shield and sword up.

The man who had lost a foot was still standing, stunned, as if unable to comprehend the enormity of his wound.

The sound of boots on the track, boots with hobnails. Soldiers converging.

The uninjured barbarian let his sword drop, got to his knees, raised his open hands in supplication. A soldier ran him through. Another cut down the one standing on one leg.

Decius glanced all around. There was no immediate threat. Pushing the point of his long *Spatha* into the ground, he bent over, leaning on the pommel.

His heart was thumping, his breath ragged. Mastering himself, he straightened, took in the situation.

Men slumped in the dirt, Romans and brigands intermingled. A pack animal standing, seemingly oblivious to the javelin protruding from its flank. Blood pooling and running down the track, as if after an imperial hecatomb. Bandits throwing away their weapons, trying to surrender. A Decurion yelling at the troopers not to kill them all. The sounds of combat from up the path. A knot of the enemy blocking the pass, the leader with the bright plume in their midst. The nearest soldiers falling back from them. Decius had to take charge. Success was almost within his grasp.

'Secure the prisoners,' he shouted at the Decurion. 'You,' he gestured at five or six troopers around him, 'with me.'

Decius walked up the path. No point in arriving yet more out of breath.

'Form line.'

Half a dozen paces away, the hill-men waited.

'Spread out. Give yourselves room to use your swords.'

The troopers shuffled across.

Decius took his place in the front.

'Are you ready for war!'

'Ready!'

The soldiers knew their trade. Three times the call and response, and they set off, Decius in the centre.

The bandit chief was taller than Decius, out-reached him. His first blow splintered the Roman's shield down to the grip. Decius threw it in his face. The brigand swatted it aside, and thrust again. This Corocotta was fast and strong. Doggedly Decius blocked. He sensed the troopers on either side giving ground. Cautiously, not leaving an opening, he followed.

Once more a space appeared between the combatants. Beyond, bandits were scampering up the track. They were driving the women and a few animals. A brigand was bellowing over his leader's shoulder, urgent and incomprehensible. Corocotta stepped back. The follower took his place. Corocotta turned, and began to move away.

'Do not let him escape,' Decius shouted. 'Once more, *pueri*. Ready? Come on, boys!'

The bandit opposite was untrained, but persistent. Decius hacked his rustic shield to pieces, wounded him three or four times. Still the hill-man fought. Decius could see the red crest vanishing up the path. He launched a volley of blows. His opponent was tiring, slowing. Decius aimed a thrust to the face, dragged his opponent's guard up, then pulled the blow, and drove his sword deep into the chest.

When Decius went to push his man away, the barbarian tried to bite his fingers. A shove, and three sharp chops to the head ended his defiance.

The bandits were down or running. Their leader was gone.

'Prisoners secured.' The Decurion was at Decius'

elbow. The rags around his helmet gave him the air of a martial vagrant.

Decius had no leisure from command. 'Put pickets out, up and down the track, up both slopes. Send twenty men to bring the horses.'

The Decurion barked out the necessary orders.

Decius walked to the side of the path, leant a hand against the black-veined trunk of a pine. The sun had burnt off the mist. Through gaps in the timber, he could see the distant peaks. He went to clean and sheath his sword. The front of his mail-shirt was clotted with blood, his forearms incarnadine. The bitter taste of disappointment in his mouth, like an old bronze coin.

'The reckoning?' he asked.

'Three dead. Seven wounded, two will not live,' the Decurion said.

'How many captured?'

'About twenty.'

Decius considered. 'Separate their wounded. We do not have time to crucify them. The ones who got away might raise the hills against us. Cut their heads off, and nail them to trees. Rope the others together. The stronger will go into the arena. The weaker can hang on a cross at the scene of their outrages.'

The Decurion went to make it so. Decius remained; for the moment there was nothing to do but nurse his frustration.

A trooper approached with a strange soldier. The latter was drawn and filthy from hard travel.

The messenger saluted, and handed over his despatch.

There was something wrong with the imperial seal. Decius broke the purple wax, opened the diptych, and read.

'How long since you left Africa?'

The messenger thought. 'Fifteen, no fourteen days. I landed at Tarraco. They told me you were holding assizes at Caesaraugusta. I got a guide to bring me here.'

'Have you told anyone this news?'

'My orders were to announce it in every community through which I passed.'

'Trooper, arrest this man.'

'Governor, I am just a messenger.'

'Yes, I am sorry for it, but you must be questioned. First by me, then you will be sent to the Emperor.'

'Governor,' he swallowed, struggling for words, 'I am only a soldier.'

'And as such, you know how things stand in Carthage.'

'I sailed from Hadrumetum.'

'How things are in Africa in general.' Little would be gained, but it had to be done. 'Tell all you know, and you will not be mistreated. Trooper, take him away.'

Decius rested his back against the rough bark, closed his eyes. What madness had possessed the Gordiani? No revolt in Africa had ever been successful. Fourteen days, the news would have reached Rome. Surely Vitalianus and Sabinus would have remained loyal. Decius felt a hollow fear in his chest. Etruscus, his eldest son, was in the imperial school on the Palatine, a hostage in all but name. Potens, his brother-in-law, commanded the Watch. Let nothing have happened to them. Etruscus was only twelve.

CHAPTER 20

ROME
THE CARINAE

The Day before the Ides of March, AD238

Timesitheus did not care to be kept waiting. The *Praefectus Annonae*, the man responsible for feeding the million inhabitants of Rome, should not be kept waiting. Especially not by an ex-slave. The accent and manner of this freedman Reverendus proclaimed his origins in some effeminate eastern province like Syria or Cappadocia. His flabby face hinted at good looks in his youth. Probably buggered senseless as a boy. It was the nature of his sort to become insufferably insolent if they served a noble family. Still, one should only make enemies if it was necessary. The situation needed delicate handling. Timesitheus did not want to alienate a member of the *familia* of the Gordiani, but over familiarity with the odious creature, let alone a rebuff, would damage his *dignitas*.

'At last the rain has stopped, and spring has arrived,' Timesitheus said.

'The weather is better,' Reverendus said.

The tone of the freedman exhibited no desire for further conversation. Timesitheus arranged his face, and turned to studying the many beaks of warships that were set in the lofty walls of the vestibule of the *Domus Rostrata* and gave the house its name. Tranquillina gave no sign of noticing the abrupt exchange. She waited with complete composure, as if bestowing a gracious favour. His wife always knew exactly how to behave. Unlike her husband, she had grown up in the great houses of the eternal city.

Timesitheus looked closely at the bronze rams. Pompey the Great had decorated the house with spoils from his campaign against the pirates. Yet these ornamental prows did not look as if they had ever seen the sea. It was always important to look closely. Few things in Rome were ever quite what they seemed.

The superstitious considered this an unlucky house. Its owners seldom came to a good end. Pompey beheaded on a beach in Egypt. Defeated and abandoned, Mark Antony falling on his sword in the same country. The aged tyrant Tiberius, worn out with perversity on Capri, smothered with a pillow. Timesitheus was not superstitious. He coveted this property. A house like this would complete his rise from relatively humble beginnings on the backwater Greek island of Corcyra. His father had just scraped together the capital necessary to qualify as an equestrian in the Census. He had owned two small trading vessels, a modest

185

house in Kassiope, and an estate of some olive groves and many barren slopes on Mount Istone. Possession of a palatial dwelling in the Carinae of Rome would seal the ascent of his son. Timesitheus would be content. Of course, he knew, Tranquillina would not. Her relentless ambition was one of the several things he loved about his wife; loved and almost feared.

Timesitheus stifled a yawn. They had got up before dawn to attend, and Tranquillina had made strenuous demands in the night. That was another thing he loved about her.

'Wake up.' Tranquillina spoke softly, so that the freedman could not overhear. Her breath was hot in Timesitheus' ear. 'Stop daydreaming. Remember why we have come. As the Gordiani are not here, we must ingratiate ourselves with their relatives and those, unlike you, who have already managed to get close to this new regime. I have no intention of remaining the wife of just another equestrian administrator.'

'Please come this way.' Another freedman had appeared. This one was called Montanus, and he had the same infuriating air of superiority.

Waiting just long enough to assert their independence, Timesitheus and Tranquillina followed Montanus into the house.

Maecia Faustina was receiving visitors sitting in the shade on one side of the broad, airy atrium. Her *salutatio* was well attended, as was only to be expected. Many wanted to be admitted and

186

recognized by a woman who was the daughter of one of the reigning Emperors and sister of the other. Few were deterred by her reputation as a cold, censorious bitch. It was said she had got worse since Maximinus had executed her husband Junius Balbus, the ineffectual governor of Syria Coele, the previous year.

The crowd eddied forward. Romans of the elite did not queue. They were brought up to dally politely. Timesitheus and Tranquillina paused by a massive, half-finished sarcophagus standing in the middle of the atrium. Tranquillina smoothed the folds of her husband's toga. Screened by the sarcophagus, she slyly ran a hand over his crotch, squeezed his prick. She grinned up at him.

By some unspoken agreement, their turn arrived to greet the mistress of the *Domus Rostrata*.

'Health and great joy, *Domina*,' Timesitheus said.

Yet another oily manumitted slave whispered to Maecia Faustina. She gave no sign of noticing her freedman Gaudianus. Necessary though it might be, to acknowledge that she needed to be reminded of her visitors' names would be a breach of etiquette.

'Health and great joy. It is a pleasure to welcome Gaius Furius Sabinius Timesitheus Aquila and his wife to our house.' Her tone belied her words.

'We are all praying for the speedy and safe arrival of our noble Emperors,' Timesitheus said.

Maecia Faustina inclined her head. 'They are safe in the hands of the gods.'

'May I say, the city is full of your praise. The imperial dignity becomes you.'

Neither the graceful words, nor Timesitheus' most winning smile, softened her forbidding demeanour.

'Duty not ambition called my father and brother to the throne. We must all do our duty, but such prominence comes at a price. I desired nothing but the solitude of a widow, to mourn my husband, and raise my son to live a virtuous life. The finest praise a woman can have is not to be talked about.'

Tranquillina spoke in the low voice of a modest young matron. 'The sarcophagus will be a fitting memorial to your husband. What will the sculptures represent?'

Maecia Faustina gazed over the heads of the throng at the great part-worked block of marble. 'Balbus' procession as Consul. A reminder of him in happier days.'

'Who are the other men?'

'His closest friends in the Senate. Men of the highest rank and *virtus*, many of them also victims of the tyrant.'

'Will your son be depicted?'

'No, it is enough for him to have to have examples of such ancestral virtue before his eyes as he grows out of childhood. The man at Balbus' right hand is Serenianus, the governor of Cappadocia, his *amicus* murdered by the Thracian.'

Maecia Faustina was more animated, her voice

softer. Superfluous to the conversation, Timesitheus glided away.

The colonnade around the open space was decorated with a famous painting of a wild-beast hunt. Long ago, Gordian the Elder had commissioned the panels to commemorate the games he had given when he held the office of Aedile. Timesitheus stood in an attitude of appreciation. Under his gaze, innumerable stags with antlers shaped like the palm of a hand met their end. His thoughts wandered as he counted them; twenty, fifty, a hundred.

Women were harder to fathom than men. He had never been as good at reading them, at winning their trust. Yet the gods knew, he should have been. His stepmother had provided him with an early training. His mother had been dead a year when she had come into the house. He was thirteen. She had not been an evil stepmother of myth. She had not tried to seduce him, murder him, or trick his father into cursing him with a false accusation of attempted rape. No bull from the sea had smashed him to death as he rode in his chariot. Not that his father's patrimony had extended to chariots. No, their relationship had been a low-intensity conflict; a war of small ambushes and raids, of petty deceptions and diplomatic truces soon betrayed. He had not liked the half-brother she produced, but he had not hated him. Of course she would never believe that it had been an accident. The boy had always been boastful and proud.

189

It was such pride that had undone him. Timesitheus had been home on leave between military commands, and the boy had challenged him to a swimming race. The currents in the straits off Kassiope were notorious. Timesitheus could not have saved him. He had nearly drowned himself.

One hundred and fifty stags, two hundred. Perhaps it was the life they led that made women so hard to understand, so much more difficult to manipulate. Unable to hold office, or make a mark in the world, never tasting success. Confined in the house; if they went out at all, it was under the watchful eyes of a *custos* and a maid. Their desires and ambitions so unimaginably narrow and point-less. Unless, of course, they were Tranquillina.

His wife was still talking to Maecia Faustina. Pity the child brought up in the joyless care of that dried-up old widow, with stern moral lessons and mementoes of death wherever he looked.

Timesitheus scanned the crowded atrium. He had hoped to find Menophilus, Valerian or Pupienus: the men at the heart of the emerging administration of the Gordiani. But they were not relatives, and there was no call for them to attend the *salutatio*. They would be busy making plans, in meetings from which Timesitheus was still excluded. In the far corner, Maecius Gordianus, second-cousin of the hostess, was holding court. Timesitheus went over, and greeted the Prefect of the Watch.

'My congratulations, the city is safe, now your

vigiles are back on the streets, and Pupienus has sent the Urban Cohorts into the Subura to arrest the worst troublemakers.'

Maecius Gordianus laughed. 'Without your help, how would he have known where to find them. It is a lesson. Around you we must all watch what escapes the prison of our teeth.'

The various clients sniggered.

Timesitheus again arranged his face. 'If one's thoughts are virtuous, there is no fear our unguarded words are dangerous.'

Tranquillina came up and spoke to the Prefect of the Watch. 'We saw Brundisinus the other day. When your brother takes the toga of manhood, women will besiege him. He has your family's looks.'

She was standing just a little too close to Maecius Gordianus, smiling up at him with her very dark eyes. The Prefect beamed down at her. Timesitheus stowed his jealousy deep in the hold of his mind. Tranquillina was not wanton, not with other men, she did nothing without calculation. They needed the friendship of this kinsman of the Emperors. Timesitheus himself had failed to win it. She would not go too far. Timesitheus moved away.

All governments were oligarchies behind the façade. A Greek *Polis* like Corcyra claimed to be a democracy. Yet power resided with a few dozen rich landowners, who monopolized all the magistracies and kept the poor out of both Council and Assembly with property qualifications. Rome was a monarchy only lacking the name in Latin. But an autocrat can not rule alone. Unless it was in front of him, he only knew what he was told. His friends decided what he heard, what was put under his nose. The question was how to penetrate that inner circle.

Timesitheus had proved himself of use to the new regime. To quell the unrest of the *plebs urbana*, he had released a huge amount of grain from the public warehouses. Much of that surplus had been marked for his own profit. Using contacts such as the young cut-purse Castricius, he had summoned up a mob so that Menophilus could drive out and liquidate Sabinus. Promptly handing over the names and domiciles of those same men had made it easy for Pupienus to arrest them, and at a stroke ended all rioting in the streets.

He had applied himself in the interest of the Gordiani, advancing various plans that could win the civil war, perhaps end it before the fighting began. His friend Axius Aelianus, the Procurator of Dacia, might be induced to overthrow the governor of that province, and thus take control of an army that could threaten Maximinus from the rear. He had suggested that the new regime might bring pressure on those officers serving in the North by seizing their relatives in Rome, especially the children being taught at the imperial school on the Palatine. Similarly both the Praetorians and the men of the 2nd Parthian Legion had left families at their Italian bases, respectively in Rome and in the Alban Hills. Even soldiers were not so heartless as to ignore the safety of their loved ones.

More direct actions might spare Italy the horrors of internecine strife. As Prefect of the Heavy Cavalry with the field army, Timesitheus' own cousin Sabinus Modestus was well placed to strike down the tyrant. Privately, Timesitheus doubted this scheme would succeed, but it was more than worth the risk to his dim-witted relative. More inventive was the plan involving his friend Catius Celer. The Senator was regarded with suspicion in Rome because his brother Clemens had been instrumental in putting Maximinus on the throne. What would be more natural in the eyes of the tyrant than Celer fleeing to the North. In his train, as a stable boy or the like, would go Castricius. The knife-boy would have no choice but to try and kill Maximinus. Now, as a prisoner, his future held only the cross or the mines. Should Castricius succeed, and, by some miracle, survive the aftermath, he would be richly rewarded.

Menophilus and Pupienus had looked askance at all the suggestions. They had said such things ran against the ways of their ancestors. The *mos maiorum* could countenance nothing so underhand. Menophilus had dredged up ancient history. The Senate had rejected offers to assassinate enemies such as Pyrrhus and Arminius. Which was rich, coming from a man who, recently having stabbed one opponent with a sword, had beaten the next to death with the leg of a chair.

Timesitheus had not spared himself on their behalf. They had rejected his proposals, and he had received nothing for what he had accomplished. He had not added the Prefecture of the Praetorians, or even the Watch, to that of the Grain Supply. He had not been admitted to the small inner circle of the unofficial oligarchy. Half-promises of the command of the fleet at Ravenna or Misenum, vague hints about the Prefecture of Egypt, some time in the future, were not enough.

What galled Timesitheus most was that he seemed to have no choice but to persevere. Maximinus had sentenced him to death. Changing sides was not an option. Thracians were strangers to mercy or forgiveness. Maximinus was most unlikely to remit the death penalty, let alone invest him with high command, embrace him with friendship, should he suddenly ride into his camp. And, worst of all, Timesitheus thought it most likely that Maximinus would prevail.

With the thought came fear. Timesitheus heard the scrabble of its claws, felt its moist breath at his throat. He walked away from his wife. He needed to be on his own, somewhere he could face down the rodent, stare back into its flat, black eyes.

The rear colonnade was deserted. Timesitheus leant his back against a column. There had to be a way out. A bold stroke to cut the apt image of the Gordian knot. Perhaps Egypt could provide the answer. Annianus the Prefect there had been appointed by Maximinus. Rome needed Egyptian grain. Without it, the plebs would riot. Annianus could make the city ungovernable. Persuade Menophilus of that danger. Timesitheus must go there now to replace Annianus. Who better than the *Praefectus Annonae* to secure the supply? Once there he would have soldiers, not just auxiliaries, but also the 2nd Legion Traiana Fortis. There were another two legions in Mesopotamia with his friend Priscus. Two more in Syria Palestina under Priscus' brother-in-law, weak old Severinus. Priscus had flirted with revolt before. No matter who won in the West, Maximinus or the Gordiani, the army of the East could challenge them. Invest a pliable Senator with the purple. Severinus might serve. Tranquillina would approve. She would become not just the wife of a friend of Caesar, but of the man who had put him on the throne.

A small movement behind him in the *lararium* made him whirl around. It was just a boy, no older than nine or ten. He looked frightened. Toy soldiers were spread across the floor of the household shrine.

Timesitheus smiled, and walked over slowly, as he did approaching a nervous horse.

'I was not doing anything wrong,' the boy said.

'No.' Timesitheus squatted down by the toys. 'May I pick them up?'

The boy nodded. 'My mother told me not to be

seen playing. She said people would think me a baby.' He was older than he first appeared, perhaps eleven or twelve, and had a slight lisp.

Timesitheus peered at a wooden soldier. 'The 10th Legion?'

'No, the 2nd Augusta. The thunderbolts on the shield are very similar.'

'They are well-painted. Better than I managed when I was your age. Did you paint them yourself?'

'No, my mother says it is not suitable for a boy of a noble family. My uncle Gordian gave them to me.'

'Perhaps when he returns to Rome, he will give you some more.'

'I think he will be too busy, now he is Emperor.' The boy said the last with pride.

'Would you like me to bring you some?'

'I can not accept gifts from strangers.'

'I will ask your mother. My name is Timesitheus.'

'I am Marcus Junius Balbus.'

Timesitheus grinned. 'I know.'

The boy looked past Timesitheus, and shrank back.

'Junius Balbus, you are late for your instruction in ethics. Your mother paid a great deal of money for the philosopher. He is waiting.' The voice of the freedman became peevish. 'Your mother told you not to play with those childish things in public. Next year, you will take the *toga virilis*.'

Timesitheus stood, and faced Montanus. 'It is my fault. I asked the boy to show me the soldiers.'

'Nevertheless, he has disobeyed an instruction. He must be punished.'

'It was my doing,' Timesitheus said. 'He should not be punished.'

The freedman bridled. 'You presume to dictate how the house of the Gordiani conducts itself?'

Timesitheus stepped up to Montanus. The freedman went to move back. Timesitheus took him by both shoulders, put his face very close, spoke quietly. 'You know who I am. You know what happened to Magnus, what happened to Valerius Apollinaris. Crushing something like you, an ex-slave who has forgotten his place, an ex-slave with scars on his back and his arse still gaping, is nothing more to me than stepping on a snail. The boy's mother need not be informed. If I hear that he has been punished, I will come for you. Believe me, I do not make idle threats.'

Montanus staggered a little, when released.

Timesitheus arranged his face into an open smile, turned back to the boy. 'Farewell, Marcus. I hope to see you again.'

'Farewell, Misitheus.' The boy blushed. 'I am sorry, some names are hard to pronounce.'

'No need to apologize. Misitheus sounds a better man than Timesitheus.'

CHAPTER 21

AFRICA
THE TOWN OF LAMBAESIS,
NUMIDIA

The Day before the Ides of March, AD238

I t was late. The early watches of the long night had come and gone, *kindle-light* and *first-sleep*. Now it was *intempesta*, the untimely hour, deep night, the time when it was unlucky to do anything. The streets should be empty.

Capelianus stretched and yawned. The initial tension of waiting had died out of him. Now he was tired. He could not afford to be drowsy. The bunch of herbs tied to the foot of the bed to deter scorpions caught his eye. That was Africa for you: scorpions and snakes, blistering heat in the summer, cold rain and clinging mud in the winter, the endless tedium of empty duties, then this bitter draught of betrayal.

Aching with weariness, he got up, and took a small wooden box from his medicine chest. He put a pinch of the powder on the back of his hand. Blocking first one nostril then the other, he snorted the compound of natron and chalcanthite. Iulius

198

Africanus, the imperial librarian, had said it held fatigue at bay. Impotence, baldness, blindness, nocturnal emissions – Africanus had a cure for every ailment.

Capelianus sat down on the bed again. Not long now. By cock-crow it would be decided, one way or the other. A few hours, a brief moment in time. The past lacked a beginning, the future lacked an end, and the present was between them, so thin and ungraspable, no more than a meeting point of what has been and what will be.

Arrian was a fool, a weak, trusting fool, like his masters the Gordiani, the pretend Emperors acclaimed by a mob of untrustworthy Africans. Arrian had said the Gordiani were merciful. In a short while, Capelianus would be allowed to retire to his estates around Cirta. For now, he was under house arrest, placed in the charge of Ballatius, the Prefect of the Syrian archers. Arrian had no foresight, had not troubled himself to investigate how things really were. The lands around Cirta were mortgaged. With no other income, they would have to be sold. Capelianus would be reduced to poverty. Simple economics combined with the noble duty of revenge to make the life of a quiet landowner impossible. Ballatius had served under Capelianus for years. The first step had been easy.

A tap at the window. Capelianus got up, his heart hammering despite himself. He blew out the lamp. The darkness was complete.

The bolts on the outside were drawn, and the

shutters opened. Pale moonlight flooded the bed-room. An arm reached in, beckoning. Awkwardly, Capelianus climbed out onto the roof.

There were two of them, soldiers in undress uniform, scarves tied around their faces. Without a word, they led him up the sloping tiles. Capelianus paused for a moment, precarious astride the ridgeline. The far side was in shadow, dark and precipitous. He was too old to be clambering about on a roof in the dead hours of the night.

There was nothing else for it. Slowly, slowly he inched down the incline. Every moment he expected a tile to skitter out beneath hand or foot, feel himself begin a painful and noisy slide, and then out and down onto the hard cobbles.

At the bottom, they steadied him, pointed where the barrels had been stacked in the ally at the side of the house. They helped him scramble to the ground, dropped down after him. Still without speaking, they trotted off into the dark, leaving him alone in the night.

This way, should everything go wrong, no one else would suffer. Neither Ballatius nor the guards on the door could be proved accountable. Capelianus had escaped with the aid of persons unknown. Even under torture, he could not describe the soldiers. Ballatius would have to claim the pain had induced Capelianus to implicate him falsely.

Thoughts of the rack and the horse, the pincers and claws, threatened to unman Capelianus. He stood in the shade of the barrels, his heart again

200

pounding. They said the heart shrinks once you were past fifty, contracted until it became no bigger than that of a child.

He could not go back. It was all on one throw of the dice. Revenge was the birthright of every Roman. Capelianus forced himself to start walking.

Cutting down the alley, he came out at the front of the house. The guards on the door looked the other way. He turned right onto the *Via Principalis*. Clouds scudded across the moon. It was strange, unnerving to be out at this time, all alone, no slaves, not even a linkman. He carried no weapons.

The tall outbuilding in front of the headquarters loomed ahead, blocking the street. The guards on duty under the gloomy arches of the *Groma* studiously ignored him. He turned right again, went up the alleyway by the side of the *Principia*.

Ballatius had said that the commanders of the other auxiliary units would back him; Fabatus of the 7th Lusitanians, Securus of the 2nd Spaniards. But Capelianus knew that it was only the Legion that counted. Tonight all depended on the senior officers of the 3rd Augusta. Should they decide against him, Arrian would not be so weakly merciful a second time. Even the *clementia* of the feeble Gordiani had its limits.

Capelianus turned left through the side gate of the *Principia*, went across the rear courtyard, and through the hangings that screened the shrine of the standards.

It was bright inside, lamplight gleaming off the

great eagle, off the other standards, many bearing the portraits of the Gordiani. The latter was to be expected, but a poor omen, one on which he must not dwell.

Capelianus looked around at those waiting. He saw five of the legionary tribunes. The sixth, the one from a Senatorial family was not present. That mattered little; he was young, had scant influence. It was a relief to see the Prefect of the Camp; a soldier of more than thirty years' service, his opinion carried weight. He counted eight of the ten senior Centurions. His spirit sank when he realized that old Firmanus the *Primus Pilus* was one of those missing.

'Tell us what you have to say,' the Prefect of the Camp said.

Capelianus nodded heavily, gathering himself. Everything hinged on the next few moments, the fleeting, unstable meeting place of what had been and what would be. His grandfather, friend of Emperors, governor of great provinces, would have known what to say. Somehow the thought reassured him.

'By now you all know Arrian was lying. Maximinus has no intention of transferring the 3rd Augusta to the North. It is the Gordiani themselves who will lead the Legion out of Africa. They will make you desert your homes and families to fight and die in support of their doomed, selfish bid for power.'

The faces of the officers were inscrutable.

Capelianus pressed on. He would not die for want of trying.

'Maximinus is a soldier, risen from the ranks. Like many of you, he served under Severus, under Caracalla. When he came to the throne, he doubled your pay. He is your brother. The Gordiani are *nobiles*, born into luxury, brought up in marble halls. They are more at home at a symposium than in an army camp. To them you are nothing.'

Men who have had a hard life, had little sympathy for those who had never toiled. Resentment might bring them round, that and greed.

'The Gordiani promised you a donative of five years' pay. Have you seen a single coin? Return to your loyalty to Maximinus, and I will see you get every *sestertius*. Return to your loyalty, and I will give you Carthage to plunder. The property of traitors is forfeit, in Carthage, Hadrumetum, and Thysdrus, in every community that has broken its oath.'

The lamps hissed. The officers were silent, but Capelianus thought perhaps he nearly had them. One more step, one more inducement.

'If we act with speed, we may yet catch the Gordiani before they sail for Rome. Imagine how Maximinus will reward us if we crush this revolt singlehanded. 3rd Legion Augusta Pia Fidelis, live up to your titles. Let Piety and Fidelity be the watchwords!'

As if waiting for the end of his speech, the curtain was pulled back, and Arrian marched into the shrine. He was backed by the *Primus Pilus*, and the other two missing officers from the 3rd. A squad of legionaries in full armour blocked the entrance.

A good oration wasted, Capelianus thought. Now for the pincers and the rack. Inconsequentially, he noted the absence of either of the young tribunes who had come from Carthage with Arrian.

'Gaius Iulius Geminius Capelianus, you are arrested, for the second time.' A look almost of sadness passed over Arrian's grooved, weathered face. 'As you have spurned their clemency, you will be confined in chains, and sent to our noble Emperors, to await their judgement.'

Be a man, Capelianus thought. Do not disgrace yourself or your ancestors.

'Chain him,' Arrian said.

'The order can not be obeyed.' The *Primus Pilus* spoke clearly.

Arrian whirled around. 'What?'

'The 3rd Augusta will reaffirm its oath to Imperator Maximinus Augustus.'

'But you have taken the *sacramentum* to the Gordiani.'

'We were misled. Our oath to Maximinus came first.'

Arrian stood, tugging at his beard, as he tried to conjure up something to retrieve the situation.

'Seize him,' Capelianus said.

Accepting its impossibility, Arrian attempted no resistance.

Capelianus stepped towards him. 'It seems, after

204

all, that it is me doing the arresting. And, I am sure you will agree, tonight has shown that house arrest is a misplaced clemency. I have many questions about the plans of the Gordiani, and you have an appointment in the cellars with men who are skilled at extracting answers.'

BRAINSE CARNAN CLOCH
DOLPHINS BARN LIBRARY
TEL. 454 0681

CHAPTER 22

AFRICA
CARTHAGE

The Ides of March, AD238

Gordian had not felt up to attending court early that morning. Sabinianus and Mauricius had sat as his father's advisors. Despite still feeling jaded, at the fifth hour Gordian had walked through the Palace to the library, where he knew his father would be working on his biography of Marcus Aurelius.

The room was scented with cedar, from the wood of the bookcases and the oil rubbed into the papyrus rolls. Progress was slow. The air was warm and heavy, sunshine streamed in from the east-facing windows. Gordian was soporific. As a younger man, his father had been a prolific poet: an epic *Antoniniad* in thirty books, a translation of Aratus from the Greek, other works on various subjects, a *Marius*, *Alcyonae*, *Uxorius*, and *Nilus*. The life of Marcus was unfinished after six years. His father cited the rigour of his research, and the demands of exact prose. Gordian knew it was advancing age.

His father missed Serenus Sammonicus, that was obvious. They had grown old together. Morning after morning closeted over their books. A lifetime of quiet, studious companionship. Now Serenus had crossed the Styx before him. It was a pity neither Philostratus nor one of the other famous Sophists with whom his father was close was present in Carthage. Gordian suspected that he was a less than wholly adequate replacement. What literary talents he had possessed mainly had been squandered in his youth. Still, one or two slave secretaries aside, it gave them a chance to be alone.

'Last night, Father, I did not mean to offend you when I spoke of the prodigy.'

'You know I do not share your Epicurean views, but nothing you could say could ever offend me.' His father ran a hand over his eyes, and looked very careworn.

'Father, the gods are far away. They have no interest in us. They are perfect in their happiness. If they cared for the vices and follies of humanity, it would disturb their equanimity, mar their perfection. The soothsayers and astrologers that have troubled you are charlatans.'

'Many are frauds,' his father agreed. 'But I have never understood how a god, or any sentient being, could be happy, if it had never experienced misery. The gods are different from us only in their power and immortality.'

'Now we are Emperors,' Gordian said, 'many will worship us as gods.'

'At least for a time.'

It was clear his father wanted to say something else. Gordian unrolled a manuscript and waited.

'It may be that such warnings only come true to those who believe. Perhaps those who do not are unaffected.'

Gordian put down the papyrus and remained silent.

'Although I do not want us to be apart, you should travel ahead alone.'

Gordian leant across, took his father's hand. 'There is no reason to hurry. Now we have the 3rd Legion, Africa is secure. Let Menophilus settle Rome, and we will travel there together.'

'I did not mean to Rome,' his father said. 'You should go to the East.'

Gordian felt the hand, thin and dry in his. 'Our ancestral estates stretch across Cappadocia. You were governor in Syria, Father. The natives love you. The East will come over.'

His father took back his hand, sat up straight, spoke with an almost youthful vigour. 'Now Rome has declared for us, Maximinus must march into Italy. Unless he abandons the frontiers, and that would mean undoing all his own labours, he will have to leave the majority of the northern armies on the Rhine and Danube. When he has gone, they may declare for us, or they may remain loyal to him. In a sense, it might matter little. Whoever wins this civil war in Italy – Maximinus or us – the army in the East could overthrow the victor.

The eastern forces have been drained for Maximinus' northern wars, but, if united, they remain strong. Governors like Priscus of Mesopotamia may decide who sits on the throne.'

Gordian considered the unwelcome argument for a time.

'I would not go without you. We should not be parted.'

'No. I am too old.'

'And an astrologer predicted you would die by drowning.'

'And the stars held the same fate for my son. You could travel overland by Cyrene and Egypt.'

Gordian picked up another papyrus roll, turned it in his hands, put it down again. 'Egnatius Lollianus in Bithynia is a loyal friend. When he declares for us, Priscus and the others will follow.'

His father was not finished. 'Maximinus is wrong. What matters is not the North, but the East. When all this is over, whoever remains to wear the purple will have to face the Persians.'

'Nothing could suit me more,' Gordian said. 'To march in the footsteps of Alexander the Great. You know I am more myself on campaign than in the Senate House.'

His father looked if anything yet more concerned. 'When Alexander went East, he left no heir in Macedonia. Before you leave, you must marry, father a son.'

Gordian felt a surge of impatience – the pusillanimous nature of the old – but smiled. 'There are more than enough home-bred slaves in the Villa Praenestina with my features. There is all the time in the world.'

As he watched the resolution drain from his father, his irritation was replaced with guilt. 'You are right. When we reach Rome, I will marry. As long as my sister is not involved in choosing my wife.'

Now his father reached over and took his hand.

They sat in silence for some moments.

'Shall we return to the virtues of the Divine Marcus?'

'I am tired,' his father said. 'Perhaps tomorrow. Now I think I will have a rest before lunch.'

CHAPTER 23

ROME
THE VILLA PUBLICA

The Ides of March, AD238

Hangover cures were all nonsense. Garlanding yourself with violets, being rubbed with aromatic oils, wearing an amethyst next to your skin, eating owls' eggs – what sort of dedicated voluptuary had such foresight or went to such lengths? – none did any good. Only time would heal. Despite his scepticism, Menophilus had ordered fried cabbage to go with the mountain of eggs and bacon the two barbarian hostages were consuming.

Zeno had counselled that the good man will not get drunk. The Stoic master had considered that an inebriated man will reveal secrets. As far as he could remember, Menophilus had let slip nothing of any importance last night. Of course he could not be sure; by the end, unable to walk straight, the whole room had been spinning as if in a cyclone.

Drunkenness inflamed and laid bare every vice, removing the reserve that acts as a check on impulses to wrong behaviour, as Seneca had written. The girl had still been there this morning. Menophilus knew he had a weakness for sex and drink. The vices were not habitual, but they were recurrent. She had been a slave girl, waiting on table, so no harm had been done. Better her than a free virgin or a respectable matron. Adultery was nothing but theft. Not that it had felt like that in Carthage with Lycaenion. At least he had been discrete, not flaunted it in the face of her husband. He wondered if he would ever see her again.

Unable to face the eggs, Menophilus tried to chew a small piece of bacon. His head throbbed, and he felt slightly sick. He was sweating, and it was difficult to swallow. Cniva the Goth and Abanchus the Sarmatian showed few ill effects of the debauch. The barbarians were shovelling in the food. Bits kept getting stuck in the Sarmatian's luxuriant moustache. It made Menophilus feel worse.

Menophilus forced himself to eat some cabbage. It would give him energy. Even without the drinking, he would have been tired. Yesterday had been a long day. But both tasks had been accomplished.

In the morning, in yet another fractious meeting, at long, long last the Twenty had apportioned out the posts among their number for the coming campaign against Maximinus. Days of wrangling had produced, at best, an imperfect strategy. Only six or seven of them could be considered military men. Factional interests had precluded their straightforward appointment to the necessary stations. In the name of Republican collegiality, amid many invocations of the *mos maiorum*, all commands were to be shared by two men. How this was to function had not been explored. The ancestral way, where two Consuls alternated days of command, had been rejected, thus laying bare the unspoken imperative that each was there as much to watch his colleague, prevent him gaining too much glory, as to fight the enemy.

At least Menophilus himself would be accompanied by Crispinus in the defence of Aquileia. He knew something of Pupienus' friend. A *novus homo*, Crispinus had entered the Senate after a long succession of equestrian military commands. As governor of Syria Phoenice, he had led troops with distinction in Alexander's Persian campaign. Things elsewhere were less satisfactory. In the Apennines, Lucius Virius was saddled with the indolent patrician Caesonius Rufinianus. Organizing the defence of Rome, Pupienus would have to contend with the philosophical ineptitude of Maecenas. The task of preventing reinforcements reaching Maximinus across the western Alps, given to Cethegillus, would not be aided by the presence of the unmilitary *nobilis* Valerius Priscillianus.

The hand of that fat fool Balbinus was in everything. His vexation at the betrothal of the plain daughter of Praetextatus – his former ally – to one of Pupienus' sons would have been comical, if it

213

had not led to still further contention, when unity was a necessity.

Yet Balbinus could not be blamed for what was possibly the worst aspect of the arrangement, the holding of the front line at the eastern Alpine Passes. The two descendants of the Divine Marcus Aurelius, Claudius Aurelius and Claudius Severus, had demanded the honour of being the first to meet the barbarian tyrant on the battlefield. It had been impossible to deny their prestige and high birth, even though it had been precisely these qualities that previously had ensured no reigning Emperor had entrusted them with any military high command. Maximinus and his veteran army might be expected to make short work of two elderly aristocrats and whatever makeshift forces had been scrapped together. Menophilus had got the Twenty to agree to Timesitheus going with them. Officially the equestrian would merely provide technical advice, while levying troops and gathering supplies in the foothills and across the plain of the river Po.

The selection of ambassadors from the remainder of the Twenty to venture abroad and win over the provinces had not been easy. The luxuries of the eternal city, and its place as the ultimate residence of legitimate power, in the minds of most, seemed to outweigh the dubious honour and the discomforts of travel. To be fair, there was also the evident danger. It was near certain that any governor who did not join the revolt would have

214

the envoys loaded with chains, bundled into a closed carriage, and conveyed post-haste to Maximinus. What the Thracian would do to them when they arrived did not bear thinking about. After some prevarication, two of the faction of the Gordiani agreed. The aged Appius Claudius Julianus would go to Gallia Narbonensis, and, if the gods were kind, the northern provinces beyond. Egnatius Marinianus – a waste of one of the rare military talents – would cross first the Adriatic to Dalmatia and the Balkan provinces, then the Hellespont to Bithynia-Pontus and Asia Minor. The independent Senator Latronianus volunteered to sail for Syria and the East. He was one of the few in the Twenty who had emerged with an enhanced reputation from the endless discussions.

Everything was concluded, but Menophilus was very aware that of those fully committed to the Gordiani only Valerian would remain in Rome. He finished the bacon and cabbage, took some more, and asked a servant to bring him some eggs. He was feeling a bit less bad, actually hungry. If you could get some food inside you, and keep it there, it helped. As did focusing your mind on something other than your physical suffering. The two barbarians were talking in some language Menophilus did not know. Despite the wine fumes in his head, he continued to reconstruct the events of the previous day.

The afternoon and evening had been the idea of Timesitheus. They had taken the northern

215

hostages to the *Equirria*. The festival's two-horse chariot races in the Stadium of Domitian on the Campus Martius always made a fine show. Cniva the Goth was from the Tervingi, Abanchus the Sarmatian an Iazyges. They had seemed to appreciate watching from the imperial box. Usually men of their tribes should consider themselves fortunate to be granted a place in the Senatorial seating. There had been drinks throughout the spectacle. Both had wagered large sums of money, and laughed without restraint, slapped their thighs, at every crash, as a barbarian would.

After sunset, when they escorted them back to their nearby lodgings in the Villa Publica, they had found Timesitheus had provided a splendid feast; huge amounts of roast meat and wine, attractive serving girls, things guaranteed to please any barbarian nobleman.

At first Menophilus and Timesitheus had talked together in Greek, confident the barbarians could not understand. Timesitheus had argued at some length that he should be sent to the East. Their conversation came back to Menophilus with a strange clarity.

'Who better than the *Praefectus Annonae* to ensure the supply of Egyptian grain?' Timesitheus had said. 'I know the East from Alexander's campaign, and since then have governed provinces there. The envoy Latronianus was the earliest patron of my career; we would work in harness like a well-schooled chariot team.'

Menophilus had been forced to interrupt. 'You had better know what is really expected of you in the North.'

'I love secrets,' Timesitheus had said.

'The Julian Alps around Mount Ocra are dominated by a landowner called Marcus Julius Corvinus. Rumour has it he is more highland chief than respectable equestrian. It is said the bandits who infest the Passes either are his men or pay him a part of their loot.'

Timesitheus had appeared interested.

'You are to go to his principal residence, a mountain fastness called Arcia. If he can be persuaded to raid the baggage trains of Maximinus' army, assure him that such a service would not be forgotten by the Gordiani.'

The Greek had still not looked totally reconciled.

'Nor will your scheme for the barbarian hostages,' Menophilus had added.

That had won over the *Graeculus*.

The next part of the evening – the business with the barbarian envoys – was more fragmentary in Menophilus' memory.

While detained in Rome, both Cniva and Abanchus had learnt enough Latin to make conversation. Late that night, well warmed by the wine, they had agreed readily to win their freedom by swearing to get their tribes to act in the interests of the Gordiani.

Menophilus worried about the morality of the arrangement. Posterity might judge it harshly.

217

Fighting for the throne, Vespasian had rejected offers of foreign aid. Any good Emperor would. But Vespasian had the armies of the Danube and the East at his back. The Gordiani had no such array. The Iazyges of Abanchus would draw troops from Maximinus' field army. The Tervingi of Cniva would prevent reinforcements reaching him from Honoratus on the lower Danube. Yet unleashing Sarmatian horsemen into the Pannonias, and Gothic warriors into Moesia Inferior would cause untold suffering to innocent Roman provincials. And a taste of plunder only incited barbarians to want more. Once you have released such animals, it was hard to call them off. In politics the things you hope for are the ones you must fear.

Menophilus had finished eating. He wondered if the hostages would ever do the same. He toyed with a piece of bread and honey.

Gordian had given him strict instructions. He had left them far behind. No one in Rome was to die, except Vitalianus. Menophilus had gone on to kill Sabinus as well, smashed his skull like a pottery vessel. Neither Gordian nor his father would have countenanced the massacre of Roman citizens by barbarians. But they were in Africa, and he was here, fighting for the empire on their behalf. Someone had to make the hard decisions. When Vespasian had taken the throne, he had cast aside the generals that had won him the civil war. Probably the Gordiani would turn from him in revulsion. He already missed their companionship.

But friends were like figs, they did not keep. Better sacrifice his good reputation, take the odium, and ensure their safety. His Stoicism enjoined that a good man will take part in politics, unless something intervened. It was an irony that he had been put in this dreadful position by a man he loved whose Epicureanism urged the opposite.

The barbarians had finished. They sat back, wiping greasy fingers, belching.

'Now you show us real drinking.'

It was the Ides of March. The day the *plebs urbana* made merry in the open parkland at the north of the Campus Martius. They erected tents, makeshift shelters of reeds. Every cup of wine a man or woman drank ensured another year of life. No one wanted to die young.

Menophilus could imagine little worse. He was leaving for Aquileia the next day. There was much to be done. But he had promised the hostages. Once you have undertaken something, it had to be seen through.

Leabharlanna Poibli Chathair Bhaile Átha Cliath
Dublin City Public Libraries

CHAPTER 24

THE NORTHERN FRONTIER
SIRMIUM

The Ides of March, AD238

*I took the victims, over the trench I cut their
throats
And the dark blood flowed in – and up out of
Hades they came,
Flocking toward me now, the ghosts of the dead
and gone . . .*

Maximinus liked to go down where the dead went.
He sat on the ivory throne in the Basilica. The
alabaster vase in his hands, his court around him.
He listened to the Sophist recite Homer.

*Brides and unwed youths and old men who had
suffered much
And girls with their tender hearts freshly scarred
by sorrow
And great armies of battle dead, stabbed by
bronze spears
Men of war still wrapped in bloody armour –
thousands*

Maximinus liked to have Apsines around him, have him recite, or talk quietly with him in the dead of night. When the world was younger – so the Sophist told him – many portals stood open to the underworld; many caves and passages, at Taenarus in Laconia, Aornum in Thesprotis, the Acherusian peninsula on the Black Sea, many places, many magical names. Now the world was older, more wicked, the gods further away. A cave was just a cave. No man could cross the Styx unless he was dead. No living man could emulate Orpheus and his doomed attempt to bring his wife back from the gloomy halls of Hades.

But I, the sharp sword drawn from beside
*   my hip,*
Sat down on alert there and never let the ghosts
Of the shambling, shiftless dead come near that
*   blood . . .*

There were so many dead. Since Maximinus was a man, Micca had always been at his side. Together they had haunted the Thracian hills, bringing violent retribution to barbarian raiders and bandits alike. In the army, they had quartered the empire. Under the African sun they had faced the Garamantes. In the perpetual drizzle of Caledonia they had waited for the savages to come screaming

221

down from the heather. Rome, the Danube, the East; all those years had come to an end on a wooded ridge in Germania. Maximinus fighting his way through to the chieftains. A flash of movement in the corner of his eye. The spear between Micca's shoulder blades. No time then to mourn, far too long afterwards.

Maximinus had no memories before Tynchanius. He had been a friend even before Micca. The son of a neighbour, a few years older, Tynchanius had been the brother every boy would want. He had known how to hunt, how to make a bow, fletch arrows. Later, he had known which girls would pull up their skirts if you talked to them sweetly, gave them a gift. They were returning from hunting – Maximinus had been no more than sixteen – when Tynchanius sensed something was wrong. Although they had passed bodies sprawled in the mud of the village street, Maximinus retained a boy's foolish hope. Rather than go to his own home first, loyally Tynchanius had gone with Maximinus. They were all dead. Maximinus' father and mother, his brother and his sisters. The females were naked. In Tynchanius' hut, it was the same.

Tynchanius had been loyal to the end. From what Maximinus had extracted, the mutineers had cut down the old man as he vainly tried to protect Paulina.

To begin with, in a part of his mind, Maximinus had believed Apsines. Time would heal. Soon he would not think of her all the time. In a sense the Sophist was right. It would be two years in June. But, if his thoughts were elsewhere, it was all the worse when the grief came flooding back. It seized his limbs, numbed his mind. Now he did not like to part from her. He held the vase with her ashes, turning it in his great, scarred hands, as he listened to endless speeches. One long-bearded Greek after another; interminable complaints of embezzlement, extortion and theft, larded with fawning flattery. It was a continued affront that the world carried on with its petty, pointless concerns.

Royal son of Laertes, Odysseus, master of exploits,
Man of pain, what now, what brings you here,
Forsaking the light of day
To see this joyless kingdom of the dead?

Maximinus had made his plan. He had questioned Apsines, but had tried not to reveal what he intended. This summer, one final campaign in Germania, and he could put up his sharp sword. His duty would be done, and he could leave the ranks. No Emperor had retired. Vitellius did not count. He had been a weakling, defeated and deserted, destined for death. But Sulla the Dictator at the height of his powers had renounced them all. Julius Caesar had been wrong. Sulla had known what he was about. Like Solon, the ancient Athenian, the Dictator had done all he could, then stepped aside. No man was Atlas, to carry the weight of the world on his shoulders forever.

Of course, Maximinus would not let his son succeed. He looked over to where Maximus sat; handsome, bejewelled, arrogant, vicious. He looked at Iunia Fadilla. You could only pity his son's wife. Volo's spies reported the cruelty was unabated, the beatings getting worse. Maximinus found it hard to imagine that Paulina had given birth to this horrible, beautiful monster. Something must have intervened; a terrible conjunction of the stars, witchcraft, some malignant daemon.

If not Maximus, then another, one capable of ruling. The succession had to be clear, arranged beyond any dispute. Civil war would encourage the barbarians, undo Maximinus' long years of struggle. He ran through those who might be *capax imperii*. Anullinus, the Praetorian Prefect, had something cold and harmful about him. Domitius, the Prefect of the Camp, was avaricious, corrupt. Sabinus Modestus, the cavalry commander, was amiable, brave and lucky, but far too stupid. Volo would reject the offer. He would continue to command the *frumentarii*, continue to gather information, make arrests, quietly guard the throne, as he had for Maximinus, as he had for Alexander before. Julius Capitollinus, the Prefect of the 2nd Legion Parthica, had the necessary qualities. But, like the others, he was but an equestrian. The Senate would only truly accept one of their own as Augustus.

Most Senators were weak, unmanned by wealth and privilege. To them the *mos maiorum* was no more than an expression. It would have to be one of the Triumvirate, one of the three who had engineered Maximinus' own elevation. Catius Clemens always complained of ill health. Honoratus' demeanour, coupled with his good looks, suggested a decadent indolence. Probably both were no more than strategies to survive under an autocracy. Apparent incapacities might deflect the suspicions of a ruler. They could be cast off if either sat on the throne. Or perhaps long dissimulation had made their appearances reality, perhaps they, and other vices, would flower once the will of their owner became law. Nothing revealed the flaws in a character like being the vicegerent of the gods, being worshipped yourself throughout the provinces. Nothing escaped such scrutiny. The superstitions of Flavius Vopiscus were genuine. Yet despite all the prayers and amulets, the fasts and incubations, the childish search for foreknowledge in random lines of Virgil, Maximinus had no doubt that Flavius Vopiscus was *capax imperii*.

On a country estate, a debilitating and disgusting disease had dragged Sulla to a slow and painful death. The *imperium* would not allow the like for Maximinius. The courtiers around his successor could see him as nothing but a threat, the figure-head of a potential rebellion. Sooner or later, Flavius Vopiscus, or whoever wore the purple, would instruct Volo to send *frumentarii* to make an end to the menace. In any event, Maximinus had no intention to linger. He would take Paulina home to Ovile, inter her in the tumulus, then unsheathe his sharp sword one last time, and fall on it.

Late one night, somewhere out on the Steppe, talking in general terms about Roman suicide, Apsines had enumerated its difficulty, the pain and squalor suffered by even the bravest of men. Mark Antony hauled by ropes as his life blood flowed out. Cato tearing at the unwanted stitches with which his friends had closed his wound, pulling out his own intestines. Maximinus was not deterred. He trusted his resolve and dexterity with a blade. For certainty, he would take Javolenus with him, reward him well. After the final service, his body-guard could vanish into comfortable obscurity.

Maximinus' mind was made up. The gods approved. He had consulted Ababa, the Druid woman summoned to the imperial court by his predecessor. Her strange rites had not raised the shade of Paulina, but she had predicted the death of Alexander Severus. The deities spoke through her. The Rider God would lead Maximinus by the hand, and reunite him with Paulina and Tynchanius and Micca. Together they would ride the wild hills of his youth, drink at upland springs, sleep safe in mountain caves. Not for them the dark meadows of the realm of Hades. The Rider God would conquer death itself.

And even if you escape, you will come home
   late
And come a broken man . . .

The baying of Maximus' hounds in their kennels near drowned the Sophist's voice. Maximinus looked at his son, silk shimmering, jewels glittering, lolling on his throne. He was Caesar. His vanity and ambition would never let him give up the title. He was incapable, would lose any contest for the throne. But if left alive, even his failure would cause untold suffering. Long ago to save the *Res Publica* Brutus had condemned his own sons to a traitor's death; stripped, flogged, beheaded under the gaze of all in the Forum. The *mos maiorum* was more than words in those days. But it had been cruel. When Maximinus renounced the throne, his son would have to die. But not in public, not at the hands of an executioner.

The hound music swelled. The pack was expensive and ostentatious – Maximus never hunted – but no one could approach the royal chambers undetected.

Sure enough, a messenger entered.

Maximinus signalled the end of the recital, and waved the soldier to approach.

As he came before the throne, the messenger bowed, and went to get to his knees.

'Stop,' Maximinus said. 'While I am Emperor, no man will print a kiss on my boots.'

The soldier stood, saluted, and held out a

227

despatch. It carried the seal of Sabinus, Prefect of Rome.

With great care, Maximinus placed the vase in its cunningly made travelling case. He took the letter, broke the seal, and handed it to Apsines.

As the Sophist read, the colour drained from his face.

'Well?' Maximinus said. Nothing good had come from Rome.

Apsines mastered himself; the resolve instilled by a lifetime of public speaking did not desert him.

'To Imperator Gaius Iulius Verus Maximinus Augustus . . .'

'Tell us the bad news,' Maximinus said.

'*Quantum libet, Imperator.*'

'Speak.'

'Whatever pleases you, Emperor,' Apsines repeated. 'Sabinus writes that the people of Africa have risen in revolt. They have proclaimed Gordian the governor and his son Emperors. Vitalianus has been murdered in Rome. The Senate . . .'

'Go on.'

'The Senate have declared you and your son enemies of the Roman people. As *hostes* you are denied fire and water . . .'

Maximinus bounded from the throne. He grabbed the despatch. Too angry to read, he hurled it at the messenger. The man ducked. It hit him on the arm. The hinges broke, and the two wooden blocks skittered away across the floor.

'You little fucker!' Maximinus had the soldier by the throat. 'Guards!'

Praetorians came running from behind the curtain.

'Arrest this traitor. Take him to the cellars. Get the inquisitors. Find out everything he knows.'

The Praetorians dragged the messenger away.

Maximinus stood, fists clenching and unclenching in his fury. Three years' fighting. Three years' hard marching and killing. All for nothing. No chance now of quiet retirement. No reunion with those he loved. Three years of fighting for Rome, and this was how the Senate repaid him. No loyalty, no honour. The fuckers, he would kill them all. Every one of them, leave no one alive to mourn them.

'Father . . .'

Maximinus seized his son's head. Pressed his thumbs into his eyes. 'If you were a man, you could have governed Rome. This would never have happened. You might have made your mother proud. I should pluck out the eyes that never wept for her.'

'Imperator, no . . .' Domitius had him by one arm, Modestus by the other. Anullinus gripped him around the throat.

Maximinus released his son, shook the others off like a great bear did yapping dogs.

'Get out! All of you, out!'

Maximinus stood still, panting, as the courtiers fled.

'Apsines, you stay.'

The Sophist stopped, stood irresolute.

'Bring me wine. Tell me stories of ancient treachery. Tell me how it was punished. But first get me wine.'

CHAPTER 25

AFRICA
CARTHAGE

The Ides of March, AD*238*

'No one with any morals has ever enjoyed a mime show.'

Gordian laughed. 'But every mime artist has been *enjoyed* by half the town.'

Sabinianus was right. For those with self-proclaimed high morals, the problem with pantomimes was always the fights in the audience, but with mimes it was the sex on stage. *The Adulterer Caught* was one of the worst, or best depending on your viewpoint.

The scenery in the small theatre was simple, just a bed and a large wooden chest. The doddering old husband had been sent on a fool's errand. To persuade him to go, his young wife had sucked his prick. Gordian and Sabinianus had hooted along with the rest of the audience when the pretty young actress had lifted up his tunic, pulled it over to cover her head. The old actor had shuddered and snorted with comic abandon, his spindly limbs trembling at the quickening rhythmic movements under the material. The actress had emerged, daintily dabbing her chin.

'She reminds me of Lycaenion.'

'I did not know you were so intimate with Menophilus' mistress.'

'Unfortunately, no.' Sabinianus grinned. 'Not all my friends are as generous as you with Chione and Parthenope.'

'Only what you give to your friends is yours forever.'

They both took another drink.

The young male lead entered. He knew his craft; appearing exaggeratedly nervous, his whole body quivering, as fear struggled with lust. After kissing her on the mouth, he ran his tongue over his lips, as if tasting something strange. The audience groaned, revolted and delighted.

'Darling,' the lover said, 'what do you want to do? Eat breakfast or have sex?'

'Whatever you want,' the wife replied, 'but there is no food in the house.'

It was good to lay down the cares of office. Gordian took another drink. Sabinianus had suggested the mimes. Going in disguise had been Gordian's idea. He was not sure how convincing they were as slaves. Sabinianus had said they should take some soldiers, just in case. Gordian had vetoed that. He wanted to be Mark Antony peeping into the pleasures of the poor, not Nero assaulting innocent passers-by.

After some of the oldest jokes in the world – *How*

chaste! How easily caught! – the play reached the navigation of Venus. The lover bent the wife over the bed, flipped up her skirts, revealing her white rounded buttocks. With a look of unbridled desire, he hauled up his clothes, and started vigorously thrusting.

'In the reign of Elagabalus that would have been real,' Sabinianus said.

'Are you sure it is not now? Anyway, when you are governor of Africa, you have imperial dispensation to make penetration the law.'

Much loud stamping and muttering announced the return of the husband.

'Quick, into the chest.'

Acting or not, the lover had a creditable erection. It bobbed in front, as he hopped across the stage and clambered into the chest.

The crowd stamped their feet in amusement.

'Possibly how he got the role,' Sabinianus said.

'What a walk.' The husband sat down on the chest. 'It was all downhill to the Forum, by the time I came back it had turned into a steep climb.'

Muffled thumps came from inside the chest.

'What is that noise?'

'Mice.'

'Never in my house.'

'I heard them. You know I am terrified of mice, darling.'

'In that case.' The old man got up, threw back the lid.

Gasping, the young man tumbled out, his tunic still up around his waist.

'What? What? Oh, now I see. A thief in my private property.' The husband looked around myopically. 'Where is my sword?'

'Darling,' the wife put her arms around him, waving over his shoulder for her lover to pull his tunic down. 'He is here to catch the mice.'

'Oh, in that case, I had better pay him.'

While the husband peered into the chest for his money, behind his back the young man bent his wife back over the bed, mounted her again.

'I am sure I put it in here,' the old man said.

'Me too,' the young man said.

The husband rummaged faster. The lover thrust quicker.

'I will not be long,' the old man said from inside the chest.

'Nor me.'

'Got it.' As the husband stood, the lovers finished, straightened, and lowered their clothes.

'Here you are.' The old man handed over some coins. 'Mind you, I still do not think there ever were any mice, but as long as my wife is satisfied.'

The Adulterer Caught was always the same. The humour came from the comfortable repetition spiced with small impromptu variations, and everything depended on timing and delivery. The latter so much more difficult without a mask.

After the show, Gordian followed Sabinianus through a labyrinth of narrow shop-lined streets.

Sabinianus said he knew just the bar for a night such as this. Most of the shops had merchandise piled up outside on rugs. Barely breaking stride, Sabinianus took a bun.

'You going to pay for that?'

'No.' Sabinianus turned to Gordian. 'Run!'

'Stop, thieves!'

One man tried to stop them. Sabinianus knocked him aside. Gordian ran after Sabinianus, side-stepping and barging down the street. They turned left and right, further into the maze. The sounds of a half-hearted pursuit soon falling behind.

'In here.'

The alley was more insalubrious than most. Gordian doubled over, hands on knees, fighting to get his breath. He was out of condition, carrying too much weight. He needed a campaign to get him back in shape. Like Antony or Alexander, he was better in the field.

'Want a bun?'

'Not really.'

'Nor me.' Sabinianus dropped it in the gutter. 'You have to say, that was almost exciting. Follow me.'

Gordian pulled the hood of his cloak back over his head, and did as he was told.

The small and grubby bar was distinguished by the inventive obscenity of its murals. Apart from the bar owner in his leather tunic, a sluttish-looking barmaid and a rat-like pot boy, there was one other customer. The latter sat in a corner, the broad brim of his travelling hat down over his eyes.

'This looks like fun.'

'We are early. It fills up later; all the low-life characters one could want.'

The wall opposite where they sat was dominated by a painting of a girl riding a man. Although not blessed with much talent, the painter had taken pains depicting their genitals. But more striking was the fact that she was exercising with weights while having sex. Gordian wondered how she managed to combine the rhythms of the two activities.

'A present.' Sabinianus pushed something across the table.

'If I did not know better, I would say you have given me a small, dead lizard.'

'A skink.'

'A skink?'

'A small, dead, dried north African lizard. Powdered, it will solve your problem.'

'I do not have a problem.'

'Far better than any amount of oysters.'

'It happened once. I was tired, had been drinking too much.'

'Far more efficacious than satyrion, rocket, nettle seed, pepper.'

'Chione should not have told you.'

'She said it had happened more than once.'

'Her demands are voracious. I am not as young as I was.'

Three soldiers swaggered in, swinging the metal weights on the ends of their military belts.

Sabinianus leant close, spoke quietly from under his hood. 'We should leave.'

'We only just got here.'

'Leave Carthage. Get to Rome. Secure the throne.'

Gordian took a long drink of wine. 'My father is reluctant to sail. The astrologer said we would be drowned at sea. And he talks much about the prodigy.'

'An animal gave birth. What could be more natural? That it did so when your father was about to sacrifice it, was no more than an unfortunate coincidence.' Sabinianus shrugged. 'An Epicurean of all people should be unconcerned.'

'Now Arrian has Numidia, there is no hurry to leave Africa.' Gordian put down his drink, held out both hands, flat palm up, then turned them palm down. 'See these? Clean hands. Menophilus will do what is necessary in Rome.'

'The East then?'

'How many times have I reassured you that Claudius Julianus in Dalmatia, Fidus in Thrace, Egnatius Lollianus in Bithynia-Pontus will all declare for us.'

'And the provinces with legions?'

'They will follow.'

'Well, that is all good,' Sabinianus said. 'I have told you before, talents such as mine should not be wasted. I have no desire to die in some doomed cause.'

The ornaments on their belts showed the soldiers

belonged to the detachment from the 3rd Augusta. They were playing *Kottabos*. The bartender had set a cup on a stool, and the legionaries were throwing the dregs of their wine at it. So far no one had succeeded in knocking it off and breaking it.

Sabinianus took a large coin from his belt. He sent it spinning across the room. It hit with a loud clink. The cup wobbled, then fell, smashing into dozens of shards.

'Set up another,' Sabinianus called.

A big soldier with a scar down his face bulked over. He set his knuckles on the table. 'A slave should not wait for his master's hand.'

Sabinianus laughed. 'An ass does not become a horse if you slit its nostrils . . .'

'Where did you steal the money, whipling?'

'. . . not if you bore its jaw, put a curb-chain between its teeth; it will still bray like an ass.'

The legionary grabbed Sabinianus by the front of his tunic, hauled him out of his seat, halfway across the table.

Gordian hit the soldier hard in the stomach. Everything moved very fast. The table went over. A chair splintered. Gordian was on the floor. The big legionary had him by the throat, was banging the back of his head on the boards. The other two soldiers were on Sabinianus.

Gordian's hood slipped off as he writhed to break free. The big legionary punched him in the face. The taste of blood in his mouth, like brass coins. The fist drew back to hit him again.

'Get off your Imperator!'

At Sabinianus' shout, the soldier paused, then brought his scarred face close to Gordian.

'Fuck me, is it really you?'

'As the fates made me. You were down at the harbour.'

'Gods below, I had no idea.' The legionary helped him up. 'Hercules' hairy arse, Imperator, I am sorry. What are you doing here?'

Gordian spat blood on the floor. 'Not looking to reap this harvest of blows.'

'Are you hurt, Imperator? I did not know.'

'Nothing that a few drinks will not mend. The imperial *fiscus* should be good for them, and for the breakages.'

'Fuck me, you really are one of us. Make way there. Get a chair for our Emperor.'

CHAPTER 26

THE NORTHERN FRONTIER
SIRMIUM

The Day after the Ides of March, AD238

As her husband drunkenly rolled off Iunia Fadilla, he gave one of her nipples a last, painful pinch.

'Barren bitch, all the men that have fucked you, and no child.'

He was on his back, his chest slick with the sweat of his rutting. 'Whore. Treacherous whore.' His eyes closed.

Iunia lay very still, hoping Maximus would fall asleep. Her breasts hurt where he had bitten them, her thighs and buttocks from his slaps and punches.

'What sort of punishment is fitting for the whore of a traitor? I should feed you to the hounds, let the kennel boys fuck you first.'

Before this hateful marriage, she remembered enjoying sex; with old Nummius, with Gordian, men who cared for her, wanted to give her pleasure, not hurt and humiliate. If she cried, Maximus would notice. Her tears aroused his lust.

Maximus' breathing became more even.

With the news of Gordian's rebellion, she had known things would be worse for her. But she had thought she would be spared a visit from her husband for a time. Surely his father would need him: there would be much to be done; plans to be made, letters written, envoys despatched, forces gathered. But the Emperor remained in his quarters, drinking. It was said only Apsines the Syrian Sophist was with him, declaiming Homer, telling stories, as if to a child.

The *consilium* had convened without the Emperor. Maximus had been summoned by Flavius Vopiscus. When he had arrived there, late, already half-drunk, Maximus had told them it was treason to meet without the Emperor, dismissed them. Another couple of hours drinking, and he had come to *get the bitch in whelp*. He had hit one of her maids, and they had fled. The first time he had taken her from behind. A doctor had told him that breasts down, genitals raised, the seed can reach where it needed to go. Afterwards, sprawling on the bed, he had told her to serve him wine and food, naked, the lamps lit, *like any whore in a cheap lupanar, like you did for Gordian*. When he was ready, she had to kneel between his legs, take him in her mouth until he was hard again.

Outside the hunting dogs howled.

Iunia prayed it would not wake him.

He stirred, but his eyes remained shut.

When he was with the army on the Steppe, she

had prayed to all the gods to let a barbarian arrow find him. Not in the heart or head, death was too quick. Let the barbed steel tear into his guts, let the poison seep into his blood, locking his jaws, leaving him to linger for days in wordless agony. Or let him be captured. The Sarmatian women were said to stake their victims out, castrate them, prise their mouths open, and force their genitals down their throats. Then they flayed the skin from their living bodies, sliver by sliver.

The gods had not heeded her prayers. Gordian was right, they were far away, and had no care for humanity. They were right to keep their distance. Anything in contact with Maximus was tainted.

He was snoring.

Now. Gods, give her the courage. Now.

Even if Eunomia had gathered the necessary potions before she died, it would have done no good. Every morning now, Maximus took a draught of *Mithridatium*, the compound of every noxious thing known to man. It made him feel sick, but gave immunity to all poisons.

Now. There would never be a better opportunity. Give her the heart of a man.

Slowly, she slid off the bed, went to the chest. The well oiled hinges did not squeak. She took out the knife.

Of course she would be caught. In the morning they would find her drenched in his blood, like an actor in a tragedy. Hers would be a terrible death, as bad as any Christian. In the arena, torn apart by wild beasts, or strapped to a metal frame, roasted and burnt. Maximinus had become inventive in his executions. She had passed one at the city gates a few days before. The condemned man had been sewn alive into the carcass of a slaughtered animal. Maximus had said the maggots fed on the living flesh and the dead. The man had been conscious, but, thank the gods, beyond speech.

She could commit suicide, use the blade on herself after Maximus. She put the thought aside. Killing Maximus, that was all that mattered. Nothing else mattered. He had to die.

With terrified caution, she climbed onto the bed. As the mattress gave, Maximus shifted slightly. He still lay naked on his back, his penis on one side, like a small, sleeping rat. If she were Sarmatian, she would hack it off, stuff it down his throat.

Gods, give her the heart of a man, the heart of Clytemnestra. She put the tip of the blade to his throat. If he woke now, she would have to go through with it. As the razor-sharp steel pricked his flesh, he grunted, moved slightly. Let him wake. She wanted to see his terror and pain, wanted her hand forced.

A bright red bead of blood. The skin so white, so delicate. Now, push home the knife, become Clytemnestra. Make a sacrifice of him.

She did not want to die. She wanted him dead,

243

but not to die herself. She wanted to live. She was no Sarmatian barbarian, no Clytemnestra.

Defeated, more frightened than before – if he woke now! – she crept off the bed, moused across the floor, and returned the knife to the chest. Silently, she slipped out through the door.

Restuta, her favourite maid, was waiting in the next room with towels, unguents, a bowl of warm water. Restuta said nothing, knowing from experience that words of sympathy can break the strongest self-control. She held her shoulders as Iunia squatted over the bowl, washed herself. Iunia looked at a lamp, tried to sneeze. Restuta patted her dry.

'Sleep in my room,' Restuta said.

'It will be the worse for me if I am not there when he wakes.'

'Let me put ointments on the marks.'

'No, he likes to see his handiwork.'

Restuta passed her the jar with the white lead, cedar resin and honey in old oil. Iunia pushed the mixture inside herself. No child would be born in the purple. The imperial household was full of spies. But she had to trust Restuta. The wife of Caesar could not buy such things in the market.

Back in the bedroom, Iunia lay beside her husband. She had failed. She could not kill him. Patient endurance would gain her nothing. The revolt of Gordian would fail. That gentle, kind man would die. Nothing could stand against

Maximinus and the northern armies. She must escape. But where would she find refuge? A sanctuary might offer asylum to any criminal, no matter how awful his crime, to the lowest runaway slave, but not to the wife of Caesar.

She thought of her journey to the North, of the high Alps, of the horseman who had given her the brooch. People said Corvinus was nothing but a brigand, a law unto himself. But would a bandit chief dare to defy an Emperor? She remembered his words. *My Lady, accept my hospitality, these wild mountains are mine.*

There was Dalmatia, not far to the south. It was governed by Claudius Julianus. He was Gordian's friend. Would compassion and friendship outweigh advantage? He commanded no legions to stand against Maximinus. Yet he was a man of honour.

Her mind drifted. Cleopatra had fled Caesar. She had ridden east. Alone among men, the King of Kings might shelter the enemy of Caesar. But the Egyptian Queen had been overtaken. Destined for a Roman Triumph, she had put the asp to her breast. Persia was beyond reach, as distant as the Isles of the Blessed.

How could she escape? Rich women often travelled; to visit relatives, attend festivals, inspect their estates. But they were accompanied by many guards, attendants and slaves. Iunia had no one but Restuta. Could she entrust her life to Restuta?

Poor women walked to market, to the next village. Only entertainers – actresses, flute girls, whores

– or beggars journeyed further. They went slowly. Iunia would have to move like the wind.

Those with access to the *cursus publicus* moved fast. Requisitioning carriages and fresh horses at every Post House, they flew free as migrating birds, a hundred and fifty or more miles a day. *Diplomata* were issued to women. She was the wife of Caesar. Unless her husband was with her, nowhere in the imperial court was debarred to her. Go to the chancery, surreptitiously get her hands on an official pass, write in whatever name she would use, take to the road.

Coming up from Rome, somewhere in the marshes of the Adriatic coast, her carriage had shed a wheel. They had spent the night in a cheap inn. Those evicted to make room for her party had been ushered in to thank her for the leftovers of her meal and for being allowed to sleep in the stables. Among the hard-eyed, rough men was a family. The mother and daughter were frightened. Iunia had thought how hard it must be for a woman to travel alone.

If she had a man with her, things would be easier. Through no choice of his own, her cousin was constrained in the entourage of the Emperor. A sweet youth, Fadillus was no man of action. Most likely his nerve would fail. His presence become a hindrance. Better to go alone.

But, when her flight was discovered, what would become of him? She could not leave him to the cellars, the rack and claws.

Maximus grunted, levered himself up. His loath-some sword was half-erect.

'Let your husband harrow that barren field so many men have ploughed. Time to perform again, bitch.'

CHAPTER 27

ROME
THE MILVIAN BRIDGE

The Day after the Ides of March, AD238

Menophilus did not really think that he had shortened his life, let alone signed his own death warrant the previous day.

Out of the carriage, off to the left, could be seen the detritus of the feast: broken amphorae and cups, empty barrels and wine skins, tattered and collapsing shelters of boughs and reeds. An army of public slaves should have been working across that beaten ground, clearing everything away. It said much about the *Res Publica* that the only people in sight were a handful of rag-pickers.

The day before the Campus Martius had worn a very different aspect. The festival of Anna Perenna was always relaxed and popular. The *plebs urbana* had come from their tenements in their tens of thousands. Reclining on the grass, they drank, got up and danced lumbering measures, sang snatches of songs they had heard in the theatre, or traditional airs of startling obscenity. Supposedly innocent young virgins sang how the old goddess had nearly tricked Mars into ramming her aged quim with his erect spear. Many couples, under the limited privacy of a cloak, reached the end denied Anna Perenna. Above all they drank. Men and women, young and old, prayed that each cup they drained granted them another year of life. The barbarian hostages had enjoyed themselves enormously. Barbarians and plebs, there was little to choose between them. Blessed with huge capacity, Cniva and Abanchas had seemed to be aiming for near immortality. Crapulous, and with a great deal to do, Menophilus had taken just three cups, before he left. It was good that he was not superstitious.

There was more traffic on the Via Flaminia as they neared the Milvian Bridge. Their carriage slowed. Timesitheus carried on reading. At least, Menophilus thought, the *Graeculus* looked like being a quiet travelling companion. There were just the two of them in the carriage. Menophilus' servant, and the gladiator who accompanied Timesitheus rode behind.

Yesterday afternoon, up on the Caelian and the Esquiline, the breezy hills where the rich lived, it had not taken long for Menophilus to ascertain that the majority of the plans of the Twenty were being implemented with no alacrity whatsoever. One or two things were in hand. Crispinus had already set out for Aquileia, and Egnatius Marinianus and Latronianus, the two envoys to the east, had sailed. Old Appius Claudius Julianus also was near ready to depart for the west. But everything else was bad.

In Rome Maecenas had vetoed Pupienus' proposal to conscript the gladiators of the Ludus Magnus and other schools into the forces being raised to defend the city. It was not only against all philosophical precepts, but against the *mos maiorum* itself, Maecenas had claimed. The Senate and People of Rome should not entrust their defence to slaves and such scum. The militia must be the citizens in arms.

Rufinianus had insisted that Lucius Virius not leave to begin constructing fortifications on the roads across the Apennines until he was ready to accompany him. Likewise the mission to close the passes of the western Alps to any reinforcements destined for Maximinus had not left Rome, Cethegillus being detained by the inertia of Valerius Priscillianus.

Worst of all, Claudius Severus and Claudius Aurelius, the interchangeable descendants of the Divine Augustus Marcus Aurelius, were far from ready to leave for what soon would be the front line on the eastern Alps. Great aristocrats did not set forth without carefully organized entourages to take care of every eventuality. *Nobiles* such as them were not to be hurried or chivvied.

It was the latter that had induced Menophilus

to summon Timesitheus to the Palatine. The Greek would accompany him as far as Aquileia. He would remain there but Timesitheus would continue to the mountains. While talking to Corvinus the arch-brigand, the *Graeculus* could gather information, survey the main routes, and, on his return, begin to levy troops and supplies. Despite the leisureliness of the two distant scions of the imperial house, there would be a commander in the Julian Alps.

Menophilus looked over at his companion. Timesitheus was reading the *Histories* by Tacitus. What a man read was a statement of how he wished to be seen, like the art in his house, or the friends with whom he passed his time. Tacitus was a classic, which made reading it a claim to be both serious and cultured. The *Histories* recounted a civil war fought in northern Italy, so it was eminently practical under the circumstances. The text was in Latin, thus indicating Timesitheus was not one of those Greeks who lived in the past, and affected to despise the modern world and all culture except their own.

Ringlets of dark hair curled over Timesitheus' forehead. His eyes were very dark, liquid. Unlike his choice of literature, nothing could be made of his looks. Menophilus had complete contempt for physiognomy. He based his judgements on deeds and words, things within a man's control, not irrelevances like fine cheekbones or a strong jaw.

No one could fail to see that Timesitheus was intelligent, energetic, and capable. But it did not call for much insight to realize that he was ruthless, ambitious, and untrustworthy. Armenius Peregrinus blamed him for an attempt on his life and the burning of his house. Most likely he was right. Valerius Priscillianus hated him for denouncing his father. That was a certainty. Others disliked him without such specific reasons. Maecia Faustina had told her kinsman Maecius Gordianus to turn him away from the *Domus Rostrata* when the Greek had arrived bearing toys for her son.

As often, when Gordian's nephew came into his mind, Menophilus felt a stab of pity for the boy: his father dead, that echoing mausoleum of a house, living under the joyless eye of that severe mother.

Maecia Faustina and all the others might mistrust Timesitheus, but, paradoxically, now in this war, and only while it lasted, Menophilus knew there was no one he could trust more. Maximinus had ordered the death of the Greek. Timesitheus could not desert. If Maximinus won, he would die, most likely a hideous death.

They were almost at the bridge when the carriage came to a halt. Timesitheus stopped reading, leant out. A dense crowd blocked the way. Timesitheus asked a bystander what was causing the delay.

'The *frumentarii* are questioning everyone.' The man put his thumb between his fingers to avert evil. 'They have taken a Christian.'

After the man stepped away, they waited.

'Many believe the Christians are the root of all our troubles,' Timesitheus said. 'If the dominion of Rome truly rests on the *Pax Deorum*, they are right. The Christians deny our gods exist. As we suffer the atheists to live among us, it is no wonder the gods withdraw their favour. When the Gordiani are safe on the throne, they should order a persecution across the empire. In any event, their confiscated property would swell the imperial coffers.'

Menophilus made a noncommittal noise. In his vision of the gods, each was an emanation of the divine intelligence that oversaw the Cosmos, far above such petty jealousies. The arrest was just bad luck on the atheist, Menophilus thought. He had told Felicio to use what Praetorians and *frumentarii* remained in Rome to prevent any spies or assassins from Maximinus getting into the city.

What a difference a few hours could make in politics. Assassination was not the Roman way. Long ago, when a man had offered to kill her great enemy Pyrrhus of Epirus, the Senate had rejected the scheme as unworthy. Even later, under Tiberius, the same answer had been given concerning Arminius, the German leader who had massacred three legions in the forest. Menophilus had every intention of following the *mos maiorum*, until yesterday when he was confronted by the sheer ineptitude of those tasked with defending the *Res*

Publica from Maximinus. *I shall meet with inter-ference, ingratitude, disloyalty, ill-will, and selfishness.* Marcus Aurelius could have added indolence, complacency, and sheer stupidity. No doubt all caused by a basic failure to distinguish between what was right and wrong.

Castricius had been brought up from his cell. The knife-boy was young. Menophilus was unin-terested in the truth of his story of the betrayals and misfortune that had led him to the Subura. Castricius talked a lot, but he was not without sense. Presented with the alternatives – the beasts, the cross, or the mines – he had readily agreed to the offer.

Menophilus had modified the original scheme proposed by Timesitheus, removing all mention of the Senator Catius Celer. Instead, Castricius would carry a straightforward despatch to Maximinus. In his own handwriting, in return for his own safety, Menophilus would propose to kill the Gordiani when they landed from Africa. That should get Castricius access to Maximinus. The dagger would be hidden in a bandage on the knife-boy's arm.

Should Castricius manage to escape in the ensuing chaos, he would be rewarded with wealth beyond his imaginings. In case he decided to slip away, a *frumentarius* would accompany him as far as the imperial camp. Of course his nerve might fail him. He was assured that if it did, when the war was over, he would be hunted down.

After the complicated plan involving Castricius, he had made another simpler one: sending a messenger to Axius Aelianus the Procurator of Dacia offering huge rewards if he removed the governor of the province by whatever necessary means.

The carriage moved forward and stopped just short of the bridge. A soldier briefly scanned their *diplomata*, saluted, and waved them through. They clattered across the bridge. Timesitheus returned to the *Histories*.

In a short while the Via Flaminia would turn right and head through Saxa Rubra towards the Apennines. They would reach the Adriatic at Fanum Fortunae, journey north through Ariminum and Ravenna to join the Via Annia, and finally the Via Postumia, which would take them to Aquileia. Seven or eight days' travel usually, using their *diplomata* to requisition fresh horses, not driving them to death. But the times were far from usual. If beasts had to founder, so be it. Perhaps he could make Aquileia in three or four days.

Three or four days out of another three years of life. Even should the vulgar superstition prove to be true, Menophilus did not fear death. Dying was a different thing. The possible pain, squalor, humiliation of the event; those might be difficult to deal with, would test all his resolve. But being dead was nothing. He had been nothing before he was born, and he would be the same after his death.

Having been dead before, he remembered no punishments or pleasures, no sentience at all. It was an area where his Stoicism met the Epicureanism of his friend Gordian. If they could hold to their principles, neither should be afraid to die.

An ordinary journey – like from Rome to Aquileia – would be incomplete if you stopped in the middle, or anywhere short of your destination. But a life was never incomplete, if it was an honourable one.

Was there any honour in killing Vitalianus or Sabinus? Would there be in striking down Maximinus? Could honour be reconciled with unleashing the Goths and Sarmatians into the empire?

A man must do his duty; to himself and his fellow men, to the *Res Publica* and the deity. Maximinus was a tyrant. He was beyond reform or redemption. It was the duty of a good man to free others from his tyranny. As far as the barbarian could, Maximinus acted against the harmony of the Cosmos. The deity would approve his removal.

There was no doubt that killing Maximinus was an honourable act. But the others? Were they too beyond redemption? Perhaps not, but they stood in the way. The world could not be freed from Maximinus unless they were eliminated. Menophilus had given Sabinus a chance, and the offer had not only been rejected, but met with treachery. Sabinus deserved to die. But what of

Vitalianus, or Licinianus the governor of Dacia, or numberless provincials along the Danube? At least, if there were no afterlife, there could be no punishment.

CHAPTER 28

THE EAST
THE TOWN OF CARRHAE

Two Days after the Ides of March, AD238

Priscus, the governor of Mesopotamia, did not appreciate being summoned from his bed well before dawn. Especially not when his bed contained a fifteen-year-old he had bought only the day before. Blond curls, soft white skin, firm thighs and buttocks; everything a man could desire to ease the cares of office. A night of pleasure, and a morning of relaxation, some drinks and poetry, all had been snatched from him. He was tired, and that did not improve his temper.

The false alarms were endless. Once, the dust from a column of Persian cavalry proved on more careful inspection to have been raised by a herd of wild asses circling to frustrate a hungry lion. Usually the reasons were more prosaic: a loose horse in the night, the wandering herds of the tent-dwellers, a lone traveller taking his life in his hands on the highway. The Sassanid spy caught climbing into the town had been revealed under interrogation as a runaway slave apprehended trying to get out. But in the truceless war in the lands between the two rivers nothing could be left to chance.

Priscus must be getting old and slow. He had got up as soon as Sporakes had woken him. With the efficiency of long practice, the bodyguard had helped him arm. They had ridden straight here from the citadel. There had been no delay. Even so, his *familia* were waiting on the battlements of the Gate of Sin.

Health and great joy.

They were all present. His brother Philip, despite the early hour, was immaculate in Roman parade armour. His heavy-lined, serious face would have looked more at home on the Palatine or in the Forum than on the defences of this fly-blown, ill-omened Mesopotamian town. Philip stood with the other two Roman commanders, Julius Julianus and Porcius Aelianus. The Prefects of the two legions in the Province were long-serving officers of equestrian status. Priscus had appointed them to their commands five years previously, after their performances in the eastern war of the late Emperor Alexander.

Health and great joy.

Priscus turned to the three men from Edessa. The portly, bejewelled figure of Manu Bear-blinder was backed by his son Abgar Prince-in-waiting and his old friend Syrmus the Scythian.

Health and great joy.

Priscus greeted Ma'na son of Sanatruq. The

259

young Prince of Hatra had come into the *imperium* as a hostage for the good behaviour of his father's client kingdom, but had proved himself time and again over the years. The same was true of the Hatrene nobleman with him, Wa'el. Priscus trusted them both, as far as he trusted any man.

There were three other men on the roof at the edges of the torchlight: Arruntius, the commander of the auxiliary unit responsible for the gate and this sector of the walls, and Iarhai and Shalamallath, the caravan-protectors. There was no love lost between the latter two. Both *Synodiarchs* had come from the town of Arete to offer the services of their mercenaries. There was only enough money for one contract.

Priscus nodded to each in turn.

'Anything?' Priscus asked.

'Not yet.'

'Is the report credible?'

Arruntius stepped forward. 'The scout has been reliable before.'

'Then we wait.'

'Drink this.' Manu passed Priscus a cup of warmed, spiced wine. 'Very restorative.' He rolled his kohl-lined eyes. 'It might be necessary, given your new purchase.'

'That is most considerate.'

Manu laughed. Philip looked uncomfortable. There had always been something priggish about Priscus' brother. It should have been the other way round. Even for these lands beyond the

260

Euphrates, the Edessenes were notorious for the strictness of their moral code. A woman even suspected of fornication would be stoned to death. And the men, while happy to be named a thief or a murderer, would go for their knives at the merest hint that they enjoyed the natural pleasures offered by boys.

Manu started to sing softly.

There is a boy across the river with a bottom like a peach. Alas I can not swim.

Perhaps it was as well that the Emperor Caracalla had abolished the small kingdom of Edessa, incorporating its territories into the Roman province of Mesopotamia-Osrhoene. If he had inherited from his father, as King the morals of Manu Bearblinder might not have squared with those of his subjects.

'Put out the torches.'

It was dark until their eyes began to adjust. Then they could make out the bulk of the ballistae hidden under their covers, the stepped line of the machicolations, the flat, black expanse of the plain beyond. The sky was beginning to lighten in the east.

Priscus was tired. Cup in both hands, he leant his forearms on the parapet and gazed out. He was in his forty-ninth year, the great climactic. An *Iatrosophist* had told him that if he got past that, most probably he would make it to at least sixty-three. Sophists were just empty words and display. They were all charlatans, whether they claimed medical knowledge or not. Anyway it was more likely he would be killed long before then, either by the Persians, or by a knife-man sent by some Emperor.

If he had been twenty years younger, he would still have been tired. After three years of relentless fighting, anyone would be tired. There had been isolated raids in the two years after Alexander had left the East, but it was news of the Emperor's death that had unleashed the true fury of the Sassanids. Since then the campaigning had been unremitting; few pitched battles, but three long years of unexpected descents, feints, surprise attacks and ambushes. So far, only the major town of Nisibis had been lost. Yet it was a war Priscus knew that his understrength Roman forces could not win. One serious defeat would lead to disaster, the loss of the whole of Mesopotamia, and the opening of the way to the West. Any number of victories meant nothing; the Sassanids could always put another army in the field.

There was a great irony to Priscus defending the eastern borderlands. He had been born out here, in an obscure village called Shahba on the desolate, sandy borders between the provinces of Syria Phoenice and Arabia. Growing up, he had more often spoken Aramaic than Greek or Latin. Unlike his brother, he had no sentimental attachment to the place, none whatsoever. Priscus had worked long and hard to rise in the imperial service, to get away from places like Shahba, get away from the dust and flies, the small-minded, choking censoriousness.

Priscus had a family in Rome. His house on the Caelian was modest, but his son was in the imperial school on the Palatine. The morals of Rome were easy and congenial. His wife was Italian, and seemed unshocked, perhaps relieved, that he had desires outside the marriage bed. He had last seen them in Antioch, three years ago. The boy must be coming up to twelve. Somehow Priscus must see him in the next two years, before he took the *toga virilis*.

'There.'

Priscus followed the pointing arm towards the north-west.

Against the deep purple sky, a thick column of black cloud could be half-seen, some miles away, in the direction of the Temple of Nikal, the bride of Sin.

'They are burning the sanctuary of the Moon Goddess.' There was hatred in young Abgar's tone. 'The Persians have the eyes of goats and the hearts of vipers. They fuck their sisters, their daughters, even their mothers. Disgusting and cruel, they kill their brothers and sons, throw their elderly out to be eaten by the dogs. May Nikal and Sin strike them all dead.'

His father interrupted the diatribe. 'When I was their captive, there was a man called Kirder, a priest, one of those they call a *Mobad*. He was much about the royal court, always whispering in

263

the ear of the Prince Shapur, trying to get near King Ardashir himself. His talk ever was of overthrowing the temples of foreign daemons, founding sacred fires to their god Mazda among the unbelievers.'

There was silence for a time, as the sky grew lighter, and the smoke more evident.

'They come at a bad time,' Shalamallath said. 'In the Spring the shepherds drive their flocks back to the settlements. Many will fall into the hands of the reptiles. There will be hunger if the Persians stay. The beans and pulses must be sown, soon the grain harvested, or the poor will starve.'

It was a pertinent comment. The *Synodiarch* was very tall and thin to the point of desiccation. Perhaps all those years of guarding camel caravans across the sands of the desert had dried him out. However he had come by his physique, Priscus thought that he was no fool.

The sun lifted clear of the distant hills. Most of the easterners blew it a kiss, performed reverence to the risen god. Priscus did not move.

The Sassanid horde was coming down from the north, dividing into two to encircle the town. Priscus could tell that they were all mounted, but not yet make out any individuals. It meant that the heads of the columns were somewhere between thirteen hundred and a thousand paces distant. Not so far that he could not judge that they rode in great numbers.

'They have no infantry or siege train, perhaps

they will burn everything outside the walls, and move on.' Shalamallath was keen to show his astuteness. Iarhai evidently was a man of fewer words.

Priscus was not reassured by the reasoning of Shalamallath. Ladders and mantlets could be quickly constructed out of materials plundered from suburban buildings and groves. By his own estimate, there were at least twenty thousand horsemen. Romans who said the Persians would not fight on foot were fools. There were more than enough to attempt a storm of the town.

Shalamallath and Iarhai had come to Carrhae looking for war, and it had found them. Priscus thought of the man in the cellars. He had not come seeking war. His ship driven by storms, the horses under him ridden until they foundered, he had raced halfway across the world to deliver a message. No one ever had crossed the *imperium* quicker. Instead of a reward, he had been loaded with chains, and thrown in a cell, where he was watched by a mute gaoler.

Priscus had not let the messenger speak to anyone else, had told no one the content of his letter. Instead the governor of Mesopotamia had gone to the agora and bought an expensive new pleasure-slave. A man needed to consider some very important things in his own time, on his own. Priscus detested summoning his *consilium* unless he was fully prepared, had turned the issues over in his own mind. Of course, now that council might never meet. The Sassanids might kill them all and the man in the cell before the staggering news the latter carried could become known or discussed. That would be one less thing for Priscus to worry about.

'The King of Kings,' Manu said.

The Sassanids had halted a little under five hundred paces from the walls. The sunlight glinted off their weapons and armour. Priscus could see bright hues of their costumes and horse trappings, the lighter-coloured spots of their faces. Banners flew above their heads. One was larger than all the others; an enormous rectangle, shimmering yellow, red and violet. It hung from a crossbar topped with a golden orb. It had to be the Drafsh-i-Kavyan, the royal battle flag of the house of Sasan.

'Which rider is Ardashir?' In none of the battles had Priscus yet faced the King of Kings.

'The one with the golden helmet in the shape of an eagle.' His time in captivity had made Manu an expert on the Persians.

'The huge man on the white horse?'

'No, that is his son, Shapur, his helmet resembles a ram. The King of Kings rides next to him on the black.'

'Can you tell the others from their banners?'

'I see the insignia of two other sons of the King of Kings, Ardashir, King of Abrenak, and Ardashir, King of Kerman. There are many great barons – Dehin Varaz, Sasan of house Suren, Sasan Lord of Andegan, Peroz of house Karen, Geliman of Demavend – and many from the court – Manzik Mard Head of Scribes, Papak Master of Ceremonies, Chilrak the Judge, Vardan of the Stables – many others. We should be honoured to have such distinguished visitors.'

'What will they do now?'

'They will sacrifice a ram, then a nobleman will ride to the gate and call on you to surrender.'

'And when we do not?'

'They will try to kill us all.'

'Thank you. Let me think.'

The members of the *consilium* respected his wish. Along the walls on both sides, Roman soldiers jeered at the Persians. The sun was warm on Priscus' right cheek. His eyes followed the foreign priests about their ceremony. Before they had finished, he had made up his mind.

'Manu, Syrmus, I am not minded to let the one who approaches the gate return from his task.'

'He will not come very close,' Manu said.

Priscus smiled. 'Are the Bear-blinder and the Scythian no longer artists with their chosen weapon?'

'Bardaisan of Edessa was the artist,' Manu said, 'we were his acolytes.'

'Use the ballista to be sure of the range,' Syrmus said.

'No,' Priscus said. 'I do not want them to know about our new ballistae just yet. It must be down to the skill of you two. Choose a position, and conceal yourselves. Wait for my order. I will shout the name of your old master.'

'As you command, My Lord.' For the first time, Manu spoke not in Greek but Syriac, as he took his leave.

Waiting, Priscus tried not to think about the prisoner in the cellar, and all that his presence implied.

'Rider coming.'

'Which one is it?'

'Sasan, Lord of Andegan.' Ma'na Prince of Hatra knew the Sassanids almost as well as Manu.

The nobleman rode a magnificent Nisean stallion. A chestnut, it had to stand at least sixteen hands tall. He was no closer than a hundred paces when he reined in his horse. It shook its head, pawed the ground.

The Persian took off his helmet, the better to be heard.

'Who commands here?'

Priscus climbed up onto the parapet, bracing himself with a hand on a merlon.

'I am Gaius Julius Priscus, governor of the province of Mesopotamia-Osrhoene. I command here.'

The Persian seemed unsurprised. 'The King of Kings Ardashir bids me tell you to heat the water and prepare his food. He would eat and bathe in his town of Carrhae tonight.'

'Bardaisan!' Priscus shouted. 'Bardaisan!'

Along the wall, off to the left, Manu and Syrmus rose up, drew and shot in one fluid movement. The first arrow took the Persian in the shoulder, the second full in the chest. The Nisean stallion wheeled, and the dying man crashed to the ground.

A roar of outrage came from the Persian ranks. 'Well,' Priscus said, 'Andegan needs a new lord.'

CHAPTER 29

THE NORTHERN FRONTIER
SIRMIUM

Two Days after the Ides of March, AD238

'The men are ready, Emperor.'

Maximinus did not acknowledge the officer. His gaze remained fixed on the fragile alabaster vase cradled in his great scarred hands. The first two days after the news had come, to get oblivion from his thoughts, he had soaked himself in wine. Neither the alcohol, nor the soft murmurings of his secretary Apsines had done any good. This morning he had stopped drinking, summoned the *consilium*, and ordered the troops to assemble on the Campus Martius outside the town.

'Emperor.'

Maximinus lifted the vase to his lips, kissed it, and with great delicacy placed the ashes of Paulina in the travelling case by the throne. He looked around the imperial pavilion as if it was all strange to him, as if he had never before seen its interior or the men assembled there.

The sacred fire burnt low. Beyond, in the purple

gloom, stood the serried ranks of the imperial friends. To the fore was Flavius Vopiscus, next to him Faltonius Nicomachus, the governor of Pannonia Inferior. A pace behind them were the great equestrian officers: Anullinus the Praetorian Prefect, Volo the commander of the *frumentarii*, Julius Capitolinus Prefect of the 2nd Parthian Legion. Further back still, merging into the shadows were the commanders of individual units: Sabinus Modestus of the heavy cavalry, Florianus of the Britons, Iotapianus of the Emesenes, and many others.

Maximinus studied each of them closely, letting nothing go unnoticed, not the way they held themselves, nor the flicker of their eyes. They were all dressed for war. Maximinus wondered if he could trust any of his so-called *amici*. Capitolinus owned an estate in Africa. The cousin of Modestus was a traitor. Iotapianus had betrayed his kinsman Alexander. Anullinus had murdered that ineffectual Emperor and his aged mother, cut off their heads, desecrated their corpses. While he had been drinking, Flavius Vopiscus had issued orders as if he, not Maximinus, wore the diadem. Old Tiberius had been right: when you sat on the throne of the Caesars you held a wolf by the ears.

'Father, we should go.'

Maximinus did not look at his son, but stood, massive and powerful. Perhaps his mere presence would overawe the *consilium*. At least he could trust the soldiers. *Enrich the soldiers, ignore everyone else.*

271

Outside the rain had stopped. The ground was mud, but it was a fine spring day. The sun shone, and a brisk wind snapped at the standards above the massed ranks.

Maximinus ascended the tribunal. His son and the *amici* fell in behind him.

The troops waited in silence.

Maximinus felt a great weariness. The gods knew, he had never wanted any of this. Everything he had done, everything he would do, none of it was for himself. It was all for duty, for Rome.

Apsines had written a speech for him, full of fine sentiments and balanced cadences. It was in his hands, but he was not going to read it. Better to speak from the heart. One soldier in front of many.

'Fellow soldiers, the Africans have broken faith. When did they ever keep it?'

The troops laughed, as he had known they would.

'They have acclaimed the two Gordians as Emperors. One is so broken with old age that he can not rise, the other so wasted with debauchery that exhaustion serves him for old age. Terrible enemies to have – an old man close to death, and a drunkard too befuddled to crawl from one dining couch to another.'

Not the sophisticated rhetoric of Apsines, but it pleased the soldiers.

'And what fearsome army do they bring against you? Not the Germans, whom we have defeated on many occasions, nor the Sarmatians who regularly

272

come to beg for peace. No, they lead the Carthaginians! Men whose hard training is in rhythmic dances, choruses and witty speeches.'

He paused, letting the spring breeze chase the wine fumes from his head.

'No one should be disturbed by the news from Rome. Vitalianus was caught and murdered by a deceitful trick. Everyone knows the fickle and cowardly nature of the Roman plebs. They only have to see two or three armed soldiers to be pushing and trampling on each other, as each man runs away to save his skin, without a thought for the common danger.

'And if that was not treachery enough, what of our glorious Senate? We fight for their safety, the safety of their wives and children, and how do they repay us? They declare us *hostes*, enemies of the *Res Publica*. We are to be denied fire and water. It should be no surprise. Our discipline offends them. They prefer the Gordiani who share their degenerate habits. They are hostile to my rule because it is sober and strict, but welcome the Gordiani, and you all know the scandals of their lives.

'These are the kind of people against whom we are at war, if war is the right name for it. I am convinced that we only have to set foot in Italy for all of them to hold out olive branches and bring their children to us, begging for mercy and falling at our feet.

'Tomorrow I will lead a flying column of cavalry

to the west. We will go by the Savus Valley, and seize the mountain passes. The next day, the Pannonian legions, in light marching order, will break camp. They will take the easier road through the valley of the Dravus. Flavius Vopiscus will have the command. Four days hence, the main body, under Julius Capitolinus, will follow them. The Prefect of the Camp Domitius already has gone ahead to secure our supplies.'

Maximinus wondered how to end. *Enrich the soldiers, ignore everyone else.*

'This will be a good campaign; easy fighting and vast rewards. I grant every man in the army a year's pay. When we have taken Rome, I grant you the property of our enemies, the wealth of all the Senate. You can take it, and enjoy it without restraint.'

As the cheers rang across the parade ground, Maximinus turned and climbed down from the tribunal. His son and *amici* jostled after him. Flavius Vopiscus was to the fore. While Maximinus had been drinking, Vopiscus had ordered Domitius ahead to gather supplies. Was that commendable foresight, or a dangerous assertion of independence? Paulina had been right; an Emperor had no friends, could not trust those closest to him.

Maximinus trudged back towards the gates of the city. He had made no mention of Sabinus and Potens. With the Urban Cohorts and the Watch at their command, they might yet crush the revolt in Rome unaided. It made no odds. When he arrived, he would keep his promise to the soldiers. The Senate was a reeking stable, mired in long generations of filth. He would scour that building, scour it remorselessly.

A woman stood in the gateway. Tall and withered, dishevelled in her attire, Ababa the Druidess did not stand aside from the Emperor.

'Maximinus.' Her face was deathly pale, like some wild revenant. Twice more she cried out his name. She said no more, but fell suddenly, as if a sacrificial beast stunned by the axe.

Maximinus knelt in the mud. He bent over. She tried to speak. He put his ear to her lips. '*Succurrite*,' she murmured. 'Help me.'

There was nothing to be done. Maximinus was alone in the roadway. The breath of life had left her.

CHAPTER 30

AFRICA
CARTHAGE

Three Days after the Ides of March, AD238

G ordian thanked the gods his hangover was mild. Even so, without the training of philosophy, it was doubtful that he could have had the discipline to withstand the wild swings of fortune the messengers had brought in one morning.

He had been having a late breakfast with Parthenope and Chione. Parthenope thought she was pregnant. It seemed to have made her more than usually lustful. The jealousy of Chione had prompted her to outrageous inventiveness in the night. Gordian had had no need of powdered lizards or oysters. When the messenger came up from the harbour, his happiness had been complete.

Had there ever been such a friend as Menophilus? He was Laelius to Gordian's Scipio, Hephaestion to his Alexander. Under the guidance of Menophilus, the Senate had elected a Board of Twenty to Defend the *Res Publica* and the rule of the Gordiani. Among them were Menophilus himself,

276

Gordian's reliable friend Valerian, and his father's close *amicus* old Appius Claudius Julianus. All the Twenty were men of status or talent. It could not be more gratifying that Senators of every shade of opinion, from the patrician Balbinus to the *novus homo* Pupienus and the Cynic idealist Gallicanus, had come together. All the factions in the Senate were united in loyalty to Gordian and his father. The dispositions for the prosecution of the war could not be in better hands. The urgings of Menophilus that the new Emperors hurry to Rome were unnecessary. Gordian had called for a drink. Parthenope and Chione were not going anywhere, and he always felt vigorous and keen in the morning, never more than when he was a touch hungover. The exact details of the military commands, which of the Twenty were going where, could be studied later.

No man appreciated being interrupted in the worship of Venus. Outside the curtain, Valens, his father's chamberlain, was most insistent. There was someone who had to talk to him. Gordian had pulled on a tunic. The girls had not bothered to cover themselves. The young officer who entered had barely glanced at the pulchritude on display. It was Geminius, one of the tribunes who had gone to Lambaesis with Arrian. He was drawn and tired, filthy from the road. Seeing him, Gordian had known the news was bad. His supposition was quickly confirmed. Four days ago Capelianus had escaped from house arrest. Numidia and the 3rd

Legion were back under his command. Arrian was a prisoner, in chains. With his forces in light marching order, Capelianus could be outside Carthage in the next five or six days.

Gordian had sent runners to summon the most trusted of the *consilium* to attend, not in the main Basilica, but the small audience chamber. Valens was despatched to request the presence of his father. Sending the girls away, Gordian had asked for a barber. This would be the hardest thing he had ever told his father. He would do so clean shaven and sober.

As the razor slid across his throat, he thought of his friend in chains. This was all his fault. *A wise man will not engage in politics*. He had known the risks, to himself, to those he loved. But he had had to intervene. Paul the Chain would have killed Mauricius. His own death and that of his father would have followed. Even if Maximinus had not condemned them at once, living in fear was insupportable. His actions were justified. The aim of life was pleasure, and fear made that impossible. Now he must face the consequences with courage.

Clad in the formal but modest white toga of a Senator, no purple robes or radiate crown or any such symbol of autocracy, he walked with Geminius to the Basilica.

They were all assembled. His father sat on the throne next to his own. He was backed by Valens and Brennus the bodyguard, and a line of secretaries.

The councillors were seated in a semi-circle; Sabinianus, Mauricius, Phillyrio, Vocula the Praetorian Prefect, Suillius of the 3rd Legion, Alfenus of the Urban Cohort, the young tribune Pedius. A small group to fight for an empire. But in war courage and unity counted for more than numbers.

Standing by the sacred fire, Gordian dismissed the secretaries. When they had left, he told the news, unadorned, all of it, the good and the bad. Only then did he sit down next to his father.

'I am sorry, Father.'

'There is nothing to apologize for.'

The aged Emperor betrayed no emotion. He asked the *consilium* to give them advice, freely spoken in accordance with the *mos maiorum*.

'The Emperors must go to Rome,' Sabinianus said. 'Menophilus requested as much from the start. He does so again in this despatch, knowing nothing of events in Numidia. As your governor of Africa Proconsularis, I will stay, delay Capelianus as long as possible. We have few troops. Some auxiliaries and a couple of detachments of legionaries and men from the Urban Cohorts do not amount to an army. Capelianus has both more auxiliaries and the main body of the 3rd Legion. It is immaterial. The fate of the empire has never been decided in Africa. I can defend the walls of Carthage for a time, but I will have a fast ship ready in the harbour.' Sabinianus grinned. 'Horatius held the bridge, but he survived. We will all meet again in the eternal city.'

279

'No.' Gordian was decisive. 'The war will be won if we contain Maximinus in northern Italy, and the provinces come over. If they hear we have lost Africa, no governor will join us. I will remain in Carthage, and my father will sail to Rome.'

Lean and tanned, Phillyrio got to his feet. 'Let Gordian the Younger hold Carthage. I am an African. All my life, I have served here on the frontier. I will gather the troops along the borders, raise allies from the tribes beyond. Nuffuzi, chief of the Cinithii, is bound to us by oath. His son Mirzi is our hostage. We can trap Capelianus before the walls of Carthage.'

Overawed by the company, and knowing his contribution would be unwelcome, Alfenus, commander of the 13th Urban Cohort asked permission to speak. 'The city is not prepared for a siege. There are no supplies laid in, no artillery. The walls are in bad repair, and they are too long to defend with the soldiers available. Unaccustomed to privation, the citizens could not be relied upon.'

The *consilium* was silent. Gordian's eyes followed the tendrils of smoke curling up from the sacred fire. *What is terrible is easy to endure.* Philosophy existed to offer consolation.

'We can not withstand a siege, and we are unable to abandon Africa, so it must be open battle,' Gordian said. 'Things may not be as bad as they first seem. Between the 13th Urban Cohort and the detachment of the Legion we have a thousand veterans in Carthage. Suillius, will your men stand against their fellow legionaries?'

'They are soldiers,' Suillius said, 'they will obey orders.'

Gordian nodded. 'The 1st Flavian Cohort from Utica and the 15th Emesene from Ammaedara can be here long before Capelianus; another thousand auxiliaries. There are five hundred in our Praetorian Guard. They are newly raised, but as Iuvenes, they have had military training. Combined, the Equites Singulares Augusti and the Scouts here with Phillyrio number several hundred. The core of our army will consist of nearly three thousand disciplined troops. Thousands of levies can be raised from the city. Hunting spears can kill men as well as animals. Weapons can be taken from the temples, blacksmiths can make more, carpenters provide shields.'

Not everyone looked convinced. Sabinianus and Suillius seemed particularly dubious. Gordian pressed on.

'Lambaesis is the headquarters of the legion, but many of its men are scattered, one Cohort is here, several more spread along the frontier. Those in southern Numidia are far away, the ones in Africa Proconsularis summoned by Phillyrio will join our cause. When battle is joined, Capelianus will be lucky to have two thousand legionaries. Numbers will be on our side.'

Gordian had omitted all mention of the auxiliaries with Capelianus in Numidia, but his intention was to persuade.

'If Phillyrio marches hard, and Capelianus does not, things may turn out better still; our army bolstered by thousands of hard fighting men from the frontier.'

He could think of nothing else to put heart into them.

'So, let us first outfit a ship to take my father to Rome, then turn our minds to putting an army in the field.'

Gordian the Elder broke the ensuing silence. 'I have never been more proud of my son. Never has an Emperor had more loyal friends. It shall be as my son says, but I will not leave for Rome.'

He ignored the babble of objections. 'I am old, past my eightieth year. I will not be parted from my son. Should he fall, why would I wish to live? The world holds nothing else for me. If the gods prove unkind, we will travel to Hades together. But come, let us turn to practicalities. *We won't go down to the House of Death, not yet, not until our day arrives.*'

Like the Romans of old, men of stern virtue, they talked of conscription, munitions and the movement of troops.

Gordian looked at his father with love and admiration. No irresolution, no talk of portents or soothsayers, instead calm courage. Old or not, such a man was born to be Emperor.

It struck him that his father had made no mention of Maecia Faustina or his young grandson. It was for the best. They were well out of it. Should things go wrong, they might survive in Rome, live on in obscurity.

He shrugged off the ill-omened thoughts of disaster. *We won't go down to the House of Death, not yet, not until our day arrives.*

CHAPTER 31

THE EAST
CARRHAE

Three Days after the Ides of March, AD*238*

Even in the dark before dawn the black shape of the eastern hills could be seen between the purple of the sky and the purple of the plain. All night Priscus and his *consilium* had watched from the battlements of the Nisibis Gate. At first a ring of white lights had marked where campfires and torches burnt. They clustered thickly where the pavilion of the King of Kings had been pitched, about five hundred paces down the road. The men on the gate had waited for the outcry, for the shadows flitting across the lights, the shouts of horror. Nothing. Through the long hours, as the fires burnt low, and the stars shone brighter, there was no alarm. Hope all gone, they remained at their post as the stars wheeled and dimmed.

'The Mazda-worshipping Ardashir will come,' Manu said.

It was best to talk of what might happen, not to speak of the failure of their first plan, the bitter disappointment of either loss or betrayal. It was best not to wonder what had happened to Shalamallath and his men.

'Divine Ardashir, King of Aryans and non-Aryans, of the race of the gods, son of King Papak, of the house of Sasan; the very pretentions of his titles impel him to come.'

'Race of the gods, my arse,' Abgar snorted, interrupting his father. 'Illegitimate by-blow of a wandering mercenary, raised by a shoemaker, he murdered his own brother, killed his rightful overlord, threw the infant son of his King from the arch at Ctesiphon.'

'Traitor and murderer he may be, but his own hubris will deliver him to us,' Priscus said, then quickly adding, 'Of course, only if the gods are willing.'

Sporakes and some of the other guards brought baskets of food up onto the fighting top. In silence, the members of the council sat, leaning against the parapet, drinking watered wine, eating warm flat bread and hard-boiled eggs.

Rather than dwell on what had gone wrong, Priscus reviewed the defences of Carrhae. There were many things that he had not had time to have his men do: dig pits with concealed stakes or flammable oil on the approaches, forge caltrops to strew under the feet of the enemy, construct cranes to swing boulders over the walls and release onto their heads. Circumstances forbade other measures, such as poisoning the wells and burning the surrounding villages and farms. The inhabitants

285

would still have to live here afterwards, those who were not dead or enslaved.

Yet, over the winter, since the fall of Nisibis, much had been achieved. Stockpiled along the wall-walks were containers of oil and sand; close by the fires were laid ready to heat them. Leaning against the battlements were pitchforks to push away siege ladders, axes to cut the ropes of grapnels, stones and pieces of broken statuary to drop. And there were more men to wield them. Two thousand locals had been conscripted, equipped, and, as far as possible, trained throughout the short daylight hours of winter. Above all, there were the new ballistae. Sixteen of them, two atop each gate, with crews seconded from the legions. Range markers of white painted stones stretched away down each road, at intervals of fifty paces.

The same had been done at the other strategic towns that secured control of Mesopotamia, at Singara, Resaina, and Edessa. All this while creating the nucleus of a mobile army. Just four-and-a-half thousand so far, but it was a start. The fledgling force was posted at Batnae in the west of the province. To guard the crossings of the Euphrates, Priscus had announced. Or, as anyone with any intelligence must realize, to withdraw over the river, when the rest of the province fell.

Everything had cost a great deal. Nothing had been forthcoming from the imperial treasury. All was earmarked for Maximinus' northern wars. Priscus had borrowed large sums from Manu. When the Bear-blinder would ask for a favour, and what form it would take, remained to be seen. It would be nothing trivial, Manu had been raised as the heir to a throne.

The plan of Carrhae itself was a rough circle bounded by a dry ditch backed by a rampart with a mud-brick wall on top. The wall, crenellated, with square towers at intervals, was pierced by six gates and two posterns. The circuit, measuring more than four thousand paces, was too long to defend easily. The irregularity of its layout meant not all lines of potential attack could be enfiladed. The citadel in the centre of the southern half of the city, and the legionary camp in the extreme south-east offered defensive strongpoints, but there were not enough troops to man them as well as the outer wall.

The light was gathering. Soon the sun would be up. The Sassanid camp was stirring. The smell of the dried dung from their fires drifted across. There were a great many of them.

Priscus had not been greatly cheered by considering the defences of Carrhae. The thought of the messenger chained beneath the governor's palace worried him further. He had still told no one. There was no point, not when they were about to fight for their lives. Let everyone concentrate on that. But what, in the names of all the gods, had possessed the Gordiani? Both father and son were voluptuaries, but neither was stupid. Yes, Maximinus was a tyrant, his rule a disaster. Either or both the

Gordiani would make a better Emperor than a blood-thirsty, half-barbarian Thracian with an obsession for fighting unwinnable wars in the North. But to start a revolt in Africa of all places?

And yet? Maximinus was hated. Rich and poor alike, Romans and provincials, everyone hated him. Everyone except the soldiers of his northern army: they were said to still love him. It was because he had doubled the troops' pay, and because he was with them, not some other army. They alone could not keep him on the throne. The reign could not last long. Priscus had flirted with revolt before, back in Samosata, when his friend Serenianus was alive and commanded the two legions in Cappadocia. New men on the throne could end the futile campaigns beyond Rhine and Danube, could turn their attentions to Ardashir and the East. Prompt adherence to a new regime would bring rewards. But declaration for failed pretenders brought nothing but death.

A hard choice had to be made, and with little delay. But one thing at a time. Defend this town. Live through this siege. Time enough afterwards. Priscus prided himself on a cold, hard pragmatism.

Maz-da! Maz-da!

The sun crested the distant hills, and the Sassanids, bellies to the ground like snakes, hailed the daily epiphany.

'Here comes Ardashir.'

The King of Kings was mounted on the same black stallion. He was wearing the same gilded helmet fashioned like an eagle. Long streamers of purple cloth fluttered from his armour. His son Shapur rode on his right hand, another son, Ardeshir of Abrenak, was on his left. Behind them flew the battle standard of the house of Sasan. It was carried by five *Mobads*. The Sassanids claimed it had been embroidered by some deity before the dawn of time. After the Drafsh-i-Kavyan came a dozen noblemen, among them Dehin Varaz, Garshasp the Lion, Zik Zabrigan, and Geliman of Demavend.

After the shooting of the Lord of Andegan, Priscus had doubted that the Persian monarch would come. But Manu had assured him Ardashir had no choice. At the start of any siege, the King of Kings had to ride close to the walls. It showed his contempt for the weapons of the besieged, and encouraged his warriors. Not to do so, would reveal the King a coward, and the Sassanids would not follow such a man into battle, would not bow down and grovel in the dirt before his boots.

'It is best if his charger paws the ground, and calls out.'

Priscus went over to the *ballistarii*, who waited by their two shrouded charges. Under the covers, the slides were already wound back, the torsion springs tight. Priscus gave the men the watchwords: *Decus et Tutamen.*

Honour and Shield, they replied.

'On my words, remove the tarpaulins. May the gods guide your aim.'

'A coin for a shave, Prefect?'

Priscus smiled. 'Kill the reptile, and I will shower you with gold.'

Ardashir, or one with him, would shoot a ceremonial arrow over the walls. Some archers could send an arrow great distances with incredible accuracy. Both Syrmus the Scythian and Manu could in their youth. The latter had saved the late King Abgar on the hunting field; two arrows, one into each eye of the charging beast. Since then he had been known as Bear-blinder. Men like that could do amazing feats, but for most bowmen to be sure of clearing the walls, they needed to be within a hundred and fifty paces.

Priscus had done everything that he could to prevent the news of his new *ballistae* being spread abroad. He prayed he had done enough. The next few moments would tell.

The wind was rising in the east. It whipped the dust raised by the hooves of their horses in front of the Persians.

The cavalcade passed the first whitewashed stones; four hundred paces, extreme range.

'Come on, you goat-eyed cocksuckers.'

No one took any notice of the obscenities mouthed by Abgar the Prince-in-waiting. No one, not even Abgar, took their eyes off the horsemen.

Three hundred and fifty paces.

'Arses like cisterns . . .'

Three hundred.

'Fuck your mothers . . .'

Two hundred and fifty.

'Silence in the ranks,' Priscus said.

Two hundred.

'Decus et Tutamen!'

Priscus and his *concilium* ducked or scrambled to the sides as the *ballistarii* hauled the covers off the catapults. The well-oiled bearings made hardly a sound. The senior artillerymen aimed.

Click-slide-thump. Two bolts accelerated away with superhuman force.

The Sassanids saw the missiles. They sawed on their reins. There was no time. One bolt transfixed the mount of the Prince of Abrenak. The horse collapsed, and young Ardashir pitched over its neck. The other sliced a hand's breadth past the head of the King of Kings. It punched through the chest of Geliman of Demavend, knocked him from his horse, impaled him in the ground.

Clack, clack went the metallic ring of the ratchets as the machines were rearmed. Faster and faster; *clack, clack, clack.*

Chaos down on the road. Horses milling. Riders shouting.

The sliders locked back, ready to shoot.

Ardashir had wheeled his horse, was spurring back the way he had come. A cloud of dust puffed up from the riders surrounding him.

The *ballistarii* placed new bolts in the grooves.

Garshasp the Lion was pulling the unhorsed Prince up behind him.

'Decus et Tutamen!'

291

A lone horseman was galloping flat out towards the gate – Shapur.

Click-slide-thump. Again, two iron-tipped shadows sped away. They vanished into the haze of the retreating King's retinue.

Shapur spun his horse around, drew his bow, and put an arrow in the wind.

Clack, clack. The noise of the ratchets was oddly inconsequential. Priscus followed the flight of the arrow. It arced high, then seemed to be coming down straight at him.

Shapur was riding hard back down towards the camp.

The arrow appeared to gain speed as it got nearer.

Priscus forced himself not to flinch.

The arrow shrieked by, and vanished behind into the town.

The road outside was empty, except for Geliman, the Lord of Demavend, pinned to the ground like an insect.

CHAPTER 32

ROME
THE PANTHEON

Three Days after the Ides of March, AD*238*

To be led into the midst of the brethren, in sackcloth and ashes, a compound of disgrace and horror, and before everyone, the elders, the widows, and all the virtuous, to grovel for their tears, clasping their knees, licking their footprints. The die-cutter was not sure he could bear the humiliation.

Twice he had been demoted to the status of a Hearer, denied instruction, made to stand by the door and plead for the prayers of the brothers and sisters as they went in and out of the building. That had been shame enough. Those punishments had been for the sin of fornication. Again he had to confess to the weakness of the flesh, but now he had broken one of the commandments. In the Street of the Sandal-makers he had tried to take a man's life. It was four years since they had made the sign over him and put the salt in his mouth and he had become an Apprentice. Four years of fasting and prayer, of being watched and judged, and he was no nearer being admitted to the Gathering. Was anything worth such trials?

Yet, if the Elders were right, the alternative was an eternity of suffering. Long ago, Hippolytus had told him what lay in store, and the words had stayed with him over the years. To those who had done well, everlasting enjoyment should be given; while to the lovers of evil should be given never ending punishment. The unquenchable and unending fire awaited the latter, and a terrible fiery worm that did not die and that did not destroy the body but continually burst forth from the body with unceasing pain. No sleep will give them rest, no night will soothe them, no death will deliver them from punishment.

Even with his limp, it was not a long walk from the Subura to the Pantheon. The die-cutter was not sure he was ready. Nevertheless, he went around to the back of the temple, but, at the last moment, hesitated outside the Basilica of Neptune.

Since the fight, he had not attended any meetings, and had put off seeing his Instructor. Still, Africanus was a mild man. Far gentler than his previous instructor Hippolytus. Although the details eluded him, the die-cutter had been unsurprised when the latter had been cast out from the Gathering. Not that it had spared Hippolytus arrest by the authorities. It was a wonder that Africanus had not been taken. Membership of the Gathering aside, Africanus was a man of prominence, wealthy and cultured, head of an imperial library, and his association with Mamaea, mother of the last Emperor, might have been enough to bring him to the attention of the regime of Maximinus.

The die-cutter summoned his resolve, and went into the Basilica.

The great hall of the library was crowded; groups of rich men deep in obscure discussion, serious scholars surrounded by papyri, slave copyists hard at work. Dressed in clean but plain clothes, the die-cutter might pass for one of the latter, but he worried that he looked out of place. He asked an attendant if Africanus could see him, and loitered, trying to look inconspicuous.

Africanus was a tall man, with the dark complexion of his Syrian origin. He arrived trailing an entourage of secretaries, but did not appear put out to see the humble petitioner. They greeted each other formally, but without intimacy, employing all the three names of a citizen. Dismissing his slaves, Africanus led the die-cutter to a private study, all the while loudly talking about the possibility that one Serenus might bequest his books – sixty-two thousand volumes! – to the library.

When the door was shut, and they were alone, Africanus' manner changed.

'News has come from the mines of Sardinia,' Africanus said. 'Unable to perform his duties in his confinement, Pontianus has stepped down.'

In his excitement, the librarian failed to notice how the die-cutter flinched at the name of Pontianus.

'He has done it for the good of the Gathering,

295

so a new man can be elected Bishop of Rome. In his wisdom and holiness, he has been reconciled with his fellow prisoner Hippolytus, brought him back to the true teaching. Praise be to God.'

They prayed together, arms outstretched as if they were crucified. Africanus' eyes gazed up, through the ceiling to the heavens. As an Apprentice, the die-cutter kept his down to the ground.

'You have been missed,' Africanus said.

'I have sinned.'

'To be an Apprentice is a trial of faith, more precious than gold which is tried by fire.'

'Father, will you hear my confession? To the Lord I will accuse myself of iniquity.'

And the die-cutter told him almost everything, the minor failings, the nights with Caenis, the attempt on a man's life; everything except his treacherous words when Pontianus was arrested.

When it was done, Africanus considered.

'We are taught to observe all things which God has commanded, and undertake to live accordingly. The flesh is weak, but a prostitute is neither a virgin nor a married woman, there is no adultery. You did not kill a man, but it was your intention. That is a grave sin. Yet in mitigation, you intervened to protect the weak. You are contrite.'

The die-cutter waited.

'You will not be brought into the Gathering in sackcloth to make public confession, nor will you be reduced to standing by the doors as a Hearer. Your instruction will continue. But you must pray and fast for twenty days. No meat, eggs, cheese or milk, no wine, nothing until sunset. And you must undergo another exorcism.'

The die-cutter was weak with relief.

Africanus waved his thanks away. 'You are a lustful man.' The Instructor's tone became less stern, more avuncular. 'There is help for that. Rue, cress and lettuce calm physical desires. Chew the roasted seeds of the Chaste-tree after your meal. After your penance, nothing is more efficacious than drinking wine in which a red mullet has been drowned. All were created by the Lord for our service.'

Walking back to the tenement in which he lived, the die-cutter pondered the cost of red mullet. All men were equal before God, but not all could afford expensive seafood. Lettuce and cress were more affordable. Christ had worked with the fisher-men, but there was nothing in the Gospels of him drowning red mullet in wine.

CHAPTER 33

THE NORTHERN FRONTIER
THE SMALL TOWN OF SALDIS IN
THE SAVUS VALLEY

Four Days after the Ides of March, AD238

Maximinus eventually had fallen asleep, despite the howling of his son's pack of hounds. They should have been silent, exhausted after the long day's run. He should never have let Maximus bring them.

Sometimes when he was very tired, after some effort of endurance, when finally he could lie down and rest, his body found it hard to accept. It ticked like a cooling stove. His heart thumped, and his muscles twitched and jumped. And then, when his resentment against those who were sound asleep had passed, he could think with a feverish clarity.

Succurrite, the Druid woman had whispered. He could no more help Ababa than anyone else. He had not been able to help Micca or Tynchanius. He had not been able to help Paulina. He was Emperor, vice-regent of the gods on earth, his will was law, and he had been unable to save those he loved, or even some barbarian priestess.

Maximinus, three times Ababa had said his name before she died. Flavius Vopiscus had been unable to hide his anxiety. The Senator had clutched at the hidden amulet he thought no one knew that he wore around his neck. What would the superstitions of Vopiscus have made of the portent? Maximinus had been on the throne for three years. Were they all the gods had allotted? Or might it mean three generations would wear the purple? Or some other triad as yet unimagined?

When he woke, it was silent. The room smelt of the waxed canvas of his travelling cloak. It was very dark, but somehow he knew it would soon be dawn. His thighs and back ached. He stretched, his huge frame overlapping the bed, and reviewed the previous day.

They had taken the more direct, although ultimately harder route. They had crossed the meandering rivers, the Savus, the Dreinos, and the Savus again, passing through riverside settlements of no fame. At times the road was built up above floodplains, where flights of duck and geese arrowed away.

Maximinus had all the cavalry with him; the cataphracts in their mail and scale, the loose-robed Moors, the Parthians and Persians with their headbands and voluminous trousers, the uniformed Roman auxiliaries, and the barbarians furnished by the recent treaties, both Sarmatians and Germans. Back in Sirmium, Vopiscus had objected to the inclusion of the latter. The Emperor Vespasian had rejected barbarian aid during civil war. Maximinus had pointed out that Vespasian had reigned before the age of iron and rust.

Among the Germans rode the young hostage that Maximinus had seen when setting out to fight the Iazyges. He had taken the son of King Isangrim as an omen that his armies would reach the northern ocean. That had not happened yet, but the purposes of the gods were slow. Maximinus liked the look of the tall youth. There was something about him that reminded Maximinus of himself.

They had left Sirmium before dawn, and halted at this undistinguished place in the Metubarbis marsh well after dark. Dozens of riders had fallen behind. Some had straggled in during the night, but many more would be left in their wake before they reached their destination. It was vital to take Emona, the first town in Italy, then cross the Alps to hold the Passes on the far side, before they could be closed by the rebels.

Somehow, with Vitalianus dead, Maximinus had little faith in the abilities of Sabinus and Potens to restore the position in Rome. If the gods willed they did, so much the better. But it was not to be relied upon.

After this headlong rush, when they descended the Alps, any number of the horses would be broken down, most never fit for service again. The north Italian plain was broad and fertile, remounts could be gathered while they waited for the infantry. Having dealt with Corvinus, the brigand whose estates dominated the mountains, Domitius should already be requisitioning horseflesh as well as provisions.

Vopiscus had ordered the Prefect of the Camp ahead without consulting Maximinus. Admittedly Maximinus had been drinking, but the assumption of power was a concern. No one knew better than Maximinus that he had only acceded to the throne because Vopiscus had put him there. Sometimes Maximinus wondered if his acclamation by the recruits had been as spontaneous as it had seemed. Certainly the response of the Triumvirate had been more than prompt. Vopiscus, Honoratus and Catius Clemens were capable men, and needed watching. Once you have made one Emperor, you might be tempted to create another.

At least there were no Senators with the cavalry. All the officers were from the equestrian order. Some of them, mainly those from obscure families, still had some ancestral virtue. To the best the *mos maiorum* was not just a figure of speech.

The imperial secretaries were all equestrians. Maximinus smiled. The ride would be hard on those intellectuals from the chanceries. They had insisted on accompanying him. The work of government did not cease when the Emperor was on campaign. Although how they expected him to find time to receive petitions and hear court cases he could not imagine.

It was still quiet. Far out in the marsh frogs croaked; *brekekekex, brekekekex*.

Maximinus got out of his camp bed, and used the chamber pot. Hearing him, Javolenus came in with some food. Maximinus told him to bring his armour.

Having washed his hands and face in cold water, Maximinus sat down stiffly on the bed. His constitution was strong, but he had lead a hard life, and was nearly sixty. He took the phial of *Mithridatium* out of its box, and swallowed some. The taste was unpleasant. Eating bread and cheese, he sent his thoughts scouting ahead.

On the other side of the mountains, once the infantry had reached him, the combined force would advance to Aquileia. The city in north-eastern Italy was the key to the campaign. From there he could move down the shore of the Adriatic. It was the obvious move, and the rebels, if they had any wit, would make some attempt to defend the roads across the Apennines. Alternatively, he could cross the plains, and take the Via Aurelia along the west coast. Again, if circumstances permitted, he could remain in Aquileia until reinforcements arrived over the Alps from Germany and the north-west. Then he could launch armies down both routes at once. It troubled him that the only officer of sufficient stature to lead the other expedition was Flavius Vopiscus. If only his son were a real man. But to entrust anything of importance to Maximus was inconceivable.

Javolenus reappeared, and Maximinus stood. As his bodyguard hung his cuirass on his shoulders, buckled the two halves tight together, Maximinus' eyes rested on the white jar in its travelling case. Paulina had not been responsible for all the happiness in his life. He had been happy as a child. His father had been a big, silent man. He had not used his belt on them more than was necessary. His mother had been somewhat less stern. As she worked, she would tell them the fables of Aesop, although less for entertainment than the morals. *Do not get above yourself, beware false friends, never be drawn into dispute with the powerful*; all the eternal resignation that made peasant life bearable. Maximinus could remember his favourites almost perfectly. A fox elected King was being carried in a litter. Deciding to test him, Zeus sent a beetle. True to his nature, the fox leapt out, and in defiance of all propriety and regal conduct jumped about attempting to catch it.

'Stand aside!'

Outside his son's voice was more petulant than ever.

'Enter.'

Maximus was red in the face, crying. How had the gods given him such a child?

'Father . . .' Maximus could not get the words out for sobbing.

'Control yourself. You are a grown man. You are Caesar.'

303

'My hounds . . .'

Maximinus waited.

'My hounds are dead.'

That explained the agreeable silence.

'All of them. They must have been poisoned. One of your barbarians must have done it.'

CHAPTER 34

THE NORTH OF ITALY
THE STRONGHOLD OF ARCIA IN
THE JULIAN ALPS

Four Days after the Ides of March, AD238

E ven in the sunshine, the home of Marcus Julius Corvinus was not a thing of beauty, nothing like the villa of a rich equestrian. A foursquare fortress, it stood on top of a steep slope, purposeful and forbidding. The walls were of rough, irregular blocks of grey stone, but they were well mortared, crenellated above, and the pines were cut back a bowshot all around. There was just one gate in the side at the top of the track. Arcia was defensible, and extremely inaccessible: the ideal lair of a bandit chief.

Low-lying clouds had prevented Timesitheus seeing much of the first stages up into the wilds of the Alps. They had had to leave the carriage at dawn and continue on horseback from the Roman fort of Ad Pirum. A local guide had led him and the gladiator Narcissus. The path had been narrow and winding, occasionally precipitous. Sometimes it branched, and often seemed to turn back on itself. Timesitheus had wondered if they were being taken by a deliberately circuitous route.

Later in the morning, when the sun had broken through, it revealed range after range of hills, stretching into the far distance, fading from green to grey to blue. They rode through grassy meadows, dotted with purple flowers on tall, delicate stems, and crossed shallow upland streams, where bright water foamed over smoothed stones. The sun shone from a pale blue sky. Spring had come to the mountains, but snow still clung on some of the higher ridges. Timesitheus thought about the remote bleakness of winter.

The gate was open, but minded by two watchful, armed guards. The three riders clattered under a low, rounded arch, and into a dark tunnel that ran through the thickness of the wall. They emerged into a small square, faced with buildings that backed onto the outer walls. The red-tiled roofs were steeply pitched, and the chimneys were covered with raised slabs. Timesitheus noted that nothing obstructed the wall walk. A grim place to stand watch in winter, worse to assault at any season.

Stable-hands held the heads of their horses. These men too were armed. The travellers dismounted. Timesitheus stretched. He was weary to the bone. Three days from Rome to Aquileia, eating and sleeping with Menophilus in the carriage, only stopping to change horses. A further long night to Ad Pirum, and then the trek to Arcia.

It would be worse for Narcissus, who had ridden the entire way. Still, it would have done the gladiator good. They were all overfed, stuffed full of beans. Every one of them carried too much weight.

'Corvinus said to take you to the hall.' The speaker made no show of deference. He was a tall man, wearing check tunic and trousers, and a long sword on his hip. He spoke Latin, but it was easy to picture him in a distant age, tattooed and screaming barbaric war cries, hurtling down a hillside with his kinsmen as they ambushed a Roman legion in some remote pass. It was not beyond imagining that, if chance offered, he might do the same nowadays.

A great table ran the length of the hall, from the doors to a massive, barbaric fireplace. Yet the room was plastered and painted, and old bronzes and fine statues stood on plinths. Timesitheus went and pretended to warm himself by the low fire. Inexplicably a lone boot stood on that end of the table. It was enormous, unworn and dyed scarlet.

Corvinus had known they were coming. It gave credence to his supposition there was a more direct route. Timesitheus yawned, and rubbed his eyes. It would have been good to wash. He was dirty, and he very much needed to be alert.

The governor's palace in Ephesus, on the hill above the theatre, had the most luxurious private bath. He thought of the afternoons there, the servants sent away, Tranquillina naked, laughing, telling him exactly what she wanted him to do.

307

Crouched between her thighs, all *dignitas* cast aside, abandoning himself to a pleasure, all the keener for its very degradation.

'Health and great joy.'

Corvinus was a tall, well built man in middle age. His face had the deep tan of a life spent outdoors. He wore a crisp linen tunic, but, like the six men at his back, he had a sword hanging from his belt.

'Health and great joy.'

Thucydides considered that only primitives carried weapons in peacetime. Yet, of course, Timesitheus came with a gladiator, and was himself armed; a sword and dagger, and a hidden blade in his boot. *O tempora, o mores*, as the more pretentious Romans often said.

'Marcus Julius Corvinus, I am—'

'Gaius Furius Sabinius Aquila Timesitheus, Prefect of the Grain Supply.'

Timesitheus produced the letter that Menophilus had given him. 'In the names of our noble Emperors, Gordian the Elder and Gordian the Younger, the Board of Twenty elected to defend the *Res Publica*, has entrusted me to deliver this message.'

He waited in silence as Corvinus broke the seal, opened the block, and read.

'Events give these lonely mountains an unexpected importance. Suddenly my remote refuge plays host to guests of the highest rank.' Corvinus closed the writing block.

Timesitheus waited. Guests was plural. He had been offered no hospitality. Visions of a closed carriage rushing him to Maximinus came into his mind. He heard the rat-like scuttle of his own fear.

At last, Corvinus spoke. 'Whether he marches by the Dravus or the Savus, Maximinus must come to Emona. Only two roads from there are practicable for an army to cross the Alps into Italy. One is the road you left at Ad Pirum. The other is longer, and runs to the north, through Virunum and Santicum. There are old fortifications on both, which, given time, could be repaired. With regular troops both could be defended. But, there is no time, and, while I have loyal tenants and clients, you know that I possess no soldiers.'

Timesitheus was too weary to think what to say.

'The sonorous phrase of this letter – give all aid to the defence of the *Res Publica* – I take it means your masters wish me to harass Maximinus, raid and delay his baggage train.'

'Yes,' Timesitheus said.

'You see that.' Corvinus pointed at the oversize boot on the table. 'Last winter a small convoy was taking supplies to Maximinus. It met with disaster. The mountains are dangerous. There were no survivors. Among the goods – incense, silk and papyrus, the types of things an Emperor might require – was that boot. Oddly, my men only recovered the one. The wagon had gone over a cliff. It is a very big boot. Not the sort I would wish to have stand on me. The boot was destined for Maximinus.'

Now, Timesitheus had to speak. 'The noble Gordiani are generous, and will remember their friends.'

Corvinus interrupted. 'The noble Gordiani are a long way away, and, I am assured, that Maximinus will be here within days.'

Timesitheus could feel the rodent breath hot on his neck, the teeth sharp, questing. 'The Emperors believe that a man of courage, one who performed dangerous service, should have a place in the Senate. The property qualification of a million sesterces would be a gift.'

'What status would such a man hold in the Senate?'

'There would be no onus to attend, but he would sit among the ex-Consuls. Anything less would be beneath his *dignitas*.'

'You have the authority to make good this promise?'

'Yes.'

Corvinus smiled. 'That is what the envoy of Maximinus said.'

Timesitheus forced his fear down out of the daylight. 'The Gordiani are still distant, but Rome has declared for them. Maximinus is a tyrant, and he is doomed. Even if he is not struck down in his own camp, everyone will turn against him. The East is in revolt. His army will not get beyond Aquileia. The Danube will rise behind him.'

Again Corvinus smiled. 'The East may rise, so may the Danubian armies. But you ask a great deal.' He went and picked up the boot, turned it in his hands. 'My ancestors were here long before Maximinus. Our citizenship was awarded seven generations ago by Augustus. We were here before Rome. I would have us here when Rome has fallen. The idea of an eternal city strikes me as improbable. The likeliest way to achieve such longevity for my family was to avoid imperial politics. But since I have no choice, my intervention should be well rewarded.'

'What would you need?' Timesitheus pushed down a surge of hope. If false, it would be too crushing.

'The Consulship, the million sesterces, tax exemption for me and my descendants in perpetuity. And it is time I took a wife. For the woman I have in mind, I would need a house in Rome, a villa on the Bay of Naples, and an estate, perhaps in Sicily.'

'Who?'

'I would marry a great-granddaughter of Marcus Aurelius, the wife of the Caesar Maximus, the soon to be widowed, Iunia Fadilla.'

'An excellent choice.'

'Splendid,' Corvinus said. 'Let us have some wine. And I will give you something. The envoy of Maximinus left this house at first light today. With four guards and a slave, he is travelling one of the less frequented paths down to the Italian plain. From his own lips, I understand that there is a particular enmity between you and the Prefect of the Camp, Domitius.'

'I have only one man.'

Corvinus shifted the boot from one hand to the other. 'You can have a guide, but this is your own affair, and my men will be occupied on imperial business, preparing a reception for Maximinus. I told Domitius that I would dedicate this boot at the shrine at Archimea. I still think I should. One must honour the gods.'

CHAPTER 35

THE EAST
CARRHAE

Four Days after the Ides of March, AD*238*

'What are the reptiles doing?'
Priscus did not like the look of this.
The *Mobads* had lit the fire at dawn.
It was about four hundred paces out from the
Nisibis Gate, at the very limit of the range of a
ballista. They had hung a cauldron over the flames.
They had fed the fire all morning. Whatever was
in the cauldron would be white hot or boiling.

Yesterday, after the Persians had recovered the
body of Geliman of Demavend, they had built a
high tribunal in front of the royal pavilion, and
placed a throne on top. It looked down on the
fire, and three wooden crosses. Holes had been
dug for the bases of these, but for now they lay
flat on the earth.

Ard-a-shir! Ard-a-shir!

Five *Mobads* hoisted the Drafsh-i-Kavyan over
the tribunal. The sun flashed off the jewels set in
its crossbar, off the golden orb at its top.

Ard-a-shir! Ard-a-shir!

The King of Kings sat on the throne under the standard of his house.

Whatever the Sassanids were about to do, it was not part of the funeral rites for either Geliman killed the previous day or the Lord of Andegan the day before that. Priscus had been told the Persians merely exposed the corpses of their dead on a high place for the birds to tear and devour. Abgar Prince-in-waiting said sometimes they did not wait for the old, ill, or unloved to stop breathing. Abgar hated the Sassanids, perhaps even more than did Ma'na of Hatra. The Sassanids had killed the elder brother of Ma'na.

A-hura-mazda! A-hura-mazda!

A group of three roped prisoners were dragged forth from the Persian lines. They struggled and fought. Their guards beat them with the butts of their spears, the flats of their blades. The prisoners wore normal eastern clothing; loose tunics, baggy breeches. Their long hair was unbound, falling over their faces. One was very tall and thin.

'Shalamallath,' said Iarhai.

So the *Synodiarch* had not betrayed them. As good as his word, he had led his chosen two warriors through the darkness into the heart of the Persian camp. Blade in hand, murder in his heart, he had failed to kill the Persian King. Somehow they had been caught. Now they would pay the price.

'A man of honour, a hard man of the desert, a noble enemy.' Iarhai sounded moved. 'He deserves better than this slave or Christian death.'

One by one the captives were forced down, tied to the crosses.

Priscus took note of that. Some crucified men could live for days, longer if bound not nailed to the cross. If cut down, they might survive. But after one night raid, the Sassanids would be more on guard.

Although ropes and labourers were ready, the crosses were not raised at once. *Mobads* busied themselves around the fire.

'The cruelty of the vipers knows no limits,' Abgar said.

With long tongs, a *Mobad* used a metal pot to scoop something from the cauldron. Walking with care, he went over to Shalamallath. Two other priests held the head of the caravan-guard, so he could not move at all. The pot tipped, liquid poured down onto his face. Shalamallath screamed.

'Olive oil,' Abgar said. 'They have blinded him with boiling olive oil.'

The *Mobad* with the tongs moved on to the other prisoners. Men hauled on ropes, put their shoulders to the wood, and Shalamallath's cross jerked upright. The other prisoners screamed.

'We should try and finish them off with the ballistae,' Abgar said.

Priscus thought for a moment, then shook his head. 'The range is very long, and it would tell the snakes that their theatre had disturbed us. They must suffer.'

Tears ran down Iarhai's cheeks, his lips moved

315

as he muttered. A prayer, a curse? Perhaps both. Priscus put a consoling hand on the shoulder of the young *Synodiarch*. Unfortunately, the King of Kings was still alive, but the dilemma of which caravan-guard would get the contract to provide mercenaries was solved. He gave Iarhai's shoulder a squeeze. From the start, he had liked him better than the more loquacious Shalamallath.

'Prefect, you promised an audience to a delegation from the *Boule* of Carrhae.' The governor might be his brother, but Philip was always very correct.

Priscus nodded. 'Let the fires on the walls be lit. Now, we will go to the citadel.'

By the time he had descended the stairs and swung up onto his horse, Priscus had dismissed the horror from his mind. Pragmatism was his great virtue. One problem at a time. The Sassanids had to attack. Ardashir could not ride away now he had killed two of his great lords, and a large number of the warriors sent to retrieve their bodies, now he had made an attempt on Ardashir's own life, It was but fourteen years since the Persian had killed his predecessor Artabanus the Arsacid. In the eyes of many across the east, he was still no King of Kings, but a pretender. Only continued military success might keep him secure on the throne. A failed attack on the city of Hatra a few years ago had provoked a wave of unrest across the Sassanid empire.

Ardashir had to attack today or tomorrow, the

day after at the latest. He had twenty-five thousand warriors with him, all mounted, and no supply train. It was early spring; neither the grass nor the crops were ready. They must move on before all the food and forage was consumed.

It was a pity Priscus had not been able to poison the wells. Something slow acting, painful and debilitating would have been best.

The Sassanids would have to try and storm the town. They had no siege engines, and neither the time nor expertise to assemble one. Yesterday they had built ladders, and felled trees to make primitive rams. They would die in droves beneath the walls and gates of the town.

As long as no Roman deserters tutored them, the Sassanids would never be better at siege warfare than the Parthians they had overthrown. Sophisticated poliorcetic endeavours would always remain beyond barbarians. It was one of the few certainties in life.

Priscus had not expected the arrival of Ardashir. Yet now the Sassanid was here, it was vital he be induced to make an attempt on the town. Of course, Priscus could not inflict a decisive defeat. There was nothing he could do to prevent Ardashir wheeling his cavalry and vanishing across the plain at any moment. But Priscus could bloody his nose; hold the town, slaughter thousands of his men, tarnish his image as a divinely favoured leader of men. When Ardashir had failed before Hatra, the much-vaunted love of Ahuramazda had been far from evident, and the eastern provinces of his empire had risen in revolt. The same could happen at Carrhae.

Ardashir had twenty-five thousand men, the defenders less than four and a half. Priscus had divided the walls into four commands. The north and north-west, from the Gate of Sin to beyond the Moon Gate, was held by the four hundred regular auxiliary infantry of 15th Arabum Cohort. With the same number, 2nd Eufratensis Cohort held the west and south-west, including the Euphrates Gate and the Mirage Postern. The latter named because, hidden in the corner of a tower, it was so hard to discern. The rest of the circuit was garrisoned by the thousand swords present under the eagle of the 1st Legion Parthica. They were assigned to two senior Centurions. The first was responsible for the Venus Gate and the Camp Postern in the south and south-east, the second the Nisibis and Lion Gates in the east and north-east. There were four ballistae in each section, and every command was supported by a hundred dismounted regular archers from the Equites Indigenae Sagittarii, and five hundred local levies.

There was no reserve beyond the hundred or so personal guards with the senior officers. These *bucellarii*, and their employers, would remain with Priscus on the citadel. It was a rigid, perimeter defence. It had no flexibility or depth. The walls of Carrhae doglegged, creating dead zones not covered by enfilading ballistae. It was very far from

318

perfect, but it was the best Priscus could achieve with what he had to hand. Pragmatism, always pragmatism.

The cavalcade clattered into the open courtyard of the governor's palace. There was a fine view out over the eastern walls and the plain beyond, today somewhat spoiled by the smoke from the Persian fires. Above, the roof-garden commanded the entire city.

Priscus handed his reins to a stable boy, and used a dismounting block.

'They are waiting for you in the Basilica, Prefect.'

Greeks, Syrians, Arabs, however they thought of themselves, Priscus had little time for the provincials under his command. Untrustworthy, cowardly, and they talked far too much. At least those who pretended to be Greek tended to be less judgemental about the pleasures of the flesh.

There were three of them. Long bearded, each clad in himation and tunic, very Hellenic. They would not have looked out of place in the ancient Athens of Demosthenes. The image seemed apposite. Demosthenes, there was another one long on words, short on courage.

Trying to suppress his irritation, Priscus sat down. The joints of the governor's ivory chair creaked under the weight of his armour. With a gesture, he indicated their spokesman should say what they had come to say.

'We owe very great thanks to our noble Emperor Maximinus Augustus, and to his noble Caesar

Maximus, for their manifold labours on our behalf – but it would not be right to admit any greater gratitude than that for sending down to us for governor such a man as yourself.'

'Very flattering,' Priscus interrupted, 'and I am as fond of rhetoric as the next soldier. But time is pressing. We are expecting a Persian attack.'

The orator rubbed his hands together. 'As you say, Prefect, as you say.' Brevity obviously did not come naturally.

'What do you want?'

'As you rightly have identified, Prefect, the Persians seem decided upon an attack. Even if it is repulsed, many citizens in the levies will die. And, despite your foresight and courage, despite the excellence of your strategies, the gods of war are fickle.'

'I have been in combat before,' Priscus said. 'I am aware a battle can have more than the one, desired result.'

'Quite so, Prefect. No one could not bow to your knowledge of the Dancing Field of Ares.'

'Good, now we have established my bona fides on the *Dancing Floor*, why did you ask for an audience?' Priscus remembered someone advising him to recite the Greek alphabet as a method of controlling his temper.

'No one should doubt the loyalty of my family to Rome.' These Greeks, like all easterners, favoured an oblique approach. 'My ancestor was none other than Hieronymos son of Nikomachos, the hero who risked his own life to offer succour and advice to young Publius Crassus, after Crassus the father had been trapped by the Parthian hordes. Like my antecedent, I offer loyal and prudent advice to the representative of the great majesty of Rome.'

Priscus briefly entertained the pleasant fantasy of having Sporakes drag the speaker outside and hurl him off the eastern terrace. It was a long way down, he was unlikely to survive.

'So I ask, is peace not preferable to war? Safety and security to danger and uncertainty? Is it necessary to face the Persians in arms? Can another way be found?'

'What other way?' Priscus made no effort to keep the asperity out of his voice. 'Tell me now, and tell me in few words.'

'Of course, Prefect, of course.' The orator bowed. 'My fellow members of the *Boule* represent the noblest families of Carrhae . . .'

'In few words.'

'We have agreed that, inspired by the love we have for our fellow citizens, and with great personal sacrifice, our *philanthropia* motivates us to raise a substantial sum of money with which to purchase peace and the safety of our beloved *Polis*. Barbarians such as Ardashir are motivated by nothing other than greed.'

'No.'

'All authorities agree their avarice . . .'

'No, we will not talk to Ardashir.'

'But, Prefect, if you opened negotiations . . .'

'He has just blinded one of my most beloved officers, burnt out his eyes and crucified him with two of his men.'

'All barbarians love money.'

'Would you like me to send you to discuss cupidity with the King of Kings?'

'Prefect, it would be better—'

'It was a rhetorical question.' Priscus touched the hilt of his sword. 'Now stop talking, and get out.' To Hades with counting from alpha to omega. Let the *Graeculus* take offense. 'The money you have so generously offered will be collected after the siege to help pay for your defence in future. Your patriotism and courage do you credit. Now, get out.'

When the delegation had left, Priscus called for food for all in the *consilium*, and for their *bucellarii* down in the courtyard. It was not yet noon, but he was hungry. Remembering the boiling oil, he was about to order something cold, but told himself to be a man and eat whatever arrived.

Philip was looking as if he had something to say.

'Yes?'

'As your legate, I would have advised you not to offend their *dignitas*.'

Priscus laughed. 'They are Greeks. They do not have *dignitas*.'

'All peoples have their pride,' Philip said.

'What does it matter? There is nothing they can do, except pay the money they offered.'

Philip had a very disapproving air.

'Perhaps they might compose an unpleasant poem about me, scribble some offensive graffiti.'

Philip did not laugh with the other members of the *consilium*.

The curtains were pulled back, but not to admit servants bearing food.

A young, nervous tribune entered and saluted.

Priscus struggled for the youth's name. Censorinus? No, that was the name of his father's friend. Caerellius, that was it.

'Prefect, the Sassanids are moving?'

'Which way?'

Caerellius looked blank for a moment. 'Towards the city, Prefect. They have ladders and rams. They are going to attack.'

'Before lunch,' Manu said. 'Our men will be hungry.'

Priscus thought that was worth remembering. If it was planned, Ardashir was no fool. Any slight advantage that could be wrung out of the enemy might be telling.

'We will go up and see.'

From the roof-garden three columns of Sassanid troops were spread out like the toys of a rich child. All were mounted. Two were already drawn up in place, about four hundred paces from the walls. The first was in the north-east, a great crescent running from the Nisibis Gate to the Gate of Sin. The second near overlapped it, stretching from just south of the former gate, past the Camp

Postern to the Venus Gate. The final body was cantering around to the Euphrates and Moon Gates.

With the dust and the distance, numbers were hard to discern. Once, in the imperial mint in Antioch, Priscus had been shown an ingenious arrangement of lenses, which made very small objects, like the writing on tiny coins, appear larger. Why had no one invented a similar device that made distant things appear closer?

Not all the Sassanid warriors had left their camp. Each of the columns seemed roughly the same size. Priscus studied the one drawn up in the south-east. Six, perhaps seven thousand horsemen. As he watched, they dismounted. One in three remained, holding the horses. The others jostled into line.

On each of the three sections of walls that would be assaulted the defenders would be outnumbered by four or five to one. The odds were not good. Experts usually reckoned a fortified place would fall to three to one. But the men on the battlements of Carrhae were well prepared, the walls were sound, the Sassanids had no siege materials beyond ladders and rams. Like always in battle – on the Dancing Floor of Ares, as the pretentious Greek had it – everything would turn on morale. If the local levies fought like men, most might live through today.

The Sassanid horde to the north-east was shifting, wavering like tall grass in the wind. Even at this distance, the Drafsh-i-Kavyan was clearly visible. Where the war standard of Sasan went, the King of Kings was to be found. The great white stallion ridden by his son Shapur was easier to see. The royal party was riding along the front line, no doubt being cheered by those about to die.

Sporakes and other *bucellarii* escorted the slaves with the food onto the roof. Meat and onions on skewers, dripping with oil and fat. Priscus took some bread. Be a man, just eat.

The sound of distant war horns and drums drifted up to the citadel. The Sassanid columns moved forward. Here and there were eddies, where, unseen from high above, artillery bolts tore through their ranks.

Priscus chewed on some lamb. It was good. He was hungry.

Clouds of arrows blew this way and that across the battlements, like showers of rain in a cross-wind. Minute figures of men pitched from the wallwalks or dropped motionless to the dusty earth outside. All oddly quiet and removed.

A deity looking down from Olympus could not have been more detached. Men fighting and dying in near silence. It was fascinating, but somehow of limited relevance.

The Persians to the south-east were hanging back, reluctant to close with the wall, enfiladed as it was by four ballistae. There was something god-like about the way the bolts struck; inhumanly fast and powerful, brushing men aside, punching through their armour, nailing them together.

Priscus took a drink, dismissed that part of the town from his mind.

Between the Gate of Sin and the Lion Gate, ladders reared against the wall. Legionaries wielded pitchforks to push them sideways and down. In two places they were not quick enough. Bright robed figures swarmed over the parapet. Steel flashed in the sun. Tight knots of men struggled. Individuals toppled back, to be dashed to ruin on the cobbles of the street below.

'Fuck the reptiles up the arse.'

Abgar's obscenities drew Priscus' attention to the north-western defences. Above the Euphrates Gate the town wall ran to the left for about a hundred paces, before snaking back to the right. After some three hundred more paces, it turned sharp right again, to head towards the Moon Gate. Its strange configuration left those three hundred paces uncovered by any shooting from the gates. Sure enough, the Sassanids already had three small, tight-packed groups of warriors on that section of wallwalk.

Two clear threats: north-east and north-west. Either could spell the end of the town. One hundred *bucellarii*. No time for discussion or careful deliberation.

'Julianus, take Manu and Iarhai and their men. Get to the north-east wall.'

No time for ceremonial salutes.

'Sporakes and my guard, Ma'na and Wa'el, the men of Hatra, with me.'

The horses were waiting. They thundered and slewed down from the acropolis. At the foot of the hill, all sight of the wall was lost behind houses. They plunged into the maze of narrow alleys. The sounds of their own hooves and rattling equipment, the roars and screams of battle, dinned back from the close, blank walls.

They skidded to a halt in the street below the wall. The fighting seethed above them. Priscus threw a leg over the horn of his saddle, dropped to the ground.

'No horse holders, hobble the horses instead.' It would take a moment longer than just turning them loose, but he had no intention of being trapped here on foot.

Still the three groups of Sassanids on the battlements, a dozen or more warriors in each. Stairs to the left, the barred door of a tower to the right. Arruntius and some of his auxiliaries were at the head of the stairs.

'Ma'na and Wa'el, you and your Hatrenes stay down here. The *bucellarii* with me.'

He waited while the men sorted themselves out.

'With Arruntius, we will clear the wallwalk from the left, drive the reptiles against the tower. Ma'na, you and Wa'el, have your archers keep pace with us, shoot the easterners as we reach them.'

He turned towards the steps.

'Prefect.' It was Sporakes. 'Your helmet.'

Gods below, in the heat of the moment, he had forgotten the thing. With fumbling fingers, he pulled it over his head, tied the laces under his chin. Finally, he retrieved his shield from one of the rear horns of his saddle. His warhorse was well trained. It stood quiet amid the uproar and confusion.

Sporakes and the *bucellarii* had used his delay to get up the stairs, and join with the auxiliaries huddled there. Priscus ran up after them. Wedged himself into the second line.

The rampart was wide enough for five fighting men abreast. *Bucellarii* and auxiliaries combined came to about thirty-five swords. A minuscule phalanx seven deep. In the confined space it might be enough. Huge battles can turn on such tiny factors.

Hunched over, they edged forward.

An arrow from outside the walls whistled past Priscus' face.

They had to stamp out the barbarian toe-holds before thousands of others joined them.

The first Sassanids were in a huddle, five paces beyond Sporakes and Arruntius. They were lobstered in plate and chain armour. These were *clibanarii*, the noble knights of Ahuramazda. Inhuman, only their kohl-lined eyes showed through animal masks, veils of mail. Streamers of silk fluttered.

A flight of arrows chinked off the metal-clad easterners.

Sporakes' shoulders were heaving, readying himself for the fight.

Another squall of arrows. One penetrated into the leg of a *clibanarius*. He was hauled to the rear.

'Come on,' Priscus shouted. 'You want to live forever?'

Arruntius and Sporakes launched themselves forward. Priscus was close behind Arruntius, but not so close as to impede him.

The ringing of steel, stamp of boots, panting breath. Priscus shifted and moved over the shoulders of Arruntius, eyeing any opening. None came. Sporakes went down, clutching an arm. Wounded, not dead. Another *bucelarrius* stepped over him. Without warning, the fight turned to butchery. The last Sassanids were hacked, almost dismembered despite their fine armour, as they fought each other to get back on their ladder.

A *bucellarius* went to push down the ladder. An arrow took him in the throat. The others crouched down below the parapet. Arrows whickered above their heads, pinging off the merlons. Priscus forced himself to his feet. Under his boots the bricks were slippery with blood. Sometimes cold pragmatism demands heroics. He stood, seized the top rung of the ladder. Arrows shrieked past. One clanged off his shoulder guard. He heaved the ladder sideways. It shifted, caught, then came free and toppled.

'Two more nests of snakes, then we are saved.' He had ducked down again.

Priscus was shoulder to shoulder with Arruntius. Together they counted out loud – alpha, beta, gamma – and charged the Persians.

The easterner opposite Priscus was quick and experienced. His dark-lined eyes followed the Roman's darting blade. Priscus redoubled his attacks, cutting and thrusting, first high then low. There had to be a way through.

Arruntius reeled across into Priscus' sword arm. The equestrian's thigh was open to the bone. In his agony, he clung to Priscus. The Sassanid thrust. Impeded, Priscus failed to get his shield across. The eastern sword scraped into the mail guarding his ribs. Links snapped, jagged iron driven into his flesh. He heaved Arruntius up, and forced him over the side. The officer's arms clawed at the air as he plummeted down to the street. Unencumbered, Priscus dropped to one knee, chopped the Sassanid's legs out from under him.

The *bucellarii* and auxiliaries surged past him. In every fight, there was an instant when the momentum tipped inevitably. Some of the Sassanids left on the wall fought to the death. It made little difference. They died with the others. The assault had failed.

CHAPTER 36

AFRICA
THE PLAIN BEFORE CARTHAGE

Five Days after the Ides of March, AD238

Disheartening was too mild an adjective, Gordian thought, as he rode with his father, inspecting the army and the new recruits. The regular troops were drawn up to the right, facing the levies, to inspire confidence in the latter. There was nothing much wrong with these regulars, except lack of numbers. The cavalry were particularly short-handed. Together the Horse Guards and *speculatores* only had just over two hundred in the saddle. Perhaps it would have been wiser not to have them on parade.

There were five units of professional infantry. The Cohort of the 3rd Legion were accoutred for war, shield covers removed to display their Pegasus emblem. Gordian had been reminded that the majority of recruits for the legion were drawn from Africa Proconsularis. They should fight harder to defend their homeland, and possibly the bulk of the legionaries with Capelianus might be more inclined to desert, if the battle turned against them.

331

The 13th Urban Cohort looked the part, yet it had to be kept in mind that their usual duties involved overseeing the docks and controlling crowds at the spectacles, rather than campaigning. The recently raised Praetorians were smartly turned out, and although their previous training in the youth organizations of the Iuvenes was minimal, no body of men were more closely bound to the Gordiani. Next to the Praetorians stood the new unit, grandiosely named the 1st Legion Gordiana Pius Fidelis. It numbered about four hundred, and consisted of veterans recalled to the standards, and *stationarii*. The latter, soldiers detached from their units, and for some reason or other present in Carthage, were likely to be better at finding easy billets than at fighting in pitched battle. The hastily painted insignia on their mismatched shields were all too visible signs that these men had not served together before. At the end of the line were the auxiliaries of the 1st Flavian Cohort, who had arrived from Utica, tired and footsore, earlier that morning. Of the other auxiliary Cohorts in the Province all but one were on the distant southern frontier. Only the 15th Emesenes would reach Carthage in time, and the army of Capelianus would be close behind them. Gordian thought it best not to mention this when he addressed the levies.

The imperial cavalcade halted at the tribunal. Gordian took his father's arm, and they ascended the steps. The senior Emperor made a short speech, stressing duty, courage, discipline. A fresh southerly breeze made his words hard to hear.

Gordian ran his eyes over the recruits. The three hundred or so mounted men were not unpleasing. They were local landowners and their well-equipped retainers, accustomed to the hardships and near military manoeuvres of hunting. The eight thousand men on foot were another story. The majority unarmed except for a knife, butcher's cleaver or pitchfork, this was nothing but a mob from the backstreets of the city. No doubt they could riot, but there would be no more than five or six days to train them to stand in the line in open battle.

His father finished, to no great discernible enthusiasm, and it was time for Gordian to speak.

'*Quirites!* Julius Caesar with that one word transformed a mutinous legion from soldiers to civilians. Today we do the opposite. *Milites!* When you take the oath, no longer shall you be citizens, but soldiers!'

Some at the front grinned and waved whatever weapons they carried. Most were silent, and appeared apprehensive.

'Do not let your lack of training distress you. You are Romans! The children of the wolf! Ausonian beasts! Your forefathers conquered the world. You are feared from the Atlantic to the Tigris. The battlefield is your birthright. It is in your blood. Cincinnatus was summoned from the plough, and he saved the state. You will save the *Res Publica!*'

Simple rhetoric, but a number cheered.

'Do not be concerned at your lack of arms. The gods themselves offer the weapons stored in their temples. Throughout the city, blacksmiths forge swords and spears, carpenters make shields. When you march out, you will be as well equipped as any Praetorian.'

A blatant lie, but that did not matter.

'Give no thought to any lack of experience. Four hundred gladiators have been granted their freedom. These heroes of the arena, skilled fighters all, will stand in the front rank between you and the enemy.'

The audience seemed somewhat encouraged. Fools, Gordian thought. A gladiator was no soldier. But the general idea should be developed.

'You are not alone. Look at the thousands of regular troops in their serried ranks opposite. These veterans will be at your side.'

With luck, the professionals were not considering how the levies might guard their flanks.

'What brings victory? Is it years of lolling in barracks, swaggering in bars, requisitioning animals, using threats and violence to oppress fellow citizens? No, it is innate courage, overwhelming numbers, good generalship, and a just cause, one which brings the certain favour of the gods. Look into your hearts, recall your native courage. Look about you. Who would stand against such overwhelming numbers? Consider my leadership. Have men under my command ever tasted defeat?

Think of the justice of our cause. We fight to free the empire from bloody tyranny. The gods will fight at our sides.

'Finally, remember you fight for your homes and families, for your ancestral gods, for all you love. Let no one think he can stand aside. There is no safety in flight. The Moorish tribesmen that Capelianus brings against Carthage could not be restrained from pillage and sacrilege, rape and slaughter, even if that bloodthirsty general, that servant of a murderous tyrant, so wished.'

Now the throng called out their willingness.

'As one take the oath, say the binding words of the *sacramentum*. Every man who stands with us for freedom will be accounted a hero. Every man will receive the pay of a Praetorian for the rest of his life.'

Prompted by the soldiers, they said the time hallowed, powerful words.

By Jupiter Optimus Maximus and all the gods, I swear to carry out the Emperors' commands, never desert the standards or shirk death, to value the safety of the Emperors above everything.

The oath administered, Gordian kissed his father, and Brennus and Valens helped the old Emperor down the steps and onto his horse. Gordian remained on the tribunal with Sabinianus. They would stay to watch the first steps in the training of the levies.

Senior officers shouted orders, and Centurions pushed clumsy recruits into some sort of formation.

Gordian again had tried to persuade his father to leave for Rome. The old man was adamant he would not go. At least Gordian had sent Parthenope away. She would bear his child in the villa on the Via Praenestina. It would grow up safe amid the marble luxuries of that beautiful and peaceful place. Chione he had kept with him. A man had needs, as much as anything companionship in these troubled nights. Before Parthenope had left, he had had a ridiculous desire to emancipate and marry her. Should the worst happen, he would leave a legitimate heir. Sabinianus had pointed out that no Senator, let alone an Emperor can wed a freedwoman. Anyway, such thoughts of death were premature. If the battle was lost, there was a fast ship crewed and waiting in the harbour.

It was ill-omened to think of defeat. The forces at his disposal were not good, but the battle would be fought on this field of his choosing. There was nothing Capelianus could do but come to him. They would make their stand here, astride the Mappalian Way. The aqueduct and burial ground and walls of Carthage would be at their backs, the villa of Sextus to their left, the fishponds further off on the right. The plain was flat and featureless, but there was time to prepare, and Gordian had to squeeze what advantage he could from the terrain.

CHAPTER 37

NORTHERN ITALY
THE TERRITORY OF THE CITY
OF AQUILEIA

Five Days after the Ides of March, AD238

The noise of the wagons strung out along the Via Gemina stunned the senses: the rumble and jolt of iron wheel rims on stone, the shriek of wood tortured against wood. One or two rustic carts would have been in keeping, but this armed convoy violated the peace of the countryside on a fine spring morning. In the sunshine the territory of Aquileia was beautiful, flat and fertile and well tended. Regimented lines of vine props, very black and tough with age, stretched away with geometric precision from fruit trees heavy with blossom. Violet flowers pricked the grass in between the rows. The land did not deserve this intrusion. With destruction its intention, this convoy was a violent harbinger of civil war.

Menophilus was tired, dog tired. He had reached Aquileia two nights before. After three days in the carriage from Rome, that first night he had been unable to sleep in an unsettlingly solid and unmoving bed. One night's sleep had not been near enough to recover. His Stoicism made him despise the weakness of his body. He hated making decisions when fatigue clouded his judgement. But decisions had had to be reached.

His colleague Crispinus had arrived in the city the day before him. Crispinus had been with a Senatorial travelling companion, an ex-Praetor called Annianus. Also at the meeting was Flavius Adiutor, the Prefect of the 1st Cohort Ulpia Galatarum. The five hundred auxiliary infantrymen temporarily stationed in Aquileia were the only regular troops available in the vicinity. Two other equestrian officers had been present, Servilianus and Laco, as well as two locals of the same social status. The latter were the heads of the Barbii and Statii families. They owned many of the estates through which the convoy was passing. Both had senatorial connections. The Barbii had provided the late Emperor Alexander with a wife for one of his brief and less than happy marriages.

Crispinus was an Italian *novus homo* like himself, and Menophilus had tried not to be prejudiced against him merely because he wore a long beard of philosophical pretentions. Although standing somewhat on his *dignitas*, Crispinus clearly was competent and energetic. It could not be easy for the older man sharing this command, especially as he might well see Menophilus as an imperial favourite promoted too fast and above his merits.

Menophilus wondered if he had acted out of personal pettiness when insisting that Crispinus' friend Annianus be sent to Mediolanum to raise recruits and see to the making of arms and armour. With the ex-Praetor gone, neither Crispinus nor he had any adherents among those in Aquileia. But the tasks were pressing, and the posting made sense, as did the other appointments. Laco was to go to secure the adherence of the fleet at Ravenna to the cause of the Gordiani. Servilianus would train the militia within Aquileia. Artillery, sulphur and other war materiel would be assembled by the troops under Flavius Adiutor. Of the civilians, Barbius had been assigned the repair of the town walls, and Statius the gathering of stockpiles of food. As nothing much could be expected of the defence of the Alpine Passes, Aquileia was likely be the front line. The city had to be ready to stand siege.

When the meeting was done, weary as he had been, Menophilus had gone to the Temple of Belenus in the centre of the town. He was not much given to the forms of traditional religion. But if, as he devoutly believed, the cosmos was guided by an omniscient intelligence, then the plethora of individual gods worshipped by the masses could be seen as imperfectly understood reflections of that one Demiurge. Menophilus could not see why God should need the reminders of prayer or the bribery of sacrifice. Nor was it likely that the deity would make His will known via the flight of birds or the entrails of beasts. The Demiurge could find simpler and more elegant methods.

Yet Belenus was strongly revered in the area, and the loyalty of the townspeople was not above suspicion. True, Maximinus had earned some unpopularity by conscripting unwilling recruits from Aquileia for his northern wars, and by ordering the rich young men of the youth organizations to the undignified and hard labour of repairing the roads. But, on the other hand, he had given gifts to the city, and already in his brief stay Menophilus had seen several inscriptions praising and thanking a *Saviour Emperor* whose recently chiselled out appellation was of the right length to contain the names Gaius Iulius Verus Maximinus.

The priests of the sanctuary had received a lavish monetary offering from Menophilus, as if granted by the Augusti Gordian Father and Son. Belenus gave oracles, and his priests conveyed them to humanity. In what lay ahead, suitably bracing divine encouragement might be invaluable, and it was not the moment to begrudge money.

The convoy shrieked and rumbled along. On either side of the road, the cut-back vines were low at this time of year. Enormous barrels stood in the vineyards, empty, waiting for the vintage. They were as big as a peasant hut, big enough to house not just a lone Cynic philosopher like Diogenes, but a number of his pupils as well.

Weariness caused images to slide without control

through Menophilus' mind. A philosopher sitting in a barrel, crawling out to tell the King to move out of the sunlight. Sabinus slumped in a dark storeroom, his head smashed like an amphora. The dazzling light from the polished walls of the court-yard on the Palatine they called Sicilia. His own reflection, disjointed and bloody, reflected back. Vitalianus pleading for the lives of his daughters.

A farm at the side of the road broke the train of unwanted thoughts. Soldiers were loading produce onto one of the wagons, strapping sacks onto pack animals, herding the occupiers away, tearing the doors from their hinges. The work of Mars had begun. War was a harsh master.

Another image came unbidden into Menophilus' mind. An itinerary of the empire, straight black lines for the roads, the mileage between halts in neat numerals, and each place illustrated with a drawing of a building, as if done by a careful child. Along the roads tiny carriages rolled, raising diminutive clouds of dust. A messenger sped with a deadly despatch towards Dacia. The knife boy Castricius crossed the Alps, rattling ever closer to Maximinus. Worst of all, two barbarians lolled drinking as their conveyances took them towards the edge of the map, where the roads ended, where began the great blankness of barbarity, and where there was nothing but large letters spelling *Sarmatia* and *Gothia*. Sleepless the other night, Menophilus had remembered that when desperate even Marcus Aurelius had stooped to putting a price on an enemy chieftain's head. The exemplum of assassination did not make Menophilus feel any better.

'We are there, Sir.'

The Aesontius river was lined with willows. Its waters were wide and fast with spring melt from the mountains, white mist spraying up where it ran over rocks and met promontories. The bridge was built of light-grey stone. Its graceful piers and arches, above the roiling water, epitomized everything that was secure and good about the rule of Rome.

The convoy halted, men climbed out of the wagons, and Menophilus gave the orders to begin the hard toil of breaking the fine spans of the bridge.

In the dark days of the Marcomannic War, Marcus Aurelius had done worse than countenance political murder. The noble Emperor had succumbed to superstition and magic. The Emperor had been persuaded victory would be his if he allowed some outlandish charlatan priest to sacrifice two lions on the banks of the Danube. The beasts had escaped, and swum across to the barbarians, never to be seen again. If the wisest of Emperors, a man fortified by a lifetime's study of the philosophy of the Stoics, could be brought so low, what chance was there for a lesser man? Menophilus knew he would never be the same again. The actions he was taking, which might secure power for his friends, would destroy that very friendship. Menophilus knew he no longer deserved the friendship of the Gordians, or of any men with claims to decency and virtue. In politics, the things you wish for, were the things you must fear. He was dying every day.

CHAPTER 38

THE NORTHERN FRONTIER
SIRMIUM

Five Days after the Ides of March, AD238

In the gloom of a room shuttered for the siesta Iunia Fadilla was dressed for travel; a long tunic, sensible shoes, a veil, and a cheap and plain but deep-hooded cloak. It was the third day since Maximus had departed. The absence of his brutality had threatened to undermine her resolve. Was it so bad? Perhaps she could endure, if she did everything he demanded, tried to avoid provoking him. But tomorrow she was due to leave for Italy, packed up with the rest of the imperial baggage. In a few days she would be delivered to his insults and beatings. The revolt would fail, and she would be trapped forever. No, she had to act, and the day and time were as propitious as could be found. Her husband and father-in-law had gone ahead, and Julius Capitolinus and everyone left were preoccupied with organizing the march. With the siesta it would be some hours before she was missed, and then uncertainty and indecision might well delay pursuit.

Restuta came in quietly. Iunia Fadilla had collected the minimum necessary for the journey; a spare tunic and pair of shoes, several changes of under-clothes, a warmer cloak, oil and nard for washing, cosmetics and perfumes, a flask of wine and some biscuits. Restuta packed them into two bundles.

Iunia Fadilla had coins, a lot of coins. She had sent Restuta to the market to sell the necklace with the nine pearls, the sapphire bracelet, and the emeralds torn from her headdress. Iunia Fadilla had wondered about the golden brooch set with garnets, but it was very distinctive, and she both did not want to part with it, and thought it might yet be useful. Most likely the merchant had cheated Restuta, assumed the items had been stolen by the maid. If it was ever discovered that the jewels he had bought were betrothal gifts given by Maximus, the merchant would more than pay for his avarice.

Some of the coins were in a belt Iunia Fadilla wore between her shift and tunic. The remainder Restuta had sown into the lining of the two cloaks. Everything was ready. Iunia Fadilla peeped out through the shutters, checking the sun. It was time. There were no excuses not to leave.

Restuta picked up both the packages, and led the way.

There was a Praetorian at the end of the corridor, near the head of the stairs to the servants' quarters. He smiled at Restuta and ignored what he had been told was another maid.

Iunia Fadilla followed Restuta down the narrow stairway. She had never been this way before. The boards were bare, and the walls unpainted. As they descended, there was a smell like stale cabbage or unwashed humanity.

Slipping out of a door by the kitchens, they crossed a muddy courtyard. There was another Praetorian by the wicket gate. He too grinned, and ostentatiously looked the other way. Iunia Fadilla had not asked how Restuta had bribed them, with money or other favours, perhaps both. Restuta was a good girl. If this ended well, she would have her liberty.

The alleyway was empty. Iunia Fadilla felt a rush of relief. She could return to her rooms, take off her disguise. Restuta could pack away the bundles, and it would be as if none of this had happened. Iunia Fadilla suppressed the cowardly thoughts. She might have lacked the courage to kill Maximus, but she would not go back and submit. In her eagerness, they were early.

A beggar, old and filthy, walked down the alley. He stopped, and looked speculatively at the two women. Restuta told him if he was bothering them when their men arrived he would get a beating. He called them both whores as he left.

They waited. More nervous than she could ever remember, Iunia Fadilla tried to ignore an urge to relieve herself. It was no good. She was desperate. She whispered to Restuta. The alley was empty. Restuta told her to be quick. Iunia Fadilla hauled up her clothes, and squatted. A great-granddaughter of Marcus Aurelius, an imperial princess, wife of Caesar, bare arsed, pissing in the mud. Doubtless she would suffer worse.

No sooner had she rearranged herself, than a covered litter carried by four slaves turned into the alley. Another servant walked at its head, carrying a valise. It stopped by them. Her cousin pulled back the curtains, helped her in beside him. They moved off.

Iunia Fadilla was not so foolish as to look out of the hangings, but she could hear that the streets were near empty. Almost everyone would be resting in the early afternoon. Thank the gods that the Romans had imported their Mediterranean customs to this bleak northern outpost of their *imperium*.

She reached over and squeezed her cousin's hand. Fadillus smiled, and silently returned her affection. He had been a revelation. When she told him, Iunia Fadilla had thought he would be scared, quite possibly so terrified that he would refuse to help. She had been prepared to offer him anything, money, her body, promises of vast rewards if they reached Gordian. None of it had been necessary. Fadillus had known Maximus mistreated her. At court it was common knowledge. People said Maximinus had rebuked his son, not that it had done any good. Fadillus wanted to kill Maximus. He would do anything to help Iunia, anything she asked. Of course they should flee, anything was better than leaving her to such cruelty. They had not been born to live as chattel.

Fadillus had been as good as his word. He had hired the litter, sworn his own body servant to secrecy, promised him both manumission and wealth when they reached safety. She wondered if any of them would live to see that day.

The litter swayed to a stop. Fadillus looked out. They were at the gate. There was a queue. Nothing to worry about, just the customs officers. They were interested in export duties, never bothered those about imperial business. They both knew the real test would come outside the gate, when they went to requisition a carriage and horses at the post of the *cursus publicus*.

Obtaining the official passes had been surprisingly easy. On a pretext, Iunia Fadilla had gone to the imperial chancery. The under secretaries who had not gone with the Emperor were not about to start questioning his daughter-in-law. Restuta had distracted them – she was an attractive and resourceful girl – and Iunia had swept two *diplomata* under her cloak. One she had filled out in the name of Fadillus, the other in that of a wife – Sextia – he did not have. Fadillus was not prominent at court, let alone with the army, and no soldier or minor official was likely to know anything about his marital state. Maximus was negligent about such duties as he was given, often leaving more or less important documents lying about. Copying his signature had not been difficult.

The litter moved forward. Despite all Fadillus' reassurances, despite everything she had told herself, her heart was pounding. She chest was hollow. She needed to relieve herself again.

The curtain was drawn back by Fadillus' servant. The customs officer was clean-shaven, and respectful. He bowed to Fadillus, did not look around the litter, barely glanced at the *diplomata*. Waving them on, he apologized for having delayed them.

After the hanging was back in place, Iunia Fadilla hugged her cousin. Just possibly this might work.

'Halt!'

Again the litter stopped.

'No travellers without *diplomata* beyond this point.'

Fadillus' servant pulled open the curtains. Her cousin got out, handed her down. Until he had finished, he did not look at the junior officer.

'I am Gaius Iunius Fadillus, *amicus* of the Emperor. This is my wife. These are our passes.'

The officer took the *diplomata*, opened and studied them. Although he was not young, he was an *Optio*. A man risen from the ranks, but he could read. Obviously this duty was not new to him. He must have seen hundreds of *diplomata*, doubtless many forged as well as genuine.

Iunia Fadilla had to force herself not to squirm.

'My instructions are to go to the Emperor with all haste.'

The *Optio* did not stop scrutinizing the documents.

Had Fadillus sounded too eager?

Iunia Fadilla prayed he would not, but her cousin spoke again. 'We need a light four-wheeled carriage, with a hood, big enough for four passengers, and two of the fastest horses in the stable.'

There were two large denomination coins in Fadillus' hand.

Now the officer looked up. The coins vanished into a purse on his belt. He gave back the *diplomata*. 'Would you care to choose the horses, Sir?'

Fadillus smiled. 'I am sure you know the best animals on the post, *Optio*.'

Hood up, Iunia Fadilla kept her eyes demurely down. It seemed an age before a carriage was brought around.

'My man will drive,' Fadillus said.

'The *cursus publicus* provides the driver.'

'That will not be necessary.' Fadillus produced another coin. 'My man used to be in the Circus with the Greens. I desire to make the best time possible.'

'As you wish, sir.'

Rattling away from the gate, Iunia Fadilla felt a strange urge to throw herself at Fadillus. At that moment she had never been more attracted to any man.

Fadillus unrolled an itinerary. 'Where to, my Lady?'

She had considered going east. It was away from Maximus, and Gordian's friend Fidus was governor of Thrace. But it was a long way, and too much of the road ran through territory ruled by men loyal to Maximinus. There were two choices to the west. In the Alps was Corvinus. The bandit chief had given her the brooch, offered her hospitality. But not under these circumstances. He might give her straight over to her husband. Otherwise there was Dalmatia. Another friend of Gordian had charge of that province. Yet Claudius Julianus commanded no legions. He was poorly equipped to defy Caesar. Neither alternative was safe, and first they had to get there.

'West along the Savus. The road divides at a place called Servitium. We do not have to decide until there.'

Servitium. She hoped the name was not an omen.

CHAPTER 39

THE NORTH OF ITALY
THE JULIAN ALPS

Five Days after the Ides of March, AD238

Timesitheus had been persuaded to spend the night at Arcia. His first thought had been to saddle fresh horses, and set off after Domitius there and then. However, Corvinus had assured him that Maximinus' Prefect of Camp was not travelling fast. Indeed it might be thought that Domitius was dawdling, and appeared somewhat reluctant to venture down onto the plains at all. Requisitioning supplies and horses in what could prove enemy territory, with just four men, was an unenviable mission, and might induce a certain temerity in anyone.

The hostility between Timesitheus and Domitius went back a long way, back to the Emperor Alexander's ineffectual campaign in the East. They had been two of the three equestrians charged with collecting supplies. The third had been a big Thracian called Maximinus. Over the years the enmity had deepened into a consuming hatred. Timesitheus had often considered the ways he would like to kill Domitius: scourged and crucified like a slave, thrown naked into the Arena for the beasts to maul and devour. The vengeance he might take in these mountains would be less public, but still immensely satisfying.

It had been the prospect of a bath, and clean clothes, as much as a meal and a bed, that had convinced Timesitheus not to give chase the previous evening. At first, without the accustomed motion of the carriage, even though the bed was soft, it had been hard to get to sleep. When one of Corvinus' men woke him before dawn, it seemed he had barely slept at all.

Although there was no ground mist, it was a dark morning. The guide led them slowly and carefully down a goat track under dripping pines. When the sun rose, it was behind black clouds. Glimpsing it shining red through brief gaps was like looking into the heart of a furnace.

After a time they came to an unmade road, and made better time. On the slopes were bare circles where charcoal burners had once made their camps. Nothing but weeds grew there, as if the earth had been blighted by the heat of their fires.

The guide never spoke, but pressed on hard. They ate and drank in the saddle, only dismounting occasionally to breathe the horses and relieve themselves.

Early in the afternoon, perhaps the seventh or eighth hour of daylight, they reached a small inn. Not part of the *cursus publicus*, its owner was under no obligation to provide them with animals or sustenance, despite the imperial *diplomata* Timesitheus carried for himself and the gladiator Narcissus. Nevertheless, at the mention of Corvinus, he found three horses and some rough wine, bread and cheese. The innkeeper had answered their questions. Yes, a party of five had stayed the night; an imperial official, four soldiers, and a slave. The official had complained about the meal, said the goat was tough, the wine sour. They had not changed animals, and left late, about the second hour of the day. Most likely they would stop tonight at a bigger inn further down, not more than twenty miles. Timesitheus tipped the man generously, although Domitius had been right about the wine.

Now they rode fast. As they descended, the pines gave way to juniper, beech and oak. The beeches were stunted, but their silvery bark, faintly luminous under the gloomy skies, reminded Timesitheus of the rougher and more gnarled trunks of the olives in his native Corcyra.

Timesitheus did not trust Corvinus. The brigand-chief had demanded astronomical rewards for his help. Timesitheus had no idea if they would be met, but in a civil war it was wise to promise anything. Refusing to provide any aid beyond a guide to hunt down Maximinus' Prefect of Camp did not argue for strong commitment to the cause of the Gordiani. It was possible Corvinus had sent him into a trap, or it could be some strange sort of test. Perhaps, once Corvinus had the signed pledge from Timesitheus, he had no further interest in him, just wanted him gone. One could be certain he had extracted something similar from Domitius. Quite probably Corvinus would sit out the war in his mountains. Then, when the fighting was over, emerge and flourish the document from whichever side had won, and claim his exorbitant dues for any number of fictitious acts of selfless heroism. The corroboration of witnesses would not be hard to find among his retainers.

On the whole Timesitheus envied Corvinus his freedom to pursue his self-interest. For now, Timesitheus was bound to the cause of the Gordiani, whether he cared for it or not, like Ixion to his wheel. At least in this desperate venture through the mountains their interests coincided with his own. But if a better chance offered, another pretender to the throne with more substantial military backing, some governor in Germany or the East, he would not be slow to untie the thongs and climb down from the wheel. Provided, of course, that he could find a way to take Tranquillina and their daughter.

About an hour of daylight remained when they spotted horsemen ahead. Apart from the occasional shepherd or boy tending goats, they had seen no one all day. Unsettled times did not encourage casual travellers. The riders, quickly vanished around a corner, had to be their quarry.

'The inn is not far.'

Without any other words, the guide turned his mount and left.

They rode down more circumspectly. Timesitheus had no wish to encounter Domitius on the road.

The sun had gone behind a distant crest when the inn came into view. They continued until they found a meadow hidden by a fold of the ground, where they tethered the horses. On foot, they graded across the hill, until they could look down on the inn just below. The valley was in shadow, and hazed by smoke from the chimneys, but there was enough light to make out the building.

The inn was not small, but nondescript, with an air of neglect. It was arranged around an open courtyard. There were stables at the front, on either side of a gate wide enough to admit wagons. The two wings must contain the accommodation; the occasional servant emerging from a door to throw out slops indicated the rear block was the kitchen. There was a dog loose in the yard, but few people about. There were no external windows at ground level, and both entrances would be barred when night fell.

Timesitheus took it all in, made his plan, and sent Narcissus off on foot.

With nothing to do but wait, he memorized what landmarks there were on the short route down, then went back, and brushed down the horses. The sweet smell of horse and the steady repetition of the routine were calming.

Narcissus had come highly recommended from

Alcimus Felicianus. So far there had been nothing to make Timesitheus question his friend's judgement. Timesitheus himself could not turn up and ask for lodgings. Obviously, Narcissus would not use his *diploma*. Instead, he would pose as an ex-gladiator, now a trainer, on his way back from Pannonia, having sold his merchandise, and looking for new stock. It was unlikely anyone would question closely the big, ugly purveyor of violence. That there was a dog was to be expected. Given his trade, Narcissus should have no great problem killing the thing.

The horses settled, Timesitheus tacked them up again, lashed the packs to the rear saddle horns, and made sure of their tethers. He checked his weapons, wrapped himself in a cloak, and went back to his point of vantage.

The clouds of the day had gone, but now there was no wind. It was very still, except for a faint sighing in the trees, as if they were breathing, evenly and softly in their sleep.

The moon tracked up across the sky, casting black shadows from the buildings and trees. Timesitheus watched the rear of the inn. It grew cold. Time lost all meaning. An owl hooted. It did not trouble Timesitheus, who despised superstition.

A bulky shade detached itself from the kitchen block. Moving cautiously, Timesitheus went down to meet it.

The blade in the hand of Narcissus shone in the

357

moonlight. The blood on it was very black. The dog had met its end, perhaps others had too.

They closed the rear door almost shut behind them. The kitchen was warm, the range kept on overnight. A potboy slept curled up in front of it. There was just enough light to see. Silently, they stepped past him.

Narcissus led him through the kitchen to a narrow corridor, and to the wing on the right. Outside a door, he stopped and pointed.

The gladiator brought his lips very close to Timesitheus' ear. 'The slave is with him, the soldiers in the other wing.'

Reversing their posture, entwined like clandestine lovers, Timesitheus whispered. 'Wait by the door into the kitchen. If there is an alarm, hold them there.'

Narcissus left.

Often Timesitheus was surprised by how quietly big men could move.

Shards of moonlight lay on the floor of the corridor from the ill-fitting shutters to the yard.

Now he was alone, and everything was to do, Timesitheus hesitated. He did not think he was afraid, more that he was in awe of the irrevocable nature of the thing. *Tempus fugit*. He wanted to be long gone before dawn.

There was a catch on the door. Odd that he had thought in Latin. Dismissing that and everything inessential from his mind, he pushed his cloak back over his shoulders, and raised the catch. A sharp click. He waited, holding his breath, listening. Nothing.

The way he did this – with stealth and silent precision, or fast in blood-splattered uproar – depended on where the slave was sleeping.

Very, very gently, he pushed open the door. It did not creak. After a couple of feet, it softly met resistance. Timesitheus pulled it back a fraction. The slave shifted in his slumber on the floor.

The slave grunted, settled. There was soft snoring from deeper in the room.

It was darker than the corridor. Timesitheus waited until his eyes could register dim shapes. He slipped through. With both hands, he lowered the catch. The faintest of sounds.

Let us be men. The words in his mind reassuringly Hellenic.

His dagger came free of its sheath with a faint hiss.

Timesitheus crouched, and, with the solicitude of a murderous doctor, put a hand over the sleeping man's mouth. He saw the white, horrified eyes. Dropping his weight on the slave's chest, he pushed the point of the dagger into the throat. Hands scrabbled at the knife. Timesitheus twisted the blade. The body lifted, slumped back. Blood pulsed hot on his forearm as he withdrew the knife.

A motion in the close, dark air. Timesitheus threw himself backwards, drawing his sword and getting to his feet in one motion. Something skittered out from under his boots.

'Thieves!' Domitius was out of bed. In a gleaming undertunic, he was hunting through his baggage.

Timesitheus crossed the room. Too slow. Domitius came up with a sword in his hand.

A thrust at the white glimmer of a face. Domitius blocked. The ring of steel.

'Murder!'

No time for subtlety. Kill him before the shock and disorientation ended. Timesitheus entangled the blade of Domitius with his cloak, punched two feet of steel deep into his stomach.

Retrieving the sword, Timesitheus pushed the dying man away. Domitius fell with a crash across the bed. It was a pity he did not know who had killed him.

Devoid of exultation, Timesitheus was wet and reeking with blood.

Loud noises from somewhere in the building. Doors thrown open. Men shouting.

Timesitheus ran back down the corridor, turned towards the kitchen door, expecting to find the hulking shape of Narcissus.

The gladiator was nowhere to be seen. Instead, boots pounding, soldiers hurtling around from the far wing.

Timesitheus doubled back. He was level with Domitius' door, when more soldiers appeared at the end of this corridor. He skidded to a halt, went to open a shutter to the yard.

'Put down your weapons.'

He was surrounded. Four of them.

'Now! Or you die!'

Words should not fail a Greek. He turned at bay, sword still in hand. Words never failed crafty Odysseus.

'I am Gaius Furius Sabinius Aquila Timesitheus, *Praefectus Annonae*, by order of our sacred Emperors Gordian the Father and Gordian the Son, the traitor Domitius has been justly executed.'

The soldiers stood, striped in slivers of moonlight.

'That is unfortunate, Prefect,' one of them said. 'We gave our oath to Imperator Maximinus. And you will answer to the Thracian.'

CHAPTER 40

ROME
THE SUBURA

Six Days after the Ides of March, AD*238*

After the customer had left, Caenis sat on the thin mattress on the narrow, hard stone platform. He had been a pig, unshaven and unwashed. The reek of him, stale sweat and goats, lingered in the tiny cubicle. She looked at the one painting set in the cracked plaster of the wall. A man and a woman made love on a high bed. It had big round bolster-like pillows, a colourful bedstead, swags of material hanging down. There was a wine jug on a table, an elaborate lampstand. The woman sat on top of him. They looked at each other with intimacy and fondness.

Caenis did not blame her mother. She remembered their conversation the morning after the first time she had been sent to a man. While her father lived, they had plenty of everything. He had been a good worker, highly thought of in their district by the Magnesian Gate. When he died, her mother had sold his anvil, tongs and hammer. That had kept them for seven months. After that life had been miserable. Her mother had barely provided for them, by weaving, by spinning thread for woof and warp. Working all hours, her mother had made sure she had enough to eat. There had been nothing for luxuries. Her mother had fed her, and waited for her hopes to be realized. She was pretty, and, now she was a woman, it would be easy for her both to keep her mother and buy herself fine clothes. She would be rich, have purple dresses and maids.

She had wept. Her mother had told her to pull herself together, thank the Graces that she had good looks. Dress attractively, look neat, smile, never cheat a visitor, never talk too much, do not drink too much, keep clean, look after her figure, be amiable and lively in bed, never sullen or slovenly; all good advice. There had been no purple dresses or maids, but the next year had not been too bad. Some of the men were young and attractive, some little more than boys, hardly older than herself. The money was good; occasionally she received presents. She had given half the coins to her mother, saved much of the remainder. When her mother died, she had been able to put aside more. Then a local pimp had tried to force her to work for him. That was when she had left Ephesus. On the ship to Rome, she had stopped being Rhodope. First she thought of calling herself Margarita, but decided against the name. A Pearl was pretty, but could be dissolved in wine. She wanted something altogether tougher. Caenis better suited the woman she wanted to become; Bitch.

The bar was quiet, but she should go down. Although Ascyltos was an easy innkeeper, he did not like his girls idle. Caenis washed herself over the chipped bowl, as much for hygiene as anything. She was not unduly worried about getting pregnant. She was careful. Every morning she drank a mixture of willow, iron rust, and iron slag diluted in water, and she wore an amulet of a pierced bean wrapped in mule hide. She put on her breastband and short tunic, a pair of sandals, nothing else. The room still stank of goat. She took some of the cheap perfume she had bought, and sprinkled some on the stained mattress. Before she left, she blew out both the lamps. Ascyltos was always moaning about the waste in his establishment.

There were only three customers in the bar. Two draymen sat in a corner, drinking and talking quietly, oblivious to everything else. The other was Musaria's regular. She was sitting on his lap, whispering into his ear. That girl was a fool. The man never had any money. The previous month, Musaria had sold two necklaces another customer had given her. They were Ionic, weighing two Darics each. She had given most of the money to this regular. It was obvious he would never take her away, marry her.

Behind the counter, Ascyltos came up behind her, put his hands on her hips, and drew her back against his crotch.

'When Musaria has dealt with him, she can watch the bar for a while. It is time you reminded me of the pleasures my customers enjoy.'

Caenis said nothing, not even when he ran his hands up under her tunic. There were worse innkeepers, and, as one of her customers said, no one misses one olive from a jar.

A couple of cronies of Ascyltos came in, and he joined them at a table. Having served them wine and water, she went back behind the counter, and cleaned some cups.

She would like to get married. Of course the law said a prostitute could not wed a freeborn citizen. But it was often ignored, and there was nothing to stop her marrying a freedman. If she had a husband, and no longer had to sell her body, the *infamia* would be gone. She would be able to make a will, receive inheritances, would have the rights of any other woman. But, unlike Musaria, she was not stupid enough to think customers came to the bar of Ascyltos looking for a wife.

She had savings. There was always the fear of theft. The bags of coins and cheap jewels were hidden in different places in her room in the tenement, two lots under floorboards, one behind a loose brick. Yet everyone in the neighbourhood knew she was in the bar almost every evening, and a determined thief would find them. She had asked the die-cutter across the corridor to keep an ear for anyone breaking in. Occasionally she let him into her bed for free to keep him well disposed.

Although how he would stop any thieves was another question. He had been of little use when she was attacked in the street.

Anyway, the money she had was not near enough. When she had more, she would leave Rome. It would be easier than it had been uprooting herself from Ephesus. If she could get hands on more, she would go to one of those magical islands the ship had called at on the voyage here; Zacynthos or Corcyra. She would say that her parents were dead, she had no family, and now her husband had died. Many men would marry an attractive young widow, one with money. If she was married, she could become Rhodope again.

A man she half-recognized came into the bar. Asked if he wanted a drink, he said maybe afterwards.

Back in the cubicle, she lit the lamps, and bolted the door. Thankfully, he was not one of those who wanted to talk. She pulled off her tunic and breastband, and took his penis in her mouth. Was it true a respectable wife would never do such a thing? When he was ready, she got on all fours on the narrow bunk, and let him take her from behind. Was that another thing a good wife would not allow?

Face down on the mattress, as the man thrust into her, she wondered how she might get the money she needed.

She knew something about the Senator Gallicanus, a shameful secret that would make a mockery of his claims to philosophy and old-style virtue, that would disgrace him in the eyes of the world. That should be worth a great deal to his political enemies. But, even if she discovered who they were, how could she gain access to them? A prostitute could not walk up to the mansions of the great and demand admittance. If they listened, why would they believe her?

Yet now fate had given her two other ways to acquire the necessary coins.

Unexpectedly, Castricius had arrived at her door that afternoon. The young knife-boy had been very full of himself, claimed he had been released from gaol by the Senator Menophilus himself, and sent on some very important secret mission to the North. But he was no fool. He had given the soldier escorting him the slip somewhere in the Apennines, and returned to Rome. He had taken new lodgings, but the Subura was teaming, and the authorities would be too busy with the war to come looking for him.

Caenis had not believed a word of the story, but she knew he was an escaped prisoner, and there would be a price on his head. It would be all the higher if she bore witness against him for the murder in the Street of the Sandal-makers.

And then there was the die-cutter. Unable to sleep, one morning before dawn she had followed him. He was so short-sighted, it had been child's play. And now she knew where he went. Later, watching them leave, she had realized what they were. Who else met in secret in the dark? And one of them had been careless enough to make one of their signs. The authorities would reward anyone who pointed them to a cell of atheist Christians.

With what was stashed away, perhaps she need only inform against one of them.

The man finished and left. The cubicle smelt of cheap perfume and goat.

CHAPTER 41

THE EAST
CARRHAE

Six Days after the Ides of March, AD*238*

Priscus kept a lamp lit in the bed chamber. Just the one, a soft light to enhance beauty, not betray its flaws. It was a hot night. The slave slept with the covers thrown back. Raised on one elbow, Priscus traced the graceful hollow of the back, the swell of a hip, firm line of a young thigh. He preferred the grapes when they were green.

The slave was fast asleep. The sleep of the innocent, of those without guilt or worries. Priscus lay back. He had not slept like that for years, if ever.

The Sassanids were still camped outside the city. Two days had passed since they had been thrown back from the walls. They had not made another assault. Priscus doubted if Ardashir could persuade them to try again. So why did the King of Kings linger? The forage must be near all eaten. The horses would soon lose condition, get thin. Perhaps Ardashir was reluctant to accept the finality of the

369

verdict. Once he broke camp, and retreated, the defeat was acknowledged. Rumour would fly ahead of him – through Media, Persis and Sistan, to distant Sogdia and Bactria, through all those eastern territories so ancient and exotic sounding to a Roman ear – and the great noble families would begin to whisper, and then the revolts would flare.

When Ardashir had left, the messenger chained in the cellar would remain, and Priscus would have no reason for further procrastination. He closed his eyes, and numbered the allegiances of Rome's governors in the East, as if a recount would alter the simple arithmetic or reveal some previously overlooked figures.

Priscus himself held Mesopotamia. One to him. His brother-in-law governed Syria Palestina. A weak man, but Severinus was closely bound to the family. When Priscus' sister had been ill, and likely to die, Philip had wed the sister of Severianus. The new union had produced a son. Philip always was dutiful. Two links by marriage and one by blood should ensure the adherence of the legions stationed in the old homeland of the Jews. Two provinces in the *amicitia* of Priscus.

The Prefect of Egypt, an equestrian called Lucretius Annianus, was accounted loyal to Maximinus. Certainly, his initial act on taking up office had been to kill his predecessor, who had been appointed by Alexander. That was one to the hostile *factio*. Pomponius Julianus, the governor of

370

Syria Phoenice, was a close friend of Flavius Vopiscus, and the latter had been one of the three Senators who had put Maximinus on the throne. Two to the enemy. Worse still, Cappadocia now was under the rule of Catius Celer, and he himself was one of the Triumvirate behind the elevation of the Thracian. Three in the wrong camp.

Aradius of Syria Coele and Domitius Valerianus of Arabia had been given their posts recently by Maximinus, but were not seen as his adherents. Rather, most had interpreted their appointments as the regime attempting to conciliate moderate senatorial feeling. Both men had pursued successful careers of unusual probity for the times, and were uncontaminated by partisanship or denunciations. They were two in the laager of the uncommitted.

If Priscus could win over Aradius and Domitius Valerianus the count would stand at four to three in his favour. If only one came over, but he somehow eliminated one of the followers of Maximinus, three to two. He thought about factors of time and distance, the merits of poison and steel. He pushed aside the fatal appeal of inaction. A choice had to be made. Blood and steel, it was the only path.

The boy turned in his sleep and muttered. Priscus opened his eyes, and regarded him. With the near perfect symmetry and harmony of his features, the curve of his shoulder, the clean limbs, he could model Ganymede for a sculptor. The beauty of a boy was natural, unadorned. Women needed artifice; cosmetics, tongs and curlers, gauzy gowns, legions of maids and hairdressers.

Reason would always choose true beauty, necessity settle for less. Not that Priscus had any time for the nonsense spouted by philosophers. The modest youth learning from the restrained older man, the combination of pleasure with virtue; such a path was nothing but condemning yourself to the punishment of Tantalus: parched, but unable to drink. And if restraint failed, there would be the fresh tortures of guilt. Far better to imitate the Emperor Trajan; take those you desire to bed, but do not hurt them.

Priscus looked at the first, golden down on the boy's face. When it became stubble, cast a shadow on his cheeks, then he would send him away. Priscus had bought estates outside Antioch and in Italy. The stewards and overseers of his properties were all good-looking young men.

'Prefect.' Sporakes was in the room, his voice calm, but urgent.

'Yes?'

'The Persians are inside the walls.'

Priscus got out of bed, reached for his tunic. 'How many?'

'Too many.' The bodyguard helped him on with his boots, passed him his sword-belt.

'The *consilium*?'

'Have been summoned to the roof-garden. I will bring your armour up.'

As he left, Priscus took a last look at the boy,

who was sitting up in bed, naked, with no false modesty.

The governor's palace was set high on the acropolis. From its roof, the scene was set out like a spectacle in the amphitheatre. Flaring torches and dark groups of men pushing through the Moon Gate and into the streets. One phalanx was moving inexorably towards the Gate of Sin in the north, another heading to the Euphrates Gate in the west. Outside many more waited for those gates to be opened. Either surprise or treachery had unbarred the Moon Gate. It made no difference now, the thing was irreversible.

Priscus stood still as Sporakes fitted his breastplate, checking buckles, tightening laces. One by one the *consilium* clattered onto the roof. Some were still getting armed, but there was no panic, no wasted words. Philip, the Prefects Julianus and Porcius, the Hatrenes Ma'na and Wa'el, the men from Edessa Manu, Abgar and Syrmus, they were all dependable. These were men too valuable to throw away in futile gestures.

'The *bucellarii* are saddling the horses in the courtyard,' Philip said.

'Good.' Priscus took his helmet from Sporakes. 'No Sassanids to the south yet. We will take the Mirage Postern.'

'We must be quick,' Philip said.

His brother was right. The Persians were nearly at the Euphrates Gate.

Down in the courtyard the horses were infected

by the nerves of the men. They stamped and barged each other, calling out in their anxiety.

A *bucellarius* held the head of Priscus' warhorse, another gave him a leg up.

As he settled himself into his saddle, the boy appeared by Priscus.

'Take me with you.' He had slung on a tunic, his hair was tousled, eyes very frightened in the torchlight.

'No.'

The boy gripped his boot. 'I love you, master.'

Priscus put his hand on the boy's head. 'You are a slave now. Tomorrow you will have a new master.' He ruffled the boy's hair. 'Your looks will save you from much harm.'

'Master . . .'

Priscus gestured to the troopers, and two of them pulled the boy away. Not looking at the boy again, he checked the men were ready, gave the order to leave.

The streets down from the citadel were narrow and winding. They went at a canter. As they cornered, the metal hipposandals of their mounts slipped on the cobbles, struck sparks. They held hard to the horns of their saddles.

As they crossed a square, Priscus saw dark words daubed across a light wall. *Such things accursed war brings in its train.* Much graffiti had appeared in the last couple of days, all of it highly literate. Priscus recognized the line as Euripides, although the context escaped him. Perhaps he had underestimated

Hieronymous and the *Boule* of Carrhae. Now it seemed they had betrayed their city for some promise of personal safety. Priscus very much hoped the Sassanids would play them false.

They had not gone far when they heard the sounds of pursuit. High eastern shouts screeched above the thunder of their own passing. At each twist and turn, the ululating war cries grew louder. They echoed off the close walls, burst from every alleyway. Priscus crouched forward over the neck of his mount, urging it on, oblivious to everything but keeping it balanced, retaining his seat.

The open space inside the postern was empty. The gate was shut. Its guards nowhere to be seen. The column skidded to a halt. The Persians were close behind. Sporakes and two *bucellarii* jumped down, lifted the bar, opened the door. Priscus and the others waited, the flanks of their horses heaving. The three on foot led their mounts out. No assailants fell on them, no arrows took them. Outside all was still quiet. Behind the streets rang with the approach of the Sassanids.

'Prefect.' It was Wa'el. 'The reptiles will run us down. With two men, I can hold the postern.'

'Thank you.'

Wa'el grinned, his face shining with conviction. 'For my Prince Ma'na. If you live, tell King Sanatruq I kept my word. Honour is not dead in Hatra.'

Priscus saluted, and went through the gate.

They rode west across the plain. They were well mounted, safe for the moment. Batnae and the

Mesopotamian field army were not far. Under the star-pricked sky, Priscus regretted the boy. He was beautiful, but he might have delayed them. No call for misguided heroics. Priscus would buy another. There were always boys for sale.

CHAPTER 42

NORTHERN ITALY
AQUILEIA

Seven Days after the Ides of March, AD238

The wall came down with the roar of a man-made avalanche. A great cloud of dust rolled out across the plain, obscuring the town. It was a paradox that builders always had to make things so much worse before they could begin their repairs. From this destruction, the defences of Aquileia would rise stronger. But at what cost?

Menophilus looked around the ravaged landscape. Every building within four hundred paces of the walls had been razed. From the huts and sheds of market gardeners and smallholders to the sumptuous villas of the rich, all that remained were pitiful mounds of debris. Having finished with the ancestral homes of families great and small, the gangs of workmen under Barbius were tearing down the tombs that lined the roads approaching the gates. All the useable materials were being dragged to piles of spoil heaped close to the sections of the wall that needed strengthening or rebuilding. Dislocated fragments of statues and relief sculpture could be seen in each jagged knoll; the works of patient hours of skill reduced to unwieldy blocks.

Menophilus let his eyes stray to a shady orchard. Men with axes, stripped to the waist against the sweat of their labour, were chopping down the trees. They went at it with a will. Whatever spark of the divine and beneficent cosmos was within them, most men had an appetite for destruction.

Turning his gaze to the bright water of the Natiso that flowed past the town, Menophilus marshalled his thoughts. That morning, Claudius Severus and Claudius Aurelius, the two most prominent living descendants of Marcus Aurelius, had reached Aquileia. Both had appeared put out to hear that the bridge over the Aesontius had been rendered impassable, as if they did not understand that their arrival from Rome was too late to begin organizing any realistic defence of the Alpine Passes against Maximinus. After lengthy negotiation, it had been decided that they would go west to look to the security of two strategic towns on the North Italian Plain: Severus to Verona and Aurelius to Mutina. Their breeding had ensured they agreed with moderately good grace. Of course, they announced, their entourages would require a rest of several days before they set out.

It would be better when they were gone. Menophilus and Crispinus had reached a *modus vivendi*, despite the latter's stiffness and irritating beard. Nothing would be gained by the presence in Aquileia of two more members of the Board of Twenty. And the two scions of the Antonine dynasty might actually be of some use in the overall strategy of the war.

Although largely symbolic, the two Claudii should assist Annianus at Mediolanum in keeping the Po Valley loyal to the new regime. If not too hampered by Valerius Priscillianus, and certainly that corpulent and indolent patrician would contribute little, Cethegillus might succeed in barring the western Alps to any reinforcements marching to Maximinus from the Provinces of Germania. If that was the case, and the Ravenna fleet under Laco controlled the Adriatic, the entire focus of the war must be centred here on Aquileia.

Maximinus would come. There could be no doubt. It was merely a question of how soon. Aquileia would be invested. A siege – its drawn out privations and constant fear – pushed those inside and outside the walls to the extreme limits of physical and mental endurance. Tempers frayed, and loyalties unravelled. After a time all standards of civilized behaviour gave way. Every advantage that ingenuity could devise must be employed.

Menophilus wondered about Timesitheus. He had heard nothing. It would help if the little Greek had managed to win over the brigand chief Corvinus. Unaided, they could not block the passes behind Maximinus' army, but they might disrupt his communications and supplies, kill or capture important messengers, loot baggage trains, create a feeling of unease and isolation.

Of course, the knife-boy Castricius might already have struck down the tyrant. It was possible, but unlikely. More probably, Castricius would be apprehended. His fate would not be pleasant. But he was of little consequence. Even if he succeeded, it was no guarantee the war would be stillborn. The northern army might replace Maximinus with another candidate for the throne, and the war would still come to Aquileia.

The worst of the dust had settled. Teams of draught animals were being driven to haul the rubble clear of the breach.

Menophilus' thoughts roamed unbidden. He was still very tired, could not imagine feeling any other way. An image of the empire unrolled in his mind like a long strip of papyrus. Lights burnt bright in Carthage and Rome, their light diffused out across the Province of Africa and the Italian peninsular. But in the gloom of the rest of the *imperium* menacing, often indistinct shapes shifted and moved. Menophilus stared into the darkness. News had come that Decius in *Hispania* had arrested the courier from the Gordiani and reaffirmed his allegiance to Maximinus. How many other governors would follow his example? With the possible exception of Dacia, the provinces bordering the Danube would remain loyal to Maximinus until his death. Honoratus in *Moesia Inferior* would see to that. There was no specific reason to believe that the armies along the Rhine or in Britain would come over. Catius Priscillianus in *Germania Superior* was brother to one of the men who had put the Thracian on the throne, and Tuccianus in *Britannia Inferior* was close friend to another. Only in the East was there a certain light, some slight chance of salvation. Timesitheus had revealed that Priscus of Mesopotamia already had flirted with revolt. Severianus in *Palestina*, his brother-in-law, had attended the treasonous meeting in Samosata, and neither Aradius in *Syria Coele* or Domitius Valerianus in Arabia were thought particularly attached to Maximinus. But there again, one of the Emperor-makers, Catius Clemens, held Cappadocia, and the governors of Syria Phoenice and Egypt were considered strong adherents of the tyrant. Menophilus was becoming ever more certain that the war would be decided here at Aquileia, and that the town would stand alone.

A stork flew across the Natiso to the south. The workmen had been reluctant to pull down the crumbling battlements of a tower on which was a nest. If the storks left Aquileia, it was an omen of the fall of the town. Menophilus had had to intervene. The best omen was to fight for your country. And there were many other nests.

Menophilus turned his horse. The animal picked its way across the gauged and scarred earth. At the corner of the wall by the Circus, the road from the north came into view. It was crammed with thousands of refugees; pathetic huddles of men, women and children, innocent victims of a war not of their making.

If there was a benevolent creator ordering a peaceful cosmos, why did he allow the evils of war? Was the strife of war caused by the foolishness and ignorance of men? Or was the disturbance superficial, just skin deep as it were, or even merely apparent, unreal, some kind of illusion? In ways too profound to be grasped by men, did the Demiurge permit some to suffer to build a more secure future for all? Either interpretation was better than the only other alternative, that there was no God, and everything was down to chance. Menophilus believed there was a divine intelligence immanent in the world. To do otherwise would be to cast himself adrift without sails or oars on the widest of seas. He preferred not to blame the Creator. That reeked of cowardice. Mankind should bear the burden of war, and he himself must take the weight of his terrible actions this past month.

CHAPTER 43

NORTHERN ITALY, BEYOND THE ALPS THE TOWN OF EMONA

Eight Days after the Ides of March, AD238

An Emperor should lead from the front. It encouraged the men, and he did not have to inhale their dust. Maximinus headed a weary column of cavalry. The forced march had taken its toll. Nine thousand strong when they left Sirmium, their number had been diminished at every halt. The regulars – the Horse Guards and auxiliaries – had suffered no more than was to be expected, and the light horse – Moors, Persians and Parthians – had stood up to the pace better than could have been hoped. But the heavy armoured troops – both the cataphracts and the Sarmatians – as well as the German allies had left a meteor trail of lame horses and stragglers the length of the Savus valley. The mounts of the former had been worn down by the weight of armour, and the latter by the sheer size of their riders. Three hacks had broken down under the Emperor himself.

Despite everything, at a bend in the road, when

he could see back down the line, Maximinus was not displeased. The riders were still in good spirits, the order of march carefully observed. A few days' rest, and if it came to battle, with the remaining men, he could ride through almost any force in the world on an open field.

That there would be fighting was now certain. The messenger from Potens had met them the previous day on the road. The news from Rome was all bad. Sabinus was murdered. The capital was lost. Potens was fleeing to Decius in Spain. The Senate had decreed a Board of Twenty to defend Italy from their rightful Emperor, although, by the time Potens had left, its members had not been elected.

Nothing in war was certain or easy. There were difficulties ahead. If the town of Emona closed its gates, accompanied only by cavalry, Maximinus would have to wait for the Panonnian Legions under Flavius Vopiscus before attempting an assault. Beyond Emona were the Alps. The mountains were covered with dense forests, and the narrow passes hemmed in by overhanging cliffs that ended in precipitous drops; easy to block, and ideal for ambush. Exhausted men would have to be pushed ahead to seize the heights and most constricted places. On the far side of the Alps stood Aquileia. The last time Maximinus had passed through, the walls had been in bad condition. He understood that the townsmen had squandered his largess on the circus and theatre rather than prudently looking to their defences. The Romans of old had clearer priorities. Even if the walls had been repaired, Maximinus would not be unduly disheartened. The siege train was with the main body of the army under Julius Capitolinus. Civilians, long used to peace, could not hope to defy well-equipped soldiers for any considerable length of time. Replenished by the resources of the city and with remounts drawn from across the North Italian Plain, the army would march on Rome. There would be hard fighting, times of danger, but Maximinus was confident. When the three bodies of the field army were reunited, even allowing for those who had fallen by the way, he should have more than thirty thousand veteran soldiers and experienced barbarian warriors at his back.

What madness had induced the Senators to acclaim the Gordiani? Could those soft, southern, treacherous aristocrats not see everything he had done had been for the good of Rome, ultimately for their own wellbeing? If only Paulina were alive, she could have explained it all. Maximinus had met the Gordiani once years before in the East, when the father was governing Syria Coele, and the son acting as his Legate. The elder had looked old even then, the younger dissolute. How could anyone imagine they could sit on the throne of the Caesars?

Maximinus stretched. His thighs were sore, and his spine ached. He was no longer young, but his stamina was still good. He looked over his shoulder at his son. Maximus was slumped in the saddle, his pretty, girlish face a picture of misery. Perhaps a hard and protracted campaign would either make a man of him or kill him. If the former did not come about, the latter would spare Maximinus a hideous duty. Certainly, as he was now – weak, vicious and depraved – his son could not be allowed to inherit the throne. It occurred to Maximinus that he should recall his second cousin to the imperial entourage. Young Rutilus was serving with Honoratus on the lower Danube. Tough, intelligent and restrained, with an uncommon sense of duty, the youth had the qualities necessary in a Caesar. On reflection, military service on the frontier was a better education than the *consilium* of an Emperor, and there was plenty of time.

They would soon be at Emona. The scouts were out in front and on both sides of the line of march. Maximinus relaxed. No point in facing problems until they were in front of you. There would be more than enough crises in the next months.

A fable of Aesop came into his mind; one his mother had told. A lion and a bear fought over the carcass of a fawn. They mauled each other so badly, they lay half-dead, unable to move. A passing fox noted their condition, and ran off with the meal. If the rebels put up a strong resistance, the same could happen here. Maximinus was convinced that he would prevail against the Senate in Italy, and the Gordiani in Africa. But at what cost? A depleted, war weary army might encourage a predator.

Who might play the fox? Honoratus held the Danube. For all his indolent good looks, he was an ambitious man. Having helped create one Emperor, it was not beyond possibility that he might bid for the throne himself. Catius Clemens was yet more of a danger. Another of those who had clothed Maximinus in the purple, Clemens might cast off his hypochondria and raise the eastern army. Worse still, his brother Priscillianus commanded in *Germania Superior*. If the Euphrates and the Rhine were stripped of troops, they might crush Maximinus' forces between them in a pincer. Paulina had been right; an Emperor could trust no one.

They rounded the shoulder of the last hill, and Emona came into sight. There were still two rivers to cross, but both bridges were intact and it was not far. Maximinus' spirits lifted. The gates were not shut. Yet there was something strange. The town was unnaturally still, and above it hung a pall of smoke.

A scout was spurring back down the road. Maximinus studied the horseman. He did not hold his cloak above his head. They had not encountered the enemy. But there was something urgent about the way he pushed his mount.

The rider reined in, sketched a salute. The flanks of his horse were flecked with foam.

'Imperator, Emona is not defended. We guard

the gate. But the town is deserted. There is no one in the streets, no one anywhere. They have torn down the doors of all the houses and temples, the gates themselves. They have burnt them. There are fires in the Forum and open spaces. They have burnt all the provisions.'

An officer behind Maximinus spoke unbidden. 'The men will go hungry. It is a bad omen at the beginning of a campaign.'

The speaker was Sabinus Modestus, a brave soldier, but a fool.

Maximinus gathered his thoughts. 'The enemy flee from us. Our approach fills them with terror. It is the best of omens. We will send out parties to forage. A keen appetite is the best relish for food.'

Despite his brave words, riding up through the town filled Maximinus with apprehension. The dark, empty doorways were like openings onto the underworld. There was a reek of burning. In the distance dogs howled. Something slunk across an alley, too low and fast to be made out.

An Emperor can not show weakness.

In the Forum, Maximinus remained in the saddle as he gave the necessary orders. The imperial standard was to be set up outside the Curia. The town hall would serve as army headquarters. Pickets were to be set in all directions, the furthest at least a mile from the walls. Lookouts were to be posted on the towers, guards on the walls and gates. Barricades were to be made ready to close the latter for the night. The men were to be assigned billets, their horses stabled or tethered nearby. The pack animals were to be brought up, corralled here in the centre, what comestibles they still carried distributed. A search was to be made for any food or forage remaining in the town. Whatever was found was to be given out with equity to all. Every unit was to designate a squad of foragers. They were to go out to the surrounding farms and villas. If any came to blows over what was discovered, they were to be executed. If any tried to keep anything back for themselves, they were to be executed. No one else was to leave Emona on pain of death.

Justice tempered with severity.

Dismounted, Maximinus went into the Curia. His footsteps echoed in the empty building. It had been stripped bare. There was no furniture, no ornaments or paintings. Motes of dust turned in the air. He told an orderly to place the folding ivory throne under the apse at one end of the council chamber, and have his camp bed set up in one of the smaller rooms, along with his few possessions.

A soldier burst in, so fast his bodyguard drew his sword.

'Report,' Maximinus said.

Javolenus sheathed his blade.

The soldier was wide-eyed, frightened.

'Speak.'

'Imperator . . .' The man mastered himself. 'Imperator, the town is full of wolves. They are everywhere, dozens of packs.'

'Kill them,' Maximinus said. It explained the howling.

Sabinus Modestus spoke. 'They are sacred to Mars.'

The man was becoming a nuisance, and his cousin Timesitheus was a traitor. Maximinus controlled his anger. 'Kill them.'

The soldier did not leave, but shifted on his feet. 'What?'

'Imperator, the men will not go near them.' The soldier hesitated, then got the words out very quickly. 'Imperator, the men say they are not natural wolves. They believe it is sorcery. The inhabitants have been changed into wolves.'

'Gods below,' Maximinus said. He never underestimated the superstitions of the troops. He was one with them. 'Take me to the nearest pack.'

Three wolves were trapped in the garden of a small temple opening off the Forum. They were loping back and forth along the back wall, searching for a non-existent way of escape.

'Give me a javelin,' Maximinus said, 'and one for my bodyguard. And bring me a jug.'

The wolves had stopped. Together, they lifted their pale muzzles, and howled.

'I want one left alive.'

Javolenus nodded.

Together, they advanced cautiously. The wolves watched them without moving.

Maximinus balanced the javelin, calculated the weight and the distance, and threw. Javolenus threw a moment later. Both casts were good. The beasts leapt too late. One was skewered to the ground. The other was down, snapping at the shaft that protruded from its chest.

The final wolf backed off into the corner of the wall.

Maximinus gestured for Javolenus to stay where he was. He unfastened his cloak, and wound it tightly around his right arm. He drew his dagger.

It was an old she-wolf. Her dugs hung down. Amber eyes regarded him with complete malevolence. She raised her hackles and snarled. Still dangerous, despite her years.

With care, and no sudden movements, Maximinus approached.

The wolf was coiled, ready to pounce.

Maximinus passed the blade across in front of her. The amber eyes followed. He feinted from the right, and she sprang. Her teeth clamped down, fastened on his right arm, biting through the cloak, into his flesh. He dropped the knife, and staggered back from the impact. Then, ignoring the pain, he got his left hand around her throat, hurled his weight on top of her, and knocked her to the ground.

Pinioned under his bulk, the wolf released her grip, tried and failed to sink her fangs into his other arm. Using all his great strength, Maximinus throttled her.

She was still alive, but limp, when Maximinus shifted, and took one of her forelegs in his right hand. He wrenched it back, until the bones snapped. Methodically, he broke her other three legs. She revived enough to scream. There was something human about the sound.

The pain coursed up Maximinus' arm. The blood was soaking through the cloak, staining it from purple to black. He felt sick, but had to see this through.

'Javolenus, the knife and the jug.'

With precision, he cut her throat, then caught the bright blood in the jug.

It was done.

When he got up, he was unsteady on his feet. His arm throbbed and bled. He passed the jug to Javolenus.

'Sprinkle a few drops all around the walls, then bury her here where she died. No wolf, nothing in the shape of a wolf, ever again will come into Emona.'

It was what they had done in his youth in the hills of Thrace.

Back in the privacy of the room he had taken for himself, an army doctor cleaned and dressed his right arm.

When the man had gone, Maximinus sat motionless on the camp bed. Already the wolf was forgotten, and his thoughts had returned to Rome and to the duty of revenge.

After Paulina had been killed, as he drank, he had had Apsines tell him stories of vengeance. The sophist had recounted terrible things from the Greek past. Decapitated heads drowned in bowls of blood. Dismembered children served to their father in a meal. When he demanded Roman tales, Maximinus had heard of enemies burnt alive in the Forum, of severed hands and tongues nailed to the Rostra. The Syrian had misjudged him. Such barbarities were unfitting for an Emperor of Rome. When the traitorous Senators and the Gordiani were in his power, his actions would be seemly and measured. No torture or gloating. The enemies of the *Res Publica* would be strangled in the dark of the Tullianum, their corpses exposed on the Gemomian Steps, their houses demolished, and everything else they owned confiscated to reward the soldiers. Nothing excessive. True Roman revenge.

CHAPTER 44

AFRICA
CARTHAGE

Nine Days after the Ides of March, AD238

'Strike with the point, not the edge of the blade.'
Gordian had raised himself up on the horns of his saddle. He had already said the same words to the other main body of recruits, and different speeches to each of the units of regular troops.

'A cut, no matter what its force, seldom kills. Often it is deflected from the vitals, if not by shield or helmet, then by a limb or by bone. A lame man or a man with one arm is still dangerous. But a thrust driven in just two inches is always fatal. Delivering a cut, your right arm and flank are exposed. When you stab, your body remains covered by your shield, and your enemy is wounded before he realizes. Thrust to the face, and the man standing against you will flinch, and then he is open to the killing blow.'

The recruits stood in a stolid mass. They had heard all this before. For the last four days, the junior officers and soldiers seconded from the regular units had been instructing them out here on the plain before the city. Of course there had been no time for marching, manoeuvres or entrenching, let alone the swimming and other advanced skills recommended by all the tactical manuals. But they had been issued with improvised equipment, and the basic arms drills had been relentless. They had complained on learning that they would work through the heat of the afternoons, like slaves or soldiers on punishment duty. The instructors had quelled that: Did they want to offer themselves up like sacrificial animals, or learn how to survive?

'When you return to your homes tonight, look at your aged parents, your wives, and your children. It is for them you are fighting. If you fight with courage, if you are men, you will return to them tomorrow night. If you let fear unman you, if you turn your backs, then you will be cut down. Be under no illusion, there is no safety in flight. If you run, you will die, Carthage will fall, and the Moorish barbarians that follow Capelianus will rape and enslave your loved ones.'

Not the right note on which to end.

'But if you stand firm, remain in your ranks, victory will be yours. Our enemies do not want to fight. They are forced into the field by the cruel servant of a monstrous tyrant. Their hearts are not in it. Some of them have families here. When they see your resolve, your numbers, your ordered, silent ranks, they may not fight at all.'

Now to finish.

'If they do fight, it will be half-heartedly, under compulsion. They have nothing for which to risk their lives. You, by contrast, have everything. You fight for homes and families, for freedom. Justice is on our side. The gods are on our side. We will be victorious!'

The recruits cheered.

Before he rode away, Gordian took time to survey the whole scene, fearful there might be something that he had overlooked, something that might unhinge all his plans.

The scouts were out of sight, some ten miles distant, watching the hills through which Capelianus would come. Similarly, the remainder of the cavalry were hidden by distance and a slight fold in the plain. Only a cloud of dust marked where the two hundred Horse Guards were teaching the three hundred levy horsemen how to keep together in the charge. Tomorrow, if Gordian's stratagem was to work, they must charge as one.

The rest of the army was close at hand, set out in the places they would occupy the next day. The line faced west, straddling the Mappalian Way. The left rested on the villa of Sextus, at their back were the aqueduct, tombs and town walls, and the fish ponds were some way off to the right. The villa was garrisoned by the newly raised 1st Legion Gordiana Pius Fidelis. Sabinianus had argued that these four hundred veterans and *stationarii* would be better employed stiffening part of the array in the open field. But Gordian had overruled him.

396

It was vital the flanks of the army were as secure as could be achieved.

Running from the villa towards the north was a solid phalanx of heavy infantry. On the left were three thousand levies. The centre consisted of two thousand regulars; the 1st Cohort Flavia Afrorum, the Cohort of the 3rd Legion Augusta, the Praetorians, and the 13th Urban Cohort. The right was held by the other three thousand levies equipped for hand-to-hand combat, and at the extremity of this wing stood the 15th Cohort Emesenorum. The latter had only arrived from Ammaedara this morning. They would be tired, but hopefully by the next morning less so than Capelianus' men. The right was the position of honour, the most exposed place in the line. Of all the army, the 15th Cohort had seen action most recently. Not a pitched battle, but the previous autumn they had been deployed chasing bandits back into the mountains.

In front of the close-order troops Gordian had had a broad swathe of pits dug. At the bottom of each was a sharpened stake. Beyond were two thousand more levies armed with bows and slings. After the opening of the battle, when they had discharged their missiles, they were to move back through the pits and the heavily armed troops. In open order, and knowing where the traps lay, with luck most should negotiate the pits. They were to retire through the regular troops in the centre. The recruits in the main battle line were not yet experienced enough to open their ranks to let others pass through. Rather than close up again, they were more likely to be swept away in a general rush to the rear and the illusory safety of the town.

Gordian looked again at the open ground to the right of his line, at the walls and buildings of the fish ponds beyond. The next day everything would depend on what happened there. Finally, he was satisfied that he had done all he could. The light was beginning to fade, and, at the head of his staff, he turned his horse's head for home.

The levies were full of enthusiasm. Only those who had not stood close to the steel ever welcomed the onset of battle. Their eagerness would not last. They were Africans, and the hot climate thinned their blood, made them reluctant to see it shed. The nature of all Africans inclined to cowardice. And they were from the city. Every military man knew country-men made better soldiers. Unlike the soft urban plebs, they were nurtured under the open sky in a life of hard work, enduring the weather, careless of comfort, unacquainted with bath houses, ignorant of luxury, simple-souled, content with but a little, their limbs toughened to withstand every kind of toil, digging entrenchments, bearing a burden; patient endurance was in their souls.

Yet he had recruited men of the right age, neither beardless adolescents, not bent old men, and the correct physique, clean-limbed, almost every one of them approaching six foot tall. Care had been taken to draw them from the better occupations. No pastry cooks or pimps: until a few days ago they had been masons, wainwrights, butchers, and huntsmen, except, of course, for the four hundred or so gladiators distributed along the front rank. Whatever the shortfall among the latter in the virtues instilled by freedom, it should be compensated by their skill at arms. All in all, if the levies stood up to the first clash, they should buy enough time for Gordian's ambush to win the battle.

At the grave of Serenus Sammonicus, he reined in to pay his respects. The monument to his old tutor was not finished. The fresh white marble was uncarved, the niche not yet tenanted by his statue. Gordian hoped he would live to see it completed. This was not the moment to dwell on death. He moved on. *We will not go down to the house of death, not yet, not until our day arrives.*

His father was waiting in the Palace. They were dining in the room called the Delphix. It was not a large party, apart from the two Emperors, just the high-ranking officers: Sabinianus, Mauricius, the Praetorian Prefect Vocula, the four commanders of the Cohorts, and the two young tribunes Pedius and Geminius. The tribunes deserved their places, although nine was the lucky number for a dinner.

Servants brought in the first plates; snails fattened on emmer meal and grape syrup, anchovies fried with sea-anemone tentacles, a relish of fish sauce, warm bread, and a salad of rocket and pepper. Gordian was relieved there was nothing unpropitious, no lentils, lettuce or beans, not even eggs, nothing pertaining to the dead. In times of tension, the superstitious could read omens in anything. As they crossed the Euphrates, the legions of Crassus had been issued with lentils and salt, the symbols of mourning. They had marched to Carrhae expecting to die.

The wine flowed – Caecuban and Falernian – and the talk was animated, even febrile. Gordian noted his father seldom joined the conversation. Towards the end of the main course, he moved across to his couch.

'Father, you are not still concerned about the prodigy?' He spoke quietly, although there was little danger of being overheard by the other now raucous guests. 'Given the number of animals an Emperor sacrifices, sooner or later one will give birth during the ceremony. It is natural, signifies nothing.'

His father touched his hand affectionately. 'The soothsayers interpretation was although I would die, my son would be Emperor. And they predicted that, like the new-born animal, you would be gentle and innocent, subject to treachery.'

In deference to his father's feelings, Gordian did not point out that at the time of the prodigy, he had already been proclaimed Emperor, and that as a mature man his nature was well known. He sought to lighten the mood. 'At least, Father, tomorrow we do not face death by drowning.'

His father squeezed his hand. 'Not all men share

your Epicureanism. My belief is that the gods exist, that they care for mankind, and send us signs of the future, hard though these are to grasp correctly. There are many astrologers in Carthage. I summoned another, a learned man. He demonstrated how the constellations at your birth prove that you will be both son and father of an Emperor. You have no child, so it follows that you will live through tomorrow. Having no desire to outlive you, it reassures me. Now, I am tired, and will go to my chamber, leaving you younger men to your dessert.'

It was a warm spring night, the curtains drawn back, and the windows open to catch the breeze. Sometime later, towards midnight, Gordian saw lights twinkling in the distance. He got up, and went over to see better. Campfires on the hills. Capelianus had come.

Drawing near the window, he heard faint music, shouts and cries from an unseen street, like a Bacchic throng.

Sabinianus was beside him. 'A troop of revellers, their course seems to lie through the city toward the Mappalian Way.'

'A good sign.'

'Perhaps.'

'Come, Sabinianus, let us drink.'

'It is late. I will go to my bed. You should take your rest.'

'Nonsense, let us drown consideration.'

'Brother, tomorrow is the day.'

'And I hope well of it, expect victory.'

Sabinianus took his arm. 'If it goes otherwise, remember I have a fast boat ready for you, fully crewed, lying off the mole of the outer harbour. Hail them with the password Safety.' He looked as if he had more to say, but did not.

'*Salus*,' Gordian repeated.

They embraced, kissed, and Sabinianus left.

Gordian turned to his remaining officers, now sitting quietly watching. 'Come, brothers, let us burn the night with torches. Fill your cups, let us toast tomorrow. *Let me not die without a struggle, inglorious, but do some big thing first, that men to come shall know of it.*'

CHAPTER 45

AFRICA
THE HILLS OUTSIDE CARTHAGE

Nine Days after the Ides of March, AD238

It was late, but Capelianus did not expect to sleep. Tomorrow was the day.

The men would be tired. The march had been along good roads, but it had been gruelling. Capelianus had driven them hard; from Lambaesis east to Thamugadi and Theveste, then north-east through Ammaedara – where the 15th Cohort had just escaped him – and Thugga, before swinging further north to approach Carthage through the hills. As they camped, the lights of the city had been laid out below them. It would do the men good to see the scale of the plunder that awaited.

In the morning, the troops might be footsore, but Capelianus had no doubt that they would be victorious. Stripping Lambaesis had produced almost two thousand legionaries. The auxiliaries stationed in or near the base had been called in: the 1st Ala of Pannonians, and seven Cohorts, the 1st Flavian, 1st Syrian archers, 2nd Spanish, 2nd Moors, 2nd Thracians, 6th Commagenes, and 7th Lusitanians.

In all he had raised six thousand infantry, and five hundred cavalry. To these he had added two thousand irregular Moorish horsemen. Admittedly more than one in ten had not completed the march. In a way Capelianus was pleased. The weak had been weeded out. Those that remained were tough, the Moorish cavalry savage, and the regulars veterans.

Those they would face were contemptible. A mob from the amphitheatre and circus. Used to sitting on soft cushions, watching others exert themselves or die, perhaps throwing the occasional stone when the spectacles did not amuse them. They were supported by a handful of auxiliaries, a few from the Urban Cohorts – men better at bullying stevedores than fighting – and a detachment from the 3rd Augusta itself. The latter had already mutinied once, and it was unlikely that they would stand against their comrades when it came to battle. When his men came close, the scant number of real soldiers who followed the Gordiani would not be able to stop the Carthaginian plebs pissing themselves, and running for the city.

The troops were only one reason to be confident. Capelianus was bred to command in war. For four years he had campaigned in the wilds of the desert and the harshest of mountains against the most bloodthirsty of tribes. There had been no defeats. The barbarians had learnt to fear his name. Tomorrow the Gordiani would learn that same hard lesson. The father was an old goat, so infirm he could no longer sit a horse or stand for more

404

than half an hour. The son had massacred a couple of villages of peasants, and had the hubris to compare himself to Alexander and Hannibal. His mind addled and constitution ruined by drink, it was said he haunted the backstreets of the city, searching out magicians and other charlatans, anyone whose potions and strange rites might promise to restore his undermined virility.

Capelianus knew justice and the gods were on his side. He had kept to his *sacramentum*, and his men had returned to their military oath. The Gordiani, and all who followed them, had broken the most sacred of promises. Capelianus fought for the lawful Emperor, the Gordiani for their own vanity and advantage. Already the gods had shown their displeasure. At the outset of their revolt, when the old satyr was sacrificing the victim had given birth. A hideous prodigy, made all the worse by the blood that had splashed the old man's toga. And the astrologers read disaster in their stars. The captive Arrian, well goaded by the pincers and the hooks, had admitted everything. The heavens foretold the Gordiani would die by drowning. It amused Capelianus to think how he would fulfil the will of the gods when the Gordiani were in his power.

Victory was assured. There was no need for elaborate plans, no need to fear some cunning stratagem. Line the troops up, and set them on the enemy. The soldiers and Moors would be eager to be unleashed. Capelianus had promised them three days of licence in Carthage, three days of

405

unrestrained rape and pillage. Capelianus knew what motivated men; lust and greed.

Outside the tent, from somewhere in the camp, came the sounds of music and laughter. Discipline was not what it had been in the past. If the revelry did not soon cease, Capelianus would get up and have the perpetrators arrested. In the morning, one or two salutary executions might concentrate the minds of the men on the task in hand.

Capelianus shifted on his camp bed. Sleep would continue to elude him. The victory won, what rewards might he expect? It was true that Maximinus was less known for generosity than punishment. Every Roman Senator had read the *Agricola* of Tacitus. Its message was not hard to grasp. A suspicious Emperor mistrusted and feared too great a military triumph won by a subordinate, no matter how loyal that general. For all his virtue, old Agricola had been lucky to be sent into retirement, not to the block of the headsman.

The Senate had declared against Maximinus. What would the Senators do when the Gordiani were dead? The vengeance of the Thracian would be terrible. To have any hopes beyond ruin, exile and death, beyond the destruction of their families, the Senators must find another candidate. Decius in Spain was wedded to Maximinus, the governors along the Rhine and Danube said to be equally committed. The Senate must look to the East then, or, just possibly to Africa? Ambition flickered in Capelianus' thoughts. He had been born to win great victories, to humble the powerful, perhaps spare the weak, to sit in judgement on the fate of peoples, cities and continents: Imperator Capelianus Augustus Pius Felix.

Yet to ascend the throne of the Caesars was to share the fate of Damocles, to sit under a sword suspended by a thread. Better someone else wore the purple. Capelianus' grandfather had been one friend among many of Antoninus Pius. Better by far to be the one man on whom the Emperor relied, to be the power behind the throne. A malleable man of noble ancestry would have to be found. If things did not go well, his confidant could change sides, but an Emperor must die. Such things might lie in the future, but now Capelianus needed to rest. Tomorrow was the day.

He must have slept. One of the guards was calling from behind the hangings. Gods below, it was early, not yet cock crow, but early. Capelianus swung his legs off the bed, sat up.

'Enter.'

The guard put his head around the curtain. 'A deserter, Sir, high ranking.'

'Have you searched him?'

'Yes Sir, we have taken his weapons.'

'Bring him in, but watch him.'

The deserter was a tall man, wearing a tunic and travelling cloak. He had an oddly supercilious air, for a man in custody. He looked vaguely familiar.

'Name?'

'Health and great joy.'

'Do not try my patience.'

'I had hoped for a warmer welcome.'

'Name?'

'Sabinianus, Legate to the Proconsul of Africa.'

Capelianus could not help himself jumping up from the bed, peering into the face of the man. There was no doubt, it was him; the other of the Cercopes, here in his tent.

'A drink would be hospitable.'

Capelianus backed away, picked up his sword. The bone hilt was reassuring in his fist.

'What are you doing here?'

Sabinianus smiled. 'Have no fear, I am not an assassin. I have never desired to die in a doomed cause. So I have come to renew my oath to our sacred Emperor Maximinus.'

Capelianus felt a surge of disgust. The world had fallen so low.

'And you think I will welcome you?'

'Perhaps not, but as the saying goes, love the treachery, hate the traitor.'

'What proof can you offer of your change of heart?'

'What proof do you want?'

Capelianus considered.

The guards watched the deserter.

Sabinianus yawned. If anything he looked bored.

'Come with me,' Capelianus said.

It was still dark.

The big game cart was parked near the general's pavilion. The feral reek grew stronger as they approached.

'Unbar the gate.'

When they did so, there was the stench of excrement.

'Bring the torches closer.' Capelianus was beginning to enjoy this, delighting in his own ingenuity. 'Take a good look.'

The guttering light revealed a man loaded with chains, lying in his own filth.

'Say *Health and great joy* to your friend Arrian.'

The figure in the cart struggled into a sitting position. His fingernails were gone, his eye sockets empty. His blind, crusted face turned towards the men.

Sabinianus betrayed no emotion.

'You have a choice,' Capelianus said. 'You can be reunited with your brother Cercopes in there, share his punishments, or you can give evidence of your redemption.'

Capelianus stepped away. 'Give him a knife.'

Sabinianus took the weapon that the guard held out.

Capelianus and the guards covered Sabinianus with their swords.

'Make your decision,' Capelianus said, 'or I will make it for you.'

Sabinianus climbed into the wagon.

Arrian reached up, ran a ruined hand over the face of his friend. Sabinianus bent close over him. Arrian said something too low for Capelianus to catch.

'Of course, brother,' Sabinianus said. 'The end is to the beginning, as the beginning is to the end.'

With great tenderness, Sabinianus cut his friend's throat.

CHAPTER 46

AFRICA
THE PLAIN OUTSIDE CARTHAGE

Ten Days after the Ides of March, AD*238*

Gordianus! Imperator! Gordianus!

It was more than passing brave to ride along the lines and hear thousands chant his name. Any man might feel a little more than mortal. Gordian reined in by every unit, and made a brief speech. Each was addressed not to the officers but the men. Have confidence in your courage, your numbers, your general. Have confidence in the justice of your cause, the favour of the gods. You fight for freedom, for your loved ones, for your city, and for eternal Rome. To hope for safety in flight was folly. In battle it was the greatest cowards who were in the greatest danger. Courage was the one sure and certain hope of protection. Stand up to the initial onslaught, and the enemy would be trapped. Silence in the ranks, listen for the commands of your officers, do not desert your friends, your kinsmen, your tentmates, your brothers. Victory will be ours!

He wished he had had more sleep. At this season

the hours of darkness and daylight were balanced. Sabinianus had been right to retire early. Gordian's head ached from too much wine and too little rest. He wondered if the other senior officers felt equally jaded.

The sun was risen, but the enemy were still no more than a smear of dust over the hills on the horizon. Capelianus was no fool. He would not launch an attack while the sun was still low in the east, slanting into the eyes of his men, dazzling them. Suspecting as much, Gordian had given instructions for food and drink to be brought out from the city. All men fought better on a full stomach, better still with a moderate amount of wine to dispel some of their fears, if not to much sharpen their courage.

Gordian reached his station, and dismounted. The Praetorian Prefect Vocula offered him some bread, a handful of olives, and a flask. He took a long pull of wine, and tried to eat. *Death is nothing to us.* He had been nothing before, and he would be nothing again. Fear must not cloud his mind.

He walked out a few paces from the line to where the pits were dug, and studied the dispositions. The standards of the 1st Legion, the Gordian, Pious and Faithful, flew over the villa of Sextus. Under the tribune Pedius the four hundred would hold the left secure. From there the main battle line of close order troops stretched towards him. First stood the three thousand or so levies under the other tribune Geminius. From a distance their makeshift shields – skins and osiers stretched over wooden frames – and their rough-and-ready weapons – a miscellany of hunting spears and axes, antique swords from temples, and whatever could be gathered from the amphitheatre or hastily forged – made them look almost like real soldiers. Alongside them were the five hundred auxiliaries of the 1st Flavian Cohort under Iulius Pullus, and next to them Suillius with the same number of legionaries from the 3rd Augusta. Gordian had taken his place in the centre with the Praetorians. As the first supporters of the Gordiani, these five hundred locals from the African youth organizations had most to fear. If the day went against them, as instigators of the revolt, the former Iuvenes could expect no mercy.

Turning to the right, Gordian ran his eyes over the 13th Urban Cohort. Another five hundred professionals, well led by Alfenus, they had an appearance of dependability. Past them was Sabinianus' command, the other three thousand levies equipped for hand-to-hand combat. On the extremity of this flank was Fuscinus with the 15th Cohort of Emesenes. These five hundred easterners probably were the best troops. That was as it should be, for beyond them, open plain stretched some three hundred paces to the walls and buildings of the complex of fish ponds. Mauricius had the cavalry concealed from view.

Men were walking forward from the ranks to relieve themselves in the pits, in advance of which the two thousand levies with missile weapons clustered in the casual disarray of light infantry in open order. The onshore breeze of dawn had already died, and soon the still air held the familiar pre-battle smell of urine and excrement.

Gordian had been concerned that the nerve of many of the levies would have failed this morning, that they would have decided to cower in their homes or try to lose themselves in the myriad backstreets of Carthage. Certainly there were not as many on the field as the day before. But most had appeared, even if some had needed to be roused out by the professional soldiers sent through the city for that purpose.

Looking out to the west, the enemy now formed a dark stain across the plain. They were still a long way off. Waiting was always difficult. Act as one prepared long since. What is terrible is easy to endure.

A small lizard or skink scuttled onto a flat rock near Gordian's boot. As he watched it bask in the sun, he heard a horseman ride up from the right. The soldier slid out of the saddle, and saluted.

'Imperator, the Legate Sabinianus has not reported for duty.'

Gordian was at a loss. Where in Hades was his friend? Perhaps he had continued drinking on his own.

'Ride into town, go to the quarters of the legate. If he is there, wake him.'

The man remounted, clattered away.

The levies on the right needed a leader. Men fight better under the eyes of senior officers. Gordian waved for another messenger to approach.

'Go to the villa of Sextus. Tell the tribune Pedius he is to take command of the levies of Sabinianus. The *Primus Pilus* of the 1st Gordiana will hold the villa.'

What had happened to Sabinianus? Lack of courage had never been an issue. He had volunteered to ride alone into the oasis of Ad Palmam. At Esuba he had been second over the wall. When Gordian was wounded, he had covered him with his shield, had single-handedly saved his life.

The enemy were much closer. Gordian could tell which bodies of troops were mounted. That meant they were within 1,300 paces. But, as individuals could not be distinguished, still more than a thousand distant. The infantry were in the centre, the cavalry on both wings; all conventional enough.

Gordian forced himself to stop straining to make out where the separate units were stationed. Time would tell. His eyes rested on the slowly diminishing empty plain between the armies. It was green with spring grass, tinted lilac with tall flowers. Soon it would be ruined and foul, worse than the excrement-soiled pits. The idyll would be stained red, littered with hacked corpses and discarded weapons. If the gods existed, if they cared, they would not let such things happen.

His father had taken the sacrifice in the Forum, outside the Palace. Thankfully, given the heightened superstitions of men going into battle, he had pronounced them propitious in the second victim. It had been hard saying goodbye to his father. There was so much he had wanted to say, but lacked the words. Somehow he felt there were more things that he did not yet know, things that might forever remain unthought and unexpressed.

He had known his father drew strength from the words of the astrologers. Today there was no danger of either of them meeting death by drowning. If Gordian was to father a son who would be Emperor, he must live through this day. Perhaps his father was right. It would be a comfort. But no, this was not the moment to let go of his Epicurean convictions. He needed a clear head, sharp focus. He took another drink of wine.

Death was nothing. Anyway, he had no intention of dying here. If the worst occurred, there was always the ship commissioned by Sabinianus. Gordian would cut his way back to the city, gather his father, and sail to Rome, or to the East. One defeat did not have to end the war.

Now individuals could be seen clearly among the enemy; the colour of their shields, the pale roundness of their faces, the bright crests of their helmets. They were less than five hundred paces away. The legionaries were massed in the centre, opposite where Gordian stood. As he had hoped, there seemed to be no more than two thousand swords with the 3rd Legion. Judging by the other standards, three Cohorts of auxiliaries marched on either side. If they were up to strength, that was another three thousand. In all five thousand heavy infantry, with a screen of probably another five hundred archers out in front. The numbers of foot favoured Gordian.

Irregular cavalry flanked the enemy infantry. Riding anyhow, without order, their numbers were impossible to judge. More than a thousand, less than three; it mattered little. These Moorish tribesmen on their little ponies would not close with well-ordered infantry, not until the latter were running. They would be as brave as lions if it came to spearing men from behind. Much more important were the cavalrymen who could be seen over the heads of the infantry. Gordian knew that the nearest regular troopers to Lambaesis were the men of the 1st Ala of Pannonians based at Gemellae. Assuming it was them, the unit had a strength on papyrus of five hundred.

Capelianus had force marched to Carthage. Many stragglers would have fallen by the wayside. The men and horses still with the standards would be tired. That was all to the good.

Trumpets rang out across the plain. Some four hundred paces away, the enemy halted. The speed of his arrival before the city showed Capelianus was eager for glory, his alacrity no doubt spurred by his old animosity to Gordian's father. Yet, as a general, the cuckold appeared cautious as well as unoriginal in his thinking.

More trumpet calls. Despatch riders galloped to

and fro. All the cavalry, the reserve of regulars and all the Moorish irregulars were moving to Capelianus' left. Gordian felt his spirits lift. His open right flank, the gap between the 15th Cohort and the walls and warehouses of the fish ponds had been temptation enough. This battle could be decided in those three hundred paces of open land – just as he intended.

Gordian walked back to the line, and mounted. The Praetorians opened their formation to let him pass through to the rear. A Roman general was not some hairy, savage chieftain inspiring his men with deeds of rash ferocity in the front rank. He needed a position from where he could survey the field, manage the battle. Whatever the barbarian Maximinus believed, in pitched battle an Imperator should only draw his weapon when things were desperate and there was no other choice. If it came to that, often it was best if he turned the blade on himself. Better to die with honour, leave an example for others to follow, than live as an object of scorn. To live as a coward was no life at all.

Reordered, spacings dressed, the enemy again were moving forward. The cavalry walked in line with the heavy infantry. Their archers jogged out in front.

Gordian's light infantry could not contain themselves. In small groups, no more than half a dozen at a time, they rushed forward, and let fly with slings and bows. All the missiles fell harmlessly.

The enemy were still some three hundred paces away, well out of effective range.

The enemy archers ran on, bent forward like men with rain in their faces. As they got closer, one or two went down. Not near enough to make a difference.

Some hundred paces from their opponents, Capelianus' bowmen came to a stop. Gordian had not heard the order. As one they drew and released. The volley scythed through Gordian's men. One missile could be dodged, a multitude was an altogether more terrible thing. The recruits broke and ran. Another volley caught them as they tried to negotiate the pits. Many were hit. Pushing and shoving, maddened by their terror, some impaled themselves on the stakes.

'Open ranks. Let the light troops go through.'

Gordian's order was repeated down the line. The Praetorians and regulars did as they were bidden. The militiamen dashed down the gaps. At least half continued running, off under the aqueduct, through the tombs, and away towards the gates.

'Close ranks. Vocula, have some Praetorians rally those that remain. Get the bowmen among them shooting back over our heads.'

The hostile archers pulled up at the pits. Now they were free to play their arrows on the main battle line. Gordian checked the lacing on the strap of his helmet, turned his horse face on to the threat, and brought his shield up to cover himself and the neck of his mount.

'Form *testudo*. Lock shields.'

The air thrummed with menace. Arrowheads thumped into the leather and wood of shields, dinked off metal armour. Some got through. Men screamed. The arrows fell thick around Gordian and the standards, as he had known they would. None found the mark.

Outgoing missiles arced overhead. One whistled past Gordian's head. Gods below, that would be a stupid way to die.

'Vocula, have them shoot higher. I do not want an arrow up my arse.'

The nearby Praetorians laughed.

A trumpet sounded out on the right.

Capelianus' cavalry were walking forward. The regulars came on in a column of fives. The irregulars cantered about as each man's will dictated. They moved to the space between Gordian's line and the fish ponds, into his cunningly prepared killing ground.

Time slowed. An arrow punched into Gordian's shield almost unheeded. Come on, you bastards. A little further, not far, just a few more paces.

An arrow hit a standard bearer full in the face. He fell. Another Praetorian took up his burden. Gordian barely noticed.

Come on, come on.

Now! The enemy were deep in the trap. Now Mauricius! Now!

Movement by the fish ponds. The flash of a scarlet standard. Gates opening. The glint of steel.

Hannibal had not done better at Trasimene. Gordian had them in his grasp.

A trumpet call cut through the din.

The Moorish irregulars were galloping to get clear.

Horsemen filing out of the gates. The Horse Guards, the levy troopers, the Scouts, Mauricius below a banner at their head. The ambush was sprung to perfection. Mauricius and his men would plough into the flank of the surprised enemy cavalry.

Another trumpet, brassy and clear.

Capelianus' regular troopers halted, and, without fuss, turned to face the new threat, as if on a parade ground, as if it had been expected.

Mauricius' men were forming up, getting ready to charge. But instead of crashing into a panicked huddle, they faced an ordered line five riders deep.

How had the enemy known? Had some deserter told them? Gordian felt hollow. His fortune giving way, all his plans turned illusions.

Mauricius' men were advancing.

Come now, as one prepared long since, courageously stand in the face of fortune. The numbers of heavy cavalry were about even. The close order infantry still stood. The issue yet to be decided.

The arrow storm slackened. The archers on both sides were watching the right.

The cavalry clashed together. In an instant the mounted melee was obscured by the dust kicked up by thousands of pounding hooves.

Gordian's stratagem had failed. He had hoped to lure Capelianus' troopers into the gap between the infantry and the fish ponds, catch them unaware, hit them in the flank, scatter them like chaff. As they fled, their panic might have infected their infantry. The whole army of Capelianus could have been swept away in the rout. Even if that had not come about, Mauricius should have been free to lead his men around behind the enemy line. Few troops, not even the best, hold their ranks when surrounded. The plan had failed. The gods had not been kind. The gods did not exist.

The issue would not be decided soon, not in time to affect the main battle. But already Gordian could see the standards of Mauricius' men giving ground, and the Moors were beginning to lap around their flanks.

As he watched a wedge of horsemen burst through the fight into the sunlight. Even at that distance, he recognized the centurion Faraxen and the twenty or so Scouts. Without slackening pace, Faraxen led them off the battlefield to the south.

Gordian felt a great heaviness. He did not blame Faraxen. Twenty riders could not alter the course of a battle. He hoped they would reach Phillyrio at the frontier. Although if the battle were lost, the gods knew what would become of them. Inconsequentially, he realized that he had never asked Aemilius Severinus why his men called him Phillyrio.

Something caught his eye to the front. Like an

421

audience at a play that no longer held its attention, Capelianus' infantry returned to its own concerns. The archers retired through the main body.

The shields of legionaries and auxiliaries snapped together. Like an implacable wall of steel, leather and wood, something quite inhuman, they began the final advance.

'Officers dismount. Turn the horses loose.'

Before he got out of the saddle, Gordian raised his voice to carry through the formation. 'Fellow-soldiers, your Imperator and your officers will stand and fight shoulder to shoulder with you. Together we will conquer, or share the same fate. Let no man turn his back, desert his brothers.'

The Praetorians around him cheered. Gordian Imperator! Victory and freedom!

Gordian took his place by the standards at the rear. A tall, big man, he could see over most of the helmets ahead.

The enemy broke into a run as they reached the line of pits. The rattle of their equipment proceeded them. The ranks of the legionaries bearing down on Gordian clattered sideways, eddied and bunched, but close packed, some still failed to avoid the pitfalls. They yelled in agony as their legs went from under them and the sharpened, splintered wood pierced them. Their tentmates trampled over them.

'Stand firm! Hold the line!'

An awful uproar on both flanks

At both ends of the array the levies were running, with not a blow struck. They had given way like a tenement in an earthquake.

Cowards! Traitors! Carthaginian catamites!

'Silence in the ranks!' Gordian tried to take in all that was happening. Everything was confusion, going too fast.

The legionaries had not charged home into the two thousand of his regulars who remained. The legionaries stood in a ragged, panting line a few paces away.

Behind Gordian on both wings the mob were throwing down their shields and weapons, the better to run. He could not see what had happened to the 15th Cohort on the far right, but to the left the standards of the 1st Gordiana still flew over the villa. If only he still had the horse. He needed an unobscured view to make sense of the chaos. If the discipline of Capelianus' auxiliaries broke, and they chased after the routing levies, the issue here in the centre might still be balanced.

Uniformed men off to the left, slashing at the backs of the fleeing plebs. Dozens of them, hundreds. The atavistic urge to slaughter the defenceless had overcome all the auxiliaries' years of training. It was the same on the right. There was still hope. Two thousand against two thousand here at the heart of the battle.

'Imperator.' Vocula was pointing.

The standards of Suillius' Cohort of the 3rd were dipping.

423

Maximinus Imperator. The shout was loud. *Maximinus Imperator.*

They were reversing their swords. The treacherous bastards were going over. They would not fight their fellow legionaries. They would rather serve a barbarian tyrant than Emperors born in Rome. Beyond them the standards of the 1st Flavian Cohort were going down as well.

Who was left? The Praetorians, on their right, the 13th Urban Cohort stood firm. One thousand men.

They would withdraw. Keep their faces to the enemy, fight their way back to the city. The aqueduct and the tombs would break up the formation of their enemies, negate their superior numbers.

But as he looked towards Carthage, hope died. Already the gates were choked with a throng of men. They were stationary, wedged together, fighting among themselves, as Capelianus' auxiliaries bore down, killing the laggards among the tombs.

Face your fate with courage. Not with the complainings and entreaties of a coward. Death is nothing.

A voice was shouting.

'Lay down your arms, fellow-soldiers. Your fight is done and over.'

It was Capelianus, sitting a horse behind his men. Just four ranks away. He was still shouting.

'Your pretend Emperor has fled. Those who led you astray have fled. No mounted officers remain

424

under your standards. Return to your *sacramentum*. You were misled. The clemency of Maximinus is boundless. I am merciful. There will be no retribution.'

Gordian tugged off his helmet, cast it aside, so he could be seen. 'I am here. Praetorians, we will stand together to the end.'

He shouldered his way to the front, drawing his sword. 'The coward Capelianus has put himself at our mercy. Some god has blinded him. Kill the cuckold, and the day is yet ours. With me, brothers.'

He could see the surprise and indecision on the face of Capelianus.

Just four ranks of soldiers. *Let me not die without a struggle, inglorious, but do some big thing first, that men to come shall know of it.*

'With me!' Vocula was beside him. 'Are you ready for war?'

Ready! All the men around him were bellowing, caught up in the intoxication of the sanguinary drama.

'Are you ready for war?'

Ready!

On the third response, Gordian charged forward.

At a run, he crashed shield to shield into the legionary opposite. The man staggered back, collided with the man behind. Gordian took a blow from the left on his shield, smashed the boss into a bearded face. He caught a sword thrust from the right on his own blade, rolled his wrist, and punched. His knuckles hit the face guard. He felt them break. But the man reeled away, impeding his fellows.

They were in the midst of their lines.

Gordian dropped to one knee, thrust under his shield into the thigh of the legionary in front. Before the man could fall, Vocula had finished him. Another Praetorian was on his other shoulder.

Three ranks to go. His own men around him. The clamour of the fighting stunned the senses.

Gordian hacked and thrust. No room or time for thought. He chopped down a man to his right with a backhand slash. Felt his shoulder-guard buckle as a blade caught him. Ignoring it, he cut down the next man in his way. His shield was splintered, jagged. His right hand throbbed.

Two ranks. He could see Capelianus turning the head of his horse. If he rode off, the morale of his men would collapse. If he stayed, Gordian would kill him.

Too fast to react, Gordian was hit on the side of the head. For a moment, his vision blurred. He struck out blindly. The point of his sword glanced off metal. Blood was running hot down his neck. He thrust again, met resistance.

Now there was only one legionary between him and Capelianus. But out of the corner of his eye he saw Vocula fall. There was no one else with him. He was alone. Steel all around him.

Something jabbed between his shoulder blades. The armour broke. A surge of pain, the breath driven out of him. A legionary aimed a swing at his head. He went to bring his shield up, but he was slow. The sword cut into his jaw, snapped his head sideways.

He brought up his sword. But it was heavy, so very heavy. The iron taste of blood filling his mouth, flooding down his throat.

He was on his knees. Men were shouting, but they were far away, as if he were at the bottom of a well.

A blow to the back of his head knocked him forward on all fours. All ways of dying are hateful to us poor mortals. No, that was wrong. Death was nothing.

He felt the next blow, but not the ones after that.

Death was nothing.

CHAPTER 47

AFRICA
CARTHAGE

Ten days after the Ides of March, AD238

T he sea was calm. The galley was waiting off the commercial harbour. He could still escape.

He would have to be quick. Capelianus' auxiliaries and the Moorish tribesmen had almost finished hacking down the throng that clogged the gates. Soon they would be inside the walls. When the raping and massacre began in the city, the more intelligent, the more avaricious, would make for the Palace.

For a time, he had hoped his son was alive, somehow had escaped death. If only he would ride up, defeated, but bloody and glorious. It had been the hope of a fool, of a young man. Marcus Antonius Gordianus Sempronianus, recently, to his cost, hailed Romanus and Africanus and Augustus as well, was over eighty, and, whatever some may have called him in his long life, he had never considered himself a fool.

His son lay dead on the battlefield, on that dreadful

plain where all their hopes had died. Gordian had watched from the battlements; the trap that failed, the cowardice of the levies – when had the Africans ever shown anything more? – the desertion of the legionaries, and that final doomed charge. He had watched until that last knot of men had been butchered. No one, not even his son, could have survived.

As the carriage had brought him back to the Palace, the plebs had shouted insults, blamed him for their plight. They did not see it was the other way about, and all the imprecations in the world would not save them. Anyway, the plebs were ever fickle, not worth considering.

There was still time to get down to the port. But there was no point. His son was dead. Some might say that he should think of Maecia Faustina and his grandson. But if he reached Rome, there would be nothing he could do to defend them. They would be in less danger without his presence. He had never cared for his daughter, and the child was a stranger. All the love he possessed had gone to his son. Perhaps love is a finite quality. Some might squander it on acquaintances, he had given it all to his son. And his son was dead.

He should not fear suicide. He was old. Many old men had taken their lives. If it was done, not in despair, but with self-control, after rational consideration, it was a praiseworthy end. In Pliny's *Letters*, Corellius Rufus had starved himself to death in the face of gathering pain and debility. Pliny had held him up as an example.

In the stern *mos maiorum*, a defeated general should seek death at the hands of the enemy, or turn his blade upon himself. His son had done the former – could he really be dead? – now it remained for Gordian to take the latter path. Even Varus, when his foolishness had led three legions to their deaths in the forests of *Germania*, had won a measure of posthumous redemption, when he fell on his sword.

Gordian had never shared his son's certainty that there was no afterlife. There could be no delight greater than walking in the Elysian Fields, reunited with his son. But would the gods admit one who had denied their existence? And he was far from sure his own limited virtues would earn him entrance to those flower-jewelled meadows. His youth had been marked by arrogance, vanity, ambition, and lust. None but the last had been tempered by age. Yet there were no greater vices against his name, and his life had been untainted by any terrible act of cruelty or impiety. He doubted he deserved eternal torment. If he went, as most did, to Hades, he could drink the waters of Lethe, and all would be forgotten. If his son was right, they would both sleep peacefully for ever.

If he took his life now, perhaps his daughter and her son would be spared, perhaps the house of the Gordiani would continue. It might be his

430

descendants would still look on the fine paintings of the *Domus Rostrata*, walk the marble halls of the villa on the Via Praenestina. Given the nature of Maximinus, it seemed unlikely.

With hindsight, he should have devoted himself to death before the battle. Long ago, the Decii, father and son, had made a compact with the gods. They had offered their lives in return for the victory of their armies. But that had been long ago, when the world was young, when the gods were closer. At his age, an old man tottering towards the enemy might have invited not divine admiration, but scorn.

From his point of vantage, a terrace high in the Palace, he could see the Hadrumetum Gate. The Moors were inside. He could see their white tunics, the bright tips of their javelins, as they stabbed down from their ponies, into the heads and shoulders of the panic-stricken and unresisting. Time was getting short.

He should try for a good death. Socrates had taken hemlock, a gradual numbness had spread from his feet up through his body. Many Senators wore a ring containing poison. Gordian was not one of them. It would have to be a blade, the Roman way. What was it young Menophilus often said? *What is the path to freedom? Any vein in your body.* There was no time for the hot bath and the leisurely and uplifting discussion of the immortality of the soul. No time to die like Seneca or Thrasea Paetus.

'Brennus!'

Gordian called again. His bodyguard did not come.

The terrace was deserted.

'Brennus!'

Gordian walked inside. The first room was empty, so was the long corridor. His footsteps echoed.

There was no one in the *Delphix*. Four years as Proconsul of Africa, twenty days since the Senate had acclaimed him Emperor, so many dinner parties in this elegant room. Now someone had stolen the cups and plates and big wine cooler.

He sat on a couch. In the further reaches of the Palace he could hear men moving, like mice behind a wainscot.

'Emperor.'

It was Valens, his *a Cubiculo*.

The last person to desert him would be the steward of the bedchamber.

'Emperor, four loyal slaves wait with the carriage. If we do not delay, we can still get you to the ship.'

A momentary surge of relief, of joy, like a servant spared a beating. No, to prolong his life was cowardice. His arrival in Rome would seal the death sentence on his daughter and grandson.

'Valens, take this ring. Go to the ship, go to Rome. Tell Menophilus and Valerian, our other friends, to look to their safety. Tell my daughter . . .'

Tell her what? Since her mother had died, their minds had been closed to each other.

'Tell her we died well.'

'Emperor . . .'

'Now go. Obey my final command.'

When Valens had gone, Gordian went to his bedchamber. It was undisturbed. He had a sharp sword, long since prepared. It should have been wielded by Brennus. But Brennus had gone.

He tested the edge with his thumb. A bright spot of blood. Razor sharp. The ivory hilt looked incongruous in his age-spotted hands.

All ways of dying are hateful to us poor mortals. He had a sudden urge to rush after Valens. Ridiculous, the *a Cubiculo* would be long gone. He would not suffer the fate of Galba or Vitellius; an old man, a deposed Emperor, dragged through the streets, stripped naked, tortured. He hefted the sword.

When the friends of Cato had bound up his wounds, urged him to live, the philosopher had ripped open the stitches, torn out his entrails with his bare hands. Cato had died slowly, in agony. Gordian threw away the sword. He could not face the steel.

He took off his belt, looked around. Nothing of use. He went back into the dining room. Taking one of the upright chairs on which the women and children sat, he dragged it under a beam. The belt was too short.

He stood uncertain, panic rising. Men were shouting somewhere in the Palace.

The curtains were held back by a long rope, ornamental, but thick. He looped it over the beam,

433

tied one end to a pillar. He clambered up onto the chair. He fashioned a noose, put it over his head, checked and tightened the knot.

There would be no one to catch his last breath, close his eyes, call his name. It did not matter.

Let me at least not die without a struggle, inglorious, but do some big thing first, that men to come shall know of it. Time would tell.

He thought of his son. Saw him as a child sleeping, the tousled fair hair, the perfection of the line of his jaw, of his mouth, the beauty of his eyes as they opened and gazed into his own. He kicked away the chair.

Withdrawn From Stock
Dublin Public Libraries